טרעפט וואס מען שפיעלט

דיענסטאג, אבענד, דען 29טען דעצעמבער, 1908

צום עהרען אבענד
פון
מאדאם
קלארא יאנג
? ? ?

צום עהרען אבענד
פון
מאדאם
קלארא יאנג
? ? ?

עס איז קיין אנדערעם וויא נור

דאס אידישע הארץ

אבער מיט מעהר פראכט אונד גלאנץ וויא עס איז נאך ביז יעצט
אויפגעפיהרם אונד געשפיעלם געוואארען.

דיא גאנצע קאמפאני פערשפרעכם
צור עהרע פון

מאדאם קלארא יאנג

צו מאכען דאם מקסעם שמיק
"דאם אידישע הארץ"

פריש, נייא אונד יאנג

פאלקסשטיק אין 4 אקטען פון ה' י. לאטיינער

אויפגעפיהרם פון הערר דייוויד העסלער

מוזיק פון מאנולעסקא אונד ברודני

מיקטעס זיינען שוין צו בעקומען אין באקס אפפים

THALIA THEATRE

טהאליא טהעאטער, 46-48 בּאוערי.   46-48 Bowery.

GORDIN, LIPZIN, MOGULESKO & MOSHKOWITZ.   Lessees & Managers.

דאנערסטאג אבענד, דען 26טען יאנואר, 1905

עהרען בענעפיטס פיר   עהרען בענעפיטס פיר

מאדאם
מאניע
ווילענסקי   מאדאם
מאניע
ווילענסקי

עם ווירד אויפגעפיהרט
צום ערשטען מאל   עם ווירד אויפגעפיהרט
צום ערשטען מאל

❧ דיא מאסקירטע פרוי ❧
אדער עממא ווייס

פערזאנען: גרויסע קאמעדיע אין 4 אקטען   פערזאנען:

מאד. בריח   אוים דעם פראנצויזידשען איבערזעצט פון   ראוויד ווייס, א באנקיער   ה' מאשקאוויטש
ה' נאראווסקי   סעם, זיין זאהן   ג. ג.
אין דיא בענעפיציאנטין מאד. ווילענסקי   מ. נאלדבערג.   אדאלף מאנינע, אין בעטטער   ה' קאהן
אין דער וואונדערבארער ראללע   צעניריטע אונד אויסגעפיהרט   קלאסמאן וואהל, אין קלערק   ה' מאביאם
עממא ווייס.   נאך אלע רענעלן דער ביהנע קונסט פון   מאד. ה'נעמאן
אום דער האנדלונג : לאנג פרויסט.   ב. ווילענסקי   טשארלי, ראווידם קוטשער   ה' היימאן
ציים: דיא נעגענוואארט.   ליא, טשארליים ווייב   מאד. מאביאם
                                                                              רוזי, א פארמער בּאי   ה' גילטמאן

פערטהאעט פובליקום! פערליערטא ניט דיא געלעגענהיים דיעזע גרויסארטיגע פארשטעללונג ביצואוואהנען, דען ,,די מאסקירטע פרוי'' איז
איינע פון דיא בעסטע אן שטארקסטע פיעסען אויף איהרער גענער. מאד. ווילענסקי צום שטענדען צו איהרע בענעפיטסע נעם אן צוהלרייכע
פיעסען אן דאם זעלבע שהוט זא אויך געגם. קאמסטען אין מאסקען אן אוים ערייגגס אויך. אבטונגסאלל, דאם מענטשטעטגעם.

Thursday Eve'g, Jan. 26, *Testimonial
Performance
tendered to* Mme M. Wilensky

For the first time

THE MASKED WOMAN
or EMMA WEISS

 ליפשיטמ פרעסם, 180 נרערד סט., ניו יארק. מיטגענומט צו בעקומען אין באקם אפים פון טהאליא טהעאטער.

BEAUTIFUL,
as the MOON,
RADIANT
as the STARS

שיין ווי די לבֿנה, ליכטיק ווי די שטערן

די פֿרוי אין דער ייִדישער דערציילונג

אַן אַנטאָלאָגיע

רעדאַקטירט פֿון

שיינע באַרק

אַרײַנפֿיר פֿון

פֿראַנסין פֿראָז

ווערנער בוקס

אַן אײַ. אָו. אֶל. טײַם וווערנער קומפּאַני

BEAUTIFUL, as the MOON, RADIANT as the STARS

JEWISH WOMEN in YIDDISH STORIES
An Anthology

Edited by
SANDRA BARK

Introduction by
FRANCINE PROSE

WARNER BOOKS

An AOL Time Warner Company

This book is a work of fiction. Names, characters, places, and incidents are the products of the authors' imaginations or are used fictitiously. Any resemblance to actual events, locales, or persons, living or dead, is coincidental.

Permission to reprint Yiddish Theater Posters from the Dorot Jewish Division, The New York Public Library, Astor, Lenox, and Tilden Foundations:
(1) *The Jewish Heart*, starring Madame Clara Young, Kessler's Thalia Theatre, December 29, 1908 (2) *The Masked Woman, or Emma Weiss*, starring Madame Manya Wilensky, Thalia Theatre, January 26, 1905 (3) *Hamlet*, starring Madame Bertha Kalish, Thalia Theatre, January 30, c. 1890 (4) Repertoire, Thalia Theatre, June 1892.

Warner Books, Inc., 1271 Avenue of the Americas, New York, NY 10020

Visit our Web site at www.twbookmark.com.

 An AOL Time Warner Company

Printed in the United States of America

First Printing: November 2003
10 9 8 7 6 5 4 3 2 1

Library of Congress Cataloging-in-Publication Data
Beautiful as the moon, radiant as the stars : Jewish women in Yiddish stories : an
   anthology / edited by Sandra Bark; introduction by Francine Prose.
      p. cm.
   Includes bibliographical references.
   ISBN 0-446-69136-4
      1. Short stories, Yiddish—Translations into English. 2. Yiddish fiction—20th
century—Translations into English. 3. Jewish women—Fiction.   I. Bark, Sandra.

PJ5191.E8B43 2003
839.1'30108352042'089924—dc21

2003052599

Book design and text composition by H Roberts Design
Cover design by Leah Lococo
Cover illustration by Melanie Marden Parks

For my mother,
who taught me to love stories.

And for my grandparents,
for whom Yiddish is not only a living language,
but the language of their lives.

Acknowledgments

This anthology would not have been possible without the support and contributions of a number of people. I will always be thankful to my sister, Mimi Bark, and my dear friends Alexis Kanfer, Sarah Masters, and Sharon Glassman for their patience and encouragement. I am indebted to Les Pockell for being the best thesis adviser ever, to Amy Einhorn for being my mentor on this and many other projects, and to Penina Sacks for her keen eye for literature and punctuation. Much thanks also goes to Brigid Pearson for coordinating this lovely cover; to Keri Friedman, for making sure people would hear about this book; to Christofer DuBois, for graciously sifting through heaps of contracts; to Faith Jones and Michael Terry at the Dorot Jewish Division of the New York Public Library for pulling out dusty archives for me to sift through; to Joseph Sherman, Sheva Zucker, Sarah Swartz, Kathryn Hellerstein, Ellen Cassedy, and Dr. Ellen Kellman, for their sound advice and suggestions; and to all the contributors, for their wonderful translations.

Contents

Foreword

by Sandra Bark

What does it mean to be a Jewish woman? According to Jewish law and tradition, she is a dutiful daughter, marries the right (Jewish) man, and becomes an *eishes chayil*, a woman of valor. Women's intelligence and contributions are not disputed—rather, they are directed toward "appropriate" outlets. "The wisdom of the woman builds the home," instructed the sages. When the primary building block of the community and the nation is the family unit, this is an honor. But what happens when women want to circumvent custom and reinvent their boundaries?

Set in Europe, Russia, Israel, and the United States during the later nineteenth and twentieth centuries, the stories in *Beautiful as the Moon, Radiant as the Stars* reflect the perspectives of male Yiddish writers on women and allow Yiddish women writers to define their own issues. The nineteenth century was accompanied by great social, political, and economic shifts. Young men opened their eyes to the rest of the world, and so did young women. Recognizing the unique struggles of women—and reading their stories—is integral to our appreciation of recent Jewish history.

Most of the stories in this volume are pre-Holocaust, full of images from a lifestyle that is now completely destroyed. Concerned largely with relationships, the stories center around women who reach beyond the limits imposed on them by their families, societies, and religion, yet feel bound to their communities. These heroines are wistful mothers, stalwart grandmothers, rebellious teenagers, desperate brides, and star-crossed lovers. They are women fighting to be students, students pretending to be boys, and boys who become brides. They make choices and mistakes. They take chances. They take revenge.

While women have been writing in Yiddish for four hundred years, they are sparsely present, if at all, when we envision the Jewish literary canon. Yet before modern Yiddish culture and literature began to flourish in the later nineteenth century, Yiddish was the voice of grandmothers, aunts, and daughters. While men conducted their religious and literary affairs in the holy Hebrew, women lived their lives in Yiddish, raising their children, running their businesses, and bargaining with God in that language. This is why Yiddish stories by and about women are especially appropriate—Yiddish, the *mame loshen*, literally, the "mother tongue," was the language of women's experience.

When I told my own mother about this collection, she suggested that I take the name from "Sheyn vi di levone," the Yiddish love song whose refrain goes, "To me, you are as beautiful as the moon, as bright as all the stars in the sky." This is the way culture is passed on—from mother to child, from generation to generation. I hope you will read this book as both an engaging piece of literature and an exciting piece of cultural history. Language and tradition tie us to our pasts and bind us to our history, as do stories. Diffusion of Jewish culture has long been the province of the women, as the sages charged, and so was the spread and development of Yiddish, the linguistic homeland of the people without a home. After all, when your mother raises you, it is her voice you will always hear in your ears and her language you will count as your first.

Introduction

by Francine Prose

Reading *Beautiful as the Moon, Radiant as the Stars*, I was reminded of a story I heard from a friend who, as a child, attended a religious Sunday school in her local Reform synagogue. Her teacher was, my friend later realized, a secret feminist, years ahead of her time (this was in the late 1950s), who was determined to do her part to challenge the tenets and assumptions of the patriarchy.

Every week, the teacher told her class, they would be studying a different biblical heroine. And so, week after week, they learned about the brave and noble deeds of Miriam, Deborah, Ruth, and Esther. But though the teacher tried valiantly to make a convincing case for the wives of the patriarchs, the list of suitable subjects was relatively brief, and they ran out of women to study within a couple of months.

"What about the other heroines?" my friend sensibly asked.

Her teacher thought for a long time. "The other heroines," she replied at last, "were women we've never heard of."

Likewise, the heroines—and heroines they truly are—of this revealing collection of Yiddish stories about Jewish women are (with the exception of a few well-known fictional characters like Isaac Bashevis Singer's Yentl) women we've never heard of. And each one certainly represents millions of real women whose lives must have resembled the brave, complicated, and difficult lives of the Jewish women—young and old, rural and urban, poor and middle-class—we encounter in these pages.

Perhaps what's most striking about *Beautiful as the Moon, Radiant as the Stars* is the force with which it reminds us that—not so very long ago and not so very far away—women had to struggle for even the smallest fraction of the autonomy and self-determination that we take for granted today. Set mostly in Europe, the United States, and Israel, mostly in the nineteenth and twentieth centuries, many of these fictions concern women who must fight just to entertain and express a simple opinion of their own or to exert the slightest influence on the shape of their own destinies.

Several of the stories concern the often insurmountable obstacles that young women were compelled to face if they found themselves inexplicably seized by the subversive and socially suspect desire for an education. "A girl only needs to learn how to read her prayers and sign her name," declares the grandmother in Rachel H. Korn's "The Sack with Pink Stripes." In Dvora Baron's "Kaddish," a child must witness her grandfather's helpless grief at not having been blessed with a son who could have said the mourner's prayer for him after his death. The girl's love for the old man inspires and intensifies her own heartfelt, well-intentioned, and ultimately futile desire to learn and recite the words of the prayer—a longing that cannot be fully satisfied because she has had the misfortune to be born female.

Like several of the selections included here, Helen Londynski's "The Four-Ruble War" portrays the wily and frequently desperate survival strategies that young women adopt in order to realize their ambitions. Hoping to raise money for the tuition that will allow her to continue her studies at a private school in Warsaw, Chayele buys cheaper shoes than the ones she has been given money to purchase. In fact, the strength of her passion for learning is so intense that she is driven to steal money from her own father. And Londynski encourages us to see these petty crimes as the rash but ultimately justified means to a worthy and justifiable end.

Even when they succeed in overcoming the prejudice against educating women, these heroines are often tormented by guilt and remorse over what they have left behind and lost. The narrator of Yente Serdatzky's "Rosh Hashanah"—a self-described "freethinker" who has abandoned the shtetl for the city—longs for the "holy, poetic stillness" of the village where she spent her youth and is devastated when she looks in the mirror and notices that her face resembles that of the grandfather she adores. Women who have successfully broken away and established autonomous lives must face new difficulties and challenges. For example, the three beautiful emancipated sisters who run the lodging establishment at the center of "In the Boardinghouse" inspire fervid gossip, rumor, speculation, and love among the men with whom they come in contact, men who simply cannot believe that the sisters are not "keeping their husbands here in Berlin, but hidden away."

Stories about girls who defy the strictures of the adult world around them seem like accounts of small, significant triumphs—until we happen to compare them to stories about male protagonists in more or less comparable circumstances. The fourteen-year-old narrator of Rochel Faygenberg's "My First Readers" scores a personal victory by ignoring her grandmother's anxious warnings against wandering around a city that suggests Odessa and by drafting letters for a servant and a wet nurse to send to their fiancés. But when we compare the girl's experience of the city with that of her male counterpart in a work such as Isaac Babel's "My First Fee"—a tale about a boy whose passion for a prostitute inspires him to invent his first piece of imaginative fiction—the girl's bid for independence seems suddenly tame, and indeed the whole story begins to sound as if it were written with the monitory grandmother looking over the author's shoulder.

Considering the determination with which the parents and grandparents in these fictions resist their daughters' educational aspirations, it's no surprise that the girls' romantic longings and their efforts to determine whom they will love and marry are consistently and fiercely overlooked and ignored. Love, we soon come to understand, too often provides the occasion for the misuses and abuse of power. Matches and betrothals reveal the hidden truths about these women's lives—namely, that they are little more than property to be traded, bargained for, and disposed of at whim or for reasons of convenience, social advancement, communal pressure, tradition, and superstition—and with little or no regard for the young women's wishes.

The stories are filled with secret passions and thwarted love affairs, with engagements broken by parental fiat, and with innocent lives ruined as a consequence. In "The Sack with Pink Stripes," the narrator discovers that her mother has never gotten over the loss of her first love—a handsome boy whom she was forbidden to wed after his sister scandalized the community by converting and marrying a blacksmith. The ironic, delicate sexual comedy of Isaac Bashevis Singer's "Yentl the Yeshiva Boy" is set in motion when Hadass's parents prevent her from marrying Avigdor—and consequently throw her into the arms of the cross-dressing Yentl, whom they believe to be a man. Read in the context of this anthology, "Yentl the Yeshiva Boy" seems even more delightful and meaningful than we may have remembered. For the sense of these women's lives that *Beautiful as the Moon, Radiant as the Stars* provides makes us realize that Yentl would have had very cogent, very strong reasons—apart from her more inchoate and irrational psycho-sexual urges and promptings—for wanting to lead the life of a man instead of the much more limited, restricted destiny of a woman.

Many of the stories function as cautionary tales—warnings about what happens when a woman refuses to follow, or, alternately, when she follows too closely, the rules and conventions that so narrowly define the manner in which a woman is supposed to behave. The eponymous heroine of I. L. Peretz's "Bryna's Mendl" is one of several in the book—among them, the milkman Tevye's daughter, the title character in Sholom Aleichem's "Hodel"—who are considerably more resourceful, more capable, smarter, and quicker to figure out the complex ways of the world than the men around them. Married to a dim and barely competent husband, Bryna wants nothing more than to be "his footstool in Paradise. She pampered him and stuffed him with food. She worked like a donkey to support him, to shoe and clothe him and their five children—three girls and two boys." Dreaming of England, which in his mind is a sort of Promised Land, Mendl fails to notice that Bryna is working—and literally starving herself—to death so that he will be properly cosseted and well fed, until at last she collapses and dies. "Bryna, who had attracted no notice in life, was barely visible on her deathbed. She was so thin!"

What's interesting about Esther Singer Kreitman's "A Satin Coat"—yet another story about underappreciated female competence and the perils of forcing, or attempting to force, a woman to marry against her will—is that it examines not only the bonds and restrictions imposed by gender, but also the prejudices and presuppositions associated with money and social class. Here, all of Yidl Glisker's misguided efforts to gentrify his sturdy peasant family—or at least to create the appearance of gentrification—pale before the intensity of his daughter's refusal to marry the suitor her father has chosen, "a gentle and silken young man from a fine family."

In a number of stories, including Sholom Aleichem's "Hodel," women are drawn to budding young Communists whose ideology offers, or appears to offer, a promise of something more closely approximating sexual equality. Celia Dropkin's "At the Rich Relatives" tracks the hopes and disappointments of a young girl whose discomfort over her allegedly inferior social and economic standing is alleviated by a charged flirtation with her attractive and politically engaged cousin—until circumstances remind her that despite her cousin's noble ideas about the role of women in the revolution and the eventual abolition of private property and class, the power balance is still tipped heavily in favor of men like her rich and privileged uncle. Likewise, the heroine of "Rosh Hashanah" discovers, to her chagrin, that all her modern, urbanized notions about politics and religion cannot match the emotional sway that her memories of her traditional family and her village home still exert over her heart and soul.

Beautiful as the Moon, Radiant as the Stars guides us through the life cycle of these perfectly ordinary and utterly exceptional women, from the child at the center of "Kaddish" to the young women discovering first love and the dawning of eroticism in Celia Dropkin's "Bella Fell in Love" and David Bergelson's "Spring," to the elderly aunt whose passing in Blume Lempel's "The Death of My Aunt" forces her surviving niece to confront issues of love and loyalty, of promises broken and kept, of what women like the narrator's aunt have brought with them from the old country to the New World.

Two of the volume's most intriguing stories concern old age. In Shira Gorshman's "Bubbe Malke," rage and righteousness inspire an elderly midwife to commit an amazing act of courage, violence, and revenge. In Dvora Baron's "Bubbe Henya," a mysterious old woman who has acquired a reputation for almost superhuman generosity and sympathy proves that her powers are far more astonishing than anyone could have imagined. The characters and actions of the two old women could not possibly be more different, yet what they have in common is power, bravery, autonomy, independence, and resourcefulness—in short, all the qualities that the younger women in these stories have been working so hard to obtain.

Reading "Bubbe Malke" and "Bubbe Henya" makes us feel that these women's struggles were not in vain, that the obstacles they overcame, the roadblocks they crashed through or circumvented, and the surrenders or defeats they were forced to endure were also sources of wisdom and strength—a difficult school in which they learned the lessons that enabled them to become the heroines they were destined to be. Reading *Beautiful as the Moon, Radiant as the Stars* makes us glad that our own lives are so different from the much more circumscribed fates of the women we are reading about. At the same time, the book makes us grateful to these heroines for having had the courage and resolve to help prepare the way for us to insist upon—and even to take for granted—the ordinary, everyday, absolutely essential freedoms that we enjoy today.

A Note on the Transliteration

There are many ways to write Yiddish in English. Over the years, standards of transliteration have been developed by organizations like YIVO that are widely used and accepted by academic institutions. When considering the approach for this volume, we opted for a more familiar style. We strived for a balance between comfort and standardization, while considering the spellings still in use in contemporary Jewish communities, Yiddish pronunciation of Jewish holidays and references, and words referenced in Merriam-Webster. For this reason, we have decided on *Chanukah* instead of *Khanike*, *Shabbes* instead of *Shabes*, and so on. While it is unlikely that everyone will be happy with our choices, we hope that all our readers will be able to look beyond the spelling to enjoy the literature presented herein.

BEAUTIFUL,
as the MOON,
RADIANT
as the STARS

White Night

Kadya Molodowsky
Translated by Adrienne Rich

White night, my painful joy,
your light is brighter than the dawn.
A white ship is sailing from East Broadway
where I see no sail by day.

A quiet star hands me a ticket
open for all the seas.
I put on my timeworn jacket
and entrust myself to the night.

Where are you taking me, ship?
Who charted us on this course?
The hieroglyphs of the map escape me,
and the arrows of your compass.

I am the one who sees and does not see.
I go along on your deck of secrets,
squeeze shut my baggage on the wreath of sorrows
from all my plucked-out homes.

—Pack in all my blackened pots,
their split lids, the chipped crockeries,
pack in my chaos with its gold-encrusted buttons
since chaos will always be in fashion.

—Pack the letters stamped *Unknown at This Address*—
vanished addresses that sear my eyes,
postmarked with more than years and days;
sucked into my bones and marrow.

—Pack up my shadow that weighs more than my body,
that comes along with its endless exhortations.
Weekdays or holidays, time of flowers or withering,
my shadow is with me, muttering its troubles.

Find me a place of honey cakes and sweetness
where angels and children picnic together
(this is the dream I love best of all),
where the sacred wine fizzes in bottles.

Let me have one sip, here on East Broadway,
for the sake of those old Jews crying in the dark.
I cry my heretic's tears with them,
their sobbing is my sobbing.

I'm a difficult passenger, my ship
is packed with the heavy horns, the *shofars* of grief.
Tighten the sails of night as far as you can,
for the daylight cannot carry me.

Take me somewhere to a place of rest,
of goats in belled hats playing on trombones—
to the Almighty's fresh white sheets
where the hunter's shadow cannot fall.

Take me . . . Yes, take me . . . But you know best
where the sea calmly opens its blue road.
I'm wearier than your oldest tower;
somewhere I've left my heart aside.

KADDISH

•

Dvora Baron

Translated by Naomi Seidman with Chana Kronfeld

My grandmother bore my grandfather ten gifts—ten children, but, alas, not a single son. They say that every time a girl was born, he would lift his thoughtful-pious eyes to heaven and sigh deeply:

It seems, Father, that you don't consider me worthy of a son, a son who could say kaddish for me when I pass on. . . .

And at nightfall, he would sit down listlessly at the table, open the big Talmud, and sadly, very softly and sadly, sing to himself. Somewhere in a far-off corner between the wall and the partition, my grandmother would sit and listen to the Talmud chant and cry in silence.

Later, after my grandmother had died and my grandfather took me in, a tiny orphan, to feed, I would often hear this very same mournful chant.

Late, very late at night, when a thick, mute, darkness would press up against our little window from outside, my grandfather would light the lamp and sit down at his Talmud. All is quiet now, and melancholy. Only occasionally, from some distant field, comes a soft *Hoo, hoo, hoo.*

1

That was the wind, chasing its tail somewhere out there in the darkness, stumbling over naked fields, and sobbing softly.

And inside the house, mute, terror-black shadows would wrap my grandfather in dark shrouds, veiling his clouded-gray face, his high forehead, his deep-set, sad eyes:

Ay, ay, Father, ay, ay, sweet Father.

And it was hard to know, at times like these, whether he was thinking about himself, about his lonesome life, and crying, dry-eyed, or whether he was really absorbed in the words he was chanting.

Ay, ay, Father dear . . .

"*Zeyde.*"

And running through the shadows with my tremulous steps, I would sneak onto his knee.

"I want to listen to you learn."

And my little body would be set loose between his cold, thin hands, which stroked and hugged me, clutching me close, close to his heart:

"Ach, Rivele, Rivele—if only you were a boy . . ." And a strange look would come over his face and his eyes would become dejected and thoughtful.

What a beard he had, my grandfather, white all over.

I remember the Sabbath days, the winter Sabbaths in my grandfather's house. Outside—a disheveled, lumbering sky over the congealed, dead earth. It's quiet and dismal. Every now and then a flock of black crows flies by, hurls a few curses into the air, and then disappears, and again it's quiet.

But now the winter sky is turning darker, a heavy, angry dusk creeps slowly and icily through the little window, enveloping in black the damp walls, the low ceiling, the table with its white tablecloth, even Grandfather's white beard.

Dark.

And soon I hear Grandfather rise from his place, scrape together the challah crumbs from the late afternoon Sabbath meal, wrap a thick scarf around his neck, and leave.

With wide-open eyes and beating heart I stay where I am, enveloped in shadow. I listen: everything around is silent. Only from farther away, from the top of the hill, can a monotonous ringing be heard.

Clang-clang-clang! . . . clang-clang-clang!

The church bells are proclaiming that our holy Sabbath is passing away, and now it's their holy day, the uphill folk's.

Clang-clang-clang!

Slowly. Every peal distinct. And the wind rocks, rocks and sways:

"Ay-ay-ay . . . ay-ay-ay . . ."

That was exactly how my mother howled the night her two sons died on her.

But now a powerful ray of light suddenly pierces the little window, covers the table, scatters into many golden threads, and stabs my eyes: the old solid-walled synagogue, which towers over the hovels around its courtyard like a giant among midgets, watches me with seven fiery eyes—its lit windows. There, in the study hall, they're praying the evening service. The winter hats sway, the men spit out the closing prayer, wish each other "a good week."

Grandfather comes in, lights two thin candles, pours himself a little glass of havdalah wine, and looks toward the door. Soon an ugly little kid walks in—he's the one who's going to be drinking that wine. He gives me a look with his small, devious eyes, waits for my grandfather to look away, and then sticks out his tongue. If it weren't for Grandfather, I'm sure that loathsome boy with his grubby paws would just stick his fist under my nose: "Here, take this."

I feel the blood rising to my head: You rotten snot-nose!

"*Zeyde*," I say, "*Zeyde*, I'll drink the wine today."

He shakes his head.

"Child, child—the havdalah wine? You forget, you're a girl. . . ."

Child, child . . . These words ring so bare, so strange. Two deep, deep creases spread across his high, pale brow, his milk-clouded eyes open wider and wider. Now all I can see are two gaping holes; they look off toward the corner between the window and partition.

"Beyla, Beyla, what did you do? You couldn't have borne me a kaddish, Beyla, huh . . . ?"

And he stretches out a palsied hand, his right hand, the fingers long, pale, the nails sharp and cold.

"Beyla, oh, Beyla."

And he bursts into tears. I can see his eyebrows trembling now, the tears rolling down.

"*Zeyde* . . ." I lift my head.

Pacified-saddened now, he sits over the open Talmud, swaying and chanting softly.

He is learning—my soul fills to the brim with happiness. Suddenly, I remember that somewhere in one of the shacks at the very bottom of the hill lives an old Jewish woman, an ancient one. For five kopecks a week she'll teach anyone who asks how to read Hebrew.

"Five kopecks a week," I say to myself, and I feel a warm flow seep slowly into my heart and gently, silently, caress it. . . .

So one beautiful summer Sabbath I go over to Grandfather with tremendous steps and raise my two eyes—full of quiet, holy joy—to his.

"Want to test me, *Zeyde*?"

Grandfather lifts his head from the Talmud and brushes his brow with his hand. I see an eyelid tremble as he looks at me:

"Child."

"*Zeyde*," I blurt out, and feel as if my heart were about to burst in my chest. "*Zeyde*, test me."

He goes to the bookshelf, takes out a prayer book, opens it, and sets it before me. I lower my eyes and look into it.

Yisgadal veyiskadash shemey raba . . . the kaddish. A sweet shudder runs through my entire body. I push the prayer book away with both hands, raise my head, and piously close my eyes.

"*Yisgadal veyiskadash shemey raba.*"

And the words flow from my lips, they pour out of me into the air so mildly, so sadly . . . I feel my face flush, break out in a heavy sweat, my heart beats and beats, and I keep reciting. . . .

And suddenly, Grandfather snatches me in both arms, lifts me up on high, to the ceiling, and rising and soaring himself, he carries the two of us floating through the house, rocking me and tossing me into the air and adorning me with psalms of praise:

"Holy Sabbath, holy Sabbath, holy Sabbath."

Purplish red are his lips, his high forehead—pure white. His long beard flies in all directions, quivering, and among the strands—two large teardrops shimmer and tremble now like a pair of diamonds.

Just a few days later I'm sitting on a big rock outside the synagogue wall with my head bowed—a congealed sorrow in my heart, two warm tears in my eyes. Over there, in our little house, a single memorial candle is burning. I can't forget that for a minute. Somewhere on the dirt floor a bundle of trampled straw has been strewn; scraps of white linen—remnants of Grandfather's shroud; on the door—a lock, a black, round lock . . . But what do I care? If only I had a black dress, an

entirely black dress, I would look more like a boy, a lot more—
this, it turns out, is the thought that's spinning in my brain.

Around me women are gathering, wagging their heads.

"So what do you suppose will happen to the orphan girl
now?"

One of them even strokes my hair. "Would you like a little
bun, maybe?"

A band of schoolboys shows up, looking at me with fasci-
nated pity, and I announce to them very earnestly: "I'm not
afraid of you."

I jump up from my place and follow them.

"Where are you going?" they ask.

"I'm going to the study hall," I say, and at once feel both
my knees start shaking. "I'm going to say kaddish."

"She's going to say kaddish," they snort, and an acrid,
stuffy whiff of boy-sweat sears my nostrils. There are men all
around me, blocking my way to the lectern, pushing me
back—out—out to the entry hall. But from above, from the
Holy Ark, two thoughtful-pious eyes look down at me:

"Child, child . . . ," so lonesome, so beseeching. "Child,
child . . . ," and only I see the light of the memorial candle by
the lectern overflow into a burning ocean, engulfing me on all
sides. My breath catches and sticks in my throat.

And when I open my eyes I find myself lying with my head
against the hard rock in the synagogue yard and around me,
like an angry stepmother, the dark, quiet night. There, on the
door to our little house, hangs a round black lock. I haven't
forgotten that, and a great fear grips my soul. I lower my face
to the damp earth and burst into tears, first softly with dry eyes,
and then louder and louder.

Somewhere high up under the synagogue eaves a bird
awakens, flutters its wings, and listens with dread.

✦ ☾ ✦

DVORA BARON *was born in a small town in Lithuania in 1887. Her father was a rabbi, and unlike most of his contemporaries, not only was he interested in educating his daughter in typical women's subjects, but he allowed her to attend the classes he taught the boys of the town (she sat behind a partition in the synagogue). She arrived on the literary scene in 1902, writing mostly in Hebrew—an instant marvel because she was female and was only fourteen years old, which was unheard of among Eastern European Hebrew writers at that time. She immigrated to Palestine in 1910. The first modern Hebrew woman writer, her stories focus on the shtetl and women's experiences in Jewish Eastern Europe. She died in 1956 in her apartment in Tel Aviv, having spent the previous thirty-three years as a shut-in and the last twenty years of her life completely bedridden. The stories reprinted in this collection are from her earlier Yiddish works.*

THE SACK WITH PINK STRIPES

Rachel H. Korn

Translated by Seymour Levitan

I t was a fairly long sack made of pink-striped linen, the kind of material that we called *gradl* and used for quilt covers and pillowcases. It was probably made out of a bit left over from my mother's trousseau. In it there was a "treasure"—various-colored balls of silk and cotton for knitting and stitching, pieces of violet canvas with started patterns of flowers and birds in cross-stitch, patterns that were never finished. Besides these, there were pieces of silk, velvet, brocade, and plain cotton print and percale, all left from my momma's trousseau and returned by the honest seamstresses in case it was necessary to fix a rip, sew on a patch, or widen a dress at the waist. As I remember, these remainders were never used because all these brocaded silk dresses intended for wear in the city hung in the wardrobe and were only removed to be aired out once a year just before Pesach. The dresses with the long trains would have been a fine sight in the mud of Fidilske.

And then it became our custom—when we had clothes

9

made for us, any pieces of material left over went into the secret depths of the sack with pink stripes. My greatest dream was to get the most colorful pieces of silk and velvet from those secret depths and sew dresses for my dolls out of them. But I didn't dare touch the sack, which was at the very bottom of the big chest in the bedroom all the way over under the window. Very deep under the shimmering "treasure" lay a bundle of letters from my mother's first betrothed. While she was searching for the right ball of thread, they would rustle under her fingers like dry November leaves.

All week I waited impatiently for Sunday afternoon. On Sunday afternoon, the hired farmhands slept in their fresh linen shirts—in the wintertime on the wide ovens and in summertime under the trees on the warm grass. Both summer and winter, the servants would be down in the village at their parents' houses and the cowherds would be busy with the cattle.

The cats that were always at my mother's side mewed and pleaded in the gathering quiet. Like a big dark spider, the clock on the wall spun the minutes and hours. The house was emptied of its weekday stir. This was the time when my mother would bend over the chest and take out the striped sack. She would begin to sew a pattern on canvas or mend a pillowcase, but in a little while her hands dropped and her glance wandered over the treetops to a place in the distance hidden from me. And my momma began to unwind the strands of her life, as if the smell of mildewed silk coming from the little sack had opened a secret door that she would never have opened on her own, afraid that it might lead her too far away from her home and children.

Ordinarily my mother didn't talk much. She was more inclined to listen to others. I never heard her complain about anything. And so the Jewish women of the village would come up to our farm on *Shabbes* to unburden themselves by talking

to her. Most often it was a cousin of my father's whom we children had to call "Aunt Chaye." She never stopped finding
fault with her husband, Chaim. He'd been cursed by his own
father, who wished Korach's fate on him, and he was stuck
with the name "Korach" for the rest of his life. Auntie Chaye
would lean her whole body against my mother's shoulder and
whisper endlessly in her ear, because everything was a secret to
Chaye. My mother would nod her head from time to time to
indicate that she was taking it in, though I'm sure that hardly
half of Chaye's grinding on and on penetrated.

It was only on Sunday afternoon that my mother gave up
her silence. To this day, I'm not sure if she was speaking to me
or to herself. Years later, as I began to understand what she told
me, it occurred to me that my mother wanted her daughter not
just to take in the details of her life, but to draw her own con-
clusions as well.

On those Sunday afternoons, in the shadow of my
mother's quiet words, I was suddenly a grown-up sharing her
youth. Till then I had been busy mainly with games, cats, dogs,
birds, trees, and dolls—I had no friends on our isolated farm.
We were far from the village, and this was my childhood
world. In contrast to the village children, who very early had
to take on their parents' worries and concerns about making a
living, I knew nothing about work or money. In our house we
never spoke about money. Money was an incidental thing. We
were never jealous of people who were better off, but when my
parents heard of an injustice, of someone being cheated or
swindled, they were outraged for a long while after. It pained
them exactly as if they'd been cheated themselves.

This was the world of my childhood, guarded by my
watchful parents. Until my father's early death left me an
orphan at ten and a half.

On those Sunday afternoons, I learned that both of my

zeydes were dead by the time I was born. My *zeyde* Leyzer Fast I know well from what my mother told me about him. He was tall, broad shouldered, with a thick blond beard that kept his smile warm. He was good-natured and ready to help. With his broad shoulders and warm smile, he would hide the crimes of his six children from Bubbe Rivka's stern eyes that darted about quick as mice. My mother truly idolized her father, and apparently my *zeyde* was especially close to her, the youngest of his three daughters.

He conducted business on a large scale. During the week, he went off into the forests he'd bought from the surrounding landowners, while my grandmother ran the farm and a tavern. Like her eyes, her hands never rested. Short, thin, with a dark complexion, she was everywhere. She ordered her sons around, her daughters, her staff. From their earliest youth, her children were expected to work. She hired the best religious and secular tutors for them, but the minute the tutor got up to go, Bubbe Rivka dispersed the group—one to the barn to do the milking, another to the granary, a third to the tavern. For her daughters, the "regime" was even stricter. "A girl only needs to learn how to read her prayers and sign her name." My mother, quiet and sensitive, couldn't stand her eternal bustling and dominating. My mother wanted to sit in a corner with a book and mull over the fate of the people she encountered in stories she read. When her mother sent her to the barn to keep an eye on the threshers, she would hide a book under her shawl and drink in the pages while the threshing tools beat the kernels of grain from the dry sheaves.

My *bubbe* was hot tempered and could blow up over the tiniest trifle. If something displeased her, she "rewarded" you for it then and there, whether or not the house was full of strangers. And then, later, calm, even smiling, as if nothing had happened, she'd go off to her work, leaving the children feeling as if they'd been beaten, shamed by their mother's unconcerned way. My mother, who took after her quiet, dreamy father, would rather have been slapped in private than humiliated in the presence of strangers. She'd wait all week for Friday, the day her father came home, and cling to his chest while her tears wet his thick broad beard.

My mother was tall and quite slender, with thin arms and legs and blond hair down to her knees. The heavy weight of her braids made her head ache, so she'd often let them hang down over her shoulders. Her little brother, Itsye, would wait for this. He would chase her all over the place and grab on to the long, heavy braids like reins.

My mother got sick when she was sixteen. There was a smallpox epidemic. The windows were curtained to shield her eyes from the light, and she pleaded to have her hands tied down to keep her from tearing at the blisters in her sleep. She knew very well that you could have the signs of the sickness all over your face for the rest of your life. When she got up and looked in the mirror for the first time, she fainted. It looked as if someone had rubbed a grater all over her pretty young face. . . . "And yet he fell in love with me. I don't know what he liked about me. He was so tall and handsome, with the kind of blue eyes you hardly ever see."

He really was as handsome as my mother said. His picture on the first page of our red satin photo album bore witness to it. "I also loved him very much, even though we weren't officially engaged, only promised to each other," my mother would add quietly with an embarrassed smile, as if she were defensive about being in love with her fiancé. My mother didn't know, or out of modesty wouldn't say, why Shmuel Rubenfeld loved her so, even though her face was no longer as fresh and sweet as it had been before her sickness. But I know why—no doubt because Shmuel Rubenfeld recognized her innate refinement and delicacy. And then, too, her graceful figure, her proud walk, her warm brown eyes, and those blond braids hadn't changed after her sickness.

The date was set for the wedding. The gown and trousseau were ready. Shmuel Rubenfeld was waiting for the day when he could bring his young wife to his small estate, Zalesia, which he'd inherited when he was orphaned at a young age. From his inheritance he had to provide a dowry and wedding for his youngest sister. Since it wasn't respectable for a young girl to live in a bachelor's house without appropriate supervision, Shmuel Rubenfeld kept her safe at his older, married sister's house in Pshemishl. In the meantime, the young landowner of Zalesia had the buggy fitted up or the horse saddled so that he could ride to Matskyevitsh to see his fiancée. Since it wouldn't look proper either to her household or to the neighbors for him to visit more than once or at most twice a week, he would send a letter by the hired hands every day. These were written so that the lines began with the letters of my mother's name read from top to bottom: Chania. My mother's name was Chana. She was called Chantsha at home. But her fiancé called her Chania. These letters from him were in the little pink-striped sack at the bottom of the chest.

Suddenly, like a bolt out of the blue, her fiancé's sister, the young girl who was staying with her older sister in the city, converted and married a blacksmith. They said that she did it to spite her sister, the wealthy, educated wife of the sawmill owner, because she didn't treat her well. When she would complain to her brother, he would plead with her, "Hold out just a bit longer. I'll be married in three weeks and you'll like living with my Chania."

One evening he came riding up, pale, upset. He found my mother on the porch and didn't make any attempt to come into the house. "You probably know what happened."

"Yes, I do."

"Your family will do everything they can to break our engagement. According to religious law, they can't do it without your consent. I want to know one thing—aside from what's happened, do you want to be my wife?"

"Yes, Shmuel."

"Can I be sure of you—you won't let them persuade you?"

"You can be sure of me."

"Then no one can tear you away from me, Chania—whatever happens, you'll be mine."

My *zeyde* Leyzer was dead by then. Just after my mother's sickness he suddenly collapsed, and in less than three days Leyzer Fast, always healthy, strong as an oak, left this world, his family, his fields and forests. When he went, my mother lost her support in life, her protector, the person who understood her so well, on whose chest she could cry her troubles away. If my *zeyde* had lived, he would have intervened for the sake of his daughter's happiness. My mother was sure of that.

The two older sons, Pinchas and Hersh, and the two younger daughters, Esther and Beyltshe, married while their father was still alive. The two youngest, who remained with my *bubbe* Rivka, were now the responsibility of her eldest son-in-law, Esther's husband, Reb Mordchele Engel, a man of few words and measured movements, with a long face, a dark complexion, almost as dark as his mother-in-law's, and a high, scholarly forehead. He knew his own worth and how to carry himself: he wanted everyone to feel he had been worth the large dowry that he received, but he also wanted them to know that he wasn't just Leyzer Matskyevitsh's son-in-law, he was Mordechai Engel. And the family went along with it. Whenever there was a business problem or an important family matter, they always asked his advice. Mordchele's word, no matter how quietly spoken, was law—and not just for his wife, who tried to read his slightest wish from his looks; even his mother-in-law brushed the dust from under his feet. This short, slight woman was the one who made the decisions when her tall, broad-shouldered husband was alive, but to her eldest son-in-law she was as submissive as if her husband's death had robbed her of all her drive, all her bustling energy.

This same Mordchele Engel, who'd come from Reyshe and spoke Polish like a true "landowner," quickly acquired a reputation throughout the region as a very clever, sedate young man, to whom one came for advice on all important matters. It didn't suit him to have the brother of a convert in the family, and he determined to use any means he could, even misrepresentation if necessary, to dissolve the match.

Without my mother knowing it, Shmuel Rubenfeld was called to the rabbi in Pshemishl. What happened there my mother never knew. Apparently the eldest brother-in-law used all his diplomatic strategies to convince her fiancé that it was all occurring with my mother's approval. And Shmuel Rubenfeld couldn't even for a moment suspect that this fine, refined man was lying. He probably thought that my mother had allowed herself to be persuaded by her family and had broken her word regardless of the fact that she'd promised him she would never agree to give up the match. When the daily visits and letters from her fiancé stopped, my mother realized that something bad had happened behind her back. She was ashamed to ask what and maybe even afraid to discover the truth. Once when she accidentally opened a dresser drawer, she saw her engagement agreement on the very bottom under all the documents and papers. These things were never discussed in our house. Shmuel Rubenfeld's name was never mentioned. "What I went through then only God in heaven knows. And what were either of us guilty of? We were going to be married three weeks later." My mother ended her story and sat quiet, deep in her own thoughts.

Yes, in three more weeks she would have been Chania Rubenfeld. Everything had been prepared.

Reb Mordchele and Bubbe Rivka began to look for a suitable match for my mother . . . "because the clothes made to order for the wedding might go out of style and they'd have had to order a new trousseau if they waited," my mother repeated bitterly a number of times. "No one thought of me. Only that the clothes might go out of style. It wasn't long before I was engaged to your father."

My parents got along very well together. I never heard them raise their voices. I only knew about arguments between husbands and wives because I was told that they happened in other families. My mother was the best, most devoted wife. She truly loved my father, she knew how to value his intellect and refinement. My father behaved with gentleness and chivalry to my mother. Not just in family matters. Even when selling grain or cattle or buying new plows or threshing machines, he would always ask his young wife's advice, though she still knew very little about such things.

My mother loved and respected my father, but she never forgot her first fiancé. Once, after she had become engaged again and had gone into Pshemishl with Bubbe Rivka to buy some things for her trousseau, she suddenly saw Shmuel Rubenfeld on the other side of the street. He was walking with his head down, as if he were afraid to lift his blue eyes to the sky. Had he noticed her, too? My mother didn't know, but she left my *bubbe* in the middle of the street and ran in the opposite direction. When she got home, she threw herself on her bed fully dressed and cried all night.

When I heard her tell all this, I wanted to scream, hammer my fists on the wall that bad people had set up between my mother and her destined one. "Why didn't you refuse instead of letting them do what they wanted with you, Momma?"

She lowered her head. "You're still a child. What do you understand about the world, about life? That's how things were done in those days. But I made a vow. That I would never keep a child of mine from marrying whoever they care to marry. A child of mine can bring me a shoemaker, a carpenter, can bring me someone off the street—I'll hold him dear. I will never stand in the way of my child's happiness."

Three weeks . . . if only Shmuel Rubenfeld's sister had waited three weeks. As it was, she not only destroyed the happiness of her brother and his fiancée, she darkened her own life. The blacksmith would go out and get drunk and beat her half to death. She stood over the washtub all day doing other people's laundry because her husband dropped all he earned at the tavern. A few years later she died of exhaustion, leaving two tiny children in Gentile hands. My father took sick three years after my parents married. They only lived together twelve years. He left behind a young widow and three small children.

Shmuel Rubenfeld remained a bachelor a few more years. When he finally did marry, he was also fated not to have an easy married life. A few years after the wedding, his wife was crippled. "Maybe everything would have been entirely different if people hadn't meddled with us." My momma sighed softly, as if even now after so many years she was trying to bargain with her fate.

The sun slanted down behind the mountain. My mother began to tie up the little striped sack. From the barn came the mooing of the cows to let us know that their udders were full and they were ready to be milked. The wives of the hired hands, who did the milking on Sundays, were banging the milking pails.

The Sunday afternoon ended.

✶ ☾ ✶

RACHEL H. KORN *was born in Podliski, East Galicia, in 1898. A writer of both prose and poetry, Korn escaped from Poland into the Soviet Union during World War II, settling in Montreal in 1948. She wrote "Dos roz-geshtrayfte zekele" [The Sack with Pink Stripes] near the end of her life. One of the two completed chapters of a memoir titled* Mayn heym un ich *[My Home and I] that she was planning on writing, this chapter has not been published before in Yiddish or in translation. The other chapter, "Dos naye hoyz" [The New House], written mainly from a child's point of view, tells of the building of the house she lived in through most of her childhood and adolescence. Korn's work has been translated into Hebrew, French, German, and English, and she was awarded the Manger Prize of the State of Israel in 1974. She died in Montreal in 1982.*

WINTER BERRIES

Fradel Schtok

Translated by Irena Klepfisz

Afresh snow covered the roofs, and the town was white. A winter happiness shone into the houses.

Reyzl wanted to go out, so when her mother gave Hessi the glass jar and five *graytsers* to buy kerosene, she offered to go instead. Everyone was taken aback that Reyzl had suddenly become such an obedient child, and her mother wondered whether perhaps something had died in the forest.

It was the season for winter berries—the first ice-cold berries. All along the streets Gentiles were hawking them, and when people caught sight of them through their windows, young and old ran out to buy clusters of berries. In almost all the bay windows, you could see bunches of icy berries displayed on white cotton.

Reyzl had a passion for winter berries, and when she remembered how they dissolved like wine in her mouth, her tongue puckered. She gave the five-note a squeeze—kerosene had to be bought.

21

Outside there was a searing frost, but the sun dazzled as it shone on the snow. Reyzl met a couple of mud-splattered boys running to the store to buy herring. The littlest one hobbled behind because his boots were too tight. Itsye Glezer with his neck all bundled up was carrying a windowpane under his arm. Somehow the frost had turned his yellow beard even more yellow. He was going somewhere to install a bay window.

Reyzl looked at his bundled-up neck and felt somewhat lonely. She remembered how at home she was considered the worst of all: wouldn't even stick her finger into cold water. At home they mockingly called her "Fraulein Paradisa." If she could only stop sleeping late, then Hessi wouldn't be waking her with "Fraulein Paradisa . . . please get up . . . Count Joseph has already gone off to church. . . . So now you too can get up." It didn't help to pretend to be sleeping. Hessi knew. And even if she had been sleeping, Hessi'd wake her up anyway. In the morning, while still in bed, she'd think about the most lovely things: about an aspiring lovelorn student, about a wonderful velvet dress trimmed with fur, or about wearing the wonderful velvet dress and dancing with a cavalier. But most of all, she'd think about running away to study in a big city and becoming a doctor—"Fraulein Doctor, excuse me . . ."

She walked through Chantsi's shop and noticed fur pieces hanging on display. Over there was a black Parisian hat that would be so becoming perched on her black head. . . . But her father is a poor man, and the brokerage's failing . . . and she's only the third in line. Everything has to go to Hessi first and to Rivtsi next and then finally to her. . . .

But what if she were to steal it? The hat's hanging so low to the ground, and right now no one's looking. But it would be recognized immediately. Her father would ask: "Where'd you get it?" "Found it." "Found it where?" "Don't know." And later? Oh, she'd have to face the humiliation . . . Reyzl the thief. Oh yes? A quiet one, can't even count to two. Go figure . . . really, a decent child. . . . The constable would take her to the town hall, and her mother and father would have to follow right behind. Mother'd cry, Father'd bite his pale lips. Surrounded by shame. Shame. And all the town's children would call after her: "Thief! Thief!"

No. She's an honest girl. She doesn't steal.

She walked farther down the street. She could sense that people were looking at her because she still wasn't quite grown-up, didn't stay close to home, respectable-like, but instead was seen everywhere. She had managed to meander to the outskirts of the city and met another Gentile woman with berries. She felt as if her throat were dying of thirst for berries. Precisely because she wasn't all grown-up, her heart was fainting, longing for something, wanting to escape out of itself and at the same time not wanting to escape at all. Why wasn't she grown-up yet? She should know why. How should she know? Besides, what does it mean to be "grown-up"? Getting up early, not thinking about the wonderful velvet dress trimmed with fur, washing the dishes, and worrying with her mother because there's no income . . . drumming it all out of her head: the aspiring, lovelorn student along with the dance and the cavalier and the dreams of becoming a doctor, of becoming respectable. Instead starting to mend socks. . . .

Oh, berries are bitter and they're juicy. . . . They're good and they're not good, the throat faints for them and the throat faints from them. . . . Where can one get a *graytser* for a cluster of berries? She'd willingly give up her life for the taste of just one berry.

Reyzl gave the five-note a strong tug and turned red. And then she simply went up to the Gentile and told her to give her five clusters of berries. The woman stopped, put her basket on the ground, and selected the clusters. Reyzl handed her the five-*graytser* note, which was damp from her hot palm, and arranged the clusters like a bouquet.

When the Gentile was already at some distance from her, Reyzl was still rooted to the same spot. She suddenly asked herself: "What have you done? *Nu*, and the kerosene?" But she muffled these questions with other voices, so she wouldn't regret spending the five *graytsers*. "*Nu*, and what will you tell them at home?" "Lost. Lost and that's that." "How did you manage to lose it? Why didn't you lose your head instead? That would've been better."

She put a berry in her mouth. The bitter wine–like sap melted coldly on her tongue, and her veins now really constricted. It seemed as if she were swallowing the clear frost, the cold sun on the snow, and in her red blood the juice dissolved and became fire.

She'd spent the five *graytsers*. Tonight there'll be no kerosene at home. They'll have to sit in the dark. There's no other five-*graytser* notes. . . . Suddenly she imagines herself becoming a good child . . . no minor task. She never obeys, but now—oh . . .

So why is her heart weeping even more? And the kerosene glass jar . . . Take it home. No, say you broke it. With each new berry that she swallows, her heart weeps more.

She plucks a berry from the cluster, as from a bouquet, and swallows—tormented. She watches as there are fewer and fewer red berries left. All that remains are brown thin little sticks, frozen and covered with snow. It pains her to tear off the berries, and with each one it feels as if she were again swallowing the five-note.

Suddenly, she noticed that people were looking up at the gate. People were stepping away to the side, and Gentiles were taking off their hats. A dog ran out in front.

The minister's young son.

All in all, he wasn't more than eighteen years old, two years older than her—very good. Look how delicate, how regal he is. Blond hair, light blond up to his neck, then turning gold. Exactly at the neck. Looking off so proudly, somewhere far beyond the city. The city belongs to his father.

With a trembling heart, she looked at the young count's knee-high hunting boots, at the rifle on his shoulder, at the hunting bag, and at the way his servant followed behind him.

She remembered their poor home and how today they wouldn't have any kerosene because she had "lost" the five *gray-tsers*. And she had an urge to run after the count, to chase after him, after his good fortune, which shone like a star in the sky because he had been born a count, a minister's son. He . . . perhaps he'll fall in love with her? Maybe he'll fall in love with her and carry her away into the forest and away from her poor home? Into the forest to the hunt . . . And afterward—to the palace beyond the gate—and later to Vienna . . . to the court, to . . .

Was she mad?

She continued some distance on the road past the shops, then ran in one breath to catch up with him.

When she got near the church, she was gasping. Her hot blood rushed thick into her blooming cheeks, which burned and tingled. She began to walk in the middle of the street with stately, carefully measured steps. She looked down on the ground and gently swung the bouquet of berries back and forth. She felt the distance between them shrinking, and her heart began to beat more loudly. Suddenly a kind of arrogance awakened in her.

"Don't raise your head, don't raise your head. No, no, don't raise your head! Don't even look at him! Not look at the minister's son? No, no, no . . ." She turned off to one side and ran away. And then she regretted that she'd run away.

"Who are you, Fraulein Paradisa?"—This heartache becomes

you. Went off for kerosene and ate up—no, lost the five-
graytser note. . . .

The berries are so bitter—"What is he? Not just as good a
person as everyone else? Is he an angel? When he undresses—
naked . . . Shhhha . . ."

His face dazzles like the snow, and he leaves here with a
proud step. It's not good here. His proud step is taking him to
another place so that people won't be able to look at him,
won't be able to draw any pleasure.

The berries torment her heart, torment her heart.

And what's to be done about the kerosene? The kerosene—
what's to be done? It's already getting dark.

Why are berries bitter? And though bitter, why so
good? . . . And if her heart faints for them, why does it faint
from them?

She turned back toward the shops, but her heart chased
after him and after the good fortune that had made him noble,
royal, so that his face dazzled like the snow. . . .

★ ☾ ★

FRADEL SCHTOK *was born in Skale, Galicia, in 1890, and immi-*
grated to the United States in 1907, where she first became noticed for
her poetry. Yankev Glatshteyn was one of the first to praise her work.
Her poetry and fiction began to appear regularly in all the major Yiddish
papers (Tsukunft, Forverts, and others). Dertseylungen [Stories], her
only collection of fiction—from which the two stories included here are
drawn—appeared in 1919. The stories are situated both in shtetlech
(in some cases Skale) and in the United States. They reflect unfulfilled
dreams of sexual and social yearnings and range in tone from repressed
rage to gentle satire. The women in her stories seem particularly thwarted
by Jewish conventions and try to rebel, usually unsuccessfully. One of
the rare writers to produce work in English, in 1927 Schtok published
For Musicians Only, a novel that drew neither praise nor attention.

For unknown reasons (perhaps depression), Schtok was institu-

tionalized sometime after the novel's appearance. Until recently, her life, beginning with this institutionalization, remains undocumented, and other writers seem to have lost contact with her. It has always been assumed, therefore, that she died while confined, though no specific date of her death has ever been given. Recently, however, correspondence and some short fiction by her written in the 1940s was discovered in the Abraham Cahan archives at YIVO. The exact date of her death is still not known, though it is assumed to be later than originally thought. Translations of other Schtok stories appear in The Tribe of Dina: A Jewish Woman's Anthology *and in* Found Treasures: Stories by Yiddish Women Writers.

My First Readers

Rochel Faygenberg

Translated by Sheva Zucker

1

I was fourteen years old when my grandmother told me that I was grown-up now and ought to be thinking about the future. But I wasn't at all interested in being serious like grown-ups. I would slip away from home and, as if intoxicated, spend the days wandering through the sunny streets of this strange city* I'd come to with my grandmother. It was springtime. The air in this sparkling city by the sea was fragrant with acacia blossoms. On both sides of the street the leaves on the trees were turning green, glistening in the sunny golden light and casting cool shadows on the brightly paved sidewalks. A festive crowd strolled by me, dressed in white, with panama hats atop smiling faces.

Everyone was so happy here, under the southern skies that

---

*The Yiddish original offers a footnote saying that the city referred to is Odessa. We also know this both from Faygenberg's biography and from the later mention of the Moldovanka, which is a section of Odessa. [Translator's note] were so fair and blue, but so alien to me, a bewildered young girl from a small town back in the dark oak forests of White Russian Polesia. It was easy for a girl like me to get lost in the crowd. But Grandma kept saying that I was grown-up now.

Without eating, I would sit all day on the boulevard under a white linden tree in full bloom. Beside me was the senti-mental Yiddish novel that I had brought from home. I gazed into the mirrorlike expanse of the blue sea and tried to think about what would become of me, but I couldn't come up with anything. I felt light-headed, intoxicated by the sunshine and the luscious acacia blossoms.

When I came home it was already after supper. I sneaked into the dining room; the doors and windows were wide open. I took something to eat from the credenza and listened to what was being said about me out on the balcony.

There was a family conference going on there. They were deliberating over my future. Grandmother clung resolutely to her opinion that I simply had to outgrow my small-town ways; in a few years she would start thinking about a match for me. To this end, she was ready to spend money so that I could learn to dance and speak Russian fluently like all big-city girls from good families.

But my grandmother's grown-up children did not agree with her. Her youngest daughter, her son-in-law, and her educated daughter-in-law from the big city were there, full of good advice. They offered a grandiose suggestion that I get a diploma as a barber-surgeon; that would give me some status in society. They also pro-posed a plan for me to learn a trade, and they explained it in the most practical terms: A good seamstress could support herself any-where. But my grandmother protested passionately, saying she would not allow it. Her daughter's child was not, God forbid, a homeless orphan who needed to earn a living. Why, tomorrow she would hire a Russian teacher for me and send me to dancing lessons.

I heard all of this through the open door of the balcony. I was sitting out of sight in the next room, at the table in the corner. Sunburned and famished from my day in the fresh air, I ate my late supper with gusto. Already I was feeling confined in the house. Once again, I wanted to roam about the exotic tree-lined streets of the city, fragrant with acacia blossoms. But now, in the evening, I was back under my grandmother's watchful eye. At any minute she could come in. After supper I buried myself in my Yiddish novel so that she might find me reading, as befitted a big-city girl from a good family. But I already knew the novel by heart, and the sadness of the fragrant spring night began to haunt me once again.

Suddenly, the door of the balcony closed. Apparently, my grandmother and her guests did not want anyone to hear what they were saying. Near the table stood my grandmother's servant girl, Hinde. She was tall and thin, with long, toil-worn hands. She had a round face with little black whiskers sprouting on her upper lip. Upset and distracted, she stared at me with her watery eyes. "Can you write Yiddish," she asked, "or just read?"

"I can write."

Hinde wrung her hands. "What a fool I am!" she blurted out angrily. "For a week I've been walking around like a dolt looking for someone to write a Yiddish letter for me. I beg of you, write a letter for me. I'll pay you."

I burst out laughing. "Pay? Who on earth pays money for writing letters?"

"No, no, child, I don't want it for nothing. They say that in the Moldovanka there is a man, a *melamed* who writes Yiddish letters. He charges a gulden for a letter, so that's what I'll pay you. I looked for him all week, but I couldn't get his address."

"Who do you want to write to?"

Hinde stared with her big watery gray eyes and answered

very quietly, "I'll tell you who, but please, I beg of you, don't tell your grandmother. The letter is for my fiancé. Do you know how to write to a fiancé?"

"No."

"So what are we going to do?" she asked, standing there and wringing her hands as she pondered the matter.

"I don't know," I said as if I were guilty of something. "At home, in our town, I wrote letters for women to their husbands in America, and I wrote one letter from a mother to a son. He's a *chazzen* and a *bal-darshn* in a synagogue in America; there he leads prayers and also delivers sermons on the Torah. He sent his mother his picture; in it he's wearing golden spectacles and a little silk tallis that looks like a woman's shawl. He's a big man in America. But writing to a fiancé is different. I don't know if I can do it."

"Maybe you could try?"

"All right. I'll try."

"Yes, yes. Try!" she interrupted hastily, as if someone were running after her.

"But I need his picture."

"What do you need his picture for?" Hinde asked in amazement.

"What do I need his picture for? I just do. When I see what he looks like, I'll know how to write to him."

"You're putting me on." The girl smiled in embarrassment.

"No, I really mean it. I would think that you have to write a certain way to a fiancé who's handsome and differently to one who's not."

"I suppose you're right. Well, all right, I'll give you his photograph. But be careful, child. Your grandmother had better not find it among your things."

"Don't worry," I reassured her.

Hinde reached her long bony hands into her bosom, took out a crumpled postcard, and handed it to me. "That's him."

It was a photo of a handsome, spiffed-up dandy, his slicked-down chestnut hair parted on the side. He was sitting in a soft armchair, one leg folded over the other. On his knees lay a newspaper.

"What is he, a bookkeeper?"

Hinde tightened her black-whiskered little mouth piously and reverently, as if she were about to say a prayer. "He could certainly be a bookkeeper. The fellow has a mind like a steel trap and his grandfather was a *shoychet* in their town, but he grew up an orphan, poor thing, with a stepmother, so he had no schooling. All he can write is Yiddish."

"So what does he do?"

The girl was silent. Then she stammered between her teeth, "You have to know that, too, to write the letter?"

"Yes."

"But you won't understand. He has the kind of work that not everyone can understand."

"Well, if you don't want to say, you don't have to. Try to find that man, the *melamed* in the Moldovanka, and he'll write you the kind of letter you want."

Hinde flared up with resentment. "What a wicked girl! She insists on having her way. She has to know what his business is, of all things. Just write the letter. Write that I'm sending him three rubles by mail, so that he can apply for a new permit at home, because without it he'll be in big trouble here again."

"And where's his old permit? Did he lose it?"

"You have to know that as well?"

"Yes, I actually have to know that as well," I said, trying to sound glib.

"You're wicked, and that's all there is to it! A person pleads with you and asks a favor, and you carry on and give her no peace. I'm sorry, you're not a bad person, you have a Jewish heart. You're always reading Yiddish books. If you don't want to be paid for writing the letter, I'll buy you something with the gulden."

"What, for instance?" I asked, leafing quietly through the novel I had already finished.

"Today in the marketplace I saw little handkerchiefs for girls in all different colors," she said, "so fine, delicate as silk, with lace borders, and in the middle there are initials stitched for any name you might want. Tomorrow I'll buy you a pink one, all right? A long day like today and you've barely finished a glass of borscht. Think what you'll look like if you keep eating like that. At least take a few dumplings left over from lunch. A wild goat, she roams about the streets alone, starving."

She ran into the kitchen and brought back a tin pan with five large cheese dumplings, browned and fried in butter. "Here, you miserable wretch. Keep this up and you'll drop dead. Your grandmother is an old woman, may she live to a ripe old age. She wants to make sure she has a share in the World to Come. She's so pious she's already preparing her place there. And your aunts have children of their own. Do you understand, child, sometimes a stranger is more devoted than family. Well, try a dumpling. You're as green as a church steeple."

But I just kept my gaze fixed on my novel. "Thanks, Hinde, but I'm not hungry. Put the dumplings away for tomorrow, and don't buy me any handkerchiefs because I won't let you pay me. If you want me to write your fiancé a letter, you'll have to tell me what he does."

Hinde began blinking her eyes and staring, numb and frightened by her own helplessness. "Fine, fine, you little witch, I'll tell you. He is . . . he is a 'banger.'"

"What is a 'banger'?"

"Every single thing she has to know. The girl is going to

drive me crazy this very day. All right, I'll explain. But your grandmother's coming. Hide the photo, hide it, girl."

She sprang out of the dining room, pan in hand, but she was not fast enough to escape notice. My two aunts were entering near the open balcony door, dressed neatly in white with big straw hats tilted over their foreheads. After them came my uncle, his silk jacket unbuttoned over his white piqué vest.

"You have nothing better to do than spend your time with Hinde?" my big-city aunt asked me in her high-toned way.

But my little old grandmother settled things. "Tomorrow I'm going to hire a teacher, so she'll have plenty to do."

I smiled a foolish, bashful smile.

2

My grandmother's maid, Hinde, was distraught. Her round face with its sunken cheeks was flushed with agitation. Ceaselessly, she would stare with her big watery eyes, helpless and dull, like a scared sheep. She caressed me as if I were a tremulous only child and ministered to my every need. She polished my shoes every morning, wouldn't let me wash my own socks and blouses, protected me from drafts whenever I sat down opposite the wide-open windows and doors of our big, sprawling dining room, and was always on the lookout for a chance to slip me a tasty morsel of food.

Hinde's devotion to me was boundless. But she did it all mutely, angrily, like a resentful but devoted mother. She constantly sought ways to break through my stubbornness so that I would write to her fiancé without knowing his occupation. There was no way that she wanted to tell me what a "banger" was.

But she couldn't hold out: one afternoon when my grandmother had gone to lie down for a while, she slowly closed the door of the bedroom where her old mistress had dozed off on her old-fashioned sofa bed, and, quietly, she asked me, "Do you have time now?"

"What is it?"

"My life depends on this letter. I'll give you some ink and a pen and a piece of paper. Since you've taken it into your head that you must know what my fiancé does, I'll do what you want, and tell you. I already told you that he is a 'banger.'"

I looked into her eyes with suspicion and exaggerated earnestness. "But what is a 'banger'?"

Hinde turned red. "What should it be?" she blurted out in a stammer. Then she began to speak quickly. "Banging is a way of making a living like any other. Sometimes better, sometimes worse. Well, how should I explain it to you? He works in the marketplace. Sometimes there are customers there who are not too smart—from the small towns and villages, or simply half-wits. So they put one over on them when they pay for the merchandise."

"I don't understand," I broke in sternly.

"Silly girl, what's not to understand? While the customers are paying they confuse them so much with the 'banging' that they knock a few coins right into their own pockets. But you have to be good at it, and my fiancé is a sharp fellow. Here, in the old marketplace, nobody bangs as well as he does. He can spot one of these suckers at a glance, some of them sell merchandise and others buy, and the 'banged-off' profit is split fifty-fifty with the 'banger.'"

Suddenly she became silent, as if short of breath. She looked down at the ground with a frozen glance, anticipating my harsh verdict. But at that moment I just wanted to laugh, without knowing why. She didn't see that I was smiling at her. "Does he make a lot of money from it?"

"It depends," Hinde replied in a guilty voice. "I told you it's a way of making a living like any other, sometimes better, sometimes worse, as God wills."

"But that's stealing." I laughed at her again.

"He says that everyone steals, the rich steal even more than the poor."

"Is that what he says, your fiancé?"

"That's what he says. He's got a real head on his shoulders. If he were educated, he might be the director of a company."

She ran into the kitchen and brought the cherished piece of stationery and the envelope that had lain under her pillow for weeks.

"So now you know what to write. Write that for the three rubles that I'm sending him, he should get a new permit, and add at the end that that she-devil of his doesn't give a damn about him. She's going around with someone else. Found herself some guy with one eye. He got the other one knocked out in the Moldovanka for his good deeds. Yup, he can forget her, that she-devil of his."

"Who is 'that she-devil'?" I asked seriously now.

"What's it to you who she is? But if you need it to write the letter, I can tell you."

"Of course I need it to write the letter."

"Okay, have it your way. You know everything anyway. She, that she-devil, is his . . . his . . . well, she's his wife. . . ."

These words put me into a playful mood again. I was laughing so hard, I could barely breathe. "Your fiancé has a wife? He's a married man?"

Hinde looked at me grimly, pursing her lips and flushed with insult and pent-up anger. "You be quiet, you wild goat. The old lady will wake up and we'll both get it. Now write, will you, you wicked girl."

"Okay, okay, I'll write. But tell me, Hinde, how can a

fiancé have a wife? Hinde dear, I'll kiss you to pieces, tell me, how can it be?"

"What a nuisance you are, like a sickness that won't go away." She sighed. "But tell me the truth, you little witch, do you really need to know that to write the letter?"

"Yes, yes, yes!"

"All right, I'll tell you. She is a wife and she isn't. He had a 'quiet wedding.' That's when you get married on the quiet in some out-of-the-way place so that nobody will know. It's valid only under Jewish law. You have that kind of wedding when you don't have a permit. Now do you get it?"

"I get it. And do you want to have a 'quiet wedding' with him, too?"

I asked this in my lighthearted joking manner, without the faintest notion that for Hinde it was now a matter of life and death. Her watery, glassy eyes started blinking furiously, and her whole face lit up as if on fire.

"Me—a 'quiet wedding'? Me? If I were set on marrying him under the chimney, I could have done it long ago. But I'm not some piece of trash. I have a family, and a respectable one, too. All his life my father was one of the rebbe's assistants, and to this day my mother visits the *rebbitsin*."

"What are you getting so steamed up about?" I asked. "Did something I say offend you? I didn't mean to."

Hinde would not be appeased. "Don't talk nonsense," she said, and gave me a heartfelt scolding. "Do you think I'm a piece chipped off of a stone? Don't think I sprang from nowhere just because here in the city if you fell into a hole no one would notice you were missing. In our town, everybody, young and old, knows me. I can take a train ride for a few hours and be home. My second cousins hold the lease on the mill. Oh, anything but a quiet wedding! I would suffer another fifteen years in strangers' houses, I would stay single until I turned gray. I'm not some loose woman. A husband has to be a husband, as God commanded, according to Jewish law and also according to the law of the land. Now do you know why I'm sending him money for a permit?"

"I know, I know everything now," I said. "Now I'll try to write your letter. But remember, if it's no good, I don't want you to complain, because I really don't know how to write to a fiancé. Back home I only wrote letters for women whose husbands were in America, and one for a mother to her son asking him to send money to repair her house."

Once again, my Hinde took from her bosom the wrinkled postcard with her fiancé's photo and laid it on the table, even though I hadn't asked her for it. Then she spread a newspaper over the checked oil tablecloth, making it comfortable for me to write, and tiptoed out of the room.

Diligently, I set to work at the new tasks that Hinde had ordered me to perform. When my grandmother woke up and came into the dining room, she found me sitting at the table, pen in hand, completely flushed. I was so engrossed in my task that I didn't notice her coming in. I saw her only when I heard her voice. "What are you so worked up about?" she asked in amazement. "What are you writing with such passion?"

I quivered and with my elbow quickly shuffled onto my knees the picture of the spiffed-up dandy that the servant girl had left on the table. I mustered up my courage so that I could answer very clearly that I was writing a letter for Hinde to her mother in the provinces.

"Fine, very nice, but why must you get so fired up about it? This sort of thing has to be done calmly. Oh, my dear child, you're still wild."

Fortunately, my grandmother didn't stay nearby for long. After gently reprimanding me, she put on her apron and her frilly black bonnet and went outside under the quivering gaze of Hinde, who waited by the door with a pounding heart to see that nothing impeded the holy work that I was doing for her. It was already dark in the house when I finished the letter. She turned off the lamp and we both sat down at the table. But I could barely finish reading the letter to her. After the first few lines, tall Hinde with the long, toil-worn hands began gaping and swallowing her tears the way a goose swallows its food. In that fashion, she managed to listen to the letter until the very end.

I was beside myself. Thinking that I had offended her with my silly, bad letter, I tried making excuses for myself. "I told you I didn't know how to write to a fiancé. I told you that before. Here, I'm going to tear up the letter—and that'll be it."

But the teary Hinde snatched the piece of paper from my hands and kissed it. "Silly girl," she said, "why, it's sweet as sugar. You've made me so happy. You're just a child, how did you know what to write? How did you know what I was thinking? I should kiss your sweet little hands for writing such a letter!"

Exuberant, she ran into the kitchen with the letter in her hand, but soon she came running back with a silver twenty-kopeck coin between her rough, toil-worn fingers. "Here, this is for your work. The *melamed* on the Moldovanka charges a gulden for writing a Yiddish letter, and I'm giving you more. You've earned it, that's for sure. If you want, I'll send you more people who need Yiddish letters and you'll be able to earn a pretty penny. Your grandmother is concerned about your future. Well, this is a very genteel occupation. Listen to me, girl, don't look for anything else."

But I didn't take the money. "I'll ask Grandma if I'm allowed to take money for writing." I barely managed to utter this, and to Hinde's amazement, I burst out crying like a small child.

3

All alone, as always. I wandered over the strange, sunny city, intoxicated by the blossoming trees and the blue gold brightness reflected in the shimmering expanse of sea.

I thought about the new future that my grandmother's servant girl, Hinde, had devised for me. She had promised to arrange many clients for me with orders for Yiddish letters, for which I would be paid the same as the old letter writer from the Moldovanka. I would be paid in cash, and I would be able to buy myself whatever I wanted. Just roaming over the sunny streets on a summer's day, I could order a cool and refreshing glass of seltzer water with a red candy. I could get myself a fruit cake filled with jam and the delicate pink handkerchiefs with the letters stitched in the middle that were so inexpensive and so pretty. A person could buy herself anything with her own money, even a new Yiddish novel.

No, I still had to ask my grandmother if it was all right to take money for writing Yiddish letters. Hinde still had the silver twenty-kopeck piece that she owed me for my work. How did one begin talking to Grandmother about these things? Somehow I did not know what to say to her. With one word she could completely undo me. She was very devout but was not kindhearted or given to tenderness. She did, however, possess an inborn intelligence and a bit of idealism with which she struggled against her hardened spirit. She was always vigilant, guarding her faults from strangers' glances, which made her feel in control of herself. She had plenty of free time, and her exemplary and genuine piety not only served to secure her place in the World to Come, but also stood her in good stead in her struggle to earn a living.

Here, in the great strange city where Jews spoke in all seventy languages, my pious grandmother had a thriving business.

She had inherited her prosperity from my grandfather. He, the learned Litvak,* taught bar mitzvah and kaddish Judaism†— that is to say, the bare rudiments of the religion—to the rich city children. It was also his job to provide his students' parents with matzos for Passover, because these rich people who lived like Gentiles all year long observed Passover with great care and trusted only him, the pious Torah scholar from Lite.

And my grandfather did his job to perfection. Every year he would provide these assimilated rich people with kosher matzos baked according to his Litvish standard of *kashres*, and he was nicely paid for it. The week of Passover brought him more income than his bar mitzvah and kaddish lessons. After his death, this continued to be a respectable livelihood for my grandmother. The assimilated Jews placed the same trust in her strict Litvish piety, and she was paid generously for the Passover Jewishness she provided.

For two or three months a year she fussed over her rich customers' Passover orders, and then she went back to doing her daily mitzvahs quietly, running to the little Litvish synagogue three times a day to hear the *kedushah* prayer. She measured the streets of the city by the psalms that she would recite by heart while walking to synagogue, and her day was complete when she managed to give the last bit of the lunch she

---

*Litvak—A Litvak is a Lithuanian Jew, but the place name Lite, which is often translated as "Lithuania," refers not only to Lithuania but also to the northeast of the European Jewish settlement area corresponding to White Russia (present-day Belarus), Latvia, and Estonia. A Litvak may be from any of these places. The heroine of this story and her family are from White Russia, hence they are still Litvish. Jews from Lite are typically non-Chasidic and are known for their strict observance of Jewish law and rationalistic approach to Judaism. [Translator's note.]

---

†Bar mitzvah and kaddish Judaism—Bar mitzvah is the ceremony marking a Jewish boy's coming of age and assumption of religious responsibility at the age of thirteen. Kaddish is the prayer for the dead. For assimilated Jews, these rituals are often all that remains of their Judaism. [Translator's note.]

had cooked to a pauper and had tossed the few copper coins in her pocket into the two charity boxes above the door.

My grandmother really didn't approve of the great sunny city that had so intoxicated me with its shimmering blue radiance and white-clad summer residents. She would frequently go home to our faraway town in White Russian Polesia to buy food and clothing. There she procured strictly kosher dried mushrooms and pears and grated a year's supply of dried yellow farfel, perfectly round bits of dough that were heavy as buckshot. She fried kosher-for-Passover fat for herself and her Passover customers, the wealthy, highly assimilated city Jews, and she would also buy them bleached thin linen for Passover towels. While there, she always made a point of having Asher the shoemaker make her two pairs of shoes. She would also have Zechariah the tailor make her two winter dresses, one for everyday and one for the Sabbath, and every three years Zechariah would have to sew a new lining into both of her overcoats. She couldn't wear shoes made in the city, nor did she think much of city sewing. Aside from not trusting the workmanship, she was very afraid of *shatnez*, the mixing of linen and wool in one garment, forbidden by Jewish law.

The old woman was very concerned about her own security. She also wanted to protect me and was particularly anxious about my fate here in the big city, which had frightened her for years with its heresy and wanton living.

One day she stopped me in the street, when I was walking, lost in thought as I looked at some boy in a light striped jacket hurrying somewhere, his heavy white shoes clattering over the cobblestone sidewalk.

"Why are you wandering around like a drunkard? Where are you going?"

I trembled and stood still. "I am going home."

"But you're going completely in the wrong direction. Oh,

young lady, you need a strong hand over you. Did you at least do your homework?"

"I did."

I set off for home with her, ashamed and angry. It was always like that. With one word she could reduce me to nothing. But when we turned into the quiet street where we lived, I was again brave and asked with exaggerated seriousness, "Grandma, may one take money for writing a Yiddish letter?"

The refined old woman just stood there on the sidewalk. With trembling hands she took her glasses out of her pocket, set them on her nose, placed the wires behind her ears, and then looked at me in amazement. Her sunken mouth drew itself together with a mean, female doggedness. She stood near me like this, pious and intelligent, her shiny black wig tucked under a gray silk kerchief with a starched pointy white collar at her thin wrinkled throat. But she controlled herself and answered me in a dignified, strict, motherly tone, "You mean that letter that you wrote for Hinde?"

"Yes," I answered, blushing. "She wants to pay me."

"How coarse can you get?" Her harsh judgment fell like a stone on my burning head. "Your father suffered in poverty his whole life because he did not want to be a rabbi. He did not want to make money off the Torah, and you are so base that you want to take money from a poor servant girl for writing a letter. You gave an old mother pleasure by sending her news from her child, suffering among strangers in the city, and you want to be paid for that? I don't know how you got to be so coarse. When your mother was your age she wasn't like that."

I listened to my stern and exemplary judge, sick with shame, but tried to defend myself. "But it was her idea to pay me for the letter. Hinde herself said that this was a job like any other job."

"Is that what she told you, the genius? And what about doing someone a favor, and the mitzvah of gladdening a mother's heart? Getting paid for writing a letter—what a coarse person won't think of next!"

But wanting to explain the thing in practical terms, I racked my brains and said that in any case I would like to earn something so that I would not be a burden on her weak shoulders.

"Are you lacking for anything, God forbid?" she asked resentfully.

"Who said I'm lacking for anything? But I'm almost grown-up, so I need my own money so that I can buy whatever I want."

"Such as?"

"Well, sometimes in the heat I feel like having a glass of seltzer water." The red candy that so tantalized me, I didn't mention.

"Is that what it's about? The things that a fourteen-year-old girl can think of."

An emotional person in her own way, she ran to the nearest general store and told them to pour me a big glass of seltzer water. Without juice and without a candy, I could barely drink even half.

"Why are you leaving so much? You were just dying for a glass of seltzer water. You don't know what you want."

She paid and set out for home. I followed her down the quiet, shady street set between tall buildings and looked up at the telegraph wires covered by a thin strip of sky.

"Girl, are you looking to see how birds fly?" someone shouted to me while passing by. "Watch out or you'll bump your nose on somebody's shoulder."

This time I was lucky. Grandmother didn't hear his remark. She had already reached the gate. But when we were inside the house, she said worriedly, "I'd like to find you a friend, but I don't trust the city girls. They all go around with boys."

"What's wrong with that? You want me to be refined like a city girl, don't you?"

Apparently she didn't like my answer one bit, because her thin lips drew together again scornfully. But she pulled back right away (oh, my grandmother knew herself very well).

"Is that what you think big-city refinement consists of?" she responded in an unassuming, pious manner. "You're mistaken, my child. There are also respectable girls in the city. Those who aren't, run around with boys. There are some girls here who are well brought up and have finer notions, but where does one find them? Your mother went to her grave a young woman, and in my old age I have to provide guidance for a small girl, here in this godforsaken, lawless city where hell burns at every step."

A tear fell from her eye onto her shriveled cheek. She washed her hands and went to say her afternoon prayers.

4

I acquired a new client.

One evening when my grandmother went to visit my aunt after saying the evening prayers in the Litvish synagogue, our maid, Hinde, brought over a small woman with a bright face and a head of curly blond hair. She smiled affably, speaking to me in a very familiar manner, as if she were an old friend. She introduced herself right away, although I already knew who she was. Here, in one of the houses in our courtyard, she nursed a child who belonged to the rich Barsky family. I would often meet her on the steps, noisily following the Barskys' two maids, who, after walking the baby, would take the carriage and the child into the house and carry them up to the third floor. The woman looked very handsome; her round white chin and her dainty hands bore witness to the generous room and board she received from her wealthy employers.

Apparently, she really liked her unusual occupation, which, as the wet nurse of her child, allowed her to lord it over her rich mistress, because she soon boasted to me of the privileges she had. She got to eat all sorts of rare delicacies, and she ruled over the two maids. If she had so much as the slightest desire to eat anything, she could wake them in the middle of the night and have them cook for her. There was only one thing that wasn't so good—she was bound to the child like a dog on a leash. She didn't have a moment to herself. She wasn't even allowed to go see her own child. Once a week he was brought to her for just an hour. But before she could turn around, the time had flown away and he was taken from her. He couldn't stay for even a minute longer or they'd be looking at their watches. But she took her revenge. After these visits she did such things to spite them that her lord and lady and their two maids spat up bile, but to no avail. She was nursing the child, and you don't change wet nurses. They had to give in to all of her whims.

The pretty woman blurted all this out in great haste, as if she were afraid that she might be pulled away to her nursing duties before she finished. Suddenly she became very serious and said, "Listen, young lady, write a letter for me to my soldier in Warsaw, and you'll see how I'll reward you."

"I won't take payment for it," I hastened to answer. "My grandmother says that one mustn't take money for writing letters."

The wet nurse broke into a smile, with both her cheeks dimpling. "Foolish child! Money? Who's talking about money? But if you do somebody a favor, that person should not be a pig. You're still a young child, and your grandmother is an old woman. Sometimes you may want to eat sweets, sometimes you may want something pretty, and such a thing would never even occur to an old woman. Taking money for writing a letter may not be nice, but there's nothing wrong with eating sweets. Have you ever written to a soldier?"

"To a soldier? No."

"It doesn't matter. I'll tell you how."

"She'll know how to do it herself!" Hinde spoke up impulsively, as she was wont to do. "She can think for herself, and she always knows exactly what you want to say. What a head she has on her shoulders!"

"The soldier, is he your husband?"

I asked this simply, without any ulterior motives, because she could also have had a brother who was serving in the military. In fact, I really did think it was her husband.

But my client didn't answer right away. Hinde looked her in the face contemptuously, as if she might burst out laughing any minute. But the wet nurse endured her silent assault. She smiled in her amiable manner and sang out in a sweet voice, "Yes, he's my husband. But the child was born when he was in the service. He doesn't know the baby yet."

Hinde made a face, swallowing the mocking laugh that was hovering on her lips. The woman shot her a sidelong glance and once again piped up. "Yes, I'm going to write him about the child right now. After all, he's already a big boy, six months old. Do you know how to write to a husband?"

"Yes, that I do know. At home I used to write letters for all the women in town whose husbands were in America."

"Very good"—the young woman was delighted—"but this time you will write a little differently. After all, he's a soldier and he's not in America. You'll write with love, as if you were writing to a fiancé."

Hinde became impatient. "Leave her alone. She'll know what to do on her own. You don't need to teach her anything."

"I know, I know! But listen, child. You have to do me a favor and write the letter in the nursery because I had better not stay here one minute longer. Besides, it's quiet there. You'll really enjoy it. I'll give you some chocolate and a piece of rye cake. . . . You'll sit there, chewing as slowly as you like and writing. All right?"

The invitation made me uncomfortable. "Should I come now?" I asked.

"Yes, now. Nobody's home. My lord and lady went to the theater."

"No, I can't come to your place now. My grandmother will be home soon and I'd better be here."

The pretty, well-fed wet nurse gave Hinde a slap on the hip with her bare hand. "Later, then—when the old lady goes to sleep, pop in to the nursery with her to see me. By the time they get home from the theater the letter will be ready. Go in right here through the back door. We'll do it quick: I'll have the pen and ink and paper ready on the table. While we're at it, we'll eat something, too. Do you hear, girl? As soon as the old lady dozes off, the two of you come up right away."

She set off toward the door, and in an instant she had disappeared.

Hinde and I were now alone. I sat with my Russian textbook; she stood by the wall, wrapped in thought.

"That girl is too much," she uttered softly. "She wants to make the world believe that she has a husband."

"What do you mean? After all, she has a child," I tried to protest.

"And if she does, so what? Does that mean that she has to have a husband whom she actually married, as God commanded? Is that the way it has to be? Oy, you're innocent as a calf. We ought to give you some straw to chew on."

Just then the wet nurse came in again. With her foot she

opened the door and hobbled in laden with food; on a plate she carried half of a big cake, iced with white cream and decorated with colorful flowers made of sugar, and in her other hand she held a pitcher full of milk.

"Here, little girl, this is for you. Eat a few pieces of this cake and you'll feel the sweetness in all of your limbs."

I felt very embarrassed about these unexpected treats. "Thank you, thank you," I stammered, turning red. "Take it away. My grandmother will yell at me."

The woman burst out laughing. "As if you need to show it to her, silly child. Hinde, give me a knife. Let's give her a piece and she'll see how delicious it is! Well, girl, why are you standing there? Get me a knife. All right, all right, I'll give you a piece, too, and while I'm at it, I'll finish my rice and milk. My little peppercorn is sleeping like he just came back from a wedding."

She sat down, rested the pitcher in her lap, and slowly started eating the sweet soup of rice and milk, licking her lips after every spoonful, like a cat. In the meantime, Hinde brought a knife to cut the cake. But just at that moment my childish curiosity got the better of me. Looking at the wet nurse with her milk-covered double chin, sitting there toying with her soup, I asked very innocently, "Did you not marry your husband because he had to go into the army?"

She flashed her radiant blue eyes and answered with a question: "What's up? What has she told you?"

"Nothing, nothing," I said hastily. "I was just asking for no reason. Nobody told me anything."

"She's talking because she's burning up with envy. The poor thing is jealous of me."

"Is that so?" Hinde spoke up with hostility in her voice. "May God protect me from such good fortune."

"What don't I have? I'm well paid. I eat all sorts of good things. Two maids are slaves to my every whim, and I lord it over a wealthy mistress. I make her life miserable, and she showers me with gifts. She's already given me a trunk full of presents. Oh, being a wet nurse is an easy way to earn your bread! You can do outrageous things, you can demand pie in the sky. A wet nurse is never fired. And how much longer can you go around as you are, an overgrown girl, working your fingers to the bone for your bosses?"

But Hinde remained resolute. "I would rather work like this forever than be a loose woman. A husband has to be a husband according to the laws of God and man, and a child has to know who its father is."

"Boy, are you smart. It's no wonder that you're already over thirty and an old maid. Guard, guard that good old hometown virtue of yours."

"What did I say? Did I insult anyone, God forbid. I'm only saying that . . . I want my child to have a father—"

But at that moment something happened that startled me like a clap of thunder. The wet nurse leapt up and flung the pitcher of soup at Hinde's head. The latter jumped to the side, shrieking, and the pitcher hit the polished carafe of water standing on the table. With a crash, white porcelain shards and pieces of glass scattered all over the room.

The wet nurse rushed from the room, slamming the door with a terrible bang, and Hinde hastened to clean up the broken pieces and to wipe up the spilled soup and water, crying all the while. She did it very quickly, so that my grandmother would not detect even the slightest trace of what had gone on. Scared, I stood in the middle of the room, holding my textbook, not knowing what to do. Only the sudden ringing of the doorbell roused me from my confusion. When my grandmother came into the room, she found me sitting at the table, very much absorbed in my textbook. Hinde had hidden herself somewhere in the kitchen, and all was quiet.

"What kind of cake is this?" she asked as soon as she came in.

I broke into a cold sweat. Out of haste and fear, Hinde had forgotten to take the cake off the table.

"I want the truth, what kind of cake is this?"

"The wet nurse brought it." I braced myself and answered simply, "The wet nurse who works for the Barskys, right up the steps near us."

"The Barskys' wet nurse? How did she happen to be here?"

"She came to ask me to write a letter for her, and so she treated me to cake. I can take that, can't I? After all, it's not money, it's food."

My grandmother considered the cake and shook her head. "True, food is not actually payment, but she could not possibly afford this cake. She probably took it from her mistress. That means she stole it, and you have a part in causing the theft. No, dear, you may not touch it. Give it back to her tomorrow. But writing a letter for a poor woman is certainly a good deed."

When she left the bedroom, I grabbed the cake off the table and ran through the kitchen and up the dimly lit steps to the Barskys', to give the cake back to the wet nurse so that she could put it back where it was supposed to be before her employers came home from the theater.

The woman looked at me in astonishment. But she burst into a smile right away, her cheeks dimpling, and said to me very tenderly, "Silly girl, you're afraid of the old lady. What a shame."

Silently, I hurried to the door and ran back down the dim stairway that was lighted only by the reflection of our window on the floor below.

My grandmother was not asleep yet. Her lamp burned above her bed. She was saying her prayers quietly and listening for my footsteps. I said good night to her and buried myself in my schoolbooks once again.

★ ☾ ★

ROCHEL FAYGENBERG *was born in 1885 in Luban, White Russia, into a very scholarly family. Her formal schooling, which* included studies in Hebrew, Yiddish, and Russian, ceased when she was twelve because she had to run the family store. When she was fifteen her mother died and she moved to Odessa, where she worked in a ladies' dress salon for four years and developed her childhood passion for literature. Her first published work, "Di kinder-yorn" [The childhood years], appeared in the journal Dos naye lebn in 1905 and later in book form in 1909. She published stories, sketches, and dramatic etudes in many of the major Yiddish periodicals of the time. After surviving the Ukrainian pogroms, she left the Ukraine in 1921, settling first in Kishenev, then in Bucharest and Warsaw, and finally in Palestine in 1924. During this period she wrote extensively on the pogroms and published the books Af di bregn fun Dniester [On the Shores of the Dniester; 1925] and A pinkes run a toyter shtot: churbn Dubove [A Record of a Dead City: the Destruction of Dubove; 1926] as well as her first novel, Af fremde vegn [Alien Paths; 1925]. In 1926, she left Palestine for Poland and Paris, returning permanently in 1933. There she wrote for both Hebrew and Yiddish publications and founded the publishing house Measef, which had as its mission the publication of Yiddish literature in Hebrew translation. Toward the end of her life she wrote mainly in Hebrew under the name Rochel Imri. She died in Tel Aviv in 1972.

AT THE RICH RELATIVES

Celia Dropkin

Translated by Faith Jones

A letter came from Madame Rabinovitch to her sister: "I've just heard of the terrible event that befell your town. There was just such a fire when I was a small child and you were still in the cradle. But don't worry, dear Feigel, I won't let you suffer. In the meantime, I implore you, come to us at the summer house."

Feigel couldn't read further through the tears welling up in her eyes. Since the fire, she and her only child, fourteen-year-old Dina, had taken shelter with another poor family in the end of town untouched by the fire. Now, in a dark room big enough for only one bed, Dina lay sleeping. She woke suddenly as Feigel came in holding the letter.

"Dina, sweetheart, see what your aunt Shifra wrote. She invited us to the estate."

Dina sat straight up in bed. "Visit Aunt Shifra? Never!"

"What's this about? What has she ever done to you?"

"I won't go visit those snobs." Dina kicked with her bare feet at the blankets.

"But she's asked us to stay with them for a while," said Feigel in irritation. "Look at the letter she sent, so sweet. Going there will revive us."

"But what will I wear? Everything was burned. How will I look compared to my cousins?"

Feigel hesitated, not wanting to say that wrapped inside the letter had been a gift of money, twenty rubles in all. She knew perfectly well that Dina couldn't stand the idea of taking charity from the rich relatives.

"We can get credit at the fabric store. Hannah the seamstress will let me pay her later, when there's more work to be had," Feigel said.

Dina sprang out of bed, instantly ready to go to the fabric store. There she picked out a blue satin and a white cambric and felt satisfied, imagining how she would look in her new clothes.

The Rabinovitch estate lay deep in the woods of Polesie. On the ride from the station, Feigel and Dina inhaled deeply the sweet perfume of pine needles. It was early morning. Woods and newly sown fields floated past the carriage, exiling memories of the town they had just deserted, the burned ruins above which tall, black chimneys survived; and now they were driving into a courtyard that was so big it could be a pasture but for the clean, broad footpaths and the round flower beds here and there. On both sides of the courtyard houses stood in a row, as on a city street. This was where the Rabinovitch family lived. No, this was merely their summer residence. In winter they traveled to the big cities or abroad.

The houses were still asleep, the shutters closed. From somewhere they could hear a rattling of dishes and pots.

Breakfast was already prepared and waiting for the master's family. A guard approached them.

"Which is Chaim Rabinovitch's house?" Feigel inquired.

He motioned to the closest house, from which spread broad verandas on either side, basking in the day's awakening. Feigel led Dina past the front door, which was, of course, closed, and looked for the entrance to the kitchen. Standing at the stove was Taiba the cook, a fat woman with red cheeks wearing a white kerchief tied under her chin. Feigel knew Taiba. Feigel had always recruited her sister's servants. Taiba, in her turn, had been sent by Feigel only a year earlier. They greeted each other joyfully.

"How is everyone?"

"Madame left yesterday for Carlsbad. Doctor's orders."

"Really!" Feigel was downcast. Who was there here for her but Shifra? Shifra's husband? As the saying goes, a man wants his wife healthy and his sister rich.

"The gentleman went with her," Taiba went on, cutting into Feigel's gloomy thoughts.

"Indeed?" Feigel said curiously.

"Just for the journey. He'll come back right away and leave Madame there."

"How are the children? Rosa, Sofia, Eliza, Alexi, David, Akiva?"

"They don't lack for anything." Taiba shrugged. "Yours, on the other hand, is looking pale and thin." She turned her eyes on Dina.

"She's tired from traveling. She's been up all night." Feigel made excuses. "And the horror we've lived through! Half the town taken."

Taiba, at the mention of the huge fire, began to shake her head and wipe her eyes. It had, after all, been her town, too. Eventually she pulled herself together. "You're both tired! I'll call the chambermaid to show you to your room. It's all ready for you. Madame asked me to make sure of everything."

The chambermaid, Anastasia, a tall, sleepy Russian girl, a Gentile, took them to a long, light room that obviously had recently been added to the house. The walls still smelled of pine tar. It made Dina drowsy, and very soon she was deeply, sweetly asleep.

The sun was standing high in the sky when Dina opened her eyes, awakened by a bell. Feigel came in. Behind her trailed Anastasia with a jug of water and a basin. The bell rang again.

"That's the call to lunch," Anastasia said.

Dina held her hands over the basin while Feigel poured cold, clear water over them.

"What a pleasure this is," Feigel said, sighing. "Just like it used to be in our town, though it's hard to believe now. You must eat well at lunch; I don't want to see any leftovers."

"I'm not going to eat more than usual," Dina said stubbornly, suddenly feeling a stab of hunger. The fresh air of the country was already working its magic on her.

Feigel and Dina walked out onto a broad veranda, where a long table and chairs stood. The veranda was shielded from the sun by a linen awning. The children were already seated at the table. They greeted the newcomers cheerfully in Russian.

"Good morning, Auntie! Good morning, Dina!"

The eldest, Rosa, waved them to their places at the table. Dina was uncomfortable among her cousins, of whom she had heard a lot but seen little. She also was aware of her cousin Akiva's thoughtful gaze. Under this scrutiny from Kiva, two years her elder, Dina's face colored. The table was laden with preserves, eggs, a variety of cheeses: every conceivable treat.

Ignoring her hunger, Dina barely took any food, though she sensed Feigel's anxiety. After the meal Kiva approached her.

"Come to the pavilion. We're all heading there." He motioned to a round glass building that stood high above the courtyard entrance, like a throne. Dina felt a rush of gratitude toward Kiva, who was so much more welcoming to her than his sisters were. With unanticipated joy Dina ran to the pavilion, Kiva behind her.

In the pavilion stood a piano; on the piano stood a brown, finely carved box from which a horn protruded. Dina had never seen such a thing.

"What's that?" she asked her cousin Sofia.

"You really don't know?" Sofia wrinkled her nose. "That is a gramophone."

Dina was humiliated by her ignorance. Her eyes sought out Kiva but couldn't find him. The pavilion was full of the youth of Rabinovitch's huge extended family—cousins and second cousins, all of them dressed in nicely tailored clothing of the best summer-weight material. Some of the young men were students in uniform. Dina reflected sadly that she had only two new dresses, and even they were not the quality of those the Rabinovitches wore. Her eyes lit on dainty tan slippers or black patent-leather shoes, and as she mentally compared them to her own stout, sensible shoes, she became enraged with herself and her mother for coming here.

Then she heard the deep, lucid notes of a piano. One of her cousins' cousins, a twelve-year-old girl, was playing. Everyone moved to stand around the piano, even the older ones among them. They applauded proudly when she finished. Dina could see how they doted on the young pianist, with her deep green-blue eyes, dark skin, and powerful hands that ranged authoritatively over the piano's black-and-white spine. The young pianist's mother, it seemed, had been deaf since childhood, which made it stranger yet that little Rebecca had such a sharp ear for music, as if the mother had made the daughter a gift of her hearing and now Rebecca listened for both of them. Dina was charmed by this story, but somewhere in her heart jealousy toward Rebecca flared up. Dina wanted to be just that brilliant and beloved.

Later on, the pavilion emptied. Dina lingered behind, tinkling ineffectually on the piano keys. She wished for a miracle to occur so that suddenly, from under her fingers, a melody so sweet would flow that all who heard it would fall to their knees and look at her as at an angel sent from God. She left the pavilion despondent. She lay down in a hammock slung between trees, and when the blue of the sky flashed among the dense green branches, she felt again calmed by the pulse of the woods and fields, far from the charred town, far from the windowless room.

The next afternoon, Kiva again invited her to the pavilion, but as they were walking over he wandered off somewhere. "What's the matter with him?" Dina wondered. "Where has he gone?" She herself was hoping Rebecca would play again, but at the pavilion Rebecca stood among the other children, carefree and laughing and making no move toward the piano.

"Look, look," one of the children yelled. They all turned their eyes to the window. A few dozen Russians, dressed in rough work clothes or the coarse homespun of peasants, were making their way to the pavilion, with Kiva in their midst. A racket broke out in the pavilion.

A girl with a round, placid face shouted, "It's impossible! He's bringing those lowlifes here again! We won't have any peace this summer!"

"Let's get out of here. I'm bored with it," a second answered her.

The older boys shuffled with embarrassment. Suddenly, one rose with a stern look and yelled over to the girls:

"These are the workers in our plant. They make you all rich. Without them you couldn't exist. You're parasites, living on them and sucking their blood."

This said, he ran out to join the group that had come to a halt outside the open door of the pavilion. Kiva was urging them to enter. The girls left in fury, their lips twisted in distaste as they edged past the workers. The workers ranged themselves along the benches inside the pavilion. Kiva turned on the gramophone, and with enormous curiosity the workers listened to the sounds coming from the box.

"Come to me in the palace," the gramophone intoned. "Oh, you lovely night, you dark lovely night," someone moaned from inside the box.

And then Kiva attempted to explain what a gramophone was.

When the workers had left the pavilion, Kiva stayed for a while, whispering in a corner with the boy who had called the girls parasites, the boy called Joseph.

As the summer days swam by, Kiva seemed distracted, often huddling in some kind of conference with Joseph. Dina wondered what was going on. Strong voices, not just curiosity, were calling to her. Something in her had awoken—new feelings throbbed inside her in this place, and the evenings filled her with unspeakable longing.

A footbridge over a meandering, almost dried-up river led to a large wood. When the sun was bowing to the west, the air around the wood turned pink and thick with the croaking of the frogs. Then Dina would run to the bridge, intoxicated by the murmurings there, to breathe in thirstily and stare greedily, demanding something.

Once Joseph ran by and tugged her braid. Her heart leapt. Joseph had red cheeks, full lips, and beautiful burning eyes. He was a typical member of Rabinovitch's well-fed family. Nothing about him appealed to Dina. Yet when, later that night, Joseph moved away from the tree he was leaning on beside the house, came over to her, and took her hand, she did not pull it away.

Later still that night—it was a very hot night—Dina bumped into one of the younger Rabinovitches on the veranda—a twelve-year-old boy, a cousin of one of her cousins—and kissed him passionately on his puffy lips. And he kissed her back.

On this kind of night, it seemed to Dina that to so much as move was to wade through hot, black tar. Even on a peaceful evening she would suddenly choke up. She became uneasy, peevish. She complained to Feigel: she wanted to leave. What was there for her to do here? After one such scene she ran to the woods, just at the time when she should have been sitting down at the table. She was the only one there. A pair of hammocks hung between trees. Dina walked past them. She started to feel hungry and every now and then bent down to take the black berries that burst up in little thickets between the pines. Cranberries flamed everywhere, too. She surveyed the scene with delight: the glorious woods!

She heard steps as Kiva approached her.

"I wanted to see you, Dina."

Dina stopped in her tracks. Kiva smiled at her.

"You know, Dina," he began slowly, "I take you to be smarter and better educated than my sisters, and so I want to ask you something. But take a while to think about what I say and what you think of it." Kiva took out a folded sheet of paper. Dina opened it and read the Russian headline:

WORKERS OF THE WORLD, UNITE!

Dina looked at him, dumbstruck. Yes, she knew what it meant. She had read this kind of pamphlet before. She used to find them discarded on the streets in her town. But how did he end up with one? She asked him, "Where did you find this, Kiva?"

"You think I found it? I printed it. I am taking a stand against my father's exploitation." He preened a little. "For as long as I'm here, I will organize his workers into a conscious rank and file."

Dina felt a worshipful tremor pass through her. She marveled at Kiva's strength to stand in opposition to his own important family.

"What do you need me to do, Kiva?" she asked quietly, aware of the pounding in her chest.

"You understand? Papa returns from traveling tomorrow. He will certainly come to my room and see the secret press. That would be bad. He won't go into your room. I could hide it in your room."

"Kiva, of course." Dina seized on it immediately. "Have no fear, I won't betray you."

"Good, Dina. We'll make a revolutionary of you yet." Kiva squeezed her hand and left. Dina went slowly back to the veranda. Her mother looked at her in fury.

"Where have you been?"

"In the woods," she answered, nonchalant.

There were still pierogies on the table. Dina sat to eat one and stood up again.

"Where are you running off to? There are roasted mushrooms, too, your favorite."

Dina couldn't stay still even long enough to answer her mother. She ran to her room, closed the door, and thought carefully about the hiding place. The corner beside her bed seemed to her the best place to store such a jewel as a secret printing press. She didn't leave the room but waited for Kiva, who came and also considered the spot. Late at night, when the whole house was asleep, Kiva and Joseph brought in the press and quietly, wordlessly, crept away.

Dina slept badly that night. Nightmares tormented her, and she woke many times in terror. Occasionally she stole a look at the printing press, crouching in the corner like a living thing, then pulled the blankets over her head so she couldn't see it.

At breakfast she saw Kiva and immediately felt strong and brave. The secret she shared with him seemed to lift her above the others sitting at the table. Looking them over now, she wondered why she had yesterday felt embarrassed by her poverty.

Kiva's eyes rested on her. Dina caught his glance, like a student being called on, and saw him making some kind of signal with his fingers. She strained to understand, broke out in a cold sweat, and could not figure out what he meant. Finally she stood up and ran to her room, with her mother calling after her, "Wait! You haven't finished your cocoa!"

Dina threw herself on her bed and tried to make the same signs with her fingers that Kiva had made to her. For the first time it occurred to her that Kiva had been teasing her, enjoying her bewilderment. He came in a few minutes later.

"This is just what I wanted, for you to be in your room before everyone had finished eating. Joseph went to get a big package of illegal literature. One of his sisters found a brochure. She threatened to search the house and burn them all. She's a huge coward. Right now, while they're all eating, he can easily bring over the literature. But watch Anastasia when she comes to clean your room."

"I won't let her in at all," Dina answered. "I can clean my own room. I do it at home." She reddened as if confessing a sin.

There was a quiet tap on the door and Joseph came in, carrying a bulging suitcase. He looked around the room.

"Under the bed is the only place for it," he said.

"May I read over some of these things?" Dina asked shyly.

Joseph looked hard at her. "Of course. But how old are you, Dina?"

"I'm fifteen," Dina fibbed, reversing the usual women's lie, since her fifteenth birthday was still three months off.

"That means you're old enough for love," Joseph said, and immediately bit his upper lip, on which the beginnings of a mustache could plainly be seen. Dina's ears turned red. Kiva looked at Joseph with unconcealed anger.

"You can cut out the Don Juan act. We have more important things to think about. Come on, Ivan is waiting for us at the sawmill."

On his way out, Kiva's eyes lingered on Dina longer than usual, and this time she felt it had nothing to do with secret signals and underground movements. She went to her mirror and gazed at herself. Anastasia came into the room.

"I'll do the cleaning myself today, Anastasia."

"Oh, miss, how can you, with your delicate hands?"

Dina glanced down at her small white hands, which here at the estate had at last become genteel. It pleased her to see them looking that way. She raised her pinkie the way she had seen Rabinovitch's daughters do. Anastasia meanwhile began making the bed. Her glance fell on the secret press.

"What is this, miss?" she asked. "I saw it yesterday in the young master's room, but I was afraid to ask. He's such a tough one. Now, Master Joseph is entirely different," she said with a giggle.

Dina laughed along, hoping Anastasia had already forgotten her question about the printing press, trying desperately to think up a lie she could tell if not.

"Anastasia, Anastasia," called a voice outside the window.

"Miss Rosa is calling you," Dina prompted. Anastasia ran out of the room.

Thank God, Dina thought, and breathed again.

The lumber mill was located about half a mile from the Rabinovitches' house. The workers lived behind the sawmill, in a street lined with shacks. No effort had been made to make the shacks look like a regular Russian town. They were built by the Rabinovitches so that the workers would be close to the sawmill until the first frost and looked more like playhouses than Russian huts. They were made of boards clapped together and stood in a low, muddy spot. Around the sawmill and in the street itself there was no bit of green in evidence. Behind the shacks here and there was a little garden.

The workers came to the sawmill from nearby villages and worked an expanse of land that belonged not to them but to the "Jewish master." Dina often saw an older woman in a lean-to with a suckling infant at her breast and other children surrounding her. The women were thin and small, like typical Polesie grandmothers; their children had distended bellies, narrow feet, and dirty blond heads.

Scabies, that terrible disease of the hair, ran rampant in this neighborhood, and from time to time she saw children with horribly matted hair. All the women wore tattered scarves on their heads. When Dina strolled a few times through the little street with Kiva, she felt the eyes of the residents on them, their gaze both dull and suspicious. It was obvious to her they did not believe Kiva and understood him even less. But Kiva was enthusiastic, noticing neither disloyalty nor lethargy.

Only one small event evoked a bitterness in him against them.

It was August. Kiva and Dina walked through buzzing woods. Kiva was mentally composing the text of a new proclamation and talking it over with Dina. She was helping him think of elegant, powerful phrasing. They wanted to sit on a bench, but it was covered with chalk graffiti. Both bent down involuntarily to read it; both faces reddened, and as if fleeing an enemy, they left the place quickly, not looking at each other.

The bench was chalked over with vulgar, pornographic words and rhymes, into which her own and Kiva's names had been inserted. When they recovered, Kiva spat, and the words were wrenched out of him: "This is what they are, these scoundrels!" And then he said:

"I'm afraid my entire work here is a waste of time. I know of only two of them who know how to write. All the others are practically illiterate. If those two can't be trusted, there's no one here to trust. A few of the Russians told me that there was a traitor among them, who intends to travel from town to town denouncing me. I didn't want to believe it. Now I must."

He took her arm and spoke with unexpected tenderness: "I think it would be best if you went away, Dina. There's no telling what's in store for you here. It's too soon for you to be a martyr for the revolution. There are things you can accomplish if you are patient, rather than being destined to languish somewhere in prison. If the printing press is found in your room, you'll be sent to Siberia."

Dina looked at him. Her face was pale. She knew deep down she couldn't leave just yet.

"I won't go, Kiva," she stammered through trembling lips.

Kiva suddenly leaned forward and kissed her; just as suddenly he reddened, hastily said, "See you," and left her.

Dina walked home in a waking dream. Her steps glided across the footbridge. It was dusk. The frogs croaked. She didn't notice them. She could feel only the melody resonating in her heart.

When Dina arrived at breakfast the next morning, the gaze she encountered at the table turned her cold. She felt her pride wounded as only a poor relation can. Her uncle, Chaim Rabinovitch, was glaring at her. In the three weeks since he had returned from Carlsbad, where he had left his wife, Dina had become accustomed to not looking at him, and he didn't look at her, either. From time to time at the table he would motion with his head toward a dish, say, "Have some!" and push it closer to Feigel and Dina without looking at them. Feigel had many times bemoaned her sister's absence, saying to Dina repeatedly:

"You know, sweetheart, we should be on our way back home soon."

"You're in some hurry to get home, Mama? At least wait until the end of August."

Now that Dina saw her uncle's glare, she realized they really had been there too long.

Kiva's gaze soon made her forget her uncle's. Yet after breakfast, just when she would normally go off with Kiva, she suddenly found herself face-to-face with Anastasia.

"The master asks you to come see him in his study."

Dina stood like one turned to stone. She looked around, seeking out Kiva, but panicked as she found him nowhere. She steeled herself and made her way to her uncle's study.

"Come in," Dina heard when she knocked. Rabinovitch scrutinized her coldly. Kiva was already there. He smiled at her, though it was obvious he was furious.

Rabinovitch drew a copy of a proclamation out of his pocket.

"Tell me everything you know about this," he said sternly to Dina.

"She doesn't know anything about that. It's mine," Kiva said, springing forward.

"Shut up!" Rabinovitch pushed Kiva so hard that he crashed back against the wall.

A heat inflamed Dina's face. Her lips and eyes felt scorched.

"Well, what do you have to say about that?" Rabinovitch emphasized each word. "The estate steward saw you bringing a big package of these to Kiva at night by the sawmill; he saw Kiva distributing them through the street, leaving one at every doorstep."

Dina clenched her lips; she heard her teeth grinding. It seemed to her that her tongue could be cut out of her head before she would speak.

"I told your aunt, I don't want any poor relations here to be a bad influence on the children. Send money, but don't bring them here. But she wouldn't heed me. 'Even the czar helped the Jews when the town burned down: how can I not help my own sister?' she cried. Well, this is gratitude for you."

Now it was Kiva's turn to shout, as if with a strength not his own: "Shut up!" Yet Rabinovitch went on as if he hadn't spoken, throwing one insult after another at Dina, who stood stock-still.

He took a check from his pocket and extended it to her. "For train fare," he said shortly.

Dina felt Kiva's pale face turn on her like a beam of light. She flashed a smile in his direction, turned her back on Rabinovitch, and left him standing with the check still in his outstretched hand as she fled the room.

"Mama, pack our bags!" she called to Feigel through numb lips.

"What? What's the matter with you, sweetheart, what's happened?"

As they met beside the steps of the veranda, Dina fell into Feigel's arms.

"Help, someone, my God! Dina has fainted!"

The Rabinovitch children came running from their porches. Taiba came waddling out from the kitchen, wringing her hands.

Joseph picked Dina up in his strong arms and carried her onto the veranda. They set her down in a deep swing, dabbed her with water, and brought her smelling salts, and she gradually came around.

Kiva stood nearby, his eyes burning with sympathy. Rabinovitch was there, too, looking guilty.

"The factory doctor should be called," he said.

"I don't want a doctor!" Dina shot back with renewed anger. She struggled up, shaking off offers of help, and walked on wobbly legs back to her room. She closed the door behind her, fell on the bed, and cried long and hard. She ignored Feigel's repeated pleas to be let in. Kiva also knocked on her door without result, but this was mere vanity: she knew she didn't look good when crying. When the storm of tears was over, she saw that the sun stood high in the sky and realized it was already too late to leave that day. The train left only once a day, early.

Dina washed her face and left the room. Everyone seemed pleased to see her, and aside from Kiva and Rabinovitch, nobody had any idea why she had fainted. Anastasia had picked up some gossip in the kitchen, but not the details; and Feigel knew even less. After Dina fainted, Rabinovitch had not been as rude to Feigel as he had felt free to be earlier. He had called Feigel to his study and said with apparent kindness that it seemed to him the local climate didn't suit Dina, and since tomorrow his brother, Jacob Rabinovitch, was going to the station anyway, they could travel with him. And he had given Feigel a full fifty rubles.

"Be well, may you have many happy years with Shifra," Feigel said, wiping her eyes, "but I'll be damned if I'll take more than half of that."

"It'll come in handy, what with everything lost in the fire. Just don't tell Dina. And take good care of her. Make sure she doesn't start hanging out with radicals, the socialists—"

"What's the matter with you, brother-in-law?" Feigel said furiously. "You think that Dina is just anybody? She's a blessing. Quiet as a mouse."

"Fine, very good," Rabinovitch replied, smiling halfway but thinking, The little devil drove Kiva from the straight and narrow. I'm already paying off half the town, and the workers have probably informed on him anyway. "Well, go in health. I won't see you tomorrow morning. And take care of Dina. Remember what I say."

Feigel took the money and walked back to her room, thinking, I'll have to leave a ruble for Taiba, and a ruble for Anastasia, and give fifty kopecks to the coach driver. With this much money you can pretend to be the rich relative instead of the poor one. She smiled happily. In the room she found Kiva sitting on the bed with Dina.

"You don't need to worry about spending another night here," he said quietly, so Feigel wouldn't hear. "And for a treat, tonight we'll read Pisarev for the group. You can see that with those of my cousins' and my sisters' sort, you can't start them off with illegal literature. You have to gradually lead them to the right way of thinking."

"What are you going to read of Pisarev's?" Dina asked, reinvigorated.

"What do you think? 'Bees,' that's a good lesson about the working class and the parasites."

Dina clapped her hands enthusiastically.

"But now come for a walk," Kiva said, standing up.

Feigel sighed as they left, thinking, Such a sweet young man, Kiva. She began to pack.

It was a bright starlit night in mid-August. The pavilion was lit up. The smaller children had been sent off to bed, and the young people, bursting with the laughter of a happily spent summer, sat on benches, tables, and even on the lid of the piano; others spilled out onto the steps, not thinking much about the reading they heard. What was the use of these readings? The audience was restless and heckled, although sometimes they would become interested in the subject and really listen. This time the reading was a huge success. The young women and men did not see in Pisarev's "Bees" a symbol of the workers versus the wealthy parasites, but they enjoyed the story of the queen with her numerous lovers, the drones. They shrieked, laughed, kissed. The boys, against their better judgment, touched their female cousins' breasts. Everyone was happy.

Only Dina sat pale, with eyes burning. The upheavals of the day made her feel like an outsider. She felt older and more serious than before. She listened to Pisarev's "Bees," which she had read before. Kiva was the reader. His face was expressive. The light streaks in his hair fluttered over his high forehead. Dina couldn't take her eyes off him. His eyes, too, often sought hers out, and when he found them his voice would become warmer and stronger. When Kiva ended and everyone noisily left the pavilion, he came straight to Dina.

"How do you feel?" he asked. "You look so tired. Come, I'll walk you to the house."

On the way, Kiva knocked on Joseph's window. Joseph hadn't come to the reading. He was studying for his exams. Joseph came out of his room, and the three of them went on tiptoe into Dina's room, where Feigel was sleeping. Joseph and Kiva carried out the printing press. Kiva came back quickly.

"Where will you hide the press now?" Dina whispered, so as not to wake her mother. "What your father said makes me nervous."

"Don't worry about a thing. He has enough money to buy my way out, if something should happen."

Kiva took Dina's hand in his and smiled calmly. "And anyway, we'll send it to the city soon, to the organization. Father hasn't found out about the press, and it's better to leave it that way."

The light of the full moon shone into the room. In the moonlight, Dina's skin was palely translucent; her eyes shone with religious fervor.

"You have to go, Kiva," she said. "Your father will come looking for you."

"Don't speak of him, Dina!"

"Good-bye, Kiva."

"Good-bye, Dina."

And as if by magic, he was silently gone.

Through the late-summer fields a carriage made its way early in the morning to the train station. The carriage was new, and three horses were harnessed to it, because one of the rich relatives was also going to the station.

✱ ☾ ✱

CELIA DROPKIN *was born Zipporah Levine in Bobruisk, White Russia, in 1888. She began writing in Russian as an adolescent and, while studying in Kiev, received encouragement from the Hebrew novelist U. N. Gnessin. She married socialist Shmaye Dropkin in 1909, and together they fled czarist persecution, relocating to New York. There she began writing in Yiddish, publishing many stories and poems in Yiddish journals and one book-length collection of poems,* In heysn vint [In the Hot Wind]. *She had six children, five of whom survived, and died in 1956. Dropkin's singular contribution to Yiddish literature* was the introduction of a bold literary discourse of sexuality most obvious in her love poems. Her pastoral poetry is marked equally by ecstatic, despairing, and even grotesque elements. Although highly regarded in the field of Yiddish literature, Dropkin is unfamiliar to English-language readers. The loosely autobiographical stories translated here for the first time into English provide fascinating insight into an artist whose candor and intensity still prove startling.

AT THE MILL

Fradel Schtok

Translated by Irena Klepfisz

Ruchtsi put her red bathing shirt and a bar of scented soap in the basket her mother had brought from Loshkovits. She took her parasol and said: "Mama, I'm going to bathe at the mill."

"With whom . . . don't you dare go alone, you hear? The current is strong at the mill. . . . Better go to the Zbrutsh."

"I'm going with Chane. The whole town's going today."

"Don't go far out into the water, you hear? Be sure to hold on to a pole."

Her mother gave her two slices of bread and butter and two *graytsers* for cherries and called after her not to dawdle.

Chane was already waiting for her at her house. They walked through the marketplace, bought some cherries, poured them into a paper bag, and set out cheerfully on the long road to the mill.

The road was covered with a thick dust, delicate and fine as flour, and their shoes turned white from the dust, from the summer dust. All along the way, they met people either going to or coming from the mill.

Ruchtsi marveled: "The whole town's going bathing today."

"Yes, the whole town."

"My mother wants me to bathe only in the Zbrutsh, just like some ninny. But it's such a pleasure at the mill. The waves beat against your back. . . ."

"I don't like the Zbrutsh either. Somehow the water seems to just sit there on one spot."

They walked through the Christian cemetery, then through the master miller's courtyard—farther and farther. Soon they could hear the clatter of the mill. When they reached the bridge beneath which water was rushing into the mill's wheel, Ruchtsi felt a slight tug at her heart, as if someone were leaving for some unknown place, the kind of tug—who knows what it wants from you.

The water under the bridge seethed and foamed. Ruchtsi looked over the railing. From the other side flowed the green, quiet water of the Zbrutsh, which, when caught in the wheel, became the water of the mill.

She peered inside the mill. There, in the darkness, the grinding of the bread was going along cheerfully. You could smell rye, barley, and corn.

They walked through the booth with the inspectors who guard the border. Burke—the station official—sat in a light pale duster in front of the booth. He looked at the Jewish girls who were going bathing and began to whistle "The Lost Happiness."

With a half glance, Ruchtsi saw that he was light haired—as light as his duster. And she had thought that he was dark. . . .

When Burke saw Ruchtsi, he called after her, "*Krasna.*"*

Ruchtsi didn't turn around, but she burned with pride. Chane choked.

Krasna means "beauty" in Russian. [Translator's note.]

Many people were already at the water bank. The spot with the trees close to the shore was strewn with clothes. On land and in the water, girls stood in their bathing shirts while women wrapped in sheets held naked children in their arms.

Ruchtsi saw their neighbor Etti holding little Yosele. He was naked and shrieking because he'd gotten soap in his eyes. Etti was trying to quiet him. "Little fool. You're a little fool. Sssh . . . sssh . . . Bathe. Bathe." But the child, frightened by the mill's noise, twisted his little body and squealed, "*Vinye, vinye.*"

Women near her clucked with wonder. "Such a little thing—and he's bathing already?"

"The doctor said to. . . . Little fool. Sssh, sssh. Bathe, bathe."

Asher's wife rejoiced over her child. "Ah, what a pleasure! Mine's bathing. May he live a long life."

She snuggled the naked body against her and pressed her face against the child's dripping little face and sudsy hair, tapped his teeth like a mother, and cried, "Ay, ay, ay . . ."

As the child babbled with pleasure, showing his new teeth and clapping his hands against his chest, crying, "Boo, boo," his mother lifted him up and rejoiced: "Does it feel good, my little one? May you have a long life. . . ."

And this was how young children were taken for the first time into the cold water; they'd twist their heads and cry, "*Tay, tay, vinye, vinye,*" and their tongues would tremble as they insisted that they did not, absolutely did not, want to be dunked.

And those who'd already gotten used to it and were wading in the water, these would cry when they were carried out, wanting to go back in because they were cold and their muddy little bodies were shivering. And with their heads dripping with water and suds from the scented soap, they'd stretch their arms and chests back toward the water.

Ruchtsi folded her clothes behind a tree, took the soap, and went in.

Young girls were bathing in pairs and in circles—three, four—accompanying each dip with an "Aaah." And the heavy sound of the water—as if coming from the lower depths—mingled with their "Aaah."

Ruchtsi drew in her arms. Each step that took her deeper made her heart feel as if it were rising higher into her throat. Chane was already bathing and calling to her, but Ruchtsi wanted to go out where it was even deeper.

Sanya's wife was floating farther out by the last pole. As always, she was propping herself up impertinently, and her sheet was blown up around her by the waves. Everyone was afraid to go that far. The waves coming from the wheel were strong and struck directly against her fat shoulders. When Sanya's wife saw that Ruchtsi had gone very deep into the water, even farther than she had, behind the bushes, she called out to her.

"Ruchtsi, don't go so far. I'll tell your mother. I'll tell your mother."

But Ruchtsi didn't listen and went to a hidden spot behind the bushes where a rock lay half-submerged in the water.

She sat herself down on the rock, and with one arm encircling the post, she stretched out. The mill clattered and made deafening noises that mingled with the squeals of the young girls and naked children.

Ruchtsi pulled one leg out of the water and examined it. Water dripped from her white foot. Suddenly she glanced at the blind windows of the mill. Who knew? Perhaps Burke was looking out. . . . She hid her leg under the water and submerged herself more deeply until her tied braids became wet. Maybe he'll go bathing—in his gray duster—swim around, whistle—a vagabond.

She pushed the water back and forth and felt pleasure from its heavy smoothness. What silkiness! She imagined that clouds must be this silky. Now the water lies in her hand—a silky ball—and then suddenly it becomes nothing. *"Krasna."*

When she came out, Chane was already waiting for her, ready to go because her mother would worry.

The sun was beginning to sink beneath the trees. Almost all the women were now out of the water. The cries had become softer. Some women were already eating their bread and butter. Everything was so fresh. The women smiled and gave off the scent of the water, the mill. Their faces were at peace. They felt benevolent toward the whole world. The neighbor with whom they had quarreled just yesterday, they wanted to patch things up with today; they ate with relish the tasty rye bread with caraway seeds, the sweet cherries, and shared it all with total strangers.

Finally, they set out on their separate roads home, some through the Christian cemetery, some through the dust. When they met the men coming from the other side, they tugged their kerchiefs farther down over their foreheads. The men walked refreshed and energized, argued over Zionism, and set off for home to eat supper.

The whole town had been bathing. The whole town smelled of the water, the mill, the fresh bread and cherries, and all were friends.

Ruchtsi went home with Neche and Mendl's wife. As she was leaving, she cast a final glance at the mill. Night was already twinkling in the blind windows. Something was whistling, something was moving among the waves, which rushed from the wheel. People said that at night the water became boiling hot, but people were afraid to bathe at night.

Halfway home, they stopped and looked back. Neche said that her strength was returning. The trees in the Christian cemetery made a noise—"Aaah, oooh, aaah, oooh." And to Ruchtsi it seemed that the returned strength was saying, "Oooh, aaah, oooh, aaah. *Krasna.*"

Neche quietly informed Mendl's wife that she was going to make fresh potatoes and honey cakes for supper. And the other said that she was going to cook green peas—that they were healthy.

It seemed to Ruchtsi that Burke was following her in his gray duster; she didn't turn around in case it was a delusion. But her manner became restless. She turned her parasol so its handle pointed down and swayed its tassels impertinently.

The renewed strength rushed to her fingertips. "A-ooh. A-ooh."

★ ☾ ★

FRADEL SCHTOK *was born in Skale, Galicia, in 1890, and immigrated to the United States in 1907, where she first became noticed for her poetry. Yankev Glatshteyn was one of the first to praise her work. Her poetry and fiction began to appear regularly in all the major Yiddish papers (Tsukunft, Forverts, and others). Dertseylungen [Stories], her only collection of fiction—from which the two stories included here are drawn—appeared in 1919. The stories are situated both in shtetlech (in some cases Skale) and in the United States. They reflect unfulfilled dreams of sexual and social yearnings and range in tone from repressed rage to gentle satire. The women in her stories seem particularly thwarted by Jewish conventions and try to rebel, usually unsuccessfully. One of the rare writers to produce work in English, in 1927 Schtok published* For Musicians Only, *a novel that drew neither praise nor attention.*

For unknown reasons (perhaps depression), Schtok was institutionalized sometime after the novel's appearance. Until recently, her life, beginning with this institutionalization, remains undocumented, and other writers seem to have lost contact with her. It has always been assumed, therefore, that she died while confined, though no spe-

cific date of her death has ever been given. Recently, however, correspondence and some short fiction by her written in the 1940s was discovered in the Abraham Cahan archives at YIVO. The exact date of her death is still not known, though it is assumed to be later than originally thought. Translations of other Schtok stories appear in The Tribe of Dina: A Jewish Woman's Anthology and in Found Treasures: Stories by Yiddish Women Writers.

THE FOUR-RUBLE WAR

Helen Londynski*

Translated by Sarah Silberstein Swartz

When I finished the fourth and final grade of Miss Fanny Pozner's Private School for Girls, I wanted to continue my studies.** This caused a tempest in my Chasidic home; it seemed as if the heavens had cracked open. My parents engaged in a cold war with me.

---

*In the original memoir, *In shpigl fun nekhtn* [In the mirror of yesterday], Helen Londynski opens her story with the following statement: "The generation gap that currently [c. 1972] exists in the United States mirrors in retrospect the generation gap that we in Poland—especially those of us from conservative Chasidic homes—experienced at the beginning of the twentieth century. In describing my life experiences within the Orthodox community and my unrelenting battle with my Chasidic father, I intend to depict the awakening of our youth as we strove to free ourselves from the constraining chains of our day." [Translator's note.]

**Around the time of this story (c. 1920), private secular elementary schools existed for Jewish girls in Warsaw, giving girls their rudimentary reading, writing, and arithmetic skills in four years. Students began at age eight or nine, completing school at age thirteen or fourteen. For those who wished to continue their studies, there were schools that went up to grade seven, after which an exam could be taken to attend the last two years of *gymnazium*, Polish high school. [Translator's note.]

I would not allow myself to be persuaded by my father's assault: "Your Pozner-shmozner, let her be a scapegoat for all my sins. Is it not enough that I let you finish her school? Now she does me a favor by sending the girls for more learning. She wants to transform them into *shikses!* No, not on my life!" He pushed his velvet skullcap farther back on his head. "You think you are privileged! Your sisters were satisfied with four grades and what do they lack today? We made good matches for them—thank God, I wish it on all my good friends. Only a few more years and, God willing, we will live to see the day when we fix you up with a fine match as well."

Nor did my mother's submissive pleading move me: "I beg you, Chayele, forget about the fifth grade. Why upset your father? He wants only what is best for you. A young girl should not study too much. The more she learns, the less she is worth. And the more likely she will become a gray-braided old maid."

On her own, my mother might have been happy to brag to her neighbors about her "learned" daughter who would go on to the fifth grade. But if Father disapproved, she was in no position to contradict him, and she continued to plead with me until the very last day of the school year.

It was the evening before the final day to notify the head-mistress about fifth-grade enrollment. At home, I sat on pins and needles. Father chanted a page of Gemora; Mother knitted socks for her newborn grandchild, Moyshele. It was time for my last-ditch effort to gain Father's approval to study further. My heart trembled; my body and soul were on fire. I tried to steady myself and drum up some courage.

"So, Mother dear, tomorrow is the last day of school. . . ."

Silence. Mother pretended not to comprehend: "You see that your father is studying. Don't disturb him. Have some respect!"

"But tomorrow"—my voice rose an octave higher—"tomorrow I must—"

"What is she expounding about again, that daughter of yours?" My father closed the Gemora with a kiss. "Still carrying on about the 'schools'? No, I already told you, enough learning!"

"It won't cost more than four rubles a month," I argued in a quivering voice. "The other girls in the fifth grade at Kaletzka's School pay much more. Only we students from Pozner's School get a discount. . . ."

"What a bargain!" Father laughed sarcastically into his short beard. "Chanele, tell your daughter that she has butterflies in her head. What a nuisance you are! I have heard enough from you about the 'schools.' "

Seeing my father's clouded face, I appealed again to my mother, who sat silently, hands folded. "Mother dear, tomorrow is the very last day. What should I tell the headmistress tomorrow?" I burst into tears.

"Tomorrow," said my father, becoming irate, "tomorrow you will tell her that, as far as I am concerned, she can die a violent death. Let her burn along with her school!"

I retorted, "Is that what it says in the Gemora?"

Father pretended not to hear and left me sitting with my mouth wide open.

The next morning, I returned to school in despair. It was a lively and joyful day in Miss Fanny Pozner's School. Finished with exams, all the students were in high spirits, in a jubilant holiday mood—especially those graduating from the fourth grade. Those students, thirteen- and fourteen-year-old girls, bade farewell to their teachers. Those who had received awards—a book clutched to their bosoms, as a religious Jew holds a Sefer Torah in shul—cheerfully acknowledged that their parents would allow them to study further. If need be, their families would even skimp on food in order to pay the tuition for Miss Sofye Kaletzka's School, which offered seven grades.

My face burned with shame and envy. Even the poor girls—Belbina, whose father was a shoemaker; Sabine, an orphan whose father had died of tuberculosis, her mother, left with four small children, now a peddler who went from house to house selling linens on credit—did not have to fight their parents to continue their studies. I hid in a far corner of the classroom, not wanting anyone to see me choke back my tears.

My thoughts were interrupted by my Polish teacher, Isabella Grosser. "Helenke, why are you so gloomy, hiding in a corner like a little mouse, gazing about with anxious eyes. Don't you want to say good-bye to me?" It had been two years since she began to teach us at our school. They said she did not take any pay. She was the only daughter of the prominent lawyer Nikudem Grosser; her only brother, Bronislaw Grosser ("Slawek"), was one of the founders of the Bund.

"So, have you registered with the headmistress? Surely you plan to attend Miss Kaletzka's School." Isabella Grosser stroked my head and looked deep into my eyes with warmth. Wanting to believe she could sense what was happening to me, I allowed the tears to roll down my face and shook my head "no." Astounded, she examined me with her blue eyes. She no longer questioned me; she merely invited me to pay her a visit at her home tomorrow. She lived with her parents on Nowy Szwiat, a fashionable street in Warsaw.

With cautious steps, I trod across the threshold of Isabella Grosser's well-lit room. Opposite the entrance hall stood a large bookcase packed with books. The wine-red colors of Matejko's oil paintings on the walls—*Kosziusko on the Outskirts of Ratslowitz, The Constitution of the Third of May*—infused the room with Polish history. At the desk near the daybed, engrossed in reading, sat Isabella Grosser in her modest black dress, her light brown hair pulled back from the front, braided as always in a Grecian bun, making her high forehead seem more prominent.

She embraced me warmly, we exchanged kisses, and she said with a smile: "Good that you have come, Helenke. You are such a quiet one. When you look at me with your big brown eyes, I sense you want to tell me something, but you are so shy. At my home, where no one sees or hears you, you can tell me everything, right?" My answer was merely a smile. "Why did you tell me yesterday that you would not continue to the fifth grade of Kaletzka's School? You are such a talented girl, a good student. What else would you do?"

My teacher pushed a nearby chair toward me. With bated breath, she listened to my descriptions of my home. For her, it was novel, almost unbelievable, that parents could not or would not want to understand their own child. She was especially moved by my account of how, while a student at Miss Pozner's School, I would have to beg tearfully for money from my parents in order to buy a new book.

I had made a point of making my appeals to my parents in our hardware store. At home, they could more readily ignore me: "Don't drive us crazy. We have no money." Instead, I would go to our store on Bagno Street and mill around until a customer paid for something.

As soon as my mother put the customer's money in her leather bag, tied around her hip in back of her apron, I would come up to her and say, "Mother dear, I need a ruble for a new arithmetic textbook."

"Why do you tell me? Ask your father."

"Father dear, I need to buy the book today. Without it, I can't do my lessons for tomorrow."

"Lessons-shmessons, you've learned enough."

"Mother dear," I would say, my voice beginning to whine, "the bookstore at Number Six Twarda Street will soon be closed. And if I have to go to the shop on Swietokrzyska Street to buy it, the book will cost a lot more than one ruble."

"So what do you say, Leybl?" my mother would ask my father, afraid to make a decision without my father's approval.

And so it was always with great tribulations that I purchased each new book. With a compassionate look in her dear eyes, my teacher asked me, "And what would you do if you were to continue to study and finish Miss Kaletzka's School?"

"I want to be independent," I replied decisively. "Maybe I would become a teacher, and maybe . . . who knows what else? Perhaps after I finish Miss Kaletzka's School I would study further, take a position so I could live independently from my parents' home."

Putting her hand on my shoulder, my teacher told me, "Helenke, don't worry, I know you will achieve whatever you wish. Four rubles a month are a pittance for me. Go to the headmistress and ask her to enroll you. When the school year begins, I will give you the first four rubles. I will pay for you until your father relents. Perhaps he will feel ashamed when someone else pays for your studies."

With tears in my eyes, I expressed my childish gratitude and took leave of my beloved teacher, feeling encouraged and with my resolve revived.

Later, when I recuperated from the astonishing suggestion of my teacher, the thought that I could not accept her offer began to prey on my mind. In all good conscience, how could I—the daughter of the rich Gerer Chasid Reb Leybele Toybenblat—allow someone else to pay for me? I kept coming to the conclusion that it would be unfair and dishonorable to do so. Now my mind began to formulate how to get the first four rubles out of my parents, at least for the first month of the fifth grade.

Luck played in my favor this time. It was a custom in our family for every child to receive something new to wear for the High Holidays. Since the holidays were fast approaching, my mother decided to buy me a new pair of shoes. Preoccupied with work in the store, my mother could not personally go shopping with the children. Instead, one of my elder sisters was to take her place.

Luckily for me, my mother chose my older sister Sorele to buy the shoes with me. Sorele was the only one of my five sisters I could trust with my secrets. She often agreed with me. She, too, was angry with our parents for not allowing her to continue her studies after the fourth grade.

"I have an idea," I said to my attractive, dark-haired sister. "Instead of buying suede shoes, as we usually do, we could buy cheaper calfskin ones. And the difference in price would be the beginning of my four-ruble savings."

I waited until Friday evening to show my new shoes to my mother. The table, covered with a snow-white tablecloth, was set in the well-lit dining room. The wineglasses sparkled, the challahs were covered with a silken, multicolored, embroidered cloth. Mother had already made the blessing over the candles in the silver menorah. Father had not yet returned from shul. Near the table, the children, with freshly shampooed heads in honor of *Shabbes*, dressed in their Sabbath finery, surrounded our mother.

At this time of week, my mother was particularly cheerful, with that special Sabbath calmness and receptiveness—ready to hear what her children had to say. I took advantage of the moment and, pretending pride, went over to my mother. "Sorele bought me such a beautiful, comfortable pair of shoes; it's a pleasure."

"*Nu*, let me see your new shoes."

Standing at a distance, I put them on quickly, so that Mother shouldn't, God forbid, touch them. She would immediately have felt the difference. Calfskin is tougher than suede; this was why my shoes cost one and a half rubles less.

"Very nice. Wear them in the best of health, Chayele!"

She had no idea how lucky I felt. Now I was only two and a half rubles short of making my dream come true. But where would I find the rest of the money? Time does not stand still. In all, only a few days remained until the doors would be opened for new students in the fifth grade of Miss Kaletzka's School. There was, of course, still the possibility of the teacher Grosser's offer—but no, under no circumstances! I pushed away the thought; it was too shameful.

My father came home with a customer whom I recognized as Mr. Wyszlitzki. He always bought leather straps for his mill from us. My father didn't keep the straps in the store. For this, he had a special room in our house.

"Come in, Chayele. You'll help me measure the straps for the customer." On the polished floor of the dining room, Father placed a whole collection of leather straps. "This strap," said Father, pointing to a cylinder that held the leather strapping, "is not so thick, but it is strong as iron."

Examining the strap, the customer didn't respond. Father saw that he had not been successful in talking him into buying this one. As he unwrapped another strap, he joked, "You've never had such a fine strap, Mr. Wyszlitzki, even at your wedding."

I became very impatient. Why did I need to sit here and listen to all this sales talk? Restless, I paced back and forth along the length of the dining room.

"If you can't appreciate this piece of merchandise"—my father pulled out an entire length of yet a third strap—"I tell you, Mr. Wyszlitzki—you should live in good health—you will go home today with no strap."

I stole a look at the customer. I was tempted to tell him, "I beg you, have mercy on me. Buy or don't buy, but finish up." Luckily, I detected a smile of satisfaction on the thick lips that projected from behind the thin, curly blond mustache of Mr. Wyszlitzki.

"Okay, good," he responded, "I'll take it. Measure it out, Mr. Toybenblat." Satisfied, my father took out a wooden measuring stick. I held the strap with both hands so that it would not slide to the side. Father measured the strap, cut it with a sharp knife, rolled it up, and packed it up. I wrote up the bill; the Gentile paid. Father needed to give him change from a five-ruble gold coin: two and a half rubles.

My heart thumped: two and a half rubles. This was exactly how much money I still needed.

Father searched in his pockets. "No, I don't have it. Chayele, go with the customer. Exchange the five rubles and give him his change." I threw on my coat and raced out energetically, accompanied by the lucky customer.

In my hand, I held the two and a half rubles tightly, the two and a half rubles that I should be returning to my father. Only a guardian angel could have brought this to me. I decided it was now or never: I did not intend to return the money to my father.

"Hide this money for me for just a few days," I told my girlfriend who lived next door. "Guard it with your life." I spoke nervously, in fragments, my tongue muddled. My hands trembled like those of my grandmother Pese when she lifted a spoonful of warm food to her puckered lips.

I ran down Krolewski Boulevard as though someone were chasing me. It was still too early to go home. Father was probably waiting for the profits from the sale. I must postpone any face-to-face contact between my father and myself. So I entered the Saxon Gardens, sat myself down on a bench in Krolewski Boulevard under a high, multibranched tree. Autumn smells permeated the air. The trees were almost bare. In the gardens, the Elul wind had scattered the fallen, yellowed leaves on the moist ground. At the moment, golden rays from the sunset illuminated them. By now, Father must be on his way to the study house for evening prayers—the best time for me to return home.

"What took you so long to exchange the gold piece?" asked Father with a searching look. "It's already time to go to pray and here I sit, waiting for you. *Nu*, hand over the two and a half rubles. It's getting late."

"Which two and a half rubles?" I stammered, pretending surprise.

"What do you mean? Are you crazy? Don't play dumb! Hand over the money that the Gentile paid you."

"Oh, that's what you mean, Father dear? But I have already given that money to Miss Kaletzka. We start classes in her school very soon."

"Impudent girl!" my father screamed, and tried to grab me by the arm. I ran around the perimeter of the table, not permitting him to catch me.

"So help me, I don't have it. I don't have the money."

Never before had my father hit me. Nor did he slap me, even now. Instead he threw fiery looks my way. *"Nu, nu"*—his short beard lifted as he bit his thin lips fiercely—"you're lucky that I must go off to pray. I'll argue this out with you tonight. I'll show you what it means to steal money from me, you wanton girl, you!"

When I heard him hastily slam the door behind him, I breathed a sigh of relief. I ran to my room and lay down to sleep, forgoing dinner, anything to divert an encounter with my father that night.

The next morning, my father would not speak to me. He got my mother to try to prevail upon me to return the money from Miss Kaletzka.

"Chayele, I beg you . . ." She cracked her knuckles tragically. "Don't upset your father. Such a disgrace, woe is me. Why can't you be satisfied with four grades? You will, God forbid, shorten your father's life! This notion of going to school will surely lead you down wayward paths," my mother lamented.

"But when you were young," I wondered, "did you never want to . . . Why is it so hard to understand? I want to learn about life, to come closer to the Truth in my own way. Father also searches for the Truth in the holy books. When he studies, he often comments, 'Tosefus says the opposite.'"

A pair of unseeing eyes stared back at me.

"Why does Father not want to understand me?" I asked.

"I don't understand you, either."

Trying to explain myself to my mother, I told her about a poem I knew by a French writer. He recounted the story of a boy who wanted to burn down a library, because he had never gone to school and didn't know how to read.

Mother shrugged her shoulders. "What nonsense! What a spiteful person you are, with absolutely no Jewish conscience." With clenched teeth, she threatened me, her finger in the air: "Just remember, your father will never forgive you!"

In reality, it is also my mother who does not understand me. A spiteful person, she calls me. On the contrary, I am in great pain over this conflict. Perhaps she is incapable of under-standing me. After all, she herself has never gone to school. I live in different times and have different expectations. She does not see the rising sun of tomorrow. In contrast, I walk on new roads toward the future—even though my heart is in pain because my parents' blessings will never accompany me.

Attending Miss Kaletzka's School, especially in the begin-ning, was nerve-racking for me. First of all, in order to avoid my father's sharp looks every morning, I had to be careful to leave my room only after Father had gone to morning prayers. Second, my new shoes had suddenly disappeared. My parents had hidden them somewhere.

All this anguished me but did not stop me from going to school. Since I didn't have my new shoes, I went in my old worn slippers. Because I didn't have ten groschen for the streetcar, I went by foot, even though it was more than a half-hour walk. With my rich Chasidic parents, I couldn't spare even a groschen. But in spite of this, I flourished at school.

The girls at school, mostly from wealthy assimilated homes, welcomed us, the new fifth graders from Miss Pozner's School, with open arms. We sat on a bench in pairs. Fela, my bench partner, told me about her parents. Her father did not wear a *kapote*. He dressed in the modern "German" fashion: a short jacket, a fedora rather than a peaked hat. He ate bareheaded and spoke to her in Polish. Yiddish, she said, she could understand but couldn't speak. Most of all, I was impressed by her stories of her older, educated *gymnazium* friends with whom she went for walks and who were even allowed to visit her at home.

In contrast, I was ashamed to describe my home to her, to tell her that I was forbidden to look a boy in the face. Probably she wouldn't have believed me, or perhaps she would make fun of me and no longer be my friend. So I remained silent about my own life. Deep in my heart, I was jealous of her and disgruntled that I was born to Chasidic parents.

Two Years Later . . .

Today, there is a tumult, an uproar, in our home. Outside, it is swelteringly hot; the air is heavy, oppressive. Anyone who can runs away from the city. Whoever must remain in the city runs to the Vistula River to cool off on its shores. As in previous years, my mother has rented a summer cottage in a villa in Falenitz on the outskirts of Warsaw, where we, the children, are to spend our summer vacation.

Our maid, Dora, sweated in the kitchen as she packed the meat dishes in one box and the dairy in another. Mother busied herself with packing the linens and the summer clothes. From time to time, she threw me a reproachful glance from her normally mild blue eyes. A deep sigh accompanied her look. It bothered her that I had decided against enjoying the summer in the fresh air of Falenitz.

"What pretensions you have! Ever since you started at Kaletzka's School, you imagine you are a 'lady.'" My mother turned her head to the left, then to the right. The blond wig on her head followed the motion, as though agreeing with her words.

"I'm sick of vacations," was my response. "I've had enough of the 'joys' of Falenitz. I'd rather spend my summer sweating in Warsaw."

In reality, my reason for not traveling to the cottage this year was connected to the most recent secret I was keeping from my parents: my decision to transfer from the sixth grade of Miss Kaletzka's School to the seventh grade of a Russian *gymnazium*. Kaletzka's private school had no legal status in Warsaw. To become a qualified schoolteacher or a university student, it was necessary to receive a diploma from a Russian school, at least for the final year—grade seven. And in order to be accepted to the Russian *gymnazium*, one had to pass certain special examinations, since their curriculum was broader than that of a private school. Thus, a group of us sixth graders had agreed to sacrifice our summer vacation to prepare for these examinations. Not wanting to raise my parents' suspicions, I studied with my friend Edja at her house.

Edja's father, a middle-class merchant, was not so religious. Although he still wore a cloth head covering, his *kapote* was only three-quarters length. He wore garters instead of boots and a stiff collar with a tie. His beard was rounded, trimmed short. He didn't mind that his daughter might someday attend *gymnazium* on the Sabbath. But he couldn't imagine how I would go about persuading my Chasidic father to do the same. He had heard that, to this day, my father had not forgiven me for my sin of two years ago—that I had not obeyed him and continued to go to school. Father's argument had remained: "A girl need learn no more than to write an address or to draw up a bill."

"I certainly do not envy you your fanatic father. Such an unworldly Chasid, just like all the other Gerer Chasidim," my friend's father stated contemptuously.

It upset me that he, supposedly an "enlightened" man, ridiculed my father, whom I still loved deep in my heart. I spat out at him with pride: "It may surprise you, Reb Yitzhak, that my father's avoidance of me actually brings me pain. When he sees me come home from school with a batch of books under my arm, he angrily bites his lips and a cloud seems to hover over his thick, downcast eyebrows. He turns his head away from me and is silent. He will not speak to me, and his silence affects me deeply. I would prefer he curse me, scream at me, even hit me. But my father has never raised his hand to any of his children. Yes, I would like to put aside these walls of silence between us, because . . . I do have great respect for my Chasidic father, despite the abyss between us which grows deeper and deeper. It is with great sadness that I realize he can never understand me."

"But how did you manage to get your way? After all, you went to school for two years against his wishes."

"As you know, my father is rich. It is no problem for him to pay for my classes at school. At first, he thought that if he did not pay for my schooling after four grades, I would be forced to give up the idea of studying further. Instead, I went to our headmistress, who was quite taken with me. After I explained the story of my family to her, she set me up to give private lessons. At fourteen years of age, I became a successful private tutor. Not only did I earn enough to pay for my school expenses, I was also able to save good money."

"Is that so? I understand this, but how will you deal with

your father now? How will the zealot Reb Leybele tolerate his daughter going to a Russian *gymnazium*, where classes are conducted on the Sabbath? Surely this must merely be a childish dream on your part." Edja's father laughed perniciously at me.

"My father must not know that I plan to switch schools. That's all I need! I will find excuses, one *Shabbes* at a time."

"God help you." Edja's father wrinkled his forehead doubtfully.

We were preoccupied with studying until the week of the examinations. It began with the written exams. We completed the languages: Russian, Polish, German. The mathematics examination, the most difficult subject for me, fell on a Friday. Terrified, I worked very hard on the exam, which lasted until evening.

When it was over, I wanted to scream, "Hurrah!" I knew I had answered all the math problems correctly. Dancing and singing, I headed for home.

In my great exultation, I had totally forgotten that it was Friday. Surprised, I saw the stores on the street had already been closed. In the windows of the houses, yellow flames twinkled from the *Shabbes* candles. The streets were illuminated by the tall gas lamps, with almost no Jewish pedestrians in sight. Now I was inside the gate of our building at Number Four Twarda Street. In the courtyard opposite the gate, the Arsidiners shul was lit, but there were no longer any worshipers.

I realized I was late for my father's kiddush: I was in deep trouble. My heart skipped a beat with fear as I ran into the house. On the steps, I heard the sounds of shouting coming from our apartment on the third floor. I didn't stop. I was still on the second floor. I heard yells: "No, Father dear, we won't let you do it." I raised my head and saw my father in his satin *kapote*, *shtreyml* on his head, tearing himself away from my sister's arms. Enraged, he ran down the steps toward me with malice.

"Impudent girl! You have desecrated the Sabbath!" he

shouted in a wild voice. I remained standing, bewildered and speechless. Furiously, he grabbed me by the collar of my coat and shook me with all his might, as though to drive the life force out of me. I wanted to defend myself, run away. But when I saw my father's red, tearful eyes, my feet became like stone. I remained standing as if nailed to the wall. My father smacked me with a blow that resounded throughout the building.

My face was on fire. My sister pulled me up the steps. I fell into my room, flung myself on my bed, and wailed.

My older sister Sorele gently took my hands away from my covered eyes and talked to me quietly, her voice trembling: "Father returned from shul, finished singing 'Sholom Aleichem,' and sat down at the head of the table, as always. All the children sat around the set table. When he noticed your chair was empty, he made no kiddush. Instead, he stood with his face to the window, and I heard—I couldn't believe it—yes, I heard him crying. Can you imagine our father in tears? Believe me, Chayele, it cut right to the heart. No doubt someone had informed on you. He knew where you had been."

But all this was only a prelude to my real problem: What would I do tomorrow on *Shabbes*? Tomorrow morning, I must take the verbal examination in German. I was the best student in German; it should be easy for me to pass the exam. But my father's tearful eyes gave me no rest. I could hardly lie still in my bed, let alone fall asleep. On the pillow, my head was spinning with thoughts: What am I to do? Not to go to the examination tomorrow means giving up the idea of *gymnazium*. Give in to my father out of sympathy? No, I cannot allow myself to be misled by sentiment. I must go!

Saturday morning, my parents had gone to pray. I got up, went downstairs. But where was my coat? Not there. My parents had hidden it somewhere. Never mind; I took my sister's coat. The sleeves were too long and I swam in it, but I had no other choice. Like a thief, I snuck away from the house.

My head downcast, I came into the classroom. My friends surrounded me: "What's up? Look at you. You look as though your ship has sunk. Why are you so pale? They say you got a 'five,' the highest mark, on your written German. Why are you afraid of the oral exam?"

I didn't answer. I sat down quietly. In front of my eyes, I could see my father with his tearful eyes. . . .

The teacher called on me. She glanced at my written examination and smiled at me approvingly. Though I looked in her direction, I did not see her. To me, she seemed enveloped in a black cloud. When she asked me a question, I was silent. She looked at me, bewildered. My lips didn't move. She asked me another question; I remained silent. Again, her eyes glanced at my written work. She shrugged and almost gave me the answer outright.

"I don't know," I replied in a choked voice.

"What do you mean?" the teacher questioned. "Don't you understand that if you refuse to answer the third question correctly"—she tried to incite me—"you will fail?"

"I know."

I couldn't even hear the third question. I could only hear the sound of my own voice: *Enough! No more gymnazium! Resign yourself and spare yourself the struggle with him! This is your destiny.*

I left the teacher with her mouth hanging wide open. Exiting from the classroom, I rushed back home, so as not to be late when my father returned from prayers. . . .

✱ ☾ ✱

HELEN LONDYNSKI *was born on May 31, 1896, and grew up in a sheltered, well-to-do Chasidic household in cosmopolitan Warsaw. After attending private secular Jewish girls' schools, she continued studying literature and psychology at Wolna Wszechnica Polska, an alternative Polish university formed by socialists in 1918–1919.*

Beginning in 1920, she worked with poet and journalist Shmuel Y. Londynski in his groundbreaking Warsaw publishing house Di Tzayt (the Times), which published Yiddish literature by such distinguished writers as I. J. Singer, Melech Ravitch, Yehoshua Perle, Uri Tzvi Greenberg, and I. M. Vaysnberg in the early days of their careers. Not long thereafter, she married Londynski. They moved to Paris in 1925, where they settled for over a decade. In 1939, they and their two young daughters had the misfortune of returning to Warsaw just as the city became occupied by the Nazis. Unable to go back to Paris, they escaped and spent the next three years as refugees, wandering through Odessa, Istanbul, Iraq, Palestine, Iran, India, Madagascar, and Cape Town, before they finally arrived in New York in August 1942. In New York City, Helen Londynski worked as secretary to Yiddish linguistic scholar Dr. Mordkhe Schaechter, all the while writing her own articles for such Yiddish journals as Undzer horizont, Di tzukunft, Nyu Yorker vokhenblat, Savar *(Tel Aviv)*, Zayn, Kanader adler, *and* Ofn shvel. *In 1972, her personal writings were published in a memoir entitled* In shpigl fun nekhtn *[In the mirror of yesterday]. Helen Londynski died on May 2, 1992.*

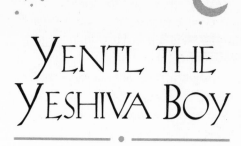

YENTL THE YESHIVA BOY

Isaac Bashevis Singer

Translated by Marion Magid and Elizabeth Pollet

1

After her father's death, Yentl had no reason to remain in Yanev. She was all alone in the house. To be sure, lodgers were willing to move in and pay rent; and the marriage brokers flocked to her door with offers from Lublin, Tomashev, Zamosc. But Yentl didn't want to get married. Inside her, a voice repeated over and over: *No!* What becomes of a girl when the wedding's over? Right away she starts bearing and rearing. And her mother-in-law lords it over her. Yentl knew she wasn't cut out for a woman's life. She couldn't sew, she couldn't knit. She let the food burn and the milk boil over; her Sabbath pudding never turned out right, and her challah dough didn't rise. Yentl much preferred men's activities to women's. Her father, Reb Todros, may he rest in peace, during many bedridden years had studied Torah with his daughter as if she were a son. He told Yentl to lock the doors and drape the windows, then together they pored over the Pentateuch, the Mishnah, the Gemora, and the Commentaries. She had proved so apt a pupil that her father used to say:

"Yentl—you have the soul of a man."

"So why was I born a woman?"

"Even heaven makes mistakes."

There was no doubt about it, Yentl was unlike any of the girls in Yanev—tall, thin, bony, with small breasts and narrow hips. On Sabbath afternoons, when her father slept, she would dress up in his trousers, his fringed garment, his silk coat, his skullcap, his velvet hat, and study her reflection in the mirror. She looked like a dark, handsome young man. There was even a slight down on her upper lip. Only her thick braids showed her womanhood—and if it came to that, hair could always be shorn. Yentl conceived a plan, and day and night she could think of nothing else. No, she had not been created for the noodle board and the pudding dish, for chattering with silly women and pushing for a place at the butcher's block. Her father had told her so many tales of yeshivas, rabbis, men of letters! Her head was full of Talmudic disputations, questions and answers, learned phrases. Secretly, she had even smoked her father's long pipe.

Yentl told the dealers she wanted to sell the house and go to live in Kalish with an aunt. The neighborhood women tried to talk her out of it, and the marriage brokers said she was crazy, that she was more likely to make a good match right here in Yanev. But Yentl was obstinate. She was in such a rush that she sold the house to the first bidder and let the furniture go for a song. All she realized from her inheritance was 140 rubles. Then late one night in the month of Av, while Yanev slept, Yentl cut off her braids, arranged sidelocks at her temples, and dressed herself in her father's clothes. After packing underclothes, phylacteries, and a few books into a straw suitcase, she started off on foot for Lublin.

On the main road, Yentl got a ride in a carriage that took her as far as Zamosc. From there, she again set out on foot. She stopped at an inn along the way, and gave her name there as Anshel, after an uncle who had died. The inn was crowded with young men journeying to study with famous rabbis. An argument was in progress over the merits of various yeshivas, some praising those of Lithuania, others claiming that study was more intensive in Poland and the board better. It was the first time Yentl had ever found herself alone in the company of young men. How different their talk was from the jabbering of women, she thought, but she was too shy to join in. One young man discussed a prospective match and the size of the dowry, while another, parodying the manner of a Purim rabbi, declaimed a passage from the Torah, adding all sorts of lewd interpretations. After a while, the company proceeded to contests of strength. One pried open another's fist; a second tried to bend a companion's arm. One student, dining on bread and tea, had no spoon and stirred his cup with his penknife.

Presently, one of the group came over to Yentl and poked her in the shoulder. "Why so quiet? Don't you have a tongue?"

"I have nothing to say."

"What's your name?"

"Anshel."

"You *are* bashful. A violet by the wayside."

And the young man tweaked Yentl's nose. She would have given him a smack in return, but her arm refused to budge. She turned white. Another student, slightly older than the rest, tall and pale, with burning eyes and a black beard, came to her rescue.

"Hey, you, why are you picking on him?"

"If you don't like it, you don't have to look."

"Want me to pull your sidelocks off?"

The bearded young man beckoned to Yentl, then asked where she came from and where she was going. Yentl told him she was looking for a yeshiva but wanted a quiet one. The young man pulled at his beard.

"Then come with me to Bechev."

He explained that he was returning to Bechev for his fourth year. The yeshiva there was small, with only thirty students, and the people in the town provided board for them all. The food was plentiful, and the housewives darned the students' socks and took care of their laundry. The Bechev rabbi, who headed the yeshiva, was a genius. He could pose ten questions and answer all ten with one proof. Most of the students eventually found wives in the town.

"Why did you leave in the middle of the term?" Yentl asked.

"My mother died. Now I'm on my way back."

"What's your name?"

"Avigdor."

"How is it you're not married?"

The young man scratched his beard. "It's a long story."

"Tell me."

Avigdor covered his eyes and thought a moment. "Are you coming to Bechev?"

"Yes."

"Then you'll find out soon enough anyway. I was engaged to the only daughter of Alter Vishkower, the richest man in town. Even the wedding date was set when suddenly they sent back the engagement contract."

"What happened?"

"I don't know. Gossips, I guess, were busy spreading tales. I had the right to ask for half the dowry, but it was against my nature. Now they're trying to talk me into another match, but the girl doesn't appeal to me."

"In Bechev, yeshiva boys look at women?"

"At Alter's house, where I ate once a week, Hadass, his daughter, always brought in the food. . . ."

"Is she good-looking?"

"She's blond."

"Brunettes can be good-looking too."

"No."

Yentl gazed at Avigdor. He was lean and bony, with sunken cheeks. He had curly sidelocks so black they appeared blue, and his eyebrows met across the bridge of his nose. He looked at her sharply with the regretful shyness of one who has just divulged a secret. His lapel was rent, according to the custom for mourners, and the lining of his gabardine showed through. He drummed restlessly on the table and hummed a tune. Behind the high, furrowed brow his thoughts seemed to race. Suddenly he spoke:

"Well, what of it. I'll become a recluse, that's all."

2

It was strange, but as soon as Yentl—or Anshel—arrived in Bechev, she was allotted one day's board a week at the house of that same rich man, Alter Vishkower, whose daughter had broken off her betrothal to Avigdor.

The students at the yeshiva studied in pairs, and Avigdor chose Anshel for a partner. He helped her with the lessons. He was also an expert swimmer and offered to teach Anshel the breaststroke and how to tread water, but she always found excuses for not going down to the river. Avigdor suggested that they share lodgings, but Anshel found a place to sleep at the house of an elderly widow who was half-blind. Tuesdays, Anshel ate at Alter Vishkower's, and Hadass waited on her. Avigdor always asked many questions: "How does Hadass look? Is she sad? Is she gay? Are they trying to marry her off? Does she ever mention my name?" Anshel reported that Hadass upset dishes on the tablecloth, forgot to bring the salt, and dipped her fingers into the plate of grits while carrying it. She ordered the servant girl around, was forever engrossed in storybooks, and changed her hairdo every week. Moreover, she must consider herself a beauty, for she was always in front of the mirror, but, in fact, she was not that good-looking.

"Two years after she's married," said Anshel, "she'll be an old bag."

"So she doesn't appeal to you?"

"Not particularly."

"Yet if she wanted you, you wouldn't turn her down."

"I can do without her."

"Don't you have evil impulses?"

The two friends, sharing a lectern in a corner of the study house, spent more time talking than learning. Occasionally Avigdor smoked, and Anshel, taking the cigarette from his lips, would have a puff. Avigdor liked baked flatcakes made with buckwheat, so Anshel stopped at the bakery every morning to buy one and wouldn't let him pay his share. Often Anshel did things that greatly surprised Avigdor. If a button came off Avigdor's coat, for example, Anshel would arrive at the yeshiva the next day with needle and thread and sew it back on. Anshel bought Avigdor all kinds of presents: a silk handkerchief, a pair of socks, a muffler. Avigdor grew more and more attached to this boy, five years younger than himself, whose beard hadn't even begun to sprout.

Once Avigdor said to Anshel: "I want you to marry Hadass."

"What good would that do *you*?"

"Better you than a total stranger."

"You'd become my enemy."

"Never."

Avigdor liked to go for walks through the town, and Anshel frequently joined him. Engrossed in conversation, they would go off to the water mill, or to the pine forest, or to the crossroads where the Christian shrine stood. Sometimes they stretched out on the grass.

"Why can't a woman be like a man?" Avigdor asked once, looking up at the sky.

"How do you mean?"

"Why couldn't Hadass be just like you?"

"How like me?"

"Oh—a good fellow."

Anshel grew playful. She plucked a flower and tore off the petals one by one. She picked up a chestnut and threw it at Avigdor. Avigdor watched a ladybug crawl across the palm of his hand.

After a while he spoke up: "They're trying to marry me off."

Anshel sat up instantly. "To whom?"

"To Feitl's daughter, Peshe."

"The widow?"

"That's the one."

"Why should you marry a widow?"

"No one else will have me."

"That's not true. Someone will turn up for you."

"Never."

Anshel told Avigdor such a match was bad. Peshe was neither good-looking nor clever, only a cow with a pair of eyes. Besides, she was bad luck, for her husband died in the first year of their marriage. Such women were husband killers. But Avigdor did not answer. He lit a cigarette, took a deep puff, and blew out smoke rings. His face had turned green.

"I need a woman. I can't sleep at night."

Anshel was startled. "Why can't you wait until the right one comes along?"

"Hadass was my destined one."

And Avigdor's eyes grew moist. Abruptly he got to his feet. "Enough lying around. Let's go."

After that, everything happened quickly. One day Avigdor was confiding his problem to Anshel, two days later he became engaged to Peshe and brought honey cake and brandy to the yeshiva. An early wedding date was set. When the bride-to-be is a widow, there's no need to wait for a trousseau. Everything is ready. The groom, moreover, was an orphan and no one's advice had to be asked. The yeshiva students drank the brandy and offered their congratulations. Anshel also took a sip but promptly choked on it.

"Oy, it burns!"

"You're not much of a man," Avigdor teased.

After the celebration, Avigdor and Anshel sat down with a volume of the Gemora, but they made little progress, and their conversation was equally slow. Avigdor rocked back and forth, pulled at his beard, muttered under his breath.

"I'm lost," he said abruptly.

"If you don't like her, why are you getting married?"

"I'd marry a she-goat."

The following day Avigdor did not appear at the study house. Feitl the leather dealer belonged to the Chasidim and he wanted his prospective son-in-law to continue his studies at the Chasidic prayer house. The yeshiva students said privately that though there was no denying the widow was short and round as a barrel, her mother the daughter of a dairyman, her father half an ignoramus, still the whole family was filthy with money. Feitl was part owner of a tannery; Peshe had invested her dowry in a shop that sold herring, tar, pots, and pans and was always crowded with peasants. Father and daughter were outfitting Avigdor and had placed orders for a fur coat, a cloth coat, a silk *kapote*, and two pairs of boots. In addition, he had received many gifts immediately, things that had belonged to Peshe's first husband: the Vilna edition of the Talmud, a gold watch, a Chanukah candelabra, a spice box. Anshel sat alone at the lectern.

On Tuesday when Anshel arrived for dinner at Alter Vishkower's house, Hadass remarked: "What do you say about your partner—back in clover, isn't he?"

"What did you expect—that no one else would want him?"

Hadass reddened. "It wasn't my fault. My father was against it."

"Why?"

"Because they found out a brother of his had hanged himself."

Anshel looked at her as she stood there—tall, blond, with a long neck, hollow cheeks, and blue eyes, wearing a cotton dress and a calico apron. Her hair, fixed in two braids, was flung back over her shoulders. A pity I'm not a man, Anshel thought.

"Do you regret it now?" Anshel asked.

"Oh, yes!"

Hadass fled from the room. The rest of the food, meat dumplings and tea, was brought in by the servant girl. Not until Anshel had finished eating and was washing her hands for the final blessings did Hadass reappear.

She came up to the table and said in a smothered voice: "Swear to me you won't tell him anything. Why should he know what goes on in my heart!"

Then she fled once more, nearly falling over the threshold.

3

The head of the yeshiva asked Anshel to choose another study partner, but weeks went by and still Anshel studied alone. There was no one in the yeshiva who could take Avigdor's place. All the others were small, in body and in spirit. They talked nonsense, bragged about trifles, grinned oafishly, behaved like *shnorrers*. Without Avigdor the study house seemed empty. At night Anshel lay on her bench at the widow's, unable to sleep. Stripped of gabardine and trousers, she was once more Yentl, a girl of marriageable age, in love with a young man who was betrothed to another. Perhaps I should have told him the truth, Anshel thought. But it was too late for that. Anshel could not go back to being a girl, could never again do without books and a study house. She lay there thinking outlandish thoughts that brought her close to madness. She fell asleep, then awoke with a start. In her dream she had been at the same time a man and a woman, wearing both a woman's bodice and a man's fringed garment. Yentl's period was late and she was suddenly afraid . . . who knew? In Midrash Talpios she had read of a woman who had conceived merely through desiring a man. Only now did Yentl grasp the meaning of the Torah's prohibition against wearing the clothes of the other sex. By doing so, one deceived not only others but also oneself. Even the soul was perplexed, finding itself incarnate in a strange body.

At night Anshel lay awake; by day she could scarcely keep her eyes open. At the houses where she had her meals, the women complained that the youth left everything on his plate. The rabbi noticed that Anshel no longer paid attention to the lectures but stared out the window, lost in private thoughts. When Tuesday came, Anshel appeared at the Vishkower house for dinner. Hadass set a bowl of soup before her and waited, but Anshel was so disturbed she did not even say thank you. She reached for a spoon but let it fall.

Hadass ventured a comment: "I hear Avigdor has deserted you."

Anshel awoke from her trance. "What do you mean?"

"He's no longer your partner."

"He's left the yeshiva."

"Do you see him at all?"

"He seems to be hiding."

"Are you at least going to the wedding?"

For a moment Anshel was silent, as though missing the meaning of the words. Then she spoke: "He's a big fool."

"Why do you say that?"

"You're beautiful, and the other one looks like a monkey."

Hadass blushed to the roots of her hair. "It's all my father's fault."

"Don't worry. You'll find someone who's worthy of you."

"There's no one I want."

"But everyone wants you. . . ."

There was a long silence. Hadass's eyes grew larger, filling with the sadness of one who knows there is no consolation.

"Your soup is getting cold."

"I, too, want you."

Anshel was astonished at what she had said. Hadass stared at her over her shoulder.

"What are you saying!"

"It's the truth."

"Someone might be listening."

"I'm not afraid."

"Eat the soup. I'll bring the meat dumplings in a moment."

Hadass turned to go, her high heels clattering. Anshel began hunting for beans in the soup, fished one up, then let it fall. Her appetite was gone; her throat had closed up. She knew very well she was getting entangled in evil, but some force kept urging her on. Hadass reappeared, carrying a platter with two meat dumplings on it.

"Why aren't you eating?"

"I'm thinking about you."

"What are you thinking?"

"I want to marry you."

Hadass made a face as though she had swallowed something.

"On such matters, you must speak to my father."

"I know."

"The custom is to send a matchmaker."

She ran from the room, letting the door slam behind her. Laughing inwardly, Anshel thought: With girls I can play as I please! She sprinkled salt on the soup and then pepper. She sat there, light-headed. What have I done? I must be going mad. There's no other explanation. . . . She forced herself to eat but could taste nothing. Only then did Anshel remember that it was Avigdor who had wanted her to marry Hadass. From her confusion, a plan emerged: She would exact vengeance for Avigdor and at the same time, through Hadass, draw him closer to herself. Hadass was a virgin: what did she know about men? A girl like that could be deceived for a long time. To be sure, Anshel too was a virgin, but she knew a lot about such matters from the Gemora and from hearing men talk. Anshel was seized by both fear and glee, as a person is who is planning to deceive the whole community. She remembered the saying "The public are fools." She stood up and said aloud: "Now I'll really start something."

That night Anshel didn't sleep a wink. Every few minutes she got up for a drink of water. Her throat was parched, her forehead burned. Her brain worked away feverishly of its own volition. A quarrel seemed to be going on inside her. Her stomach throbbed and her knees ached. It was as if she had sealed a pact with Satan, the Evil One who plays tricks on human beings, who sets stumbling blocks and traps in their paths. By the time Anshel fell asleep, it was morning. She awoke more exhausted than before. But she could not go on sleeping on the bench at the widow's. With an effort she rose and, taking the bag that held her phylacteries, set out for the study house. On the way, whom should she meet but Hadass's father. Anshel bade him a respectful good morning and received a friendly greeting in return. Reb Alter stroked his beard and engaged her in conversation:

"My daughter Hadass must be serving you leftovers. You look starved."

"Your daughter is a fine girl, and very generous."

"So why are you so pale?"

Anshel was silent for a minute. "Reb Alter, there's something I must say to you."

"Well, go ahead, say it."

"Reb Alter, your daughter pleases me."

Alter Vishkower came to a halt. "Oh, does she? I thought yeshiva students didn't talk about such things."

His eyes were full of laughter.

"But it's the truth."

"One doesn't discuss these matters with the young man himself."

"But I'm an orphan."

"Well . . . in that case, the custom is to send a marriage broker."

"Yes. . . ."

"What do you see in her?"

"She's beautiful . . . fine . . . intelligent . . ."

"Well, well, well . . . Come along, tell me something about your family."

Alter Vishkower put his arm around Anshel, and in this fashion the two continued walking until they reached the courtyard of the synagogue.

4

Once you say "A," you must say "B." Thoughts lead to words, words lead to deeds. Reb Alter Vishkower gave his consent to the match. Hadass's mother, Freyda Leah, held back for a while. She said she wanted no more Bechev yeshiva students for her daughter and would rather have someone from Lublin or Zamosc; but Hadass gave warning that if she were shamed publicly once more (the way she had been with Avigdor), she would throw herself into the well. As often happens with such ill-advised matches, everyone was strongly in favor of it—the rabbi, the relatives, Hadass's girlfriends. For some time the girls of Bechev had been eyeing Anshel longingly, watching from their windows when the youth passed by on the street. Anshel kept his boots well polished and did not drop his eyes in the presence of women. Stopping in at Beila the baker's to buy a *pletzl*, he joked with them in such a worldly fashion that they marveled. The women agreed there was something special about Anshel: his sidelocks curled like nobody else's, and he tied his neck scarf differently; his eyes, smiling yet distant, seemed always fixed on some faraway point. And the fact that Avigdor had become betrothed to Feitl's daughter, Peshe, forsaking Anshel, had endeared him all the more to the people of the town. Alter Vishkower had a provisional contract drawn up for the betrothal, promising Anshel a bigger dowry, more presents, and an even longer period of maintenance than he had promised Avigdor. The girls of Bechev threw their arms around Hadass and congratulated her. Hadass immediately began crocheting a sack for Anshel's phylacteries, a challah cloth, a matzo bag. When Avigdor heard the news of Anshel's betrothal, he came to the study house to offer his congratulations. The past few weeks had aged him. His beard was disheveled, his eyes were red.

He said to Anshel: "I knew it would happen this way. Right from the beginning. As soon as I met you at the inn."

"But it was you who suggested it."

"I know that."

"Why did you desert me? You went away without even saying good-bye."

"I wanted to burn my bridges behind me."

Avigdor asked Anshel to go for a walk. Though it was already past Succos the day was bright with sunshine. Avigdor, friendlier than ever, opened his heart to Anshel. Yes, it was true, a brother of his had succumbed to melancholy and hanged himself. Now he too felt himself near the edge of the abyss. Peshe had a lot of money and her father was a rich man, yet he couldn't sleep nights. He didn't want to be a storekeeper. He couldn't forget Hadass. She appeared in his dreams. Sabbath night when her name occurred in the havdalah prayer, he turned dizzy. Still, it was good that Anshel and no one else was to marry her. . . . At least she would fall into decent hands. Avigdor stooped and tore aimlessly at the shriveled grass. His speech was incoherent, like that of a man possessed.

Suddenly he said: "I have thought of doing what my brother did."

"Do you love her *that* much?"

"She's engraved in my heart."

The two pledged their friendship and promised never again to part. Anshel proposed that after they were both married, they should live next door or even share the same house. They would study together every day, perhaps even become partners in a shop.

"Do you want to know the truth?" asked Avigdor. "It's like the story of Jacob and Benjamin: my life is bound up in your life."

"Then why did you leave me?"

"Perhaps for that very reason."

Though the day had turned cold and windy, they continued to walk until they reached the pine forest, not turning back until dusk when it was time for the evening prayer. The girls of Bechev, from their posts at the windows, watched them going by with their arms round each other's shoulders and so engrossed in conversation that they walked through puddles and piles of trash without noticing. Avigdor looked pale, disheveled, and the wind whipped one sidelock about; Anshel chewed his fingernails. Hadass, too, ran to the window, took one look, and her eyes filled with tears.

Events followed quickly. Avigdor was the first to marry. Because the bride was a widow, the wedding was a quiet one, with no musicians, no wedding jester, no ceremonial veiling of the bride. One day Peshe stood beneath the marriage canopy, the next she was back at the shop, dispensing tar with greasy hands. Avigdor prayed at the Chasidic assembly house in his new prayer shawl. Afternoons, Anshel went to visit him, and the two whispered and talked until evening. The date of Anshel's wedding to Hadass was set for the Sabbath in Chanukah week, though the prospective father-in-law wanted it sooner. Hadass had already been betrothed once. Besides, the groom was an orphan. Why should he toss about on a makeshift bed at the widow's when he could have a wife and home of his own?

Many times each day Anshel warned herself that what she was about to do was sinful, mad, an act of utter depravity. She was entangling both Hadass and herself in a chain of deception and committing so many transgressions that she would never be able to do penance. One lie followed another. Repeatedly Anshel made up her mind to flee Bechev in time, to put an end to this weird comedy that was more the work of an imp than a human being. But she was in the grip of a power she could not resist. She grew more and more attached to Avigdor and could not bring herself to destroy Hadass's illusory happiness. Now that he was married, Avigdor's desire to study was greater than ever, and the friends met twice each day: in the mornings they studied the Gemora and the Commentaries, in the afternoons the Legal Codes with their glosses. Alter Vishkower and Feitl the leather dealer were pleased and compared Avigdor and Anshel to David and Jonathan. With all the complications, Anshel went about as though drunk. The tailors took her measurements for a new wardrobe, and she was forced into all kinds of subterfuge to keep them from discovering she was not a man. Though the imposture had lasted many weeks, Anshel still could not believe it: How was it possible? Fooling the community had become a game, but how long could it go on? And in what way would the truth come to the surface? Inside, Anshel laughed and wept. She had turned into a sprite brought into the world to mock people and trick them. I'm wicked, a transgressor, a Jeroboam ben Nabat, she told herself. Her only justification was that she had taken all these burdens upon herself because her soul thirsted to study Torah.

Avigdor soon began to complain that Peshe treated him badly. She called him an idler, a shlemiel, just another mouth to feed. She tried to tie him to the store, assigned him tasks for which he hadn't the slightest inclination, begrudged him pocket money. Instead of consoling Avigdor, Anshel goaded him on against Peshe. She called his wife an eyesore, a shrew, a miser, and said that Peshe had no doubt nagged her first husband to death and would Avigdor also. At the same time, Anshel enumerated Avigdor's virtues: his height and manliness, his wit, his erudition.

"If I were a woman and married to you," said Anshel, "I'd know how to appreciate you."

"Well, but you aren't. . . ."

Avigdor sighed.

Meanwhile, Anshel's wedding date drew near.

On the Sabbath before Chanukah, Anshel was called to the pulpit to read from the Torah. The women showered her with raisins and almonds. On the day of the wedding, Alter Vishkower gave a feast for the young men. Avigdor sat at Anshel's right hand. The bridegroom delivered a Talmudic discourse, and the rest of the company argued the points, while smoking cigarettes and drinking wine, liqueurs, tea with lemon or raspberry jam. Then followed the ceremony of veiling the bride, after which the bridegroom was led to the wedding canopy that had been set up at the side of the synagogue. The night was frosty and clear, the sky full of stars. The musicians struck up a tune. Two rows of girls held lighted tapers and braided wax candles. After the wedding ceremony, the bride and groom broke their fast with golden chicken broth. Then the dancing began and the announcement of the wedding gifts, all according to custom. The gifts were many and costly. The wedding jester depicted the joys and sorrows that were in store for the bride. Avigdor's wife, Peshe, was one of the guests, but though she was bedecked with jewels, she still looked ugly in a wig that sat low on her forehead, wearing an enormous fur cape, and with traces of tar on her hands that no amount of washing could ever remove. After the virtue dance, the bride and groom were led separately to the marriage chamber. The wedding attendants instructed the couple in the proper conduct and enjoined them to "be fruitful and multiply."

At daybreak Anshel's mother-in-law and her band descended upon the marriage chamber and tore the bedsheets from beneath Hadass to make sure the marriage had been consummated. When traces of blood were discovered, the company grew merry and began kissing and congratulating the bride.

Then, brandishing the sheet, they flocked outside and danced a kosher dance in the newly fallen snow. Anshel had found a way to deflower the bride. Hadass in her innocence was unaware that things weren't quite as they should have been. She was already deeply in love with Anshel. It is commanded that the bride and groom remain apart for seven days after the first intercourse. The next day Anshel and Avigdor took up the study of the Tractate on Menstruous Women. When the other men had departed and the two were left to themselves in the synagogue, Avigdor shyly questioned Anshel about his night with Hadass. Anshel gratified his curiosity and they whispered together until nightfall.

5

Anshel had fallen into good hands. Hadass was a devoted wife, and her parents indulged their son-in-law's every wish and boasted of his accomplishments. To be sure, several months went by and Hadass was still not with child, but no one took it to heart. On the other hand, Avigdor's lot grew steadily worse. Peshe tormented him and finally would not give him enough to eat and even refused him a clean shirt. Since he was always penniless, Anshel again brought him a daily buckwheat cake. Because Peshe was too busy to cook and too stingy to hire a servant, Anshel asked Avigdor to dine at his house. Reb Alter Vishkower and his wife disapproved, arguing that it was wrong for the rejected suitor to visit the house of his former fiancée. The town had plenty to talk about. But Anshel cited precedents to show that it was not prohibited by the law. Most of the townspeople sided with Avigdor and blamed Peshe for everything. Avigdor soon began pressing Peshe for a divorce, and because he did not want to have a child by such a fury, he acted like Onan, or, as the

Gemora translates it, He threshed on the inside and cast his seed without. He confided in Anshel, told him how Peshe came to bed unwashed and snored like a buzz saw, of how she was so occupied with the cash taken in at the store that she babbled about it even in her sleep.

"Oh, Anshel, how I envy you," he said.

"There's no reason for envying me."

"You have everything. I wish your good fortune were mine—with no loss to you, of course."

"Everyone has troubles of his own."

"What sort of troubles do *you* have? Don't tempt Providence."

How could Avigdor have guessed that Anshel could not sleep at night and thought constantly of running away? Lying with Hadass and deceiving her had become more and more painful. Hadass's love and tenderness shamed her. The devotion of her mother- and father-in-law and their hopes for a grand-child were a burden. On Friday afternoons all of the towns-people went to the baths, and every week Anshel had to find a new excuse. But this was beginning to awaken suspicions. There was talk that Anshel must have an unsightly birthmark, or a rupture, or perhaps was not properly circumcised. Judging by the youth's years, his beard should certainly have begun to sprout, yet his cheeks remained smooth. It was already Purim, and Passover was approaching. Soon it would be summer. Not far from Bechev there was a river where all the yeshiva students and young men went swimming as soon as it was warm enough. The lie was swelling like an abscess, and one of these days it must surely burst. Anshel knew she had to find a way to free herself.

It was customary for the young men boarding with their in-laws to travel to nearby cities during the half holidays in the middle of Passover week. They enjoyed the change, refreshed themselves, looked around for business opportunities, bought books or other things a young man might need. Bechev was not far from Lublin, and Anshel persuaded Avigdor to make the journey with her at her expense. Avigdor was delighted at the prospect of being rid for a few days of the shrew he had at home. The trip by carriage was a merry one. The fields were turning green; storks, back from the warm countries, swooped across the sky in great arcs. Streams rushed toward the valleys. The birds chirped. The windmills turned. Spring flowers were beginning to bloom in the fields. Here and there a cow was already grazing. The companions, chatting, ate the fruit and little cakes that Hadass had packed, told each other jokes, and exchanged confidences until they reached Lublin. There they went to an inn and took a room for two. In the journey, Anshel had promised to reveal an astonishing secret to Avigdor in Lublin. Avigdor had joked: What sort of secret could it be? Had Anshel discovered a hidden treasure? Had he written an essay? By studying the kabbalah, had he created a dove?

Now they entered the room, and while Anshel carefully locked the door, Avigdor said teasingly: "Well, let's hear your great secret."

"Prepare yourself for the most incredible thing that ever was."

"I'm prepared for anything."

"I'm not a man but a woman," said Anshel. "My name isn't Anshel, it's Yentl."

Avigdor burst out laughing. "I knew it was a hoax."

"But it's true."

"Even if I'm a fool, I won't swallow this."

"Do you want me to show you?"

"Yes."

"Then I'll get undressed."

Avigdor's eyes widened. It occurred to him that Anshel might want to practice pederasty. Anshel took off the gabardine and the fringed garment and threw off her underclothes. Avigdor took one look and turned first white, then fiery red. Anshel covered herself hastily.

"I've done this only so that you can testify at the court-house. Otherwise, Hadass will have to stay a grass widow."

Avigdor had lost his tongue. He was seized by a fit of trembling. He wanted to speak, but his lips moved and nothing came out. He sat down quickly, for his legs would not support him.

Finally he murmured: "How is it possible? I don't believe it!"

"Should I get undressed again?"

"No!"

Yentl proceeded to tell the whole story: how her father, bedridden, had studied Torah with her; how she had never had the patience for women and their silly chatter; how she had sold the house and all the furnishings, left the town, made her way disguised as a man to Lublin, and on the road met Avigdor. Avigdor sat speechless, gazing at the storyteller. Yentl was by now wearing men's clothes once more.

Avigdor spoke: "It must be a dream."

He pinched himself on the cheek.

"It isn't a dream."

"That such a thing should happen to me!"

"It's all true."

"Why did you do it? *Nu*, I'd better keep still."

"I didn't want to waste my life on a baking shovel and a kneading trough."

"And what about Hadass—why did you do that?"

"I did it for your sake. I knew that Peshe would torment you and at our house you would have some peace."

Avigdor was silent for a long time. He bowed his head, pressed his hands to his temples, shook his head. "What will you do now?"

"I'll go away to a different yeshiva."

"What? If you had only told me earlier, we could have—"

Avigdor broke off in the middle.

"No—it wouldn't have been good."

"Why not?"

"I'm neither one nor the other."

"What a dilemma I'm in!"

"Get a divorce from that horror. Marry Hadass."

"She'll never divorce me, and Hadass won't have me."

"Hadass loves you. She won't listen to her father again."

Avigdor stood up suddenly but then sat down. "I won't be able to forget you. Ever. . . ."

6

According to the law, Avigdor was now forbidden to spend another moment alone with Yentl; yet dressed in the gabardine and trousers, she was again the familiar Anshel.

They resumed their conversation on the old footing: "How could you bring yourself to violate the commandment every day: 'A woman shall not wear that which pertaineth to a man'?"

"I wasn't created for plucking feathers and chattering with females."

"Would you rather lose your share in the World to Come?"

"Perhaps. . . ."

Avigdor raised his eyes. Only now did he realize that Anshel's cheeks were too smooth for a man's, the hair too abundant, the hands too small. Even so, he could not believe that such a thing could have happened. At any moment he expected to wake up. He bit his lips, pinched his thigh. He was seized by shyness and could not speak without stammering. His friendship with Anshel, their intimate talk, their confidences, had been turned into a sham and delusion. The thought even occurred to him that Anshel might be a demon. He shook himself as if to cast off a nightmare; yet that power which knows the difference between dream and reality told him it was all true. He summoned up his courage. He and Anshel could never be strangers to one another, even though Anshel was in fact Yentl. . . .

He ventured a comment: "It seems to me that the witness who testifies for a deserted woman may not marry her, for the law calls him 'a party to the .' "

"What? That didn't occur to me!"

"We must look it up in Eben Ezer."

"I'm not even sure that the rules pertaining to a deserted woman apply in this case," said Anshel in the manner of a scholar.

"If you don't want Hadass to be a grass widow, you must reveal the secret to her directly."

"That I can't do."

"In any event, you must get another witness."

Gradually the two went back to their Talmudic conversation. It seemed strange at first to Avigdor to be disputing holy writ with a woman, yet before long the Torah had reunited them. Though their bodies were different, their souls were of one kind. Anshel spoke in a singsong, gesticulated with her thumb, clutched her sidelocks, plucked at her beardless chin, made all the customary gestures of a yeshiva student. In the heat of argument she even seized Avigdor by the lapel and called him stupid. A great love for Anshel took hold of Avigdor mixed with shame, remorse, anxiety. If I had only known this before, he said to himself. In his thoughts he likened Anshel (or Yentl) to Bruria, the wife of Reb Meir, and to Yalta, the wife of Reb Nachman. For the first time he saw clearly that this was what he had always wanted: a wife whose mind was not taken up with material things. . . . His desire for Hadass was gone now, and he knew he would long for Yentl, but he dared not say so. He felt hot and knew that his face was burning. He could no longer meet Anshel's eyes. He began to enumerate Anshel's sins and saw that he too was implicated, for he had sat next to

Yentl and had touched her during her unclean days. *Nu,* and what could be said about her marriage to Hadass? What a multitude of transgressions there! Willful deception, false vows, misrepresentation! Heaven knew what else.

He asked suddenly: "Tell the truth, are you a heretic?"

"God forbid!"

"Then how could you bring yourself to do such a thing?"

The longer Anshel talked, the less Avigdor understood. All Anshel's explanations seemed to point to one thing: She had the soul of a man and the body of a woman. Anshel said she had married Hadass only in order to be near Avigdor.

"You could have married me," Avigdor said.

"I wanted to study the Gemora and Commentaries with you, not darn your socks!"

For a long time neither spoke. Then Avigdor broke the silence: "I'm afraid Hadass will get sick from all this, God forbid!"

"I'm afraid of that, too."

"What's going to happen now?"

Dusk fell and the two began to recite the evening prayer. In his confusion Avigdor mixed up the blessings, omitted some and repeated others. He glanced sideways at Anshel, who was rocking back and forth, beating her breast, bowing her head. He saw her, eyes closed, lift her face to heaven, as though beseeching: You, Father in heaven, know the truth. . . . When their prayers were finished, they sat down on opposite chairs, facing one another yet a good distance apart. The room filled with shadows. Reflections of the sunset, like purple embroidery, shook on the wall opposite the window. Avigdor again wanted to speak, but at first the words, trembling on the tip of his tongue, would not come.

Suddenly they burst forth: "Maybe it's still not too late? I can't go on living with that accursed woman. . . . You . . ."

"No, Avigdor, it's impossible."

"Why?"

"I'll live out my time as I am. . . ."

"I'll miss you. Terribly."

"And I'll miss you."

"What's the sense of all this?"

Anshel did not answer. Night fell and the light faded. In the darkness they seemed to be listening to each other's thoughts. The law forbade Avigdor to stay in the room alone with Anshel, but he could not think of her just as a woman. What a strange power there is in clothing, he thought.

But he spoke of something else: "I would advise you simply to send Hadass a divorce."

"How can I do that?"

"Since the marriage sacraments weren't valid, what difference does it make?"

"I suppose you're right."

"There'll be time enough later for her to find out the truth."

The maidservant came in with a lamp, but as soon as she had gone, Avigdor put it out. Their predicament and the words which they must speak to one another could not endure light. In the blackness Anshel related all the particulars. She answered all Avigdor's questions. The clock struck two, and still they talked. Anshel told Avigdor that Hadass had never forgotten him. She talked of him frequently, worried about his health, was sorry—though not without a certain satisfaction—about the way things had turned out with Peshe.

"She'll be a good wife," said Anshel. "I don't even know how to bake a pudding."

"Nevertheless, if you're willing . . ."

"No, Avigdor. It wasn't destined to be. . . ."

7

It was all a great riddle to the town: the messenger who arrived bringing Hadass the divorce papers; Avigdor's remaining in Lublin until after the holidays; his return to Bechev with slumping shoulders and lifeless eyes, as if he had been ill. Hadass took to her bed and was visited by the doctor three times a day. Avigdor went into seclusion. If someone ran across him by chance and addressed him, he did not answer. Peshe complained to her parents that Avigdor paced back and forth, smoking all night long. When he finally collapsed from sheer fatigue, in his sleep he called out the name of an unknown female—Yentl. Peshe began talking of a divorce. The town thought Avigdor wouldn't grant her one or would demand money at the very least, but he agreed to everything.

In Bechev the people were not used to having mysteries stay mysteries for long. How can you keep secrets in a little town where everyone knows what's cooking in everyone else's pots? Yet, though there were plenty of persons who made a practice of looking through keyholes and laying an ear to shutters, what happened remained an enigma. Hadass lay in her bed and wept. Chanina the herb doctor reported that she was wasting away. Anshel had disappeared without a trace. Reb Alter Vishkower sent for Avigdor and he arrived, but those who stood straining beneath the window couldn't catch a word of what passed between them. Those individuals who habitually pry into other people's affairs came up with all sorts of theories, but not one of them was consistent.

One party came to the conclusion that Anshel had fallen into the hands of Catholic priests and had been converted. That might have made sense. But where could Anshel have found time for the priests, since he was always studying in the yeshiva? And apart from that, since when does an apostate send his wife a divorce?

Another group whispered that Anshel had cast an eye on another woman. But who could it be? There were no love affairs conducted in Bechev. And none of the young women had recently left town—neither a Jewish woman nor a Gentile one.

Somebody else offered the suggestion that Anshel had been carried away by evil spirits or was even one of them himself. As proof he cited the fact that Anshel had never come either to the bathhouse or to the river. It is well-known that demons have the feet of geese. Well, but had Hadass never seen him barefoot? And who ever heard of a demon sending his wife a divorce? When a demon marries a daughter of mortals, he usually lets her remain a grass widow.

It occurred to someone else that Anshel had committed a major transgression and gone into exile in order to do penance. But what sort of transgression could it have been? And why had he not entrusted it to the rabbi? And why did Avigdor wander about like a ghost?

The hypothesis of Tevel the musician was closest to the truth. Tevel maintained that Avigdor had been unable to forget Hadass and that Anshel had divorced her so that his friend would be able to marry her. But was such friendship possible in this world? And in that case, why had Anshel divorced Hadass even before Avigdor divorced Peshe? Furthermore, such a thing can be accomplished only if the wife has been informed of the arrangement and is willing, yet all signs pointed to Hadass's great love for Anshel, and in fact she was ill from sorrow.

One thing was clear to all: Avigdor knew the truth. But it was impossible to get anything out of him. He remained in seclusion and kept silent with an obstinacy that was a reproof to the whole town.

Close friends urged Peshe not to divorce Avigdor, though they had severed all relations and no longer lived as man and wife. He did not even, on Friday night, perform the kiddush blessing for her. He spent his nights either at the study house or at the widow's where Anshel had found lodgings. When Peshe spoke to him he didn't answer but stood with bowed head. The tradeswoman Peshe had no patience for such goings-on. She needed a young man to help her out in the store, not a yeshiva student who had fallen into melancholy. Someone of that sort might even take it into his head to depart and leave her deserted. Peshe agreed to a divorce.

In the meantime, Hadass had recovered, and Reb Alter Vishkower let it be known that a marriage contract was being drawn up. Hadass was to marry Avigdor. The town was agog. A marriage between a man and a woman who had once been engaged and their betrothal broken off was unheard of. The wedding was held on the first Sabbath after Tishe Bov and included all that is customary at the marriage of a virgin: the banquet for the poor, the canopy before the synagogue, the musicians, the wedding jester, the virtue dance. Only one thing was lacking: joy. The bridegroom stood beneath the marriage canopy, a figure of desolation. The bride had recovered from her sickness but had remained pale and thin. Her tears fell into the golden chicken broth. From all eyes the same question looked out: Why had Anshel done it?

After Avigdor's marriage to Hadass, Peshe spread the rumor that Anshel had sold his wife to Avigdor for a price and that the money had been supplied by Alter Vishkower. One young man pondered the riddle at great length until he finally arrived at the conclusion that Anshel had lost his beloved wife to Avigdor at cards or even on a spin of the Chanukah dreidel. It is a general rule that when the grain of truth cannot be found, men will swallow great helpings of falsehood. Truth itself is often concealed in such a way that the harder you look for it, the harder it is to find.

Not long after the wedding, Hadass became pregnant. The child was a boy, and those assembled at the circumcision could scarcely believe their ears when they heard the father name his son Anshel.

★ ☾ ★

ISAAC BASHEVIS SINGER *was the only Yiddish writer ever to receive the Nobel Prize for Literature. Born the son and grandson of generations of rabbis in the small Polish town of Leoncin in 1904, Singer grew up in Warsaw and became a prominent young writer there before he immigrated to the United States in 1936. In New York, where he lived for the rest of his life, Singer became a regular contributor to New York's leading Yiddish daily, Forverts, and set about making his work widely known through translation into English. By the time of his death, he had published, in English translation, ten novels, ten volumes of short stories, five volumes of memoirs, fourteen books for children, and three anthologies of selected writings. Four more of his novels, originally serialized in Forverts, were published posthumously. For the most part, his work is concerned with memorializing the lost world of Eastern Jewry, with its piety and superstitions. He died in 1991.*

A SATIN COAT

Esther Singer Kreitman

Translated by Ellen Cassedy

The Gliskers had lived in the village since the beginning of time. Yidl Glisker's store, which had been in the family for generations, supplied the peasants of the surrounding countryside with everything they needed. Yidl ran the business single-handedly. Tall and broad shouldered, he could hold his own against all comers, and for this the local people respected him.

He wouldn't allow his wife in the shop, except when he had to go out of town to replenish his stock. A Jewish woman, Yidl believed, should stay at home and look after the children. That way was best for all concerned.

His wife, Rochel, believed just the opposite. But when Yidl said no, he meant no, so she didn't argue. Instead, she started her own dairy as an outlet for her energies.

Yidl didn't stand in her way. As long as she stayed out of his affairs, he didn't care what she did. Indeed, he was glad—the milk business gave his three girls something to do. He helped Rochel select several head of cattle, paid for them, and drank a celebratory glass of whiskey with the farmers to seal the deal.

Rochel managed her business no less successfully than Yidl. Like him, she took care of everything herself. Alone she milked the cows, warmed the pans of sour milk, lugged the heavy stones used for pressing the cheeses. Alone she churned the butter and sewed the cheese bags.

All her daughters did was tend the cows in the field. After feasting on the tallest and most succulent grasses, the cows would make their way home every evening with their udders full to bursting. Then, with the greatest satisfaction, Rochel would seat herself on the three-legged milking stool. As her nimble fingers tugged on the pink-and-brown teats, she would scoot forward on the stool and shift the bucket with every release of the overflowing abundance. The cows would express their thanks by licking her hands with their wet tongues. The warm milk in the buckets and the smell of manure in the stable awakened all of Rochel's powers. At such times she felt she could bend iron with her bare hands.

All summer, the girls lay in the meadow under the heavens. Warmed and browned by the bright sunshine, they shot up like the pines in the neighboring forest.

The dairymen from town who drove up in their rickety horse-drawn carts to buy Rochel's milk, her butter, and her immense cheeses—they saw the way the Gliskers were living, and they were not pleased. Themselves afraid to venture too close to the stable for fear of being caught on the horns of some animal, they couldn't bear to watch the three Glisker girls growing up like peasants, Yidl paying heed only to his business and Rochel looking for all the world like a healthy peasant woman—instead of a daughter of the Jewish people.

Particularly on those occasions when Rochel refused to lower the price of her milk or cheese, the customers would take Yidl aside and attempt to point out his transgressions.

"What will become of the children, Reb Yidl?" they would

say. "How can a Jew permit his daughters to grow up in the field? Are they Gentiles? Jewish children are not meant to tend cattle, Reb Yidl—especially not the children of a fine man like you. If things go on like this, Reb Yidl, you'll never be able to marry them off when the time comes. And how will that be, Reb Yidl? Eh?"

Yidl paid them no attention. He had half a mind to grab these sorry townsmen by their withered throats and shake them until they lost their appetite for meddling in the affairs of others. He knew perfectly well that they didn't mean a word they said; they were simply irked that his wife wouldn't sell to them at half price—even though back in town they didn't think twice about gouging the poor women who came to them for half an ounce of butter or a quart of milk. They couldn't bear the sight of the Gliskers' prosperity: that was why they yammered on.

And Yidl would have continued to pay them no mind—had he not happened upon his oldest daughter, Rosa, lying in the open field like a beast with her arms around a Gentile boy. After that, he no longer laughed off his wife's customers but instead attended with great seriousness to every word out of their mouths, brooding over even the most trivial remarks. And at the end of the summer, when the Days of Awe drew near, instead of heading into the town on the other side of the forest for only a brief visit (like the little pears, the *yengalkes*, that appeared so fleetingly in the shops at this time of year), the Gliskers sold their house in the village, packed their belongings into high, latticed wagons, roped the cattle to plod along behind, and moved to a cottage on the outskirts of town—for good.

Once there, Yidl allowed himself to recall the many stories he had heard about Jewish girls and boys who took up with peasants in the countryside. A friendship began, one thing led to another, and by the time the parents took notice, it was too late. Thinking along these lines made Yidl feel closer to his new neighbors in town, especially the more "respectable" ones. He looked upon these folk more favorably than he had when they'd come to him to buy timber (for he also traded in wood). Even his wife's customers, the dairymen, now appeared in a different light. Here in town, he noticed that some of them sat every evening in the house of prayer and studied—studied what, he didn't know, but the sexton told him that the fellow with the scrawny neck was quite a scholar, and the others, too, were learning a chapter of the Commentaries.

Yidl cast a furtive glance into the volumes of the Talmud lying on the long scratched table that was greasy with tallow. He understood not a word—couldn't even make out the letters. Suddenly he was seized with a fierce desire to know what was contained in the yellowed pages of these tattered books. He would find himself a teacher, he decided, and pay whatever it cost—more—on condition that no one must know. He was tired of being a country bumpkin.

Everyone in town knew that Yidl was a wealthy man. On the very first *Shabbes*, the sexton showed him to one of the most prominent seats, and he was honored by being called up to the pulpit during the reading of the Torah.

Life in town pleased Yidl. Business was good. He had a teacher and was already making progress as a student of the Torah. Why, then, he wondered, should he be the only one in the front rows who was clothed in a worsted-woolen coat? As he swayed in prayer among the silk and satin, he worried that his six-foot frame, his broad shoulders, must surely look out of place clad in wool. It was a simple matter. All he had to do was order a few yards of silk, send them to Fishl the tailor. . . . But for Yidl, who could do almost anything in the world, putting on a silk coat was no small matter.

Every *Shabbes*, after praying, he would stretch his legs by pacing back and forth in the space near his seat and mumble a quiet, wistful tune, half to himself and half to the men in silk and satin: "*Gut Shabbes! Gut Shabbes! Oy, gut Shabbes! Gut Shabbes!*"

One eminent member of the congregation smiled into his eminent beard and muttered something through his nose, offering a rather vulgar commentary on Yidl's striding with his great fists clasped behind his back and his red country-style handkerchief tangled in his iron fingers. . . . At this, Simchele, the Talmud master's son, a pipsqueak of thirteen, took to falling in step behind Yidl's broad shoulders, turning his skinny little body to and fro, lifting his long nose in the air, and droning: "*Gut Shabbes, gut Shabbes! Oy,* good stuffing, good stuffing! *Gut cholent, gut cholent!*"

Once Yidl had taken off his prayer shawl, handed it to the sexton, and gone out, the congregation chortled openly, while scolding the Talmud master's son: "Shame on you, you little rascal! Imagine making fun of such a man—and on *Shabbes*, too!"

Little did they know that it was Simchele who was Yidl's secret teacher. Every *Shabbes* afternoon, the boy earned two gulden for instructing him in the weekly Torah portion. Each week, Simchele would steal through the blue-white shadows to Yidl's house, which stood waiting for him under the vast sky, buried in the snowdrifts at the very edge of town.

There he would find Yidl sitting up in bed, wide-awake and well rested, issuing a fatherly command to his middle daughter, Feyge: "Bring me a glass of water, Fetche. And clearr as crrystal, please—no worms!"

Before Simchele's eyes there appeared first the limpid sparkle of a running brook—then a stagnant mud puddle crawling with worms. But when Feyge returned with a thick, smudged glass of ordinary water, he came down to earth with a thump. He mimicked Yidl under his breath: "Do you hear, Fetche, clearr as crrystal—no worms!"

Still sunk deep in his *Shabbes* repose, Yidl neither heard nor saw. With every sip, he held up the glass between his cracked fingers and examined it closely for worms. Finally he put the glass on the floor, wiped the silver drops from his beard with the edge of a sheet—and suddenly took note of Simchele's arrival.

"Ah, Simchele, *gut Shabbes!*" he cried with delight, and went to awaken his wife. "Rochel, get up—he's here!"

Across the room, on a high bed with carved posts just like Yidl's, Rochel lay crosswise, her legs sticking out and propped on a milking stool. Nearly as big as Yidl and almost as solidly built, she lay fully dressed in a white linen blouse with a red-checkered skirt, a red kerchief tied under her chin, and at her throat a long string of red coral beads. She looked like a country woman who came to town only on Sundays.

At Yidl's cry, Rochel began to stir, and the stool began to slide. With every creak it moved farther away, until finally, when the tips of Rochel's heavy shoes were barely holding on, it wobbled and toppled over with a crash.

At this Rochel awoke, heaved her ample frame into a sitting position, and smiled. "Ah, Reb Simchele!"

"*Gut Shabbes!*" Simchele replied. He pretended not to look but couldn't help observing that her red kerchief had slipped down, disclosing her black hair and the broad white stripe where it was parted—something he had never seen on a married Jewish woman. He was astonished. Almost every *Shabbes* it was the same. She never seemed to notice that her uncovered hair was in plain view.

Simchele was not the only one who was surprised at Rochel's bold behavior. The whole town was bewildered by the Gliskers. They were Jews—and pious ones at that—yet at the same time they were not Jews at all. The man was more robust than a peasant, with daughters as tall and straight as trees—giants, really, with massive shoulders and bosoms and eyes so bright it was actually unpleasant to look upon them. They worked harder than any Jewish children ever seen. The mother was equally strapping, healthy and robust, and her eyes shone like the girls'.

Here in town, Yidl entrusted the store entirely to Rochel. All week she stood in the shop, counting herring. The peasants would patronize no other store. It was "Rochela this!" and "Rochela that!" Who knew why they were so taken with her—unless (God forgive the thought) she was actually one of them. "Rochela this!" and "Rochela that!"—and through it all Rochel paid them no attention whatsoever, except perhaps when a greedy peasant woman damaged the herring while searching for the best pieces or concealed something in her bosom and tried to walk out with it.

When Rochel stepped away from the herring barrels to her green upright scale, she would lift the heavy sacks as if they contained nothing but feathers, rather than the lumpy soda and coarse salt that the peasants bought for their horses and cows. She carried the casks of kerosene, cod liver oil, and cooking oil over the slippery black floor of the store as though they were empty. If, as sometimes happened, a load got stuck on a loose board, she simply gave a tug and pulled it free without effort.

Since the girls worked as hard as their mother, it didn't matter that there was so much to do. With all the customers running to Rochel's, the other shopkeepers sat empty-handed, eating themselves up with jealousy. The floors in their little stores were barren, the herring grew soft, and the brine along with the hoops on the barrels turned red with rust. The salt shrank and hardened in the bags, even the oil seemed to dry up, and the women's envy grew all the more bitter.

Meanwhile, the Gliskers became more prosperous with every passing day. It was not long before the store was so stuffed with merchandise that there was not room for one more item, and the *Shabbes* at Yidl's became all the more festive, the *Shabbes* repose all the more luxurious, the *Shabbes* treats all the more delicious.

And so, on this *Shabbes*, as Simchele waited to begin the lesson, Rochel got down from bed, smoothed the quilt back into place, and went to the front room to wash her hands.

Yidl meanwhile had finished dressing and gone to the front room, too, leaving Dvoyre, the youngest, who was twelve years old but looked twenty, to make his bed, smoothing out the wrinkles just like her mother. Upon his return, he stretched and picked several feathers from his beard, rolled them into crumbs and flicked them away, and smiled at Simchele.

They sat down at the table.

"Eh, Simchele," Yidl asked, as if the boy were a tailor, "how many yards of silk do you figure I'd need for a coat, hmm?"

Simchele looked Yidl over, sizing him up at a glance. About thirty yards, he estimated to himself.

"I'd say maybe fifteen," he said, and blushed a fiery red.

Yidl said nothing. He was sorry he'd asked. He went to the glass cabinet and took down the Pentateuch bound in calfskin with big gold letters engraved on its spine. He located the weekly reading, laid the stiff red ribbon between the pages, and carried the open book to the table, where Simchele was seated at his right side. Dvoyre sat opposite, her elbows planted on the table and her fists dug into her cheeks. Not once did she take her eyes off the teacher.

Simchele pretended he didn't know she was there. He ran his skinny index finger over the text.

"'*Vayeytsey yankev mib'eyr shova,*'" he read—"'And Jacob went out from Beer Sheva'—'*vayeylech chorono*'—'and went toward Haran.'"

This Yidl could understand. What was not to understand? Jacob went out from Beer Sheva, just as he, Yidl, had moved out of the village of Bozshenits, but what he couldn't fathom was the meaning of each individual word, and he was ashamed to ask. When he made a mistake, mixing up one thing with another, Simchele was annoyed. Like a born teacher, he did his heartfelt best, attempting to pound into Yidl's head the meaning of each and every word, but all too often his efforts were in vain.

Yidl was patient. He tried and tried again, and when he finally succeeded, he beamed all over, and Simchele was so pleased that he forgot himself and threw a look at Dvoyre, a flash of teacherly triumph in his eyes.

Dvoyre stared back with her gray Gentile eyes. She couldn't imagine what the two were so excited about. Why all the rejoicing all of a sudden? And why was her grown-up father allowing himself to be instructed by a mere boy?

Meanwhile, without turning around, Simchele could tell that Rochel was passing by with a platter of delectable things to eat. He moved his thin finger more rapidly over the page.

"'*Vayeytsey yankev mib'eyr shova—*'"

"Mmmm!" Yidl rubbed his hands together. "Let's have a bite to eat, shall we?" He replaced the stiff ribbon between the pages and gave the holy book to Rochel, who carried it reverently to the bed. She laid it down on the green quilt as tenderly as if it were a coddled child and began to serve the *Shabbes* treats.

"Eat, Simchele! Don't be bashful! What does it say in the

book?" Yidl became a lost soul once again. "How is it written?" He furrowed his brow fiercely, as if expecting to extract the answer from his forehead.

Simchele helped him out: "'Im ein kemach, ein toyre'— 'Without bread there is no Torah.'"

"But of course!" Yidl slipped Simchele a poppyseed cookie. "Enjoy!" Brimming with pleasure, he began to eat with gusto.

"Eat, Reb Simchele." Rochel placed a piece of golden brown strudel before him. "Here you are." She added a few slices of almond bread to his plate and poured him a glass of tea.

On winter days, immediately after the lesson, Yidl and Simchele would go to the house of prayer together. That is, Yidl went in first, and then came Simchele, far enough behind that the two appeared to have nothing to do with each other. Meanwhile, Rochel barely had time to stumble through the "God of Abraham" prayer for the end of Shabbes before dark. Then a yellow fire flickered in all the compartments of the stove. On one burner bubbled a big iron pot of potato peelings for the cows, on another, almost as large a pot of potatoes for the family. A red borscht filled the room with a tart warmth, and as Rochel set herself to mixing a bowl of bran, the hens came fluttering down from the shelves and out from under the beds, clustering around her like a band of demons, clucking, pecking, gobbling, and snatching the food out of one another's beaks, even though there was more than enough to go around. Sometimes a fight broke out and feathers went flying, but as soon as Rochel showed her temper, the birds settled down and behaved themselves, as if they could tell that their mistress knew best.

By now the cows in their stalls were bellowing, especially Rochel's favorite. She had always raised fine-looking cows, but never such a blessed beauty as this one, which she had brought up from a calf. The animal's hide was brown, with white spots that glistened glamorously in the sun. Truly, she looked like a princess—and such udders! No limp rags these, but as firm and healthy as could be, and milk as rich as cream.

On these Saturday nights, Rochel was nearly out of her mind with work. "Feyge, more wood!" she would call, hoping against hope that her daughter was around somewhere. "The potatoes aren't cooking! Feyge, the cow is starving! Have pity on the dumb thing! Feyge—one what-do-you-call-it is enough!"

Feyge tried not to be at home on Saturday nights. She took off after the midday meal and came back only long after dark. As for Yidl, he would often hitch up his horses as soon as *Shabbes* ended and go off on business. So the minute the sun went down, Rochel had to feed her husband along with the cows and the chickens. Not knowing whom to attend to first, she became more than a little scattered, and when Rochel became scattered she lost the ability to call things—cows, horses, husband, children—by name.

"Yidl, did you give the what-do-you-call-it to the what-do-you-call-it?" she would ask, meaning, "Have you fed the horse?"

"Whatsit, the thingums are what-do-you-call-it" meant "Feyge, the potatoes are getting soggy." (Rochel had another weakness as well—no sooner had she put a pot of potatoes on the range than she became convinced they were overcooking.)

In time, Yidl had been studying Torah with Simchele for so long that the town matchmaker came up with the idea of marrying off his oldest daughter, Rosa, to Simchele's older brother, Menashe, who was sixteen.

As soon as the two became engaged, Rochel gave up ordering her daughter to help with the household chores. The bride-to-be was a delicate creature, Yidl declared, who must not be allowed to do any rough work whatsoever. As the future wife of the Talmud master's son, she was to perform only dainty work—and plenty of it.

So Rosa sat all day long tracing monograms on pillowcases for herself and the groom (naturally, Yidl had agreed to outfit the two of them entirely at his own expense). She embroidered matzo covers for herself and her in-laws, knitted challah cloths, sewed a bag for the groom's prayer shawl, and stitched an intricate linen apron for her future mother-in-law. Rosa worked and Yidl paid, because the groom's father, the Talmud master, was quite an important fellow, a learned scholar, fastidious, with a mighty temper—and an utter pauper.

It was no easy task to convince Rosa that she was a fragile flower, because as it happened she took great pride in her iron constitution. She loved hard work and the *Shabbes* rest that followed, and she loved more than life itself the Saturday nights after *Shabbes* when she was supposed to be at home helping Mother but instead sneaked out to go walking with a Gentile boy. She hated like poison to prick her fingers with the embroidery needle. She hated to loll around the house dressed in fancy clothes like a mannequin. She hated being a lady. And more than anything on earth, she hated her future husband.

Bit by bit, however, she became reconciled to her fate—or so it seemed. One thing was certain: She had become a new person, no longer under her mother's thumb.

So Rochel did the work of ten, especially during the winter. In the summertime the daylight lasted so long that after the end of *Shabbes* there was nothing left of Saturday night. In summer she would wait for Yidl to come home from the evening prayer and end the Sabbath; she would say the "God of Abraham" prayer, followed immediately by the "Hear, O Israel" bedtime prayer—and then it was off to sleep. In summer she didn't need to cook potato peelings or mix bran.

The cows were content to graze all day in the meadow, and she almost never saw the chickens, which spent all day outside laying their eggs. Yidl didn't need to rush off at sundown, and life was good.

Yidl, too, loved the summer *Shabbes* even more than the winter. In summer, he did not go with Simchele to the house of worship after his lesson—it was far too early for afternoon prayers. He was not one to refrain from the enjoyment of *Shabbes*, so he sent Simchele away on some pretext. Behind the back wall of the spacious wooden house, his tall stacks of lumber took up more and more of the yard. There he strolled among the boards, measuring them with his eye.

Counting was forbidden on *Shabbes*, he reminded himself as he cast an appraising look at his holdings and swelled with pride. No evil eye! Soon the tall stacks would completely cover the grass. Already they'd overtaken part of the pasture and forced the cows to graze all the way down by the river—which was all for the best, Yidl figured; the grasses were juicier there.

But why was it forbidden to count? Let's say he were to count just one stack; then he would be able to estimate the rest. Well. He could see he had too much pine—but the alder and the birch—why shouldn't he count them? He felt such a powerful urge to do so that he quickly clasped his hands behind him and went over to pat the cow, so as not to commit a sin.

The cows were begging to be milked, poor things. The grass was so lush here, Yidl thought tenderly, that their udders must be stinging as the Sabbath lingered. He went back to his lumber. There certainly was a lot of it, no evil eye! He walked the narrow passageways between the stacks. How he loved his timber. He adored the scent of it, especially on hot days, when the resin was as soft as honey and smelled as if it had just been cut from the stump.

A man is only human, however. So Yidl shuttled back and forth, here giving the cow a slap on the back, there making a quick calculation with the boards. Who knew—maybe it *was* permitted to count, after all? He would ask the rabbi, who would no doubt be surprised at his ignorance. "Of course one must not count wood on *Shabbes*," he would say. "By no means! Not with the mouth and not with the eye." The rabbi would smile in a friendly way but inside would think Yidl a fool for asking a question a little child would be able to answer, and no doubt he would take him for a rube. . . .

Yidl sighed and turned onto the road leading to the house of prayer. The chickens followed as if he'd invited them along. Annoyed, he swatted them away with his red handkerchief. "Shoo! Shoo!" He looked around to see whether anyone was watching. "Shoo!"

He hated looking like a peasant. Nonetheless, who should appear at his side nearly every *Shabbes* but Boruchel the pinhead—Boruchel, who also loved to spend a summer day strolling through Yidl's timber, sniffing the sweet smell of the resin, and gazing up into the cheerful blue sky.

"*Gut Shabbes*, Reb Yidl!" Boruchel extended his small hairy hand from a paper cuff, his black eyes glittering beneath the damp thicket of hair that extended over his ears into his paper collar. His little beard and bushy black sideburns jiggled when he smiled.

"*Gut Shabbes! Gut Shabbes!*" Yidl grabbed Boruchel's scrawny little hand, swallowed it up in his massive paw, and administered a friendly squeeze that lifted Boruchel into the air.

"Owww! How are things with you, Reb Yidl?" Boruchel tried to free his bones from Yidl's iron grip.

"Not bad, praise be to the Almighty!"

"And when is the wedding, God willing?"

"And what is it to you, if I may ask?"

"Nothing—but a good friend would like to know."

"It's not yet arranged," answered Yidl. "Perhaps later in the summer, God willing, after Tishe Bov." And they made their way across the scuffed and trampled lawn that looked like a balding head with its parched grass, heading for the afternoon prayers. Boruchel cast a glance at Yidl's giant shadow, which stretched almost across the entire length of the field, and then at his puny one, which danced along daintily as he strained to keep up with Yidl's colossal strides. Much to his dismay, his head didn't even reach as high as Yidl's shoulders. Perspiring heavily, he raised himself up on tiptoe and spoke into Yidl's ear, his tiny hands making crazy shadows on the scruffy grass.

Almost every *Shabbes* found the two of them proceeding in this fashion to the afternoon prayers. Each time, Yidl was in agony because he could not work up the courage to ask even Boruchel the question that was tormenting him: whether one was or was not allowed to count lumber on *Shabbes*. Boruchel suffered, too, on account of his pitifully small stature.

This *Shabbes*, Yidl had yet another source of distress to contend with. On the way to the house of worship, he had overheard a group of women chatting with Chana-Rochel on the long bench outside her house. They were gossiping about him and his household.

"Here he is in the flesh," Chana-Rochel had said as she'd pointed him out with a skinny finger. "I ask you, does that man look like a Jew? Would a Jew be so successful? Would a Jew have such good fortune? And the rest of them—are Jewish girls so big and strong? Does a Jewish woman kiss the cow? Hair should grow on my hands if those people are Jews." And here Chana-Rochel displayed her palm, as if in so doing she could prove that the Gliskers were not Jews at all, but peasants who had converted to Judaism.

The sun was still high in the sky when Yidl and Boruchel

entered the house of prayer. The rabbi himself came over to pay his respects. "*Gut Shabbes*, Reb Yidl."

The little house of worship was splashed with light. A sunny column of dust slanted in through the window and extended all the way to the pulpit, where the menorah stood gleaming.

Yidl felt a wave of joy overtake him. His troubles floated away like a cloud melting in the hot sun.

"*Gut Shabbes! Gut Shabbes!*" he roared, delighted that the rabbi had honored him with a greeting and that the golden sun had chosen to rest atop the menorah like a crown. It was Yidl himself who had donated the menorah to the congregation—a solid silver one of considerable size. If the sun had sought out the menorah, well, no wonder: gold was always drawn to silver.

And so Yidl lived in wealth and in honor, succeeding in everything that he did. Even the Torah lessons went smoothly; with each passing week, Simchele was increasingly pleased.

Late in the summer, the special day arrived at last. Yidl's big front room was cleared, and long wooden benches were placed around the walls. From the freshly whitewashed ceiling hung a large twinkling lamp and a dozen little lanterns. The floor was spread with fine sand and the walls trimmed with paper streamers, smooth and curled, twisted and crimped. Green, red, yellow, orange—the swirl of colors was dazzling to the eyes.

Instead of her usual kerchief, Rochel was wearing a lustrous black wig with a white silk bow tied at the bun, as on Rosh Hashanah.

As for Yidl, in honor of his daughter's union with a gentle and silken young man from a fine family, he had finally managed to take the plunge. Having cast off his old worsted-woolen coat, he now made his entrance—in satin. The fabric shimmered on his massive body. His shy, open face was red and shining. Indeed, the coat suited him. It lay across his broad shoulders as if it had been poured on and seemed to rejoice along with its owner.

Rochel was helping the hired woman to fill the platters with cakes and other sweetmeats. Perfectly composed, she called everything by its rightful name: no "what-do-you-call-it" on this day. Feyge and Dvoyre were wearing white ribbons in their hair and yellow batiste frocks trimmed with myriad ruffles and pleats.

On a stuffed armchair sat the bride, dressed all in white, with her feet resting on a small stool.

The guests began to arrive—young women starched and shampooed, bedecked and berouged; pious matrons dressed to the nines. The musicians stood by with their instruments: Gimpel with his fiddle, Hersh-Leyb with his bass, Dovidl with his bow.

The groom was due to arrive any minute in the company of the finest young men: local boys as well as fellow students from his yeshiva, including Simchele, who was, after all, already a bar mitzvah boy.

Yidl was so full of joy that he couldn't sit still. He paced from room to room, pausing before the overladen tables, checking the lamps to assure himself that they were burning properly, taking out his red handkerchief to give another swipe to the place of honor where the groom would soon be sitting, peeking one more time at the bride.

But what was this? The bride was writhing in her seat and moaning softly into her white veil. At first no one took any notice. Her piteous stifled moans were drowned out by the shower of kisses, embraces, and blessings from the women. Young girls conveyed their good wishes, inspecting her wedding gown, her long veil, and her white shoes—without noticing that her face was contorted with agony, first a chalky white, then a sickly green—and now the band struck up a tune, and the cries rang out:

"*Mazel tov!* The groom has arrived! Musicians, a merry tune!"

Women clapped their hands and chanted: "Here comes the groom! Here comes the groom!"

Leaving Rosa moaning on the white armchair, Yidl hurried to welcome the young man as he crossed the threshold.

He was pale and painfully thin, no taller than his brother Simchele, with the same pointy nose. Covered completely in satin, he stood surrounded by the throng of youths, who were also in satin. The music played on.

Twisting and turning on her stuffed seat, Rosa stared through the open door as the groom was led by. Such a tiny scrap of a thing! He looked like a doll—a doll swaddled in satin.

All at once a sense of pity for the poor boy took hold of her—pity mixed with a savage rage. She almost broke out into a strange laughter, but then a fearsome pain in the pit of her stomach overwhelmed every other sensation, and she howled at the top of her lungs. At this the women rushed to her side and a great commotion filled the room. In her anguish, the bride kicked and wept like a child. Chana-Rochel, the town gossip, was sobbing. Rochel kept begging someone to run for the "what-do-you-call-it," forgetting entirely that the town had no doctor. The groom, scared to death, was led from the room. His friends were flabbergasted. What was happening was simply inconceivable.

Someone commanded the musicians to play for all they were worth.

The groom's mother plucked at her gaunt cheeks and pulled at her hair. Giving a sudden tug to her satin bonnet, she stood bald-headed in the middle of the frightened, babbling, helpless crowd.

The only one who did not lose his wits was Yidl. He looked closely at his daughter, and a terrible suspicion entered his mind, so terrible that he would gladly have seen his accursed house tumble to the ground and bury him along with his own flesh and blood and every last one of the hateful guests.

The rabbi advised that the bride be put to bed with hot compresses. If a canopy was set up and the wedding performed on the spot, he said, the Lord would provide and the bride would recover.

At that moment the Talmud master lost his famous temper and began to holler.

Yidl spoke neither to the rabbi nor to the father of the groom. Still in his satin coat, he ran to the stable and harnessed two glossy black horses. Then he bundled his daughter into a white down quilt snatched from the bridal bed, carried her out in his arms, and tucked her into the wagon. Before Rochel had time to understand what was happening and try to jump in herself, he leapt up into his seat, cracked his whip, and set out for the forest.

A deathly stillness fell upon the crowd. All eyes were fixed on the wagon with its bizarre load. Across Yidl's broad shoulders, the satin coat reflected the setting sun as he wielded the whip like a man possessed. Finally a cloud of dust enveloped the wagon and it vanished from view.

The forest stood in the distance, as silent and mysterious as ever.

As the whole town knew full well, the forest was home to a host of evil spirits. In the summer they rode through the tree-tops on broomsticks, and on winter days they took the form of wolves.

Outlandish tales had been told about the forest, but none stranger than what Yidl had to say when, after half an hour, he came riding back home.

The cottage was hushed and evil tongues fell silent when once again the wagon appeared with its cloud of dust.

Rosa was sitting beside her father. The color had returned to her face. She climbed down from the wagon without assistance.

"The wedding is off," Yidl announced to the groom's father without ceremony.

The tumult that followed these four words was such that later no one could remember exactly what happened. But one thing was clear to all. The woods had exerted their demonic power over Yidl. It was the evil spirits that had made him commit such a grievous sin on his own daughter's wedding day. And when demons were mixed up in things, there was no point trying to resist.

Only Yidl knew what had occurred in the forest. Only he could see in his mind's eye the bough of the tree where— driven by the terrible suspicion that had turned out not to be true—he had come perilously close to committing a most dreadful act.

Again and again that evening, Yidl broke out into a wild weeping mixed with laughter. Rochel was convinced that her husband had lost his mind.

That same night, after he had finally driven away the last guest, he barred the door to the front room, tore the satin coat off his back—and became his former self once more.

The family ate their supper from plain earthen bowls, the way they used to back in the village.

And to this day, the satin coat languishes in Yidl's loft, abandoned among other useless things. Every evening, the rays of the sun steal over the discarded garment and cover it with a golden blanket of dust. There it lies, silent and neglected, a relic of a forgotten dream.

✳ ☾ ✳

ESTHER SINGER KREITMAN *was born in Bilgoray, Poland, in
1891. Her brothers, I. J. and I. B. Singer, became internationally
acclaimed writers. Unlike them, she had no formal schooling; I. B.
Singer's story "Yentl the Yeshiva Boy" is thought to have been based on
her unrealized desire for education. Her marriage to an Antwerp dia-
mond cutter ended in 1926, after which she lived in Warsaw and,
finally, London. Her stories and serialized novels were widely published
in the Yiddish press. Der sheydim tants [The Devils' Dance], an autobiographical novel, was published in 1936 and reissued in 1983 as
Deborah. Brilyantn [Diamonds], another novel, appeared in 1944
and Yikhes [Pedigree], a collection of short stories, in 1950. She died in
London in 1954.*

ANDROGYNOUS

Isaac Bashevis Singer

Translated by Joseph Sherman

1

Chasidim sat around swapping Chasidic anec-
dotes. Someone called attention to a rebbe
who taught that a Jew ought to be prepared at
every moment to lay down his life for Kiddush
Hashem. Reb Leyzer Walden, an old Kotsker
Chasid, took hold of his beard, which had once been white but
had later started turning yellow again—no doubt from puffing
away all day at his pipe and taking snuff—and muttered:

"So? . . ."

When Reb Leyzer said, "So?" it was not simply some kind
of mannerism, a grunt, a snort. It was well-known in the Pilever
study house that Reb Leyzer was sparing of words. When he
gestured with a hand, shrugged a shoulder, or merely raised an
eyebrow, youngsters had to guess at his meaning. Usually
people were afraid to ask him. In his old age, Reb Leyzer had
grown persnickety. He didn't think much of modern Chasidism, of the "grandchildren," as he called the small-time

rebbes, of the fawning over the rich, the written notes asking for advice, the payments that had to accompany them. He enjoyed being irritating. On Purim, when the whole congregation was seated at the festive meal and everyone had begun passing along the challah and drinking the festive wine by the light of thick candles, Reb Leyzer Walden was quite capable of settling down to study the civil laws in the second part of the Shulchan Aruch, complete with notes and additions—for no other purpose than to rile the good-time Jews, the overpious and the weak-kneed. It was said that on Tishe Bov he used to smear cheese on his mustache so that the anti-Chasidic rationalists would think he was eating on the fast day. He deliberately dressed in the fashion of bygone times: a hat with a high crown, a caftan to his ankles, knee breeches, slippers, and white stockings. He said his morning prayers at sunset and delayed his afternoon and evening prayers until late at night. People were aware that he knew the Talmud by heart and that Reb Abraham Sokhatshever wrote asking for his opinion on questions of rabbinical law. Well and good; but why should he say, "So?" about a pious Jew who believed in laying down his life? The Chasidim glanced at one another in astonishment.

Among those in the Pilever study house was a young man familiarly known as Shloymele Mischief. The son of a rich man, the son-in-law of a man even richer, and a young genius in the bargain, this Shloymele had a reputation for being an impudent fellow. Perhaps he wanted to show how smart he was, for he asked:

"Reb Leyzer, what do you mean by 'So'? Do you regard self-sacrifice as a matter of no importance?"

Reb Leyzer cast a withering glance at him. Others were shocked. Reb Leyzer Walden was equally capable of slapping someone or even of throwing a cheeky youth over a bench and thrashing him. For a long time he sat staring quietly in front of him, far into the distance, as if he could see things on the other side of the wall. Eventually he said:

"You're an insolent whippersnapper, and you deserve to be taken down a good few pegs, but one is nevertheless obliged to provide a justification for a question regarding faith. Draw up a little closer, small fry—I've no strength to shout."

All drew closer, mouths shut and ears open. Reb Leyzer took out his handkerchief and tobacco tin and laid them on the table. He shook some coarse cut into his pipe and lit up. After a pause, he said:

"Certainly self-sacrifice is a matter of grave importance, but the manner of it is not significant. In 1648, at the time of the Chmielnicki massacres, and at other times, whole communities sacrificed themselves. One dare not say it, but the custom is common even among Gentiles. One general sends a whole camp of soldiers to battle, and they fight to the last drop of blood. Life is not at all as precious to people as we imagine. The greatest strength in the service of God is rejoicing in His commandments. The truly righteous man needs no reward. He is quite willing to forgo, if it were possible, Leviathan and the Wild Ox, the Holy Wine, even the Resurrection from the dead. He who knows the true taste of being a Jew doesn't need to be encouraged with a pinch on the cheek. In Shebreshin at one time there was a heretic, Yekel Rayfman, an atheist, who used to wear a rabbinical fur hat and spend day and night absorbed in Torah study. It was said that on the Sabbath he would read over the portion of the week while smoking a cigar. I can't say—I wasn't standing next to him. His followers among the secularists came and asked him: 'Is this possible? What can you be thinking of?' And he answered: 'What's the reward of eating dumplings? The Torah,' he said, 'is dumplings, and the Targum is chicken soup, and Rashi is compote. Two pins for the World to Come,' he said. 'For me, Jewishness is of this world.' He had a devout wife, and she traveled out to seek advice from Reb Sholem Belzer as to whether or not she should divorce her husband. Reb Sholem patiently heard out all her wifely complaints, and he apparently replied in only two words:

"'Divorce? Pity.'

"So she stayed and bore good children by him. One son, Reb Nathan, as I remember, later became a rabbi.

"But Yekel Rayfman is another matter. I really want to tell you about Reb Mottele Partsever. Who knows about Reb Mottele Partsever today? Even in his younger years he never had much of a following. In his old age he was left with only a handful of Chasidim, including those who lived with him. Reb Mottele used to say that he had prayed on the *mezuzah* that no followers should travel out to visit him. 'Six hundred thousand,' he used to say, 'journeyed out of Egypt, and as a result they made the golden calf and longed for the fleshpots. Why is unity the chief principle of Judaism? Because one is enough. The Gentiles believe in three, and three is nothing.' This Reb Mottele picked an ongoing quarrel with the Master of the Universe. He used to complain to Him: 'Just because You're great and I'm a speck of dust, do I have to keep creeping under Your nails? You didn't make Yourself great, and I didn't make myself a speck of dust. Given the fact that You're unique, what's the great achievement? To an Almighty Being, nothing's a surprise.' He said such radical things that conventional Jews fled to the other ends of the earth. In Partsev they weren't short of anti-Chasidic rationalists, and this crowd raised an outcry that Reb Mottele was blaspheming. They also smashed in his windows. He had only one attendant, Reb Alter, an old drunkard. When Reb Alter took a drink he would curse God and all His works in the foulest language. Partsev combined worship and rebellion. Reb Mottele used to say that 'an apostate out of spite is a righteous man with an appetite.' As long as he knows who his Master is, it does no harm that he's determined to be a rebel. What was Job? What was Korach? Why did Moses break the Tablets? Commonplace Jews don't pray—they only flatter; and it's quite likely that God despises flattery. In Partsev they placed the emphasis on forsaking God and keeping His Commandments. The Torah is for this world, and Paradise doesn't come to this world.

"Reb Mottele didn't believe in sleeping. Even in his youth, he didn't undress at night. His wife passed away a year after their marriage. Reb Mottele didn't need any replacement. Piety and property aren't a pair. His intimates said that for sleep he actually did little more than doze fitfully. Since Jewishness is of this world, why sleep it away? In Partsev, every day was Simchas Torah. They danced in the morning and they danced at night. They danced on Yom Kippur, and it's more than likely that even on Tishe Bov they didn't hesitate to dance a little dance as well. 'Torah is rejoicing, and rejoicing is Torah,' Reb Mottele said. Other rebbes each had their own special devotional melodies, but tunes came down to Partsev straight from the upper sphere of music itself, and everyone's tune sprang from his own inner being, both for prayer and for study. In Partsev no one sent in written requests asking for the rebbe's guidance, and payment for advice given was strongly discouraged. Reb Mottele literally didn't know what a coin looked like. His house started falling to pieces; the roof leaked. When it rained, water poured into the synagogue. The stove in the ritual bathhouse broke down, and it wasn't heated even in winter. In any case, there was nothing to heat it with. Well, who paid attention to such trivialities anyway? Reb Alter, the beadle, was descended from a brewer, and he could distill brandy—from barley, from potatoes, from apples. The rebbe had an orchard that yielded apples as hard as wood from which Reb Alter concocted a liquor, the secret of which no one could discover. Even though no one ever saw Reb Alta opening a holy book, he was an outstanding scholar. An ignoramus had no place in Partsev.

"When Reb Mottele became aware that there was no one with whom to sit down to meals, he locked himself away and stopped communicating with everyone. But in Partsev they believed it wasn't necessary to meet at table together. In any event, the Partsever rebbe never organized communal eating anyway. Even during the High Holy Days, no more than twenty or thirty people ever went there. They ate either in the middle of the night or just before dawn, or they forgot about eating altogether. In Partsev everything was turned inside out and upside down. A young joker who lived there used to say, 'In Partsev we pray so late that it turns out early.' Quips were very popular in Partsev, and they believed that heaven enjoyed these quips as well. They sit in heaven and make jokes. . . ."

2

"When the rebbe's wife died, he was still a young man— barely twenty, as I recall. His intimates busied themselves with matchmaking, but Reb Mottele wouldn't hear of it. Mating, he used to say, is contempt of the Torah. The Litvaks have recluses, but their hermits are steeped in melancholy. They live in terror of Gehenna. In Partsev they scoffed at Gehenna. 'If they want to be whipped in the World to Come,' Reb Mottele would say, 'let them be whipped. It's their backsides, not mine.' Once a Chasid came to him for advice on how to become God-fearing, Reb Mottele answered: 'One doesn't need to fear God. What's there to be scared of? Jewishness is coziness, not terror. Let the angels quiver and quake. They have no option.'

"In the early years, before people knew what Partsev was, Chasidim still came to synagogue to commemorate certain days in one way or another—one's wife was sick, another's child had died, the squire didn't want to extend the lease on someone else's land. These Jews wanted the rebbe to pray for them. But Reb Mottele gave them such contrary responses that they hurried away bitterly disappointed.

"Reb Mottele was now in his sixties. In earlier years, people still spoke of him, Chasidim and Misnagdim alike. Other pietists slandered him. Later they stopped doing even this. The world forgot there was such a place as Partsev, and Partsev forgot there was such a thing as the world. No women were ever admitted into the court. What did a woman have to do in Partsev? The rebbe never ever wished for the sight of any women. Female is flesh, and flesh is slavery.

"Now hear a story. Not far from Partsev is a little village called Laptsev. It's not even a village; it's just a settlement that belonged to a lunatic squire, where a handful of Jews had established themselves. After some time, the squire dropped dead and the settlement was taken over by a relative of his, a libertine who spent all his time in Paris. He left everything in the hands of a lessee, Reb Yossele Tsivkever, who literally ruled as the undisputed king there. He did exactly as he pleased. Twice a year he sent money to Paris, where the sot of a landlord drank it all away. So the years passed. Reb Yossele was an honest man, kept scrupulous accounts, didn't treat the peasants unjustly. He wasn't a Chasid himself, just an ordinary house-holder, but from time to time he sent to the court in Partsev a wagonload of corn, barley, and potatoes from which Reb Alter fermented his liquor. On Passover he provided the court with special flour from which to bake matzos. Reb Mottele truly didn't know there was such a person as Reb Yossele. Of what concern to him were the doings of the world?

"This Reb Yossele had five daughters and an only son, Ley-bele, who was a totally single-minded merchant. He often traveled to fairs in Lublin, in Danzig, in Leipzig. He leased land from other squires. He became so skilled that his father turned over to his son all his own business affairs and occupied himself instead with studying some Talmud and observing the precepts of the law. Great matches were proposed to Leybele, but he was in no hurry to marry. Then one day he returned from a long trip and brought a bride with him. In those days, and what's more in such a tiny place as Laptsev, for a young man to arrive with a bride-to-be and to announce that this was his choice without asking permission of his parents was an unheard-of thing. But when a young man has already made himself very rich, and deals with the most influential businessmen, he's his own master. The bride-to-be was called Shevach—an uncommon name—and she was an orphan, utterly alone in the world. He'd met her somewhere in a big city—Lublin, I think, or even Warsaw. His parents asked, 'Who was the matchmaker?' and Leybele answered, 'There wasn't any matchmaker. We met at an inn and chatted.' You know yourselves how the worldly folk of today conduct themselves. The whole of Laptsev went to stare at the bride-to-be—she was no beauty, but everyone could see that she was clever, sophisticated, spoke nineteen to the dozen, and peppered her speech with Hebrew expressions. Not only were there no in-laws, but the prospective bride also had no dowry. What was the sense in waiting? The betrothal contract was quickly drawn up, and, in celebration, plates were broken in the traditional way. Someone took this Shevach in as a houseguest to prepare her for the wedding. She had no clothes, either—just a dress, a bit of linen, and some trifles. People quickly put together a trousseau for her and fixed the wedding date. Those with whom the bride was boarding related that she read holy booklets. The woman of the house tried to teach her cooking, sewing, and darning and to instruct her in the duties of female purity, but Shevach poked fun at her. According to custom, girls came to inspect and to question her before her marriage, but Shevach answered them at cross-purposes and they went away embarrassed.

"Leybele himself wasn't much of a student, but a teacher was hired to coach him for the Talmudic discourse the groom traditionally delivers after the golden soup has been served. A wedding feast was prepared, the canopy was set up, and everything was as it should be. When it came to the discourse, however, Leybele started forgetting his words and muddled everything up. People glanced at him: the bride, now his wife, nudged his elbow and prompted him in what he had to say. Shevach knew the discourse better than he did. Such a thing had never been heard of, even in the biggest cities, let alone in such a dump as Laptsev. Everyone stared openmouthed. Leybele became so confused that he couldn't remember a thing, so Shevach delivered the whole discourse from beginning to end and even added an original bit of her own. A wedding jester was in attendance, a certain Reb Zelmele whom they had specially brought down from Janov, and in performing his function, he poked fun at the whole affair in minute detail. A great many wedding gifts had been presented; Reb Yossele had given his son a complete set of the Talmud, and the wedding jester, already a bit tipsy, gibed that if the volumes were no use to the bridegroom, they would come in handy for the bride, a remark that was received with an uproar of hilarity and ridicule. I know about it because my late father attended the wedding. He used to buy wheat from Reb Yossele. He was a grain merchant and we had a granary.

"As is the custom, after the Virtue Dance the wedding attendants escorted first the bride and then the bridegroom to the bedroom. The assembled guests danced and made merry. As usually happened, the free and easy types used to station themselves at the window of the room in which the bride and groom were secluded after the ceremony, listen in, and try to peep through the cracks in the shutters. How can one peep in when it's pitch dark? But boors remain boors. The traditional practice was that an hour or two after the nuptial couple had been led in to lie together, women from both the bride's side and the groom's side would burst in on the young pair, drag the sheet out from under them, and—if things had taken their natural course and the bride had been a virgin—dance a Kosher Dance outside with it. I'll make it short: Screaming and shouting could be heard from the bedroom—not the cries that a virgin makes when she's hurt, but quarreling, yelling, swearing, cursing. The door was flung open and the bride dashed out, with the groom chasing after her. 'What's this?' demanded the guests, and the groom bawled out, 'She's not a woman!' 'What is she, then?' they asked—'A man?' And he answered, 'Either a eunuch or an androgyne!' Laptsev had no lack of ruffians. They grabbed Shevach and immediately began to examine her body. Yes, poor Leybele was unfortunately correct. This Shevach was an androgyne, half man, half woman, neither one thing nor the other. Only now did everyone remember that she had a masculine voice. It was summer, and a mob rushed together from all the houses. Even the peasants heard what had happened. That night nobody shut an eye. They asked Shevach: 'How could such a thing be?' And she answered: 'I don't want to be a woman. I'm a man. The whole thing,' said she, 'was a blind buy, and a transaction of that kind can always be put to rights.' They took her to the rabbi, where she was examined again. It soon became apparent that no bread would rise from this dough. Leybele immediately demanded a divorce. It's not the easiest thing in the world to arrange a divorce for a bride who's an androgyne. But the rabbi of Laptsev was learned enough, he had lots of holy books, and he dug up all the relevant laws. The rabbi's wife shut herself up in a room with Shevach and asked her: 'Why did you fool that bachelor?' And Shevach replied: 'I've fooled only myself. I imagined,' said she, 'that perhaps if I married, it would help, but I see now that I'm lost.'

"Everyone imagined that Shevach would demand money, and she certainly could've pulled a packet out of Leybele. But she didn't say a word about money. She sat next to the mistress of the house, waited for the bill of divorcement, and browsed through some holy books. One thing she did demand: men's clothing. As soon as she could, she put on ritual fringes. She even wanted to put on phylacteries. The rabbi called her in and said, 'You can do as you please, but not here in Laptsev.' He reminded her of the passage in Isaiah regarding eunuchs. In those days Reb Hanoch Aleksandrover was already a rebbe, and everybody knew that he was a eunuch. You're all well aware that Reb Hanoch was not only a saint but a great sage as well. The body is a body and the soul is a soul. The couple were divorced, and Leybele, as a gesture of goodwill, gave the unfortunate woman a few hundred zlotys. She put together a bundle and went off on foot to Partsev. From Partsev one could get a covered wagon to Lublin."

Reb Leyzer Walden started knocking the ash out of his pipe and cleaning its stem with a skewer.

He grunted:

"Have patience, youngsters. I must have a smoke first."

3

Reb Leyzer Walden lit his pipe, puffed away, blew smoke straight into the faces of his listeners, and said:

"How far is Laptsev from Partsev? Partsev had already heard about the whole thing. Reb Mottele paid little attention to the goings-on in town. First of all, there was nobody to tell him. Secondly, he didn't care about anything. He was concerned only with settling accounts with the Master of the Universe and with no one else. The few Chasidim who still followed him came only on the High Holy Days. Of those who lived with him, some were deaf, some were blind, and the rest were senile. Reb Alter was always drunk. There could've been a conflagration in Partsev, but as long as the flames didn't reach the court, the rebbe wouldn't have known anything about it. Twice a year, during Passover and after Succos, the river overflowed, but since the water never washed up to the rebbe's study house, he went on with his own affairs. To this day, I don't know who told him about Shevach. But someone did tell him, and for the first time in years the rebbe listened attentively and didn't say, 'What difference does it make?' Instead he replied, 'If she comes here, I want to come to an understanding with her.' She did arrive, and they immediately confronted her with the message. That Reb Mottele should receive a woman was staggeringly incomprehensible. They brought her in, and despite the fact that this might constitute the forbidden situation of a man remaining alone with a single woman, Reb Mottele locked himself up in his study with her. Reb Mottele Partsever had never kept anyone with him for longer than fifteen minutes; Shevach, however, remained closeted with him for three hours. Everyone thought that immediately after that she would travel back to where she'd come from, but Reb Mottele gave instructions that she should be given a room in the court, and he told the beadle, who was also the cook and the housekeeper—he had a lame old woman who helped him—to provide Shevach with everything she needed. Not long afterward, the beadle, Reb Alter, died, and Shevach took over his duties. For a woman to be a rebbe's beadle had never been heard of before, but in what way is an androgyne more a woman than a man? In the same way as the body possesses both genders, so does the soul. There are such things as twin souls.

"I once looked up the whole matter in the holy books, and it would seem that an androgyne can choose for himself what he wants to be, male or female. If he wants to be female, then he is relieved of performing the daily ritual duties demanded of men. If he takes manhood upon himself, then he takes on the obligation of fulfilling all six hundred and thirteen commandments. I can't remember now whether I found this in the codes of Joseph Caro, of Maimonides, or simply in a responsum. It appears that not every androgyne is the same. In some, the male qualities are dominant; in others, the female. The kabbalah makes it clear that both male and female attributes are present in every human being. In Hrubishev there was a woman, Genendele, the wife of Shmuel Eli, who started to grow a beard. It began to sprout while she was still a girl, and because it would've harmed her chances of making a marriage, the rabbi of Hrubishev gave her permission to shave. The Torah's prohibition against shaving does not apply in the case of women. In her old age she stopped shaving, grew a white beard, and didn't cut it. She called the beard 'my jewelry.'"

"I suppose the rebbe married Shevach," called out one of the youths.

"Do you know, or are you just asking?"

"No, I don't know."

"You guessed it, smart aleck."

"What possible sense could it make?"

"There isn't sense in everything. And even if there is sense, you don't have to know it. The nub of the matter was as follows. Shevach began to behave like a man. She put on ritual fringes. It was said that she secretly also put on phylacteries. The beadle had died, and Shevach as good as took over his duties. Those who lived in the court and ate from the communal pot began to come to life again. Reb Alter, with all due respect, would get drunk and forget to prepare meals. The residents suffered greatly as a result, getting by on a slice of bread and an onion. Shevach took over the housekeeping with devotion and energy. She prepared stews and puddings that could be savored all over the court. But then who ever heard of a woman being a rebbe's beadle? Even in Partsev this would have appeared too peculiar. Crude jokers turned up to jeer and mock. Overpious Misnagdim threatened to have them all cut off from the community of Israel and to drive Reb Mottele out of town on an ox wagon. With my very own eyes I myself saw Shevach wearing a caftan and a rabbinical fur hat. She partook of the remnants of the rebbe's food and danced with all the other Chasidim like Hodel, the Bal Shem's daughter. Suddenly we heard that Reb Mottele was going to marry her. Partsev was thrown into total confusion. Half of Poland was agog with the news. How was it possible? For fifty years Reb Mottele had remained a widower, and suddenly he wanted to get married—and to whom? To an androgyne! The rabbi of Laptsev, a Misnaged himself and half an unbeliever, sent to tell Reb Mottele that it was forbidden to marry an androgyne because the sanctification of marriage and the seven blessings would be rendered null and void. Reb Mottele wrote off asking for a responsum from the Sochatshever rebbe. For years and years, Partsev had been stuck away somewhere in the poorest province of Poland. People hardly knew that such a place as Partsev existed in the whole world. Now suddenly the whole world was seething with Partsev. People immediately took sides. Shevach herself laid aside her fur hat and went back to wearing a skirt and bonnet. Now the modern radicals really had something to wag their tongues about. According to them, it was obvious that Reb Mottele had simply surrendered himself to lust. Nonsense! The whole core of that union was spirit, not flesh. The body is nothing more than a garment. When they are naming souls in the upper world and they call out 'so-and-so, the daughter of such-and-such,' no body yet exists, not even in the womb. Not only that—what about the couplings in heaven? The books of the kabbalah are full of couplings—face-to-face, back-to-back—all of them mysteries of mysteries, secrets of secrets. I wasn't there, I was still a youth at the time, but it came to a match. The Sochatshever rebbe gave his permission. The rabbi of Laptsev, half Litvak that he was, refused to perform the marriage ceremony, so they found an assistant. When a widower and a divorcée marry, the wedding is normally a quiet affair, but the layabouts of Partsev made a commotion of it. It was even written up in the newfangled newspapers. There've always been scoffers in every generation, even in the time of our father Abraham.

"I could sit and talk to you about it for hours, but I'll cut it short. You asked about sense. The thought doesn't always precede the act. As in the Bible, 'We will do' comes before 'We will hear': people are often prepared to do what is necessary without discussion or debate. Shevach became a celebrity. In the few years during which she was the rebbe's wife, she was up and stirring all the time. She had the synagogue and the study house rebuilt; she repaired the ritual bath. The old holy volumes used for study had been torn to pieces over the years, and Shevach bought new ones. From the start she'd known how to find her way about in books; later on she became a great scholar. Reb Mottele had never written down his teachings. He didn't believe in publishing. Shevach began to transcribe everything Reb Mottele said, even his everyday conversation. She had an immaculate handwriting. Had it not been for her, nobody would ever have known about Reb Mottele's greatness. His proficiency and insight in holy studies go without saying, but he was also as profoundly conversant with secular learning as any of the ancients. As a young man he'd been a brilliant mathematician. He played chess as well. I've looked into Shevach's tracts. They reveal that Reb Mottele discoursed about medicine and Christianity. He knew philology and philosophy. From where? How did the Gaon of Vilna master all the seven sciences? How did King Solomon come to understand the language of the hoopoe, the legendary bird who carried his messages? How was he able to converse with the queen of Sheba and with Asmodai? One letter in the Torah contains more wisdom and profundity than all secular books put together. During the last three years of his life, Reb Mottele went blind and deaf. Had it not been for Shevach, he would have been forced to cut himself off from the words of the Torah. Shevach studied with him. She had a voice that he could hear.

"Throughout all the years during which the rebbe suffered sickness, he never lost his joy for a moment. He ordered his bed set up in the synagogue, Chasidim danced around it, and Reb Mottele's face shone with a bliss that could only have come from the upper world. The more feeble his body became, the more joyful grew his soul. He danced on swollen feet. His Chasidim drew Shevach into the circle of dance with them. Once again rationalists had something to bark at. In the last weeks, the rebbe lost his power of speech, but he indicated with gestures that he was elated. When the Chasidim grew faint from their ceaseless dancing and wordless singing, the rebbe opened an eye and murmured, 'So? What's wrong? Why are you quiet?' Many times he started humming a tune. Those who heard the rebbe singing on his deathbed said that no ear had ever heard such sounds before. Angels sing that way. Shevach never left Reb Mottele's bedside. The Chasidim sang, and she sang with them. There was never a question of any hidden sinful thought. When the rebbe passed away, she recited kaddish. Then the Chasidim drank brandy and danced around the grave.

"After the rebbe's death, his wife went to Warsaw to have his books printed. She'd collected subscriptions by sending out pamphlets to rabbis and Chasidim. Because Chasidic leaders and scholars would never have engaged in any kind of conversation with a woman, she once again put on men's clothing— not all at once, but little by little. The prohibition against cross-dressing does not apply to an androgyne. She became so famous that a great many wanted to come and establish a following around her, but she didn't ever stay in one place; she continually wandered about. She published seven books of Reb Mottele's teachings, commentaries, and sayings. Even more of them remained in manuscript. When she herself passed away, after the ritual cleansing of the corpse a whole to-do broke out among members of the Burial Society as to whether, like a man, she should be interred in a prayer shawl or not. A prayer shawl and phylacteries had been found among her possessions. She'd worn a ritual undergarment with a double set of eight fringes.

"Reb Mottele's books shared the same fate as Reb Mottele himself: they remained hidden. You very rarely come across one of his monographs. I've got them all on my own bookshelf. There are certain lights that must remain hidden, otherwise human free will would come to an end. There are certain unions that have no need ever to couple. There are certain truths that, the more evident they become, the less we perceive them. The real truth is: The whole world is joy. In heaven, the whole year is one long festival. Of all lies, the greatest falsehood is melancholy. . . ."

✳ ☾ ✳

ISAAC BASHEVIS SINGER *was the only Yiddish writer ever to receive the Nobel Prize for Literature. Born the son and grandson of generations of rabbis in the small Polish town of Leoncin in 1904, Singer grew up in Warsaw and became a prominent young writer there before he immigrated to the United States in 1936. In New*

York, where he lived for the rest of his life, Singer became a regular contributor to New York's leading Yiddish daily, Forverts, and set about making his work widely known through translation into English. By the time of his death, he had published, in English translation, ten novels, ten volumes of short stories, five volumes of memoirs, fourteen books for children, and three anthologies of selected writings. Four more of his novels, originally serialized in Forverts, were published posthumously. For the most part, his work is concerned with memorializing the lost world of Eastern European Jewry, with its piety and superstitions. He died in 1991.

HODEL

Sholom Aleichem

Translated by Frances Butwin

You look, Mr. Sholom Aleichem, as though you were surprised that you hadn't seen me for such a long time. . . . You're thinking that Tevye has aged all at once, his hair has turned gray. . . .

Ah, well, if you only knew the troubles and heartaches he has endured of late! How is it written in our holy books? "Man comes from dust, and to dust he returns. Man is weaker than a fly and stronger than iron." Whatever plague there is, whatever trouble, whatever misfortune—it never misses me. Why does it happen that way? Maybe because I am a simple soul who believes everything that everyone says. Tevye forgets that our wise men have told us a thousand times: "Beware of dogs. . . ."

But I ask you, what can I do if that's my nature? I am, as you know, a trusting person, and I never question God's ways. Whatever He ordains is good. Besides, if you do complain, will it do you any good? That's what I always tell my wife. "Golde," I say, "you're sinning. We have a midrash—"

"What do I care about a midrash?" she says. "We have a

171

daughter to marry off. And after her are two more almost ready. And after these two—three more—may the evil eye spare them!"

"Tut," I say. "What's that? Don't you know, Golde, that our sages have thought of that also? There is a midrash for that, too—"

But she doesn't let me finish. "Daughters to be married off," she says, "are a stiff midrash in themselves."

So try to explain something to a woman!

Where does that leave us? Oh, yes, with a houseful of daughters, bless the Lord. Each one prettier than the next. It may not be proper for me to praise my own children, but I can't help hearing what the whole world calls them, can I? Beauties, every one of them! And especially Hodel, the one that comes after Tzeitl, who, you remember, fell in love with the tailor. And is this Hodel beautiful. . . . How can I describe her to you? Like Esther in the Bible, "of beautiful form and fair to look upon." And as if that weren't bad enough, she has to have brains, too. She can write and she can read—Yiddish and Russian both. And books—she swallows like dumplings. You may be wondering how a daughter of Tevye happens to be reading books, when her father deals in butter and cheese? That's what I'd like to know myself. . . .

But that's the way it is these days. Look at these lads who haven't got a pair of pants to their name, and still they want to study! Ask them, "What are you studying? Why are you studying?" They can't tell you. It's their nature, just as it's a goat's nature to jump into gardens. Especially since they aren't even allowed in the schools. "Keep off the grass!" read all the signs as far as they're concerned. And yet you ought to see how they go after it! And who are they? Workers' children. Tailors' and cobblers', so help me God! They go away to Yehupetz or to Odessa, sleep in garrets, eat what Pharaoh ate during the plagues—frogs and vermin—and for months on end do not see a piece of meat before their eyes. Six of them can make a banquet on a loaf of bread and a herring. Eat, drink, and be merry! That's the life!

Well, so one of that band had to lose himself in our corner of the world. I used to know his father—he was a cigarette maker, and as poor as a man could be. But that is nothing against the young fellow. For if Rabbi Jochanan wasn't too proud to mend boots, what is wrong with having a father who makes cigarettes? There is only one thing I can't understand: Why should a pauper like that be so anxious to study? True, to give the devil his due, the boy has a good head on his shoulders, an excellent head. Pertschik, his name was, but we called him "Feferel"—"Peppercorn." And he looked like a peppercorn, little, dark, dried up, and homely, but full of confidence and with a quick, sharp tongue.

Well, one day I was driving home from Boiberik, where I had got rid of my load of milk and butter and cheese, and as usual I sat lost in thought, dreaming of many things, of this and that, and of the rich people of Yehupetz who had everything their own way while Tevye, the *shlimazl*, and his wretched little horse slaved and hungered all their days. It was summer, the sun was hot, the flies were biting, on all sides the world stretched endlessly. I felt like spreading out my arms and flying!

I lift up my eyes, and there on the road ahead of me I see a young man trudging along with a package under his arm, sweating and panting. "'Rise, O Yokel the son of Flekel,' as we say in the synagogue," I called out to him. "Climb into my wagon and I'll give you a ride. I have plenty of room. How is it written? 'If you see the ass of him that hateth thee lying under its burden, thou shalt forbear to pass it by.' Then how about a human being?"

At this the *shlimazl* laughs and climbs into the wagon.

"Where might the young gentleman be coming from?" I ask.

"From Yehupetz."

"And what might a young gentleman like you be doing in Yehupetz?" I ask.

"A young gentleman like me is getting ready for his examinations."

"And what might a young gentleman like you be studying?"

"I only wish I knew!"

"Then why does a young gentleman like you bother his head for nothing?"

"Don't worry, Reb Tevye. A young gentleman like me knows what he's doing."

"So—if you know who *I* am, tell me who *you* are!"

"Who am I? I'm a man."

"I can see that you're not a horse. I mean, as we Jews say, *whose* are you?"

"Whose should I be but God's?"

"I know that you're God's. It is written: 'All living things are His.' I mean, whom are you descended from? Are you from around here, or from Lithuania?"

"I am *descended*," he says, "from Adam, our father. I *come* from right around here. You know who we are."

"Well then, who is your father? Come, tell me."

"My father," he says, "was called Pertschik."

I spat with disgust. "Did you have to torture me like this all that time? Then you must be Pertschik the cigarette maker's son!"

"Yes, that's who I am. Pertschik the cigarette maker's son."

"And you go to the university?"

"Yes—the university."

"Well," I said, "I'm glad to hear it. Man and fish and fowl—you're all trying to better yourselves! But tell me, my lad, what do you live on, for instance?"

"I live on what I eat."

"That's good," I say. "And what do you eat?"

"I eat anything I can get."

"I understand," I say. "You're not particular. If there is something to eat, you eat. If not, you bite your lip and go to bed hungry. But it's all worthwhile as long as you can attend the university. You're comparing yourself to those rich people of Yehupetz—"

At these words Pertschik bursts out, "Don't you dare compare me to them! They can go to hell as far as I care!"

"You seem to be somewhat prejudiced against the rich," I say. "Did they divide your father's inheritance among themselves?"

"Let me tell you," says he, "it may well be that you and I and all the rest of us have no small share in *their* inheritance."

"Listen to me," I answer. "Let your enemies talk like that. But one thing I can see: You're not a bashful lad. You know what a tongue is for. If you have the time, stop at my house tonight and we'll talk a little more. And if you come early, you can have supper with us, too."

Our young friend didn't have to be asked twice. He arrived at the right moment—when the borscht was on the table and the knishes were baking in the oven. "Just in time!" I said. "Sit down. You can say grace or not, just as you please. I'm not God's watchman; I won't be punished for your sins." And as I talk to him I feel myself drawn to the fellow somehow; I don't know why. Maybe it's because I like a person one can talk to, a person who can understand a quotation and follow an argument about philosophy or this or that or something else. . . . That's the kind of person I am.

And from that evening on our young friend began coming to our house almost every day. He had a few private students, and when he was through giving his lessons he'd come to our house to rest up and visit for a while. What the poor fellow got for his lessons you can imagine for yourself, if I tell you that the very richest people used to pay their tutors three rubles a month; and besides their regular duties they were expected to read telegrams for them, write out addresses, and even run errands at times. Why not? As the passage says, "If you eat bread, you have to earn it." It was lucky for him that most of the time he used to eat with us. For this he used to give my daughters lessons, too. One good turn deserves another. And in this way he became almost a member of the family. The girls saw to it that he had enough to eat, and my wife kept his shirts clean and his socks mended. And it was at this time that we changed his Russian name of Pertschik to Feferel. And it can truthfully be said that we all came to love him as though he were one of us, for by nature he was a likable young man, simple, straightforward, generous. Whatever he had he shared with us.

There was only one thing I didn't like about him, and that was the way he had of suddenly disappearing. Without warning he would get up and go off; we looked around, and there was no Feferel. When he came back I would ask, "Where were you, my fine-feathered friend?" And he wouldn't say a word. I don't know how you are, but as for me, I dislike a person with secrets. I like a person to be willing to tell what he's been up to. But you can say this for him: When he did start talking, you couldn't stop him. He poured out everything. What a tongue he had! "Against the Lord and against His anointed; let us break their bands asunder." And the main thing was to break the bands. . . . He had the wildest notions, the most peculiar ideas. Everything was upside down, topsy-turvy. For instance, according to his way of thinking, a poor man was far more important than a rich one, and if he happened to be a worker, too, then he was really the brightest jewel in the diadem! He who toiled with his hands stood first in his estimation.

"That's good," I say, "but will that get you any money?"

At this he becomes very angry and tries to tell me that money is the root of all evil. Money, he says, is the source of all falsehood, and as long as money amounts to something, nothing will ever be done in this world in the spirit of justice. And he gives me thousands of examples and illustrations that make no sense whatever.

"According to your crazy notions," I tell him, "there is no justice in the fact that my cow gives milk and my horse draws a load." I didn't let him get away with anything. That's the kind of man Tevye is. . . .

But my Feferel can argue, too. And how he can argue! If there is something on his mind, he comes right out with it. One evening we were sitting on my stoop talking things over—discussing philosophic matters—when he suddenly said, "Do you know, Reb Tevye, you have very fine daughters."

"Is that so?" said I. "Thanks for telling me. After all, they have someone to take after."

"The oldest one especially is a very bright girl," said he. "She's all there!"

"I know without your telling me," said I. "The apple never falls very far from the tree."

And I glowed with pride. What father isn't happy when his children are praised? How should I have known that from such an innocent remark would grow such fiery love?

Well, one summer twilight I was driving through Boiberik, going from dacha to dacha with my goods, when someone stopped me. I looked up and saw that it was Ephraim the matchmaker. And Ephraim, like all matchmakers, was concerned with only one thing—arranging marriages. So when he sees me here in Boiberik he stops me and says, "Excuse me, Reb Tevye, I'd like to tell you something."

"Go ahead," I say, stopping my horse, "as long as it's good news."

"You have," says he, "a daughter."

"I have," I answer, "seven daughters."

"I know," says he. "I have seven, too."

"Then together," I tell him, "we have fourteen."

"But joking aside," he says, "here is what I have to tell you. As you know, I am a matchmaker; and I have a young man for you to consider, the very best there is, a regular prince. There's not another like him anywhere."

"Well," I say, "that sounds good enough to me. But what do you consider a prince? If he's a tailor or a shoemaker or a teacher, you can keep him. I'll find my equal or I won't have anything. As the midrash says—"

"Ah, Reb Tevye," says he, "you're beginning with your quotations already! If a person wants to talk to you, he has to study up first. . . . But better listen to the sort of match Ephraim has to offer you. Just listen and be quiet."

And then he begins to rattle off all his client's virtues. And it really sounds like something. . . . First of all, he comes from a very fine family. And that is very important to me, for I am not just a nobody either. In our family you will find all sorts of people, spotted, striped, and speckled, as the Bible says. There are plain, ordinary people, there are workers, and there are property owners. . . . Secondly, he is a learned man who can read small print as well as large; he knows all the Commentaries by heart. And that is certainly not a small thing, either, for an ignorant man I hate even worse than pork itself. To me an unlettered man is worse—a thousand times worse—than a hoodlum. You can go around bareheaded, you can even walk on your head if you like, but if you know what Rashi and the others have said, you are a man after my own heart. . . . And on top of everything, Ephraim tells me, this man of his is rich as can be. He has his own carriage drawn by two horses so

spirited that you can see a vapor rising from them. And that I
don't object to, either. Better a rich man than a poor one! God
Himself must hate a poor man, for if he did not, would He
have made him poor?

"Well," I ask, "what more do you have to say?"

"What more can I say? He wants me to arrange a match
with you. He is dying, he's so eager. Not for you, naturally, but
for your daughter. He wants a pretty girl."

"He is dying?" I say. "Then let him keep dying. . . . And
who is this treasure of yours? What is he? A bachelor? A widower? Is he divorced? What's wrong with him?"

"He is a bachelor," says Ephraim. "Not so young anymore,
but he's never been married."

"And what is his name, may I ask?"

But this he wouldn't tell me. "Bring the girl to Boiberik,"
he says, "and then I'll tell you."

"Bring her?" says I. "That's the way one talks about a horse
or a cow that's being brought to market. Not a girl!"

Well, you know what these matchmakers are. They can
talk a stone wall into moving. So we agreed that early next
week I would bring my daughter to Boiberik. And driving
home, all sorts of wonderful thoughts came to me, and I imagined my Hodel riding in a carriage drawn by spirited horses.
The whole world envied me, not so much for the carriage and
horses as for the good deeds I accomplished through my
wealthy daughter. I helped the needy with money—let this
one have twenty-five rubles, that one fifty, another a hundred.
How do we say it? "Other people have to live, too. . . ." That's
what I think to myself as I ride home in the evening, and I
whip my horse and talk to him in his own language.

"Hurry, my little horse," I say, "move your legs a little faster
and you'll get your oats that much sooner. As the Bible says, 'If
you don't work, you don't eat.' . . ."

Suddenly I see two people coming out of the woods—a man and a woman. Their heads are close together and they are whispering to each other. Who could they be? I wonder. And I look at them through the dazzling rays of the setting sun. I could swear the man was Feferel. But whom was he walking with so late in the day? I put my hand up and shield my eyes and look closely. Who was the damsel? Could it be Hodel? Yes, that's who it was! Hodel! So? So that's how they'd been studying their grammar and reading their books together? Oh, Tevye, what a fool you are. . . .

I stop the horse and call out: "Good evening! And what's the latest news of the war? How do you happen to be out here this time of the day? What are you looking for—the day before yesterday?"

At this the couple stops, not knowing what to do or say. They stand there, awkward and blushing, with their eyes lowered. Then they look up at me, I look at them, and they look at each other. . . .

"Well," I say, "you look as if you hadn't seen me in a long time. I am the same Tevye as ever, I haven't changed by a hair."

I speak to them half-angrily, half-jokingly. Then my daughter, blushing harder than ever, speaks up: "Father, you can congratulate us."

"Congratulate you?" I say. "What's happened? Did you find a treasure buried in the woods? Or were you just saved from some terrible danger?"

"Congratulate us," says Feferel this time. "We're engaged."

"What do you mean—engaged?"

"Don't you know what engaged means?" says Feferel, looking me straight in the eye. "It means that I'm going to marry her and she's going to marry me."

I look him back in the eye and say, "When was the contract signed? And why didn't you invite me to the ceremony? Don't you think I have a slight interest in the matter?" I joke with them, and yet my heart is breaking. But Tevye is not a weakling. He wants to hear everything out. "Getting married," I say, "without matchmakers, without an engagement feast?"

"What do we need matchmakers for?" says Feferel. "We arranged it between ourselves."

"So?" I say. "That's one of God's wonders! But why were you so silent about it?"

"What was there to shout about?" says he. "We wouldn't have told you now, either, but since we have to part soon, we decided to have the wedding first."

This really hurt. How do they say it? It hurt to the quick. Becoming engaged without my knowledge—that was bad enough, but I could stand it. He loves her; she loves him—that I'm glad to hear. But getting married? That was too much for me. . . .

The young man seemed to realize that I wasn't too well pleased with the news. "You see, Reb Tevye," he offered, "this is the reason: I am about to go away."

"When are you going?"

"Very soon."

"And where are you going?"

"That I can't tell you. It's a secret."

What do you think of that? A secret! A young man named Feferel comes into our lives—small, dark, homely, disguises himself as a bridegroom, wants to marry my daughter and then leave her—and he won't even say where he's going! Isn't that enough to drive you crazy?

"All right," I say. "A secret is a secret. Everything you do seems to be a secret. But explain this to me, my friend. You are a man of such—what do you call it?—integrity; you wallow in justice. So tell me, how does it happen that you suddenly marry Tevye's daughter and then leave her? Is that integrity? Is that justice? It's lucky that you didn't decide to rob me or burn my house down!"

"Father," says Hodel, "you don't know how happy we are now that we've told you our secret. It's like a weight off our chests. Come, Father, kiss me."

And they both grab hold of me, she on one side, he on the other, and they begin to kiss and embrace me, and I to kiss them in return. And in their great excitement they begin to kiss each other. It was like going to a play. "Well," I say at last, "maybe you've done enough kissing already? It's time to talk about practical things."

"What, for instance?" they ask.

"For instance," I say, "the dowry, clothes, wedding expenses, this, that, and the other. . . ."

"We don't need a thing," they tell me. "We don't need anything. No this, no that, no other."

"Well then, what do you need?" I ask.

"Only the wedding ceremony," they tell me.

What do you think of that! . . . Well, to make a long story short, nothing I said did any good. They went ahead and had their wedding, if you want to call it a wedding. Naturally it wasn't the sort that I would have liked. A quiet little wedding—no fun at all. And besides, there was a wife I had to do something about. She kept plaguing me: What were they in such a hurry about? Go try to explain their haste to a woman. But don't worry. I invented a story—"great, powerful, and marvelous," as the Bible says—about a rich aunt in Yehupetz, an inheritance, all sorts of foolishness.

And a couple of hours after this wonderful wedding, I hitched up my horse and wagon and the three of us got in— that is, my daughter, my son-in-law, and I—and off we went to the station at Boiberik. Sitting in the wagon, I steal a look at the young couple, and I think to myself: What a great and powerful Lord we have, and how cleverly He rules the world. What strange and fantastic beings He has created. Here you have a new young couple, just hatched; he is going off, the good Lord alone knows where, and is leaving her behind—and do you see either one of them shed a tear, even for appearance' sake? But never mind—Tevye is not a curious old woman. He can wait. He can watch and see. . . .

At the station I see a couple of young fellows, shabbily dressed, down at the heels, coming to see my happy bridegroom off. One of them is dressed like a peasant, with his blouse worn like a smock over his trousers. The two whisper together mysteriously for several minutes. "Look out, Tevye," I say to myself. "You have fallen among a band of horse thieves, pickpockets, housebreakers, or counterfeiters."

Coming home from Boiberik, I can't keep still any longer and tell Hodel what I suspect. She bursts out laughing and tries to assure me that they were very honest young men, honorable men, whose whole life was devoted to the welfare of humanity; their own private welfare meant nothing to them. For instance, the one with his blouse over his trousers was a rich man's son. He had left his parents in Yehupetz and wouldn't take a penny from them.

"Oh," said I, "that's just wonderful. An excellent young man! All he needs, now that he has his blouse over his trousers and wears his hair long, is a harmonica, or a dog to follow him, and then he would really be a beautiful sight!" I thought I was getting even with her for the pain she and this new husband of hers had caused me; but did she care? Not at all! She pretended not to understand what I was saying. I talked to her about Feferel, and she answered me with "the cause of humanity" and "workers" and other such talk.

"What good is your humanity and your workers," I say, "if

it's all a secret? There is a proverb: 'Where there are secrets, there is knavery.' But tell me the truth now. Where did he go, and why?"

"I'll tell you anything," she says, "but not that. Better don't ask. Believe me, you'll find out yourself in good time. You'll hear the news—and maybe very soon—and good news at that."

"Amen," I say. "From your mouth into God's ears! But may our enemies understand as little about it as I do."

"That," says she, "is the whole trouble. You'll never understand."

"Why not?" say I. "Is it so complicated? It seems to me that I can understand even more difficult things."

"These things you can't understand with your brain alone," she says. "You have to feel them, you have to feel them in your heart."

And when she said this to me, you should have seen how her face shone and her eyes burned. Ah, those daughters of mine! They don't do anything halfway. When they become involved in anything, it's with their hearts and minds, their bodies and souls.

Well, a week passed, then two weeks—five—six—seven . . . and we heard nothing. There was no letter, no news of any kind. "Feferel is gone for good," I said, and glanced over at Hodel. There wasn't a trace of color in her face. And at the same time she didn't rest at all; she found something to do every minute of the day, as though trying to forget her troubles. And she never once mentioned his name, as if there never had been a Feferel in the world!

But one day when I came home from work I found Hodel going about with her eyes swollen from weeping. I made a few inquiries and found out that someone had been to see her, a long-haired young man who had taken her aside and talked to

her for some time. Ah! That must have been the young fellow
who had disowned his rich parents and pulled his blouse down
over his trousers. Without further delay I called Hodel out into
the yard and bluntly asked her: "Tell me, daughter, have you
heard from him?"

"Yes."

"Where is he—your predestined one?"

"He is far away."

"What is he doing there?"

"He is serving time."

"Serving time?"

"Yes."

"Why? What did he do?"

She doesn't answer me. She looks me straight in the eyes
and doesn't say a word.

"Tell me, my dear daughter," I say, "according to what I
can understand, he is not serving for a theft. So if he is neither
a thief nor a swindler, why is he serving? For what good deeds?"

She doesn't answer. So I think to myself, If you don't want
to, you don't have to. He is your headache, not mine. But my
heart aches for her. No matter what you say, I'm still her
father. . . .

Well, it was the evening of Hoshanah Rabbah. On a holiday
I'm in the habit of resting, and my horse rests, too. As it is written
in the Bible: "Thou shalt rest from thy labors, and so shall thy wife
and thine ass. . . ." Besides, by that time of the year there is very
little for me to do in Boiberik. As soon as the holidays come and
the shofar sounds, all the summer dachas close down and
Boiberik becomes a desert. At that season I like to sit at home on
my own stoop. To me it is the finest time of the year. Each day is
a gift from heaven. The sun no longer bakes like an oven, but
caresses with a heavenly softness. The woods are still green, the

pines give out a pungent smell. In my yard stands the succah—
the booth I have built for the holiday, covered with branches,
and around me the forest looks like a huge succah designed for
God Himself. Here, I think, God celebrates His Succos, here and
not in town, in the noise and tumult where people run this way
and that, panting for breath as they chase after a small crust of
bread, and all you hear is money, money, money. . . .

As I said, it is the evening of Hoshanah Rabbah. The sky is
a deep blue, and myriad stars twinkle and shine and blink. From
time to time a star falls through the sky, leaving behind it a long
green band of light. This means that someone's luck has
fallen. . . . I hope it isn't my star that is falling, and somehow
Hodel comes to mind. She has changed in the last few days, has
come to life again. Someone, it seems, has brought her a letter
from him, from over there. I wish I knew what he had written,
but I won't ask. If she won't speak, I won't, either. Tevye is not
a curious old woman. Tevye can wait.

And as I sit thinking of Hodel, she comes out of the house
and sits down near me on the stoop. She looks around cautiously
and then whispers, "I have something to tell you, Father. I have
to say good-bye to you, and I think it's for always."

She spoke so softly that I could barely hear her, and she
looked at me in a way that I shall never forget.

"What do you mean, good-bye for always?" I say to her,
and turn my face aside.

"I mean I am going away early tomorrow morning, and we
shall possibly never see each other again."

"Where are you going, if I may be so bold as to ask?"

"I am going to him."

"To him? And where is he?"

"He is still serving, but soon they'll be sending him away."

"And you're going there to say good-bye to him?" I ask,
pretending not to understand.

"No. I am going to follow him," she says. "Over there."

"There? Where is that? What do they call the place?"

"We don't know the exact name of the place, but we know that it's far—terribly, terribly far."

And she speaks, it seems to me, with great joy and pride, as though he had done something for which he deserved a medal. What can I say to her? Most fathers would scold a child for such talk, punish her, even beat her, maybe. But Tevye is not a fool. To my way of thinking, anger doesn't get you anywhere. So I tell her a story.

"I see, my daughter, as the Bible says, 'Therefore shalt thou leave thy father and mother'—for a Feferel you are ready to forsake your parents and go off to a strange land, to some desert across the frozen wastes, where Alexander of Macedon, as I once read in a storybook, once found himself stranded among savages. . . .'"

I speak to her half in fun and half in anger, and all the time my heart weeps. But Tevye is no weakling; I control myself. And Hodel doesn't lose her dignity, either; she answers me word for word, speaking quietly and thoughtfully. And Tevye's daughters can talk.

And though my head is lowered and my eyes are shut, still I seem to see her—her face is pale and lifeless like the moon, but her voice trembles. . . . Shall I fall on her neck and plead with her not to go? I know it won't help. Those daughters of mine—when they fall in love with somebody, it is with their heads and hearts, their bodies and souls.

Well, we sat on the doorstep a long time—maybe all night. Most of the time we were silent, and when we did speak it was in snatches, a word here, a word there. I said to her, "I want to ask you only one thing: Did you ever hear of a girl marrying a man so that she could follow him to the ends of the earth?" And she answered, "With him I'd go anywhere." I pointed out how foolish that was. And she said, "Father, you will never understand." So I told her a little fable—about a hen that hatched some ducklings. As soon as the ducklings could move they took to the water and swam, and the poor hen stood on shore, clucking and clucking.

"What do you say to that, my daughter?"

"What can I say?" she answered. "I am sorry for the poor hen; but just because she stood there clucking, should the ducklings have stopped swimming?"

There is an answer for you. She's not stupid, that daughter of mine.

But time does not stand still. It was beginning to get light already, and from within the house my old woman was muttering. More than once she had called out that it was time to go to bed, but seeing that it didn't help, she stuck her head out of the window and said to me, with her usual benediction, "Tevye, what's keeping you?"

"Be quiet, Golde," I answered. "Remember what the psalm says, 'Why are the nations in an uproar, and why do the peoples mutter in vain?' Have you forgotten that it's Hoshanah Rabbah tonight? Tonight all our fates are decided and the verdict is sealed. We stay up tonight. . . . Listen to me, Golde, you light the samovar and make some tea while I go to get the horse and wagon ready. I am taking Hodel to the station in the morning." And once more I make up a story about how she has to go to Yehupetz, and from there farther on, because of that same old inheritance. It is possible, I say, that she may have to stay there through the winter and maybe the summer, too, and maybe even another winter; and so we ought to give her something to take along—some linen, a dress, a couple of pillows, some pillow slips, and things like that.

And as I give these orders, I tell her not to cry. "It's Hoshanah Rabbah, and on Hoshanah Rabbah one mustn't weep. It's a law." But naturally they don't pay any attention to me, and when the time comes to say good-bye they all start weeping—their mother, the children, and even Hodel herself. And when she came to say good-bye to her older sister, Tzeitl (Tzeitl and her husband spend their holidays with us), they fell on each other's necks and you could hardly tear them apart.

I was the only one who did not break down. I was firm as steel—though inside I was more like a boiling samovar. All the way to Boiberik we were silent, and when we came near the station I asked her for the last time to tell me what it was that Feferel had really done. If they were sending him away, there must have been a reason. At this she became angry and swore by all that was holy that he was innocent. He was a man, she insisted, who cared nothing about himself. Everything he did was for humanity at large, especially for those who toiled with their hands—that is, the workers. That made no sense to me. "So he worries about the world," I told her. "Why doesn't the world worry a little about him? Nevertheless, give him my regards, that Alexander of Macedon of yours, and tell him I rely on his honor—for he is a man of honor, isn't he?—to treat my daughter well. And write to your old father sometimes."

When I finish talking she falls on my neck and begins to weep. "Good-bye, Father," she cries. "Good-bye! God alone knows when we shall see each other again."

Well, that was too much for me. I remembered this Hodel when she was still a baby and I carried her in my arms, I carried her in my arms. . . . Forgive me, Mr. Sholom Aleichem, for acting like an old woman. If you only knew what a daughter she is. If you could only see the letters she writes. Oh, what a daughter. . . .

And now, let's talk about more cheerful things. Tell me, what news is there about the cholera in Odessa?

✦ ☾ ✦

SHOLOM ALEICHEM—*a Hebrew greeting meaning "Peace be unto you"—was the pen name of Sholom Rabinowitz, born in Russia in 1859. One of the great Yiddish writers, he helped to usher in a new age of Yiddish literature and was well loved by the Jews of Eastern Europe and the United States, who considered him the "Jewish Mark Twain." He wrote his first Yiddish short story in 1883 after beginning his career writing in Russian and Hebrew and has written plays, five novels, and around three hundred short stories. In 1888, he became the editor of an annual literary publication, Di yudishe folksbibliotek, in which he published other great Yiddish writers like Mendele and Peretz, including his own work. For the last few years of his life, Aleichem lived in the United States, where he helped to found the Yiddish Art Theater in New York City. He died in New York City in 1916.*

SPRING

David Bergelson

Translated by Joseph Sherman

1

From very early that morning, Polly Ratner had been looking for a book that she urgently needed for her final examinations in the Faculty of Medicine.

Polly was single-mindedly preparing for her finals, with great zest and with all the cloudy passions that can possess the life of a young woman of twenty-eight. To pass these examinations, Polly was now obliged to carry in her head all the lessons she had ever crammed into it during the course of her whole life, and quite apart from those, she also needed to remember that outside the skies were blue and sunny and the day was mild and delightful and that somewhere in the great city opposite the open window, some kind of strange, invisible musical box was tinkling ceaselessly, day and night playing the last heartfelt melody of spring. . . .

Polly's head very early in the morning when she began studying:

Clear, fresh, like a glossy white sheet of paper—everything noted down on it would, it seemed, remain legible forever and ever.

Polly's head at night, after a long day spent studying:

A confused jumble, like the drawers of a distracted housewife before a journey—whole chapters of assorted books laboriously memorized drifted about in a chaotic muddle—and now, as though out of spite, the very chapter most urgently needed would not come readily to mind. And on top of this, that much-needed book had now disappeared—a thick book that dealt with all manner of male and female venereal diseases. Polly could not imagine who could possibly have lugged that book out of her room, and more than anything else she was deeply agitated about the fact that, in searching for the book, she was losing the best few hours of the early morning—the hours between five and seven—when everyone else in the same house was fast asleep, when everything one crammed into one's head remained fixed there permanently, like a firmly anchored nail.

As a result of her great distraction, she had even forgotten the great compassion she felt for her father since her mother had died and he had found increasing difficulty in earning enough . . . great difficulty. She had already gone to see him several times in his darkened bedroom. In the kitchen, she had also tried to rouse the soundly sleeping maid. Now she was acutely preoccupied with her agitated searching. On tiptoe she went into the night-darkened nursery and remained standing uncertainly in the doorway, as though she had already searched in there many times and found nothing. There, in the nursery, the windows were obscured with dark shutters. Somewhere high up in a corner, a fly that Polly had awakened with her entrance buzzed about. The breath of sleeping children blended in the air with the scent of hyacinth blooms withering on the ornamental table. In the largest of the three children's beds, with her reddish black locks tousled, her fourteen-year-old sister, Mura, a high school student, was fast asleep—she slept with traces of a happy, mischievous smile playing round her pretty, stubborn little mouth. Her plump, fresh cheeks were ruddy, as though inflamed by youthful, passionate heat, and on a pale patch near her left cheek, a little lower than her mouth, bloomed a hot, sharp beauty mark—a beauty mark that one way or another also had much to tell about youthful, hot passion. . . .

And so—it seemed that Polly hadn't come all this way here for nothing: she finally found the missing book, right there in the children's room. It had been shoved deep under the fourteen-year-old Mura's bed and was open at the most dangerous place—exactly where photographs were printed of a variety of venereal diseases.

Polly was obliged to stretch out on her stomach on the floor in order to drag the book out from under the bed. All her blood—the blood that was better left at rest when examinations were being prepared—rushed into her face. Afterward she stood in front of Mura's bed with the open book in her hands and regarded more closely than anything else the blooming beauty mark on the pale patch near Mura's mouth. . . . As with all female students who studied medicine, the first thought that flashed into her mind at that moment was frightful and horrible: it occurred to her that her sister—the fourteen-year-old high school student Mura—was infected with an unspeakable venereal disease and was afraid to say so at home. . . . All on her own, Mura had wanted to find out from the medical textbook what its symptoms were. . . .

What was to be done?

It seemed to Polly that she ought to run instantly to her father's bedroom and wake him, that she ought to ensure that very soon the whole household was in an uproar, loud with shouting. . . . But when she returned to her own small room with the textbook she had recovered, she was soon calmed by the pictures on the walls, the surrounding tranquillity of the books, and the board games lying on both little tables. All this made her feel that it was utter madness suddenly to start thinking, completely out of the blue, such black, shocking thoughts . . . madness . . . madness . . . but nevertheless:

This fourteen-year-old imp Mura . . . she was more inquisitive than forty thousand demons—she had to poke her nose in everywhere. . . .

She, the elder sister, was totally irresponsible in leaving such books lying openly about and not locked up to prevent that prying child Mura from stealing glances in them. Now it was all too late. . . . Mura already knew in general terms everything written in that book and had with great curiosity already examined every one of those corrupting pictures it included. . . .

Feh! . . . How ugly. . . .

Polly was mentally obliged to add this "Feh! How ugly" because even for her, at twenty-eight years old, it was healthier that even now, during this period of her examinations, she looked as little as possible at these photographs. . . . Half lying on the sofa, she began leafing through the textbook, in order to cram into her mind the contents of various important chapters, but suddenly, when she was almost completely relaxed, she discovered a thick rectangular note tucked in among its pages, written in the large, unfamiliar letters of a firm, masculine hand. The note read:

"Mura!—Mura, you dear smudgy-faced puppy, it's now been three days since I've seen you. I'm burning up. I've been waiting for you every evening in the park of the sports club (on the right, next to the orchestra, on the first bench). Tomorrow I'll wait there again. If you don't come, I certainly won't drown myself, but I'll get up to a great many other mad antics. I con-jure you to come, and you must obey. Don't forget: I'm exactly twice as old as you are. . . ."

Reading this note, Polly felt her heart beating violently. She turned pale, as though all this had a profound connection to her and to that invisible musical box somewhere that played the heartfelt melody of spring all day. . . . To begin with, she could remember only that the sports club's park was large and overgrown, that a sizable orchestra played there every night, that all around there were many dark, tree-lined alleys, and that in order to get there, one had to be ferried across the river in a little steamboat decorated with myriad small flags and red, green, and blue paper lanterns. Then she reminded herself that on Mura's delicate upper lip sprouted young, barely noticeable feminine little whiskers and that as a result her little mouth really did look a little smudgy, just as it did on Polly herself, just as it did on all girls in the Ratner family. In her heart she felt a pang of yearning toward her own smudgy-faced femininity and toward the heartfelt springtime melody of the invisible musical box. The days of study that lay ahead suddenly seemed long and hard . . . unendurably hard. . . .

In order to rid herself more quickly of this feeling, she once again considered that her father ought to be awakened, that an uproar ought to be raised. . . . Soon, however, she reminded herself that she was a member of the Ratner family—a quiet, intellectual family. In their home, no one among them had ever shouted at anyone else, not even at the maid. Instead of crying or shouting, they always prevailed over one another with quiet and logical, rational arguments. They always spoke to one another in studied, velvet tones and always, on every occasion when a child, for example, upset an inkwell on the white tablecloth, assumed smiling, almost cheerful expressions, as though to say: "Well, well, it's not a disaster, not a disaster, but all the same . . . one needn't do things like that a second time. . . ."

Moreover, since Polly had taken her mother's place for Mura during the last few years, one had to tread carefully and with good sense; one dared not be overhasty. . . . Imagining that fourteen-year-old Mura was infected with an ugly disease was not simply foolishness; it was quite plainly lethal. Mura was a dear, clever child filled with joie de vivre.

Mura was as sharp as a needle—everyone said so.

There was nothing more in all this than that Mura was halfway through high school, and among high school students of her age, there were certainly no girls who were not in love: a high school student who wasn't in love was ashamed to show her face among her friends. . . .

Polly was relieved that these thoughts made her smile, that she felt herself falling into that mood with which everyone in their home responded whenever one of the children upset an inkwell on the white tablecloth. . . . She began studying various chapters from her thick textbook in the same state of mind, as though she already knew for certain that later, when Mura awoke, she would say to her: "Well, well . . . it's not dangerous . . . there's nothing to get upset about, but one ought not to do such things. . . ."

But now, having read the note, Polly found studying very difficult: the important chapters from the thick textbook were like nails with blunted points—however many attempts one made to knock them into a fatigued mind, they refused to remain lodged there. Instead of the memorized medical phrases that still hung on her lips, in her mind other words whirled ceaselessly round:

Mura, you dear smudgy-faced puppy . . .

I'm burning up . . .

I'm exactly twice as old as you are. . . .

Polly thought: A simple calculation: twice as old as Mura means . . . exactly twenty-eight.

The calculation "twenty-eight" could in no way be made to square with a second calculation about an abnormal temperature printed in the textbook. What was more, her mind kept incessantly recalling that in the nursery Mura was sleeping with disheveled hair, with blooming, passionate, youthful heat on her face, and that on the pale patch below her mouth could be found a hot, sharp beauty mark. . . . In other words, Mura was in love with a man of twenty-eight. . . .

A fine tale . . .

That's all anyone in this household is short of. . . .

Polly wanted to drive all extraneous matters from her head and to fix her mind only on one thing:

To study industriously. . . .

But now nothing else occupied her mind but the thought: Who could this be? . . . A seducer, a debaucher, an outcast . . . No respectable man would declare his love for a fourteen-year-old child with such audacious notes and with outrageous statements like "I'm burning up." . . . Libertines did things like that, blackguards. . . . And yet, perhaps he truly was in love with Mura? . . . Perhaps he was indeed a respectable man? . . . Whatever the case, Mura was lost. . . .

Polly paced back and forth in agitation and with chagrin at herself: she had already gone up to the mirror twice and had already twice convinced herself that on account of the small feminine mustache on her upper lip, her mouth looked a little smudgy, just as Mura's did, and only her eyes were different— forlorn eyes . . . of quite another type. . . . Here was something odd: No one had noticed this smudgy-looking face except "him," that twenty-eight-year-old who wrote audacious notes to Mura.

Polly thought: Steps must be taken. . . . The main thing was not to make a fuss. . . . Mura might be shocked and imagine that she was already lost. . . .

In any case, the early morning was already ruined. Nothing could be done until Mura was up. Polly felt tired, so as she waited, she lay back on the sofa and began dozing off.

Now it was already eleven o'clock in the morning. Her father had breakfasted long before and had already left the house; so had the maid. The children who had awakened were playing. Through the open window could be heard the heart-felt springtime melody of the unseen, eternally wakeful musical box. Mura had by now also awakened. Polly snapped awake with the remembrance that some unknown man was burning up because he was twenty-eight years old. . . . At first sight, it seemed as though all this were closely connected to her in some way. She listened: the newly risen Mura was singing with the voice of a girl who would grow up to be a great beauty but without any musical talent, yet even so, her singing made it clear that she was tremendously happy—she was in love. . . . Polly was convinced that a certain man burning up because he was twenty-eight years old had definitely, absolutely, positively, a direct bearing on Mura, and on her singing. . . . Polly popped her head out of the doorway of her little room and called out, in the voice of an elder sister who could also serve as the voice of a mother:

"Children! Send Mura to me!"

2

Freshly washed, with a newly powdered beauty mark, Mura stood in Polly's room. Polly sat at her desk with a studiedly earnest expression on her face, as though earlier, before Mura had come in, she had refined and administered a moral lecture to at least ten such little vixens as Mura. She began didactically, very quietly, avoiding Mura's glances; she tapped a lead pencil against her fingernails.

"Listen here, Mura: I found my medical textbook, which you shouldn't be reading, under your bed . . . that's ugly. That's really quite unacceptable. . . . I've told you many times that among the books here in my room there are some that even I, a young woman of twenty-eight, would never have dared to read if I weren't studying medicine and didn't have to cram them for my final exams. I want to know how on earth this book found its way under your bed. Look me square in the eyes, Mura. . . ."

But Mura suddenly turned as pale as the powdered area around her beauty mark. Instead of looking at her sister, she stared with great, widely opened eyes at the thick, open textbook lying on the desk. She was beside herself.

"You found the book?" she demanded.

Incensed, she reached out to snatch it from the desk. With her own arm outstretched, Polly blocked her way, feeling suddenly intensely irritated as she did so, as though she and her fourteen-year-old sister were acting out a stock scene that had already been performed thousands of times in the theater.

"Wait," she said deliberately, with great coldness, a little haltingly. "I found a note in the book. . . . Someone, some sort of twenty-eight-year-old man, writes to instruct you to meet him this evening in the sports club park. . . ."

For an instant, Mura seemed incredulous.

"What? . . . Have you read the letter? . . . What a despicable thing! . . . Show me the letter at once—show it to me, I say!"

Now, Polly felt, was exactly the time to give the very smile that was always given in this house whenever someone had upset an inkwell on the white tablecloth.

"Mura!" she said. "Aren't you ashamed? In what tone are you speaking to me?"

She recognized that the ironic little smile that played around her mouth and lips was really far more effective than any amount of shouting or threats could have been. Polly was satisfied. In a little while Mura lay back defeated on the sofa, her face on fire, tears flowing unchecked from her eyes. Her breast heaved with great sobs as though over an immeasurably great, irreversible catastrophe. Near her, with folded arms and the expression of one who had succeeded in completing a difficult task very easily, stood Polly. Her voice sounded a little weary, but her mouth still continued to utter rebukes:

"Oh, you mischievous, naughty, disgusting little girl! You permit yourself to do such things, and you never give a thought to their consequences for you. It's all the same to me. Go and drown yourself together with him, with that libertine who dares to write such notes to fourteen-year-old children."

"Yes, yes. . . ." Mura wept bitterly, sobbing with enormous great gasps. "I'm lost . . . lost . . . believe me . . . I haven't done anything ugly, but I'm lost all the same . . . eternally lost, lost forever. . . ."

"Lost!" Polly pretended not to understand. "Why? You say yourself that you've done nothing ugly. . . ."

"No . . . not that, not that," gasped Mura, almost choking herself with sobs. "Don't think such evil things of me. . . ."

And falling on Polly's breast, she suddenly burst into an even greater wail: "I love him! . . ."

"Oh, is that so? . . ."

Polly looked up at the ceiling as though seeking some kind of solution up there—she suddenly felt that the time had come to give Mura the customary second ironic smile.

"If that's the case, dear little Mura . . . if that's the case, let's tell Papa. . . . Perhaps he'll arrange for the two of you to get married. . . . That man is, after all, twice as old as you are: that man is twenty-eight, and you—you're fourteen. . . ."

"Stop it, Polly . . . you've got no heart . . . you're making fun of me."

Polly breathed easily. Everything was going very smoothly, and the main thing—since everything was developing in a highly didactic manner—was that Mura herself had concluded that she'd done something ridiculous and made a laughing-stock of herself. Now nothing remained but the other half of the problem—to go to this twenty-eight-year-old seducer and scoundrel and see whether Polly could persuade him to disappear and desist from sending outrageous letters to fourteen-year-old children, setting up trysts with them in the dark alleys of the sports club park.

"Who is he?"

"An artist," Mura wailed. "A painter. He doesn't come from these parts. . . ."

"Good. What brings him here?"

"He was invited to come because the local museum is exhibiting his paintings. . . . He's been written up in all the newspapers . . . with so much praise . . . so much praise. . . ."

Polly bustled about the room. Her whole plan of operation was now ready. Tonight Mura would stay at home, that went without saying—that was point one. For Polly herself, her whole day's studying was already lost, as it was—that was point two. This evening, instead of Mura, she, the older sister, would take the steamboat across the river to the sports club's park, and there, on the first bench, on the right next to the orchestra, she would give a piece of her mind to that scoundrel, the painter. . . . That would put an end to the matter. Tomorrow Polly would once again spend the whole day studying hard, very hard, and would no longer remember that her mouth appeared somewhat smudgy. . . . And how did Mura respond to all this? She consented to everything, weeping with a strange heart-rending cry torn from deep in her breast, like an adult. . . . That was good . . . Mura wasn't the first and wouldn't be the last. . . . Every fourteen-year-old child had to experience the same thing, had to mourn from the depths of their hearts for the very thing Mura was mourning now. . . .

3

It was around seven o'clock in the evening. In order to avoid meeting anyone she knew on the way, the older sister took the steamboat across the river completely alone. She was wearing a white summer straw hat and last season's narrow-cut suit, a suit one wore as an act of deliberate deprivation whenever one had to go out during examination time. She had the feeling that she was now on her way to a rendezvous that no young woman in the whole world had ever kept before her—a meeting she was obliged to go through with in exactly the same way as she was obliged to go through with exams. In each case, one's mind was elsewhere, and one had no idea whether one derived pleasure from it or not. Below, from the river bank on the city side from which she embarked, the city's evening shadows swam out after her. Shortly before sunset, the spires of the churches glowed on the mountaintops; it seemed as though at nightfall, all around on the river, the invisible musical box was rapidly playing the last heartfelt melody of spring; this melody was already weary, very weary, and it merged with the waves of music pouring from the orchestra opposite, in the sports club's spacious park.

Disembarking slowly from the little boat and stepping onto the green grass of the park, Polly gazed around her distractedly, reminding herself that she hadn't studied all day. She had the vague feeling that she'd been tardy and neglected something. The orchestra had evidently been playing for some time. Soon she looked about her: very few people were strolling in the park, and the first bench on the right next to the orchestra was still unoccupied. Now she regretted having come so early. In order not to make herself conspicuous, she sat at one of the little tables not far from the refreshment counter and ordered something. Sitting like that at the table, she forgot completely about everything. She felt strangely at peace, as though she had come down here as to a health resort where no one knew her. Tired after a whole month of strenuous study, she was suddenly aware of spring all around her, of the fresh greenness of the trees, and of something else, something new. The colorful variety of the blooms in the flower beds, the purity of the whitewashed stones under her feet and of the white tablecloths spread over the surrounding little tables—all this, it seemed to her, she had never seen before in her life. She had the urge to sit like this for a long, long time, to rest without the slightest movement. Now it was even regrettable that on the right, on the first bench next to the orchestra, an unknown young man had appeared—not very tall, sturdy, darkly attractive. His long, pitch-black hair peered out from under his broad-brimmed hat, his overcoat had been hastily thrown over his right shoulder, and he himself was animated by uncommon, unperturbed, comically joyful movements that proclaimed him to be a very good-natured person, affable and generally self-satisfied. . . . From a distance it seemed as though his black eyebrows had grown together over the bridge of his nose and were of one piece. The first unbidden thought about him that sprang to mind was that he was handsome . . . somehow fresher than others. Now she recalled once more that her own mouth appeared a little smudgy. . . . Then, suddenly and very quickly, she reminded herself that this was certainly "he"—that man with whom Mura was in love. She smiled, as they always smiled in her home whenever someone upset an inkwell.

She's got taste, that impish little Mura. . . .

She broke off her smile abruptly. It was inappropriate for the situation in which she, as the older sister, now found herself. . . .

Later she recalled that she'd approached him very uncertainly, as though merely passing by. He was noticeably astonished when he learned that she was Mura's older sister, but afterward, out of pure good nature, he was noticeably pleased. This very pleasure of his confused her and seemed unexpectedly to deprive her of speech.

From her first few words he understood why she'd come. He appeared to be physically very strong, and the fact that he'd grasped everything so swiftly seemed to emanate not from his understanding, but from his physical strength.

"Correct, correct," he said, amazed at himself. "You're quite right."

Afterward he seemed discomfited and lost himself so deeply in thought that casual passersby began staring both at him and at her.

"Come," she said to him then. "Let's walk a little."

"Yes indeed," he replied, seeming to rouse himself. "Come."

But again, nothing emerged from their laborious progress through the tree-lined alleys and their sitting on another bench among them. He needed to be spoken to far more severely, to be berated vigorously, but it disturbed her that, to judge from all his movements, from his whole demeanor, he gave the impression of being oddly well-meaning. By now it even looked as if he'd become involved in this whole messy business with Mura out of inattention. . . . She looked at him severely, but he didn't notice.

Suddenly he started talking a great deal about himself, about the fact that he, the young painter, had not long before locked himself up for eighteen months in a garret where he'd painted his pictures—those pictures that were now on exhibition here in the local museum. Did she understand or not? All his friends, also painters, had sat about talking and talking, had mulled over various directions in painting day and night, but he had thought: Talk . . . talk . . . I'll work in the meantime. Polly barely understood a single word. She was prepared to write all this off as empty daydreaming, but he was speaking volubly and with great passion. "On the contrary," he was asking her, Mura's sister, "does anything positive ever come from talking?" He was a painter who loved people. . . . He painted people, only people. . . . Polly had now plucked up her courage and was ready to begin, but he had already drawn fresh breath and was once again speaking about how much he liked people:

Take the way he was looking full in the face at her, at Mura's sister, and the way he was attracted to her in exactly the same way as he'd first been attracted to Mura, on the very first day he'd seen her in company with other high school girls there in the museum, walking around and viewing those of his paintings on exhibition. He found that Polly's eyes, the eyes of Mura's sister, were exactly the same as Mura's, but a little more care-laden, and whenever he saw care-laden eyes, he was ready to lay down his soul for them . . . to surrender his soul so completely that nothing of it should be left to him. Earlier, when he'd seen Mura for the first time, it had been the same: earlier, it chanced that Mura had come up to him at the exhibition and asked him to explain one of his pictures to her. He'd done this with great pleasure, with joy, in fact, that a complete stranger, one so young and with such eyes as Mura, had been interested in one of those pictures he'd painted during the time he'd confined himself in a garret for eighteen months.

The way it turned out, all Mura's high school friends were soon ready to leave the exhibition, but Mura had lingered on, with her gaze fixed on that one picture. Standing apart, he'd overheard how Mura had answered them: "Leave me alone; you go off on your own. I'll stay here for a while." Afterward they'd started shutting up the exhibition for the day. The way things had turned out, he and Mura had been the very last to leave and had, as though by chance, lingered together in the street. This had happened on the very day the newspapers had written so positively about him, and he'd sold a great many paintings. He'd told Mura how he'd spent eighteen months confined to the garret. In response, Mura had said: "I couldn't have done that," but then she'd thought for a moment and added: "And yet, perhaps I might've been able to do it." He'd been particularly moved by the fact that she'd paused and thought for a moment in the midst of all this; if she hadn't paused in thought for a moment like that, then perhaps nothing might've happened. . . . At that time, he'd been ready to burst into tears over the fact that she'd paused in thought for a moment. . . . And perhaps he'd been ready to burst into tears because Mura had just such a dear little face as she had, and no other face. . . . Perhaps for that very reason he was a painter. . . . He couldn't be absolutely sure, as he looked back on it now, whether or not he'd paid Mura many compliments at that time, but this he did remember: At that time, he was ready to surrender to her everything he'd gained from his eighteen months of confinement in the garret, as well as everything he might gain from all future months during which he might subsequently be confined. And so . . . it had started from then on. . . . He'd fallen deeply in love with Mura and she with him. He'd forgotten how old Mura was and how old he was himself. True, Mura was only fourteen years old, but what did that matter? . . . Who didn't know that such children as Mura always ripen young? They had to fall in love with someone, so what was the tragedy that he—that he had been the first? . . . She, Mura's older sister, demanded that he should leave their city as soon as possible? . . .

Good, he was prepared to do that . . . with pleasure . . . he himself felt that he ought to do this. . . . Yet . . . she, Mura's older sister, kept on looking at him with such sadness in her eyes . . . with such sadness. . . .

All the time he was pouring out this flood of words, he never stopped moving closer and closer to her on the bench where they were sitting. It seemed as though, quite unconsciously, in the very midst of pouring out his heart, he was unaware that every now and then he took hold of one or the other of Polly's hands and began fondling and caressing it. All around, in the surrounding tree-lined alleys, darkness had already fallen. By now the orchestra behind them had several times stopped playing and several times started up again, and he was still talking. Every now and then he paused for breath and then resumed talking wearily, very wearily. It seemed as though he would never stop.

And suddenly, as though unexpectedly to himself as well, he embraced Polly swiftly with his powerful muscular arms and pressed his mouth tightly, so tightly, to her lips. All this happened so oddly quickly that she had no time to think about whether or not she ought to defend herself. In consequence of the unexpected suddenness with which she felt herself in his strong arms, she was obliged to lower her head and shut her eyes; she didn't know whether she wanted the situation in which she found herself to go on longer or to end as quickly as possible. She only found it intensely pleasurable that somewhere far from the bench and from the dark, tree-lined alley in which they found themselves, the orchestra was fading away very quietly and pensively, and it strongly recalled the invisible musical box that ceaselessly poured out the last, heartfelt melody of spring. . . .

4

When the older sister returned home, it was already very late. The entire household was asleep by then, and only her little room was still illuminated. With disheveled hair and a blooming beauty mark on her flushed, tearstained face, Mura was sleeping on the sofa.

The older sister entered the room on tiptoe in order not to awaken her, but Mura started unexpectedly and sat up on the sofa with her great eyes wide open, turning on Polly as though in fear.

"Have you seen him?" she asked rapidly, as though with a beating heart. "Well, what?"

Polly didn't look at her and began taking off her jacket. She answered coldly:

"Nothing. He's going away. . . . Go to sleep, Mura."

Mura didn't move. She sat on the sofa and stared into the lamp with great, widely opened eyes. She sat like that for a long time. Polly had already undressed. Without another word, Polly lay down in her bed.

"When is he leaving? Eh? . . . Polly?"

Polly's temper flared.

"Today . . . tomorrow . . . it's all the same. I've told you: Go to sleep, Mura."

Mura, however, seemed abruptly shocked by these words.

"Polly, dearest," she implored, "d'you know what? Tonight I'll sleep here with you. . . ."

Polly was silent.

"Please let me, dearest?"

"Very well," Polly returned shortly. "But hurry up. Put out the lamp."

Now it was very late. The small sofa was too short for Mura, so she'd made up a bed for herself on the floor. She wasn't asleep. It was quiet.

"D'you know what, Polly? He's very odd . . . somehow so sincere. . . ."

A pause. Polly was silent.

"D'you know what, Polly? Until he did, no one else had even noticed it . . . the fact that my mouth looks smudgy. Yours also, Polly . . . your mouth also looks like that."

"Go to sleep; go to sleep!" Polly answered angrily.

Again a pause.

"D'you know what, Polly? . . . One meets someone like him once only . . . once in a lifetime. . . ."

Polly was suddenly beside herself with rage.

"Won't you shut up, you . . ."

She suddenly fell to abusing Mura with sharp words such as no one in this house had ever before used to anyone else. She shocked herself with such words. Mura wept, at first quietly, then later more and more loudly and heartrendingly. Polly was obliged to get out of bed and apologize to her. She embraced and kissed Mura more forcefully than she had ever before kissed her. Their bare hands entwined with one another. Later Polly returned to her bed, and then she herself also began weeping over something, at first quietly, then more and more loudly and heartrendingly.

Outside, day was already dawning. Mura sat next to Polly on the bed and preached at her in almost the identical words with which, that morning, Polly had preached at Mura.

"Ah, you," she admonished Polly. "Foolish little girl! . . . Ah, you . . ."

★ ☾ ★

DAVID BERGELSON *is one of the best prose stylists in Yiddish fiction. Born into a wealthy Chasidic family in the Ukraine in 1884, he received a traditional Jewish education and was fluent in Yiddish, Hebrew, and Russian by the time he was a teenager. He started writing in early youth in both Russian and Hebrew but soon settled on Yiddish, his mother tongue, the language he used for the rest of his writing career. I. L. Peretz encouraged his first work, and he published his first story, "Arum vokzal" [At the Depot], in Warsaw in*

1909. Much of his best work, published before the Russian Revolution of 1917, dealt with the decay of the traditional Jewish shtetl and the plight of the wealthy Jewish bourgeoisie, who were fully at home neither in the traditional world of Orthodox Jewish observance nor in the Gentile world of czarist Russia. Bergelson, along with a dozen other writers and artists, was arrested during Stalin's anti-Jewish purges in 1948, and he was murdered, together with the cream of Soviet Yiddish literary talent, in August 1952.

BELLA FELL IN LOVE

Celia Dropkin

Translated by Samuel Solomon

1

Gray day. Filthy, packed-down snow on the sidewalks. Soldiers marching by to the music of flutes. The thin sounds cut into the gray-cold air and then into one another like a muted toothache. Words, the same ones Bella had just pored over in a booklet of poetry, now read to the fluted melody of the soldiers stomping by:

> The day was a gray one.
> Gray, like sadness.
> Two hearts have hidden
> In a warm room.

The military music, the filthy white sidewalks, and the gray sky evoked in her a gnawing sadness. Something within her silently revolted: *No, not this!*

211

A pair of soldiers with rifles slung at their shoulders followed the musicians.

It would be nice to be killed, she speculated, to fall down here in the snow, to speckle it with blood.

Bella felt crowded by the huge city—hemmed in, the way she'd felt back in her hometown. Learning no longer excited her; she didn't have the mind for it. She was hoping for a miracle—something had to help her rise above her drab existence.

Once, sitting at her schoolbook, she suddenly put out the lamp's smoking wick and ran toward Genia's house. Everything was simple with her; sadness dissipated. Genia came from a small village and had been sent away with next to nothing to keep her alive. Her father, a village Jew, paid for her courses and figured that was enough. So Bella shared her meals with Genia—it was nice to eat with Genia in the café for students. Genia couldn't afford her own room and had moved in with some other students she knew. She lived with them in one room—it was much cheaper that way.

Bella was on her way to Genia's.

There were three beds in Genia's room.

"I'm now living with the Bichovski sisters; I met them at the theater," said Genia.

"Are they interesting?"

Genia smiled, curling her upper lip. "Alone they're boring, but when they come together with their friend Stisson, they actually get interesting. The older one, Nina, is openly in love with him. The smart one, Sarah, says that she hates him more than death. But I think she loves him just as much as Nina."

This wasn't the first time Bella had heard the name Stisson. "Which one is he in love with?"

Genia laughed knowingly. "Him fall in love? It wouldn't ever occur to him. He's 'introspective,' locked up in himself—

so of course people are interested in him. He has a power over them; they open up their hearts to him. I'm actually afraid of him—he can get you to tell what you most want to keep secret. Sarah says that's why she hates him—she told him something that she never wanted to tell anyone. She calls him 'God's thief.'"

"What does he need strangers' secrets for?"

"He's interested in lives, because"—Genia glanced at her with caution—"because he's a writer, Bella."

Bella's eyes brightened. She had never seen a writer except in pictures. "Have you read him, Genia?"

"He writes in Hebrew. Unfortunately we don't know that language. I only know that he writes novels. The journal that prints his work seems to think he's good."

"Does he come here often?"

"I'll introduce you two. I'm jealous he's the first writer you'll know. You won't be disappointed."

"What do you mean?"

"Look—I already had a relationship with a writer. That writer did not instill any great respect for literature in me. He noticed nothing about you except for the womanly parts."

"And this Stisson, is *he* uninterested in women?"

Genia gave her a knowing look. "Be quiet around him. He'll notice your pretty eyes—and maybe something else."

Bella remained sitting deep in thought, teased by the image of Stisson that Genia had painted for her.

"There's a girl," Genia continued after the silence, "who follows him from town to town, even house to house. Sarah says that she wouldn't bring this girl in front of their more upstanding relations, if you get my drift, but you can't always believe everything she says—because she 'hates' him."

"But you said he doesn't love anyone." The words tore hastily out of Bella's mouth.

"See—you're already in love with him, and you haven't even seen him!"

Bella got angry. "You're a little witch, Genia."

When Bella, tired and frozen through, came home and lay down in bed, dreams came to her, dreams that drew themselves from her early childhood through the present, piling up joy inside of her.

She continued to dream into the morning: a wonderful man was healing her heart, her soul, her body; he was fatherly, charming—like a good husband. What good is a man? His kiss could make her whole. Only a year ago, she had thought that kissing got you pregnant. But his kiss now filled her with joy, even if there was more to come. What else? Genia seemed to know.

Unconscious, her head hot, she let him torture her body. She was a naughty girl, and she had to be punished. She was seldom whipped as a child; only once, in fact, did her father lose his temper; she still couldn't forget the sharp lashes on her thin flesh. She didn't forget the shame, but there was something in it that made her instantly holy, purged her of her wrongdoings and obstinacy.

It happened on a Friday. The candles that her mother lit shone like sun rays before her still-crying eyes. The angels fondled her with their flaming wings, consoling and comforting her. A fiery, holy love for her father, the first man to whip her, now burned in her heart.

She had been six years old when she kissed her father's hand, the one that lashed her. She was now almost seventeen. She would have kissed the hands, the lips, the feet, of the great, fatherly shadow-man if only he would whip her now.

Bella lay motionless in bed for a long time; finally she

stood up. The samovar had long been cold. "He who wakes up early gets God," said her landlady pedantically.

She walked into a small basement café. Then she sat for a while in the park across from Pushkin's statue. And her courses? The exams? What would they say when she returned to her village without passing the state exams? Let them say what they will.

She walked for a long time facing the sun; in the western sky it looked like a golden knight.

In the corridor outside of Genia's apartment it was already dark, and Bella couldn't find the door. Someone entered the hall and struck a match; then she could see the numbers on the door. They both stood before the same door—she was certain that this was Stisson, this tall, slender figure in the black corridor. The door was opened. Sarah Bichovski stood in the doorway.

"Stisson? Good evening!"

He took off his hat. Bella studied his face: light hair; an even lighter mustache falling onto his upper lip; his forehead broad and high—the gold of his hair was shaped like a triangle over his brow and made him look like a sphinx. Two quiet blue eyes were chiseled deep into his face. Was this the face she had dreamed of? No. The face in her dreams breathed with a magnetic force, with burning blackness and the deep blue of its eyes.

"Oh, pardon me"—Sarah suddenly remembered—"I forgot that you haven't met."

Stisson bowed politely. Nina and Genia came in. Bella didn't look at Stisson again, but she felt his blue eyes on her more than once. A spontaneous happiness took hold of her. And, as always, when such happiness came to her, her movements quickened; words—the poetry of her favorite poets—tore themselves tensely from her mouth along with feverish laughter.

The Bichovski sisters seemed to be displeased with her behavior, but Stisson came closer to her. He sat next to her, and his eyes no longer looked indifferent. They flung blue sparks over her. She trembled and laughed hysterically. The patience of the Bichovski sisters was about to give.

"I don't understand what's so funny," said Nina in a weak, frightened voice.

Sarah's protest was more energetic. She straight up asked Bella to stop immediately. Bella didn't understand—stop what? When? She couldn't tear herself away from Stisson's gaze. As if hypnotized, she stared at him and couldn't stop laughing. Stisson met her every word with laughter. He laughed the way one might at a child's unexpected wit, a successful joke, or a silly comedy. His laughter was unforced, quiet, and heartfelt. The sisters seemed flustered by the laughter.

Bella proposed that they all go for a walk. Before anyone had gotten dressed to go, she stopped laughing; she had picked up a small hand mirror from the table and cried out, "I look terrible!"

Her braids, having fallen off her head, lay like tamed snakes on her shoulders. She looked for her bobby pins on the floor. Stisson handed her one, and she met his curious, laughing glance with her embarrassed one.

In the street they separated from the others. Stisson was much taller than Bella, and he looked down at her, kindly bowing his head. His figure was elegant and his stride smooth. Her small feet deliberately lifted and fell with his. Her step also felt smooth and elastic; it was as if they were walking on a carpet. Her mood was still uplifted, but she was quiet and no longer ebullient—the streets had depleted her laughter.

"Where are we going?" Nina approached and tugged at Stisson's sleeve.

"We'll walk Bella home."

Now they all walked together in silence. Bella looked to the night sky. She had never seen such a strange grid of clouds before. Like a person's rattled brain, she thought, and wanted to say it to Stisson, but she only turned her head to him, saying nothing. In the waning light of the evening, his profile was sphinxlike. And still separate from his profile, from his figure, there was somewhere else in him hard as stone. He looked like a dark cloud to Bella; he was near as night. Everywhere was the languor of silence and night.

2

Two days of sadness and stubborn inactivity followed. But happiness came, a strange happiness. Genia hadn't waited for Bella to visit; she came herself to share the news. Stisson had visited them the day before—he had talked about her, Bella.

Spoken about her? Her lethargy vanished. Her blood quickened. "'I marveled at her; I enjoyed myself so much with her,'" said Genia with passion, trying to imitate Stisson.

A joyful color flushed Bella's face. That meant he understood her. All her mischief, her outbursts of untamed happiness or fieriness, for which she had the reputation for being wild and for which she was always patronized—he marveled at it, appreciated all of it. He wasn't a part of the people who can't smile, the ones who had judged her—he was quiet, but joy sparked in his eyes when he looked at her. She recalled how he had suddenly walked over to her that night—

"Tomorrow they're performing *La Traviata*," Genia interrupted her thoughts. "If we want to stand outside the box office now, we might be able to get tickets."

"Who wants to stand a whole day at the box office?" asked Bella like a spoiled child.

"Stisson and the Bichovskis will be there. They already have tickets."

"Very well, Genia; let's go get them."

They arrived at the beginning of the overture. The theater was dark. It didn't take long for the sweet sounds of the overture to completely overtake Bella. The violins sang to her: *You're in love, you're in love! Feel how sweet love is? Do you feel how painful love is? You want love, huh? You want to die, eh?*

Her heart awakened, growing inside her as if there weren't enough space in her small body; it mixed in with the violins, cried, begged for mercy—it loved. It was not the bloodless love of her dreams; it loved with each breath, with each heartbeat. The first scene after the overture didn't disrupt Bella's ardor, although the prima donna was very stout. The curtain fell. It became light.

Genia poked her quietly. "He's sitting there with Sima Albertstein."

Bella started.

"That's the girl," continued Genia, "who follows him from town to town." Bella looked where Genia pointed and spotted Stisson's fair head near a dark woman's. Something within Bella raged against the dark girl. Were these the first bites of jealousy? She was stubborn and wanted to preserve her desire, which had bloomed in the theater. The violins had so betrothed her, she didn't know to whom, to the point where she couldn't see Stisson's head as it gracefully and good-humoredly nodded at her in pleasure.

Stisson and the girl got up. "Come," said Genia, "we'll meet them in the corridor."

In the huge, brightly lit corridor they saw Stisson, the Bichovski sisters, and the girl with whom Stisson had been sitting. The three girls were standing in front of him, forming a living wall. Bella and Genia joined the circle. Stisson introduced them to Sima Albertstein.

Stisson's appearance was elegant and handsome. His golden hair was combed snugly over his striking sphinx brow, hair like threads of gold, the beautiful face of a sphinx, only bathed in a warmer color. A pair of mild blue eyes, the eyes of a dove, God's mild, all-seeing eyes. But a warm mouth, sensual, with finely etched lips as gently colored, it seemed to Bella, as if they were behind a veil. His beautiful mouth had breathed an idea into Bella: He is like everyone.

Stisson saw Bella's thought about him in her eyes. "What are you thinking about, Bella?"

A person had just looked at her with all of his senses. How strange—not his eyes, but his mouth, it seemed to Bella, now looked at her small breasts heaving clearly under her light, thin blouse. Bella felt her young body rising beneath her blouse; she felt how her lips were also formed to be sensual, like his; she felt a sphinx smile on her own lips. He asked her again: "What were you just thinking about, Bella?"

She remained silent. Her smile, her eyes, spoke—she would not answer him in words. He turned away from her, toward Nina.

Nina, with pale hair, pale eyes, and a weak mouth, who was as entirely pale as cotton, was thrilled and tugged tenderly at his sleeve. She noticed a loose thread and told him that the button it held in place would soon fall off. Her speech sounded of melancholy—it was almost philosophical, and Stisson promised with a sad smile that, yes, she was entirely correct. Bella saw that he looked at Nina, who was not young, very affectionately.

The younger one, Sarah, moved away from them with a scornful smile. Sarah was the opposite of Nina. Everything about her was hardened: her voice, eyes, lips, her rigid white figure. She was very pretty, with small features, pretty in a harsh, distant way.

Upon meeting Sima Albertstein, Bella saw that she had thick arms, a disproportioned, awkward figure, and a double chin. Bella instantly converted each of her defects into joy. Stisson's eyes, Stisson's whole body, had consumed her so that she forgot entirely about Sima Albertstein. But as he stood with Nina, she looked at Sima again, and a pair of brown eyes burned a hole in her; a sea of womanliness lay in those eyes—eyes that loved and surrendered themselves—eyes like burning velvet.

At the end of the last act, Bella realized that she had left home without a key. It disrupted her pleasure at seeing and hearing the heroine die.

When the curtain fell and the theater resounded with applause, she told Genia about the key. In spite of Bella's dignified voice, Genia could immediately understand the practical meaning of not having a key. "Then where will you sleep? One of their friends is already sleeping at our place. Wait!" Genia searched with her eyes for Stisson and Sima Albertstein.

"Come . . ." She tugged Bella. "They've already walked out."

Pushing forward through rows of seats still filled by the applauding audience, they caught up with Stisson in the corridor by the exit. He was still with Sima, who had stopped to fix the collar of his coat, fearful that he would, in his excitement, catch cold.

Genia told Sima that Bella didn't have her key with her, that the landlady was a Christian and moreover very strict. Sima quickly invited Bella to stay with her. Stisson looked ahead indifferently, it seemed, not hearing what the girls were saying. Genia said good-bye and walked over to the Bichovskis, who were waiting for her in the street.

Stisson made a few comments about the opera along the way, praising the prima donna. Sima looked at him when he spoke as if he were a god. Her upraised eyes looked at Stisson in the moonlight like a Madonna's.

Bella would have loved to hear Stisson's quiet dove voice, as she called it, speak longer. But he didn't speak for long.

Now, after hearing how the prima donna sounded like a nightingale, Bella thought that in every person's voice there was something birdlike, but Stisson's voice was more than a single bird sound. His voice is like a drowned clock in the deep sea, like sounds through fog, or through the crashing of distant waves.

Bella was satisfied with the last comparison. She sat on the small couch that Sima had prepared for her to sleep on and thought of Stisson: his eyes, the thin nostrils of his longish nose, his mouth, his fine, manly figure—it followed her with a strange bewitching into Sima's room. His shadow reigned in the room. Bella felt it now; he was always with Sima, even when he was away.

Bella shivered and looked around her. The room was very poorly decorated, with dirty, pale walls from which the paper had long ago fallen. She couldn't imagine Stisson's elegant, neatly dressed figure in that room. He himself was a rabbi's son—a writer. Was it true, as Genia told her, that he starved in the streets? Genia said that the money sent to him for his novels was spent on trips, on clothing himself, on friends. She had once seen him all blue, with slightly swollen lips. She imagined that he didn't eat most days, but his appearance didn't show it.

"What are you so pensive for, Bella?" Sima suddenly woke her from her thoughts. "Go to sleep. I still have to work for a few hours."

Bella raised her head and noticed Sima's figure tilted toward a cloud of silken tulle. The cloud was shaped like a magnificent dress; it was colored a pale pink. Bella walked closer to the table on which the dress lay and delightedly contemplated the noble hem, the graceful folds, the fluttering puffs and ruffles. How did that dress get in a room where everything spoke of poverty? Nowhere in Sima's room, or in her style of dress, were there any signs of luxury. The gown in which she had gone to the opera, the beads that she had worn on her throat—they were too modest even for a student.

Sima didn't let Bella wonder for very long. "I do work for a seamstress and need to bring this back to her tomorrow. Living here costs money. No one at home can send me any."

Bella woke up determined to see Stisson. "I overslept," she said loudly. "Sima! Tell me, where does Stisson live?"

Sima looked at her curiously. "Uri lives across from here. I'll show you if you can get dressed quickly."

Bella began to dress. The name Uri, the way that Sima had said it, and the way her long eyelashes fluttered as she did, made Bella feel like a believer who hears a prayer. She heard his first name for the first time—and from the very lips that loved him. How strangely beautiful it sounded—*Uri*.

She didn't think about whether it was acceptable to arrive unannounced in his room. Would he have time for her? Sima led her to his place. His room was already tidied for the day, and the dark hangings on the walls and green table gave it the ambience of a writer's room. His hair combed, ready to start the day, Stisson sat at the table with an open letter in his hands. He greeted the girls quietly.

"A letter from home?" asked Sima.

"Yeah, a letter from my mother," he said with a great softness in his eyes. "She tells me to drink milk and go to bed early."

"It's not a bad idea, Uri," replied Sima with a loving smile. "I should go—see you later." And she went.

Stisson looked now at Bella. His eyes seemed frozen to her. His entire face suddenly looked brutal and frozen, although strangely beautiful, and more than usual he resembled the sphinx.

"Did I disturb you?" she asked straightforwardly. "I wanted to see where you live."

"What for?" Stisson yawned indifferently.

Bella was silent. She tried to force a smile but couldn't.

"See you," she said suddenly, and stretched out her hand to him.

He pressed it weakly in his hand, and Bella left.

Why did she go in the morning? She was so stupid.

She stared bleakly ahead.

Why had he been so cold? In the theater his eyes had looked like burning embers. She decided that he was afraid of romance and for a moment had to try not to laugh out loud. Or is he really as indifferent, as cold, as he seemed? Something pinched her sharply; her pride was wounded. No more. I can't see him anymore.

Bella didn't stop going to Genia's, pretending to ignore the possibility that Stisson would be there with the Bichovskis.

Bella's time at Genia's always felt strained now. She sat on the bed, periodically turning her gaze to the door, against her will. She became slightly depressed from the extended waiting, and her eyes would squint, as if in a strong spotlight, the moment Stisson's short black hat appeared in the clear glass door pane.

He was restrained as always, quiet and courteous, only now he paid her no attention. Bella felt cheerful when he arrived, but her happiness was hidden, her sparkling voice hinting at her feelings.

She once beckoned dramatically to the Gentile boy who

brought in the samovar each evening and whispered sadly with pathos Nekrasov's words:

I'm sorry for the world
And it pains me to tears.

In time Stisson's eyes shot blue sparks at Bella again when she looked at him. She knew that Stisson avoided a too close friendship with her—that way he would never love her; he didn't even want her to love him. But she was bound in the web of her longing. She had already admitted to herself that she went to Genia's only to see Stisson. Genia's company now meant nothing to her if he didn't come.

Genia had taken to saying that Stisson was still interested in Bella, that he studied her and threw stealthily attentive glances her way. "You'll get him soon," Genia assured her; she constantly mentioned him to Bella.

"Have you ever seen him eat?" Genia asked once. "It's hard to imagine him eating; I haven't seen it once! He must eat sometimes; it's just that no one sees him. He's from another planet, I swear."

Genia told Bella about the third Bichovski sister, who was still at home; she was fifteen and had been Stisson's pupil. Of course, she fell madly in love with him. The sisters said that they had once caught little Mina kissing Stisson's jacket devotedly when he left it at their house.

Everyone's in love with him, thought Bella, feeling her love for him flare. She did not go to the Bichovskis' that evening but wandered instead in the streets. She was unbearably lonely and could no longer find excitement in the busy streets, avidly searching the crowds of people lest Stisson be among them. She fought to breathe—no, it wasn't he. The entire evening she was alert, searching for signs of his presence.

She saw everything before her as Stisson. He swam toward her the way that white waves approach the shore. She saw him leaning lightly on her breast—his head; his eyes—though in reality cold and indifferent—would be kind and alert; his lips, under a veil, would wear a trembling smile.

The quiet of the few days when she stopped herself from going to Genia's soon burst. She got out of bed stormily: she had to see him. "My desire is my keeper," she said out loud, as if for someone to hear. She chose to go at night, not in the morning like the first time, when he had been as cruel as the bitter, cold morning.

Filled with a terrible excitement, she knocked on his door.

"Come in!" She heard his dovelike voice. The setting sun poured its last rays through his window, but his face, turned toward the door, was left in total darkness. He asked her to sit. In the corner of the room Bella noticed a tall, slender plant with healthy leaves. "What a nice tree," she said.

He narrowed his nostrils to convey a smile; he often did this instead of smiling with his mouth. This smile suited him, but, Bella thought, it denoted darkness rather than warmth. He lifted himself up and stood at the white wall of the stove that warmed the room.

"Do you want to say something, Bella?" he inquired, his eyes forming a melancholy smile.

Bella walked closer to him. He took her by the shoulders, looked a while at her face, and placed her a little bit farther away. Bella's entire body thrilled with his touch. "I feel a little bit in love with you," she announced boldly.

"It's not needed. . . ." He shook his head. "Don't fall in love, Bella. Come, let's try to be friends, I love friendship," he said genuinely. He looked at the clock. "I have an appointment to tutor a Hebrew student. I need to go there soon."

"If it's a girl, she's probably a victim of love for you."

"Thank God it's a boy." He chuckled.

It was completely dark in the room as they both pulled on their coats. Stisson helped her with hers. "Have you ever seen such pretty hands?" Bella stretched her dainty, elegant hands toward Stisson.

He lit a match and drew it close to her hand. "Nice fingers," he remarked.

"You can tell just by looking?" Bella resented his maneuvering to avoid taking her hand in his.

"I'm nearsighted and it's dark in the room."

"Why don't you wear glasses?"

"I hate glasses."

They went out. Bella was infuriated by her second failure. She wanted to hurt Stisson, to make a fool of him.

"Do you always treat women so harshly?" she asked.

"Am I harsh?" he asked in the same tone he always used.

"You're a rabbi's son," she continued with the audacity of a spoiled child. "Why do you need so many women for friends?"

He didn't answer, and she went on. "Oh, I understand, you need to describe them, these ladies, you must have subjects for your writing. Tell me," she scoffed at him, "do you have enough brick, lime, cement, and whatever else you need to build a story about me, or are you still lacking materials?"

He was silent. She felt very impudent—he must have wanted to leave. At the intersection he walked away. She realized that she had to rid herself of Stisson forever. It was hard for her to imagine.

By morning she had sobered up. She grabbed a paper and pen and wrote Stisson a letter. Like a river in summertime, she happily clapped down words and phrases. Not one word escaped the stain of her love.

3

Genia lost her place with the Bichovski sisters. They chose to rent a nicer room and no longer needed a third roommate. Bella took Genia in; they shared her small bed, staying up every night to talk. They walked together to the Bichovskis'.

Once Stisson came and said that he had received a letter from Mina, the youngest Bichovski sister, and that there was a message for Nina and Sarah. Cautiously, almost religiously, he took out the letter. He read a few words out loud to the sisters and then put the note back in his pocket. Bella felt the ground beneath her spinning violently. She couldn't stand to see Stisson holding another girl's letter in his hands.

Suddenly Bella's eyes met Stisson's. Her entire body was shaken upon spotting the letter in his hands; it was as if she had been struck by lightning. She turned deep red but soon felt better, as if his gaze could heal her wounds.

4

Bella's mother sent a letter: everyone said that Bella ran around idly, doing nothing. She should be very sorry and come back at once. Enclosed was money for her expenses.

Bella knew that her mother was right. What had she accomplished in the city? The man she loved didn't need her. Her heart began to feel full again: the failure with Stisson had helped Bella to see herself as a whole person. The taste of sorrow was distinctly intimate, and she didn't want to part with it. But she had to leave. She decided: I will leave in three days.

When Genia got home from her classes, Bella informed her that she was going away. Genia looked at her with such wide, lonely eyes that Bella felt her throat tighten, preparing to weep.

"Genia!" she cried in despair. "How can I contact Stisson? I have to see him."

Genia looked at Bella attentively and said, "He stopped going to the Bichovskis'."

"I want to see him alone."

"I think he's in his apartment at around eight every night."

"How do you know that?"

"I go there sometimes with Nina and Sarah."

Bella decided to see him that day, but she didn't tell Genia. Something gnawed at her heart; it was like snow melting in the spring. Bella could say nothing to Genia. She felt a need to be holy, untouched by his words and the end of their affair. *The end?* Her heart didn't want to believe it. She couldn't believe in the conclusion of their romance; she was like someone who is deathly ill and at the end of her life—she couldn't believe in death. But she would never see Stisson again; it was a long distance from his town to hers. It was an even longer distance to the big city. She waited impatiently for the evening, washing her face again so that it wouldn't shine with nervous sweat.

The green lampshade sent colored light onto part of the table and on Stisson's face. Bella and Stisson sat down to a glass of tea. She had already told him that she was going away and felt that her visit had been justified.

She had drunk only a quarter of the glass, but she felt drunk, as if she had been drinking wine and not tea. Her face lit up. She was unsettled but would not speak. He was silent, too, but looked at her. Her blood rushed loudly. She heard a tick-tock from somewhere nearby. Was it a clock? No. Just a vein in her throat.

On the side of the chair hung a scarf; she turned her head and noticed it. It was red, so red that it stunned her eyes. She grabbed it and wrapped it around her head, tying the ends together under her chin.

She took Stisson's yet untouched glass of tea and handed it to him. "Baron, would you care for some tea?" she said mock deferentially. And suddenly, with a soft groan, and as if not herself, she fell onto his lap, grabbed him by the throat, and covered his face with quick, short kisses. He did not defend himself but held her waist loosely. Finally he composed himself and tried to free his throat from her hands, but they were locked together. She felt a fearful power filling her delicate, well-groomed hands.

It was not her, but her power: not her body, not her hands. It was the strange, primitive power of a "She" in the face of an obstacle to her passion.

She was not She, but something foreign, an other.

Finally he disentangled himself from her. He held her hands and guided her, like a blind woman, to the seat across from his. Her hair had fallen while he had tried to free himself. She looked at him now from the depths of her eyes, which had grown to immense proportions.

"You are insane," he spoke up; in his voice was a stilled excitement. His eyes were now like two blue wells. She remained silent for a while, as if guilty of a crime.

"But I feel completely pure," she said, trying to defend herself.

"You talk like a high school girl."

"But I'm—"

"Why are your hands so cold?"

She remembered that he had just held her hands. She trembled. "Because my heart is so hot," she answered quietly. He apparently liked her answer and smiled good-naturedly. She said she wanted to sit at the window, to cool her head on the cold glass. He showed her the way and closed the shutters.

"Yes, people can still see us," she said as if in a dream. And as she sat by the inside of the closed window, and he stood close to her, she kissed him again. She felt the prickliness of his unshaven cheek, and her whole body quivered with a new revelation—the realization of the man within him.

"Amazing," she said with wonder and delight.

"This is good for you? I'm glad." He looked at her, his eyes now deep, boiling wells. And she fell into his open arms.

Like a tree beneath a storm, with his entire, broad-boned body, he snaked down over her and began to rock her in his arms. His eyes, above hers, were so open—such fiery blue eyes. She bathed herself in them as if in hot springs. He was the stormy wind, and she felt she would soon break like a thin branch in his arms.

He held her firmly; she was beneath two big wings—she was protected by him.

My protector! she wanted to cry out, but instead she said, "I might break."

With her words he started to regain control of himself. He rocked her more slowly and put her down. His eyes were as stormy as before; now a light color flooded his face. She stood on a stool near him and said, "I'm flying!"

He lifted her into the air and carried her for a moment.

"Oh, Mama, Mama," she screamed out from too much joy. He put her down.

"Why did you call for 'Mama'?"

She didn't know why.

"Why?"

"Because I wanted my mother to know how happy I am."

He laughed. "You know you need to leave, right?"

Instinctively, she sensed that she should be afraid of him, but she said, "I'm not afraid of you."

He stood near her, and she shoved him away impulsively. She saw his face become still, his eyes extinguished, no longer stormy. Quietly, he handed her coat to her. She obeyed him, like a child, and put it on. He put on his coat as well, and they both left the apartment.

He was now pale, transparent. He was silent, as if he were hiding and could not make a noise, could not even breathe. He led her to the streetcar. When they said good-bye, he looked at her with unseeing eyes. Now he was like a huge, stormy wave that, breaking upon the shore, remains only in the form of white, fluffy foam. He was now just white, fluffy foam.

"My invisible one, my lightness, my lover," whispered Bella.

A day passes. Bella can't bear that much joy. The entire world is pale blue. Every place she turns reflects such a paleness, a blueness, that it suffocates her; she can't breathe. Thus Bella bears the burden of delight. She is too small, too delicate, for such joy. She can't handle herself with it. She can't contain it.

She wanted to overflow with tears. At night, when Genia came back from classes, she didn't notice anything extraordinary in Bella. But when they lay down together in the narrow bed, she could feel how Bella's shoulders quivered from crying. Genia got up.

"Why are you crying, Bella?"

Bella could only weep louder.

"What happened?"

Bella tried to calm herself. She felt how weak she was, defenseless in the face of her joy, weak even to the questioning of her friend. Should she indulge Genia's curiosity?

A little devil told her *yes*. Genia should know, too, should revel in her happiness. But what should she say to her?

"Tell me, Bella!" Genia demanded.

Bella felt now an open well of music, but she could utter only these few words: "He held me and kissed me."

✦ ☾ ✦

CELIA DROPKIN *was born Zipporah Levine in Bobruisk, White Russia, in 1888. She began writing in Russian as an adolescent and, while studying in Kiev, received encouragement from the Hebrew novelist U. N. Gnessin. She married socialist Shmaye Dropkin in 1909, and together they fled czarist persecution, relocating to New York. There she began writing in Yiddish, publishing many stories and poems in Yiddish journals and one book-length collection of poems, In heysn vint [In the Hot Wind]. She had six children, five of whom survived, and died in 1956. Dropkin's singular contribution to Yiddish literature was the introduction of a bold literary discourse of sexuality most obvious in her love poems. Her pastoral poetry is marked equally by ecstatic, despairing, and even grotesque elements. Although highly regarded in the field of Yiddish literature, Dropkin is unfamiliar to English-language readers. The loosely autobiographical stories translated here for the first time into English provide fascinating insight into an artist whose candor and intensity still prove startling.*

ROSH HASHANAH

Yente Serdatzky
(As Told by a Homespun Intellectual)

Translated by Ellen Cassedy

Two years ago I was at home during the High Holidays.
(Immediately afterward, I was planning to move to the
city, where I spent the holidays last year—but more
about that later.)

I was already a freethinker by then, my young mind full of
new ideals and aspirations. Yet for the entire month before
the holidays, I felt restless. Why, I'm not sure. Perhaps our
shtetl was having an effect on me. In these small towns, the
atmosphere before a holiday becomes drenched in holiness.
Away from the smoke-blackened sky and the deafening noise of the
big city, you find yourself getting caught up in the spirit of
the special occasion.

A week before Rosh Hashanah, when we began saying the
sliches, my mother, a pale and dreamy woman, became unusu-
ally serious. My father, by nature a person with a temper,
turned mild and generous. In the shop, he even promised
twenty pounds of flour to Rochel Leah, the seamstress, who
owed him a long-standing debt.

But most marvelous of all was my grandfather. Oh, Grandfather—my "silver" grandfather—how can I hold back the tears as I think of you? My grandfather's beard is so long and white, his face so pure and pale, that no other name will do but "silver." Oh, how I love him!

With the approach of the holiday, a hallowed tranquillity stole over our household. Grandfather seldom spoke. As he gazed dreamily into the distance from under bushy silver brows, his face shone with a pious solemnity. In those days, I am sure, he was living not in this world, but in that beautiful, fantastic other world, where God is enveloped in the light of the Divine Presence and angels sing songs of praise.

I felt somewhat ashamed in front of them all, especially my grandfather, because by that point I no longer believed in the other world. So I would leave the house to visit a friend or just stand in the street looking into the blue distance. As the holiday drew closer, I became more and more unsettled.

Before a holiday I always used to help my mother with the housework, but this year I couldn't. My mother—my pale, dreamy mother—said nothing. Perhaps her maternal heart could sense what was happening in her daughter's soul.

On the evening before the holiday, the house felt both sorrowful and festive. Mother had put no raisins in the challah, no saffron in the fish. It is forbidden to decorate on Rosh Hashanah, so the house was decked out in white: white curtains, white tablecloths, white pillowcases and sheets, but no colorful flowers or ribbons; these Mother was saving for Succos.

We ate in silence, our faces festive but grave. I had selected a book to read during the meal, but I didn't even bring it to the table. I didn't want to insult the prayer books that my dear family members were taking with them to the synagogue.

After dinner my father sat sighing quietly. Mother was weeping. My grandfather drew close to me. When his delicate, trembling hands touched my hair, I shivered as if a holy current were flowing through me. And when he began to recite the blessing over me in his tender, mournful voice, I couldn't restrain my tears.

I didn't sleep well that night, and the next morning I woke early. Standing by the open window, I looked out into the street. The peaceful blue sky covered the shtetl, and the sun, just emerging from the rosy dawn, gazed calmly over the holiday street, which was already crowded with people. The whole town was on the way to the synagogue, yet everyone was as quiet as if led by a host of silent angels.

There went Bendet, one of the town fathers, a tall, handsome man in his middle years. A light breeze toyed with his long blond beard, sunbeams played around his slim frame, and long shadows grew from his feet. How fine he looked! And here came Leah Esther, the oldest woman in town, wearing a white dress and a white bonnet with sky blue ribbons that fluttered in the breeze like a flag of honor. Walking straight and tall in spite of her age, she looked proud: at her age she had sung more praises to the Almighty than anyone else. A constellation of white dresses sparkled before my eyes, blue ribbons fluttered in the air, colorful kerchiefs shimmered in the sun, and the faces were so pensive, so holy. . . . Looking at it all, I felt my heart grow tender and sad and at the same time wonderfully light.

That was two years ago.

Last year, in the big, noisy city of V., I didn't even know the holidays were approaching. I was giving lessons to four pupils, studying for exams, and working in our political circle. We wouldn't have known it was Rosh Hashanah if not for the fact that most of our employers were Jews; workers and tutors alike had the two days off.

We scheduled meetings for both days: every free moment

had to be used for agitation. On the first day of the New Year, we went to a remote corner of the city and crammed ourselves into one tiny room. The air was thick with tobacco smoke, yet we emerged with shining faces. We were living in the future.

The next day we were arrested. For three months we sat in prison. After that, some of us were exiled to the cold villages of Siberia. Others they set free, including me, on the condition that we leave Russia for good. We had comrades who had fled to America, so we crossed the ocean and came here.

I asked my landlady not to wake me, because I wasn't going to work. A pious woman with no children of her own, she threw me a grateful look. "At least she still has a Jewish heart," I read in her face.

I'd made up my mind to sleep late, yet as soon as the sun peeked in my window I was awake, full of jitters. Today is the first day of Rosh Hashanah, was my first thought. I'd felt unsettled for days, ever since I heard my landlady chopping noodles for the holiday. It's funny what can set a person off—for me that sound brought back my old home with a rush.

After a while, my landlady and her husband left for services. In the silence, I felt more uneasy than ever. I turned to the wall, pulled the blanket over my head, and tried to go back to sleep, but it was hopeless. My memories—of last year and especially of the year before—wouldn't leave me alone.

"Grandfather, dear Grandfather!" The words came bursting forth. "How confusing and strange and lonely life can be!" My melancholy thoughts bored into my head and a gnawing pain filled my heart.

My friends from home, Helenka and Manya, had planned to work today. (These two are all I have—the rest are scattered to the four winds.) "Who cares about the holiday?" they said. "It's a waste of time."

"For me," Helenka added with a sarcastic smile, "the holidays were over a long time ago."

I adore Helenka: she's clever, lively, and sensitive. Manya, on the other hand, I find quite irritating. She has a strong character, but everything she does comes out vulgar and graceless.

For them, staying home for the day would indeed have been a waste. They're barely supporting themselves as it is. I'm no better off—yet on this day I just couldn't bring myself to go to work.

Nor could I go back to sleep. Feeling gloomier than ever, I turned toward the window. A few rays of sunshine crept in through the crack in the green curtains and lingered on the green-plastered walls. The green and the sunshine awakened something inside me, and my heart began to throb. Exactly what I was reminded of, I don't know—maybe the green, sun-dappled meadow where I loved to spend long hours tending our goat when I was small. . . .

On the wall over the little table I'd put up pictures of my acquaintances from V. A sunbeam glided over the photos, and my heart beat faster. My dear, beloved comrades—together we had struggled and hoped. When would we see one another again?

Never, never! a voice in my heart responded. *Volodya is in Siberia, Solomon and Sonya are in prison. Who knows if the rest of them are still alive?*

The room felt too confining, so I dressed and went out. It was early; people were still on their way to the synagogue.

I looked thirstily into the face of every passerby, searching for a resemblance to Bendet, to Leah Esther, to my mother (I don't want to compare anyone to my grandfather—to me he is holy), but in vain. Old women with skin like parchment shuffled along, more like ghosts than human beings. Once in a while, an old, thin man with a long, pointed beard went by, and then some plump, roly-poly women and well-fed men. Yes, they were carrying holy books under their arms, but something didn't look right. The sorrowful holiness of two years past was missing, and so were the idealistic strivings of last year. Here all was crude and crass. The faces said nothing, neither good nor bad. My heart grew heavier and sadder than ever, and muffled sighs erupted from my breast.

Across the street, two young women were sitting on the stoop. Both had little babies, which was why they couldn't go to the synagogue. One of them I knew a little—we often ran into each other. Once as I passed by I'd heard her aim a curse in my direction. She'd run away from home because of the pogroms, I figured, and now that things were going well for her here, she thought that if only people like us would stop stirring things up, there'd be no more troubles for the Jews. Now as she talked to her friend she flicked her eyes at me like daggers, her lips moved, and I had the feeling she was cursing me again.

As an "enlightened" person, I'm accustomed to laughing off curses, but now I felt as if the hair on my head were standing on end. I looked away. To the left, I spied the black bridge of the elevated train; off to the right went the trolley cars with their mournful clatter. I lifted my eyes to the cheerless sky; it was gray with smoke and dust.

I went back into the house and sat down to read, but the words wiggled on the page. I lit the stove and put on water for tea. When it was ready, I lifted my glass, but I couldn't drink. My throat was tight with tears.

All of a sudden there was a timid knock at the door.

"Come in!"

It was Helenka. I breathed a little easier.

"Come, Emma," she said without looking at me. "Let's go."

I examined her face, which was twitching nervously. How sad she looked! My hands dropped to my lap. "Where to?" I asked.

"Anywhere," she blurted out. "A park, a street—anything not to sit at home."

"I thought you were working today," I said.

"I couldn't." A sad smile flickered around her mouth. "I got halfway there and had to turn around."

I didn't need to ask more; her voice told me everything. "All right," I said, "let's go."

I had to put a few stitches in my dress, and as Helenka waited she paced restlessly around the room. She began to sing, her voice sounding nervous, not quite right. "Arise, ye prisoners of starvation!" she sang. "Arise, ye wretched of the earth. . . ." But instead of finishing the stanza, she switched to another, then to a mazurka, then a love song, and then suddenly she was singing in a stirring, poignant voice: *"Faryomert, farklogt, fun zayn heym faryogt . . ."* ("Wailing, betrayed, and driven from home . . ."). Her voice began to quaver, and she fell silent. I could feel the tears coming. Afraid to look at her, I began hastily to change my clothes as she continued pacing around the room.

My hair needed combing; I went to the mirror in the front room, where the light was murky and dim. Here and there, a ray of sun pierced the green curtains and fell on the patterned rug, the flowered wallpaper, the glass dishes. As I stood in the doorway, all the colors swirled together and cast a spell. My heart aching, I dropped my hands once again and stood lost in thought.

Why am I living here? I asked myself. What do I have in my life? Not the holy, poetic stillness of the shtetl and not the exhilaration of the struggle. Not my dear family members from home and not my beloved comrades. Here is only loneliness, smoke, noise, sweat, rudeness—and the reward for it all? Nothing but a crust of bread.

From the kitchen, Helenka's pacing grew more restless

still. I felt sorry for her, my only friend in the world, and although I felt like throwing myself on her and pouring out all my thoughts in a flood of tears, I didn't want to make things harder for her. And so, standing before the mirror in the dimness, I forced myself to begin combing my hair. But suddenly my body began to tremble: at that moment, my face bore an uncanny resemblance to my grandfather's.

There was a roaring in my ears and the blood rushed to my face. A rainbow-colored mist shimmered before the mirror and a wavering column of pale figures began to emerge from afar. Volodya, Sonya, Solomon . . . all at once I could plainly see the tall, refined figure of my grandfather, the velvet skullcap perched high on his head and the deep wrinkles creasing his pure white forehead. Raising his silver brows, he looked at me, his eyes so sad. He tottered toward me, and now I could feel him. I wanted to turn to him but could not. In the mirror I saw him lift his trembling hands over my head. His tender voice whispered in my ear: "May the Lord bless you and keep you in good health, may He cause His countenance to shine upon you, and may He give you peace." I felt a violent pain in my breast. My legs buckled under me and my head grew heavy. "Grandfather!" I wanted to call out, but the words stuck in my throat. I leaned my head backward—I wanted to rest against his chest and weep. But he was too far away, and my head fell back, back, back. . . .

I feel a commotion around me and a sharp pain in the temples. They're sticking me with pins. They've resuscitated me. You may ask—why?

★ ☾ ★

YENTE SERDATZKY *was born outside Kaunas, Lithuania, in 1877. In 1905, she left her husband and children and went to Warsaw to pursue a literary career, in which she was encouraged by*

I. L. Peretz. In 1907, she came to the United States. She ran soup kitchens in Chicago and New York while publishing stories and one-act plays in many Yiddish periodicals. Her only book, Geklibene shriftn [Selected Works], was published in 1913. She worked for the New York Yiddish newspaper Forverts until 1922, when she was dismissed in a quarrel with the editor. She withdrew from the literary world until 1949, when she began writing again and was published in the Nyu yorker vokhenblat. She died in 1962.

Two Heads

Yente Serdatzky

Translated by Sheva Zucker

G ray and lonely, her solitary life drags on. . . . Slowly the sad winter days slip by. . . . A great stripe of sky comes through the window into the house and flows onto the whitewashed gray walls. A powerful sadness hovers over everything: over the iron bed, the hunchbacked chair and table, and the books without covers, and she herself is also wrapped in foggy gray shadows.

She looks into the mirror and sees brownish circles under her melancholy black eyes and a tired sick redness that spills from under her eyes onto her whole face, and she becomes even sadder: something is gnawing at her heart and pressing her poor blood into her face. . . . The winter night drags on longer, longer and more sorrowfully, by the pale glow of the little lamp. She waits for no one and no one comes to her. She has cut herself off from the world.

When life began to pulsate so irresistibly below that the windowpanes of her lonely little room quivered and reverberated from the turbulent street, she woke up, left the world of

243

books, and threw herself into the seething current. But it was too late. The current did not take her in. Fervent belief was required. . . . She had only criticism and doubt.

She came back even sadder than before. There she sits, lonely, in her room, in the pale glow of the little lamp, amid the shadows that flitter over the walls: lonely and with no purpose in life.

One day she hears laughter through the wall. The adjoining room had been empty until now. Now somebody was occupying it—and laughing!

It galls her: all around there is such loneliness—and he's laughing! Her skinny hands clench themselves into fists . . . she knocks on the wall . . . rap, rap, rap . . . as if to say, "My heart is aching . . . help me, suffer with me, feel what I am feeling. . . ." And from the other side of the wall there bounces back like an echo, rap, rap, rap—"Yes, yes!" And the laughing stops. After that she taps on the wall frequently . . . rap, rap, rap . . . meaning, "How heavy is my heart, how sad my soul." Rap, rap, rap, comes the knock from the other side of the wall, and it seems to her that someone is answering her, "Me too!" "Me too!" Rap, rap, rap—"How miserably life drags on. . . . If only one had something to live for. . . ." "Me too, me too, me too," comes the reply from the other side.

That other person must also be lonely. She sighs, and starts thinking about him.

He must be so lonely. She wants his name to be "Lazar"— she likes that name . . . how old would he be? About twenty-five! He must be tall and slender . . . his face, pale . . . delicate features . . . hair, golden and curly, a bit tousled . . . especially around the forehead. He must have big, pensive, blue eyes . . . and they must gaze out so wonderfully from beneath his thick brows.

How does he live? His room is certainly as gray and sad as

hers . . . there must also be a lot of books there . . . also unbound! And he reads . . . day and night he reads. And he reads with passion . . . with excitement . . . as if he were searching for lost treasures, forfeited riches, and holy things impossible to recover; the wrinkles deepen on his high brow . . . his blue eyes become more doleful . . . more pensive . . .

And an unfamiliar feeling goes through her . . . she takes pity on him . . . so lonely!

Through the wall she hears him sighing. . . . Now it seems to her that she sees him clearly through the wall. Tears spill from his eyes onto his pale countenance. . . .

What does he need? . . . Why does he suffer? And she presses her hot brow to the damp gray wall; perhaps the wall will tell her something about him. . . . And gentleness and compassion well up in her and overtake her. Such a wonderful sorrow grows in her heart . . . and warm tears trickle down . . . and it seems to her that something cold in her heart is melting . . . something heavy in her heart is becoming lighter and lighter. It is no longer pressing on her, it becomes so light . . . so light . . . and her pity for her lonely neighbor grows. She wants to be near him. . . . Gladly would she kiss away the tears from his eyes . . . with her slender hands fix his curls . . . stroke his head. . . . She would look him in the eye with such kindness, like a sister . . . she would certainly come to love him. . . . Together, it would be easier to live, to find a purpose in life. . . .

And her rapping on the wall becomes softer, gentler, and from the other side, notes full of hope, comfort, and love echo back. She wants to see him . . . she is full of longing . . . but she won't go in to see him. . . . There are books where they do things like that, but in real life it's difficult, she can't. . . . In the summer she will open her window, so will he. . . .

And new golden dreams begin to take shape within her. . . . Just let the first sun come, the first sun! He'll appear at his window. . . . His golden hair!

And when springtime came, and specks of gold lay on the gray walls and on the shabby furniture, and a pillar of sun dust slanted into the room, sparkling colorfully, there was a sweet tremor in her heart . . . a joyful tug, rap, rap, rap—"Spring is calling, to love, to life, to happiness. . . ."

And from the other side there echoed back, "Me too, me too, me too," and she saw him clearly with his hand on his pining heart . . . with sweet tears in his yearning eyes!

"Me too! Me too!" And she threw open the window—

And she could hear that there, too . . . there, too—

And indeed, she was not the only one leaning her head out. . . .

Two heads suddenly appeared side by side at the window . . . two pale, longing countenances, two pairs of eyes full of yearning . . . but the heads of two maidens!

★ ☾ ★

YENTE SERDATZKY *was born outside Kaunas, Lithuania, in 1877. In 1905, she left her husband and children and went to Warsaw to pursue a literary career, in which she was encouraged by I. L. Peretz. In 1907, she came to the United States. She ran soup kitchens in Chicago and New York while publishing stories and one-act plays in many Yiddish periodicals. Her only book,* Geklibene shriftn *[Selected works], was published in 1913. She worked for the New York Yiddish newspaper* Forverts *until 1922, when she was dismissed in a quarrel with the editor. She withdrew from the literary world until 1949, when she began writing again and was published in the* Nyu Yorker vokhen-blat. *She died in 1962.*

In the Boardinghouse

David Bergelson

Translated by Joseph Sherman

hen one rings the bell of the boardinghouse, a pretty maid opens the door. Studiedly courteous, highly trained in all the intimate customs of the establishment, she casts an eye over the new arrival with a glance that acknowledges something more in him than other glances might discern. She helps him take off his overcoat with movements that make him feel as though he has finally reached a cozy home, as though he has swum to a safe haven; she answers in a tone that intends to reply, quite apart from all other inquiries, to one question only—a question that is never put into words. Conscious of carpets beneath, feet lose no time in making their way softly forward, as though treading on springs. All around, from the walls in the adjoining and warmly furnished open room, photographs and paintings of women with enraptured faces, with heads thrown back and eyes intense with passion, gaze down. From a half-darkened corridor, one such portrait, one too explicit in its depiction of nudity, stays in the mind, and in a moment one feels both in the center of the city yet strangely far away and cut off from all its millions of inhabitants. A thought about the boardinghouse flashes instantly through the mind:

Highly respectable, certainly.

But on the other hand . . .

Soon it becomes apparent why, of all the streets in Berlin, this boardinghouse has intentionally sought out this street, where everything around is neither too noisy nor too quiet. The house itself is at one with this ambience—it admonishes every person who enters it:

Let us have neither too much noise nor too much quiet.

Everything one sees around one simultaneously calls forth a vague suspicion and a vague doubt, as though the whole boardinghouse has perhaps deliberately been organized in this fashion, to awaken a vague suspicion, and immediately thereafter, to cast doubt on that suspicion.

In the reception room, the eldest of the three beautiful sisters, Liuba, a tall, stately brunette, receives the new lodger. Though somewhat pale and too heavily powdered, she is younger and more beautiful than her portrait, which hangs on the wall here. She turns on the unfamiliar guest a glance suggesting that she wishes to decide at once whether or not he will suit her, not solely as a lodger, but also—if things turn out that way—as a close friend, as a person capable of living more expansively outside conventional constraints than all the rest of the world lives. . . . For that reason, a short pause ensues before she begins to speak with him. She shuts her eyes and rapidly and monotonously runs through details of the costly tariff he will be obliged to pay for a room with board here; she concludes with a smile, as though she and he both know that all this has nothing to do with quibbling over prices—this is simply a formality designed to ease the beginning of an acquaintanceship. Immediately thereafter, with another smile, she gives him her hand and invites him to be seated. She settles down with him in one of the coziest corners of the room but soon changes her mind and leads him over to another corner, one even cozier. She rings and orders refreshments to be brought, right here to this corner on the low little table that has been especially pulled up, and she says to him:

"Wait, wait, let me guess what you prefer—tea or coffee."

That is the very moment at which a newcomer heedlessly determines to pay the exorbitant cost of board and lodging here. From childhood on, one might have been indifferent about drinking either tea or coffee, but when for a single instant she glances smilingly straight into one's eyes and suddenly guesses out loud:

"Coffee!"

All one's senses unite in making one feel that this was the pure truth—one's favorite drink is unquestionably coffee, and one is moreover amazed at having been such a fool as to drink tea all these years. Then one feels strangely stimulated; one forgets whether or not one's resources can accommodate the exorbitant cost of living here; one even forgets one's own age.

Sima, the second of the attractive young siblings, then enters—blond, with short, almost boyishly cut hair, she is the antithesis of her brown-haired elder sister. All her features are like herself, charmingly elongated. She is able to smile only with a little dimple on the side of her nose, and this smiling little dimple approaches the new lodger well before she herself approaches him in person. She gives him her hand, glancing simultaneously both at him and at her older sister with an expression of pleased and contented cordiality, as though she has known from the start that the two of them, the new lodger and her sister, would take a great liking to each other here in this very room; as though she envies both of them for their *rapport*. . . . In consequence, the new lodger promptly begins feeling as warmly toward this unknown Sima as though she were very closely related to him on his wife's side of the family. One does not willingly seek to weigh up which of them, the elder or the younger, is the more beautiful; on the contrary, one feels an ill-defined regret, as though one has made too hasty a judgment, too hurriedly chosen the elder.

There is not much time to ponder this, however. . . . All the time the muted, enraptured playing of a piano has made itself heard from a nearby room. Tones drift across that every now and then die away from excess of feeling, from languishing heartache, as from the memorial prayer, "God full of mercy . . . ," tones that palpitate and revive one another with fresh hope, with new questions: perhaps, possibly . . . The refreshments on the little table expand to include liquor, nuts with metal nut-crackers, and all the while, the rinds of oranges and the shells of almonds pile up on the little plates. The atmosphere is convivial, festive. Then the tones of the piano die away completely, and the third sister enters the room—young, lissome with the body of a girl desperate to be trained as a dancer, she lingers in the doorway with her arms thrown casually over her head, looking for all the world as though she wishes to stretch herself, but knowing in advance that however much she might stretch herself, she will still remain stiff and cramped. A blend of both her older sisters, she is neither blond nor brown haired, yet her eyes simultaneously express Liuba's veiled passion and Sima's blithe coquettishness.

"Julia!?" Both older sisters call out to her at the same time, and both in tandem turn wondering eyes upon her, as upon a dearly loved favorite. "Why don't you come closer, Julia?"

Thereupon, seemingly of their own accord, the new

lodger's eyes also fasten wonderingly upon Julia, as though upon a dearly loved favorite. Pondering over which of the three is the most beautiful, the lodger once again feels an ill-defined regret that he has been overhasty in deciding that he liked the older two so very much; at any rate, no one is forcing him to make a final decision, after all—he still has time to decide.

Now both sisters feel the time has come to take the new lodger to his room. It makes no matter; now he is bemused, stupefied, as on one of the first sunny days in spring. Any room they might show him here will please him immediately. It makes no matter; he will sleep through a happy rainy night, full of confused thoughts about all three sisters in general, and about each of them in particular, full of the recognition that no one is forcing him to make a final decision; he will make a long stay here in this boardinghouse. He will have plenty of time to make up his mind.

Liuba and Sima, the eldest of the three sisters, give the impression of being half widowed, half deserted. Some years before, on their journey together out of Russia, they mislaid their husbands somewhere in Riga or in Bialystok. But they have no regrets about this, it seems.

The letters they subsequently wrote to their husbands from their boardinghouse were at first very lengthy and full of longing; later, they grew brief and tepid; still later, they dwindled into nothing more than stiff, brightly colored postcards of landscapes; to make up for that, however, they carried with them heartfelt, deeply heartfelt, regards.

But they also sent postcards of landscapes carrying heartfelt, deeply heartfelt, regards to various other young men—former lodgers, future lodgers. The stiff postcards of landscapes they dispatched to unknown young men commingled for so long with the postcards of landscapes they wrote to their husbands that eventually the feelings with which the cards were written commingled as well. The husbands expressed a desire to come, whereupon the sisters, working in league together, began once again to write long letters to each of them, giving their husbands to understand that it would be best for them to remain exactly where they were, feeling as they did that no sooner were their husbands to come than their boardinghouse would become commonplace and run-of-the-mill, like all the others, and the credit accounts they held in their own names in two banks would summarily stop increasing. Their husbands felt grossly insulted at this and ceased writing, so that in the end it was not they, the sisters, who remained forever half widowed, half deserted, but their husbands, whom they had mislaid somewhere in Riga or in Bialystok, on their journey out of Russia.

Nevertheless, very early one morning, when the entire boardinghouse was still asleep, something very frightening befell the two sisters. The front doorbell was rung very insolently, as though some landlord were demanding admittance. The maid, who opened the front door, reacted vigorously against the person who rang the doorbell—she hurried off to the sisters in their darkened bedrooms and prattled on about someone who had only just arrived from Bialystok—he had come directly here with all his belongings, straight from the train station. . . .

"Straight from the train station? . . . With his belongings? . . ."

Thereupon the sisters, wearing only their nightdresses, instantly leapt from their beds with their teeth chattering in fear. But it turned out that this was a totally unknown young man from Bialystok—he had only brought a greeting, that was all he had brought; he had only needed to ask advice, that was all he had needed, because he was a stranger here and knew no one. . . .

The sisters sent the young man packing—they got rid of him with some difficulty, once again undressed, and once again returned to their beds in their nightdresses, but they were wholly unable to fall asleep again, smoked cigarettes on empty stomachs, and reviled him:

"Tfu! May he go to the devil!"

"What an idiot can do!"

"There's a Bialystok layabout for you!"

They were pale for the rest of the day after that, felt faint and indisposed, like people in need of rest at a health spa. But the fact that the shock was groundless, nothing more than a false alarm, somehow convinced them for good and all that it could never have been anything else and that from now on they could rest completely assured that neither of their husbands would ever return to them again.

Especially for the sake of one of their rich lodgers, they had subsequently written home sending for their third sister—this very Julia, who was younger and more beautiful than both of them, who regarded the world with a limitless, passionate loneliness, who possessed a body that seemed to tear garments from itself with unseen hands and moved with longing to be trained as a dancer, and who played the piano with the languishing tones of the memorial prayer "God full of mercy . . ."

Julia had been summoned from home by letter on account of a lodger named Tartakover.

He lived in three rooms for which, all on his own, he paid far more than three rich lodgers individually. His legs were paralyzed, so the interleading doors of his three expensively furnished rooms were always left wide open; their floors were covered throughout with very soft carpets so that, as need arose, he could move about unassisted in a wheelchair. At first glance, he appeared to be a handsome Tatar or a Persian, an impression reinforced by the fact that he always wore a small black hat, a little skullcap; he was receiving treatment here from medical specialists, who assured him that he was not helpless, but that it was essential for him never to get worked up about anything; absolute rest was of paramount importance. Here, in the rooms around him, the sisters had contrived to create an ambience suggesting that to have paralyzed legs was a particular pleasure not all people were worthy enough to enjoy. Their quiet hovering about him possessed its own distinct, earnest rhythm, as in music. Here Julia played the piano for him, and for a few hours each day, she read to him from soothing books with great longing in her voice while he sat in his mobile chair with his eyes shut and his legs covered. It was clear that her velvet tones calmed him a great deal more than the contents of the books she read. From time to time, he slowly opened his drowsy black Persian eyes and glanced at the way she smoothed out the soft folds over his legs, and at such times it seemed as if everything had long ago been determined and decided—when he recovered his health, he would marry Julia. For that reason, it was widely believed that for a long time now everything Julia possessed belonged to him, even the expensive fur she wore whenever she went out, and that Julia herself was inexplicably poor—Julia possessed nothing.

But there were other lodgers in the house who took quite a different view of all this.

One of the largest, most costly rooms was occupied by the permanent lodger, whose name in the old country had been Moyshe Levenberg, but who, for the sake of genteel euphony, was addressed in brief as Herr Moses. He was a curious black-bearded, black-clothed, very wealthy man who cut out coupons and, with great connoisseurship, endlessly consumed different kinds of oranges: from Messina, from Jaffa, and every variety from Italy. As a result, he himself, his black clothes, and everything that had a place in his opulently furnished room reeked perpetually of orange peel. He carried his pince-nez on a broad ribbon as black as his beard, and it was obvious from all his movements that in his old home in Russia, where he had abandoned his family for good, he had been an observant Jew.

Since he had been the first lodger to take up permanent residence with the sisters, he certainly had the right frequently to open his door into the corridor a narrow crack, to stand there with an uneaten orange in his hand, and to observe with beaming delight everything that went on in the sisters' boardinghouse.

He was often visited in his spacious room by his neighbor Dr. Bremen—the lodger on his left—a balding, blond, extremely tall doctor of economic science, who had been within a hairbreadth of becoming a professor but had remained instead nothing more than a director of a not very large bank and who spent his entire limited salary each month on paying the sisters for his exorbitantly costly lodging. This was apparently why the tall, balding, blond Dr. Bremen's nose was always blocked with catarrh—simply because, after he had settled his monthly bill for his lodgings with the sisters, he was left without a single groschen of his entire month's salary.

In his own room, Herr Moses shared a joke in a prim, high-pitched nasal cackle, ridiculing all the lodgers who, once they had found their way in here, believed that they had stumbled straight into Paradise . . . the Paradise promised by Muhammad! . . .

He peeled an apple with so much festive gusto, it seemed he wanted to offer it whole and entire to a beloved, but when the apple was completely peeled, he sliced it in pieces that he popped into his own mouth with the same festive gusto:

"I'll tell you," he added, laughing with his high-pitched nasal cackle, "there's something very wrong with the whole reckoning here."

He spoke very slowly, because he was a man who cut out coupons and had time.

"There's something very wrong with the whole reckoning here . . . it's a hopeless business. Let's only be as healthy as I'm certain of what I'm talking about. D'you know what I want to tell you? No one here gets a single thing from the sisters. . . . Listen carefully to what I'm telling you: I believe the whole business here is a lie. . . . It's very probable that the sisters aren't really sisters at all. *Khe-khe-khe!* . . . Let's only be as healthy as there's something very fishy here. It's been deliberately fabricated to bamboozle everyone. I was the very first lodger here, I can tell you, and all the time I've had a good look at what goes on here. I'm an expert on obfuscation, I can tell you . . . *khe-khe-khe*. What's troubling you? When I speak, I know what I'm talking about, I can tell you . . . *khe-khe-khe!* The whole business has been deliberately and ingeniously contrived to encourage you to believe that *I'm* getting something from the sisters . . . and I, on the other hand, am meant to believe that *you're* getting something from them. . . . D'you understand what goes on here? They're quite simply thieves . . . they're nothing more than pickpockets . . . *khe-khe-khe!* . . .

"Take that room in which you're living at the moment—previously it was occupied by a rich Greek—when I arrived, he was living here already—so in the evenings the sisters used to visit him in his room and play out such scenes in there that I used to jump out of my bed—right out of it, I can tell you. Wearing only my nightshirt, I used to stand and listen in for as long as it all lasted—it used to go on for hours. And only later on did it dawn on me that during all those evenings, the Greek wasn't at home at all. *Khe-khe-khe!* . . . He'd actually gone off somewhere for a whole week, I can tell you—one whole week away. . . . Wait! Shush! I'll tell you another story, I definitely will. You've seen the new lodger? That young man, that Lipschitz? He's a student from Romania. Well, he's fallen in love

with the sisters—with all three of them . . . *khe-khe-khe*. . . .
You've seen the way he walks about, as though he's in a daze?
His rich parents send him more than enough money, but he
still hasn't enough to pay for his lodgings here every week. So
he's always sending telegrams home, saying that if they don't
send him any more money, he'll take his own life. . . ."

As Herr Moses popped the peeled slices of apple into his
mouth, the tall, balding, blond Dr. Bremen looked on, rapt in
thought, as though also caught up in festive enthusiasm. He
snuffled meditatively through his nasal catarrh, and it seemed
as though he were drawing up an account of all those many of
his monthly salaries the sisters had, until that very day,
snapped up with none of the anticipated gain to himself. Both
lodgers were all ears; every few minutes they would fall silent
and listen attentively to the slightest shuffle that drifted across
from the surrounding rooms.

"Do you understand or not?" Herr Moses peered closely at
the fresh orange he had picked up. "What more can I tell you?
All around, it's been very cunningly arranged. . . . Three sisters—five lodgers—how can one know? Where? What? . . .
Who with whom? . . . *khe-khe-khe!* Go get to the bottom of it,
when they're on lovey-dovey terms with each one individually
and with all together. . . . And the cost of living here! . . .
That's no small matter, that outlay! . . . Before you've turned
round, for every little thing you've laid down another fiver,
another tenner. And shall I tell you something else? I've got
another suspicion entirely. . . ."

But first Herr Moses got up and went to listen at the door.
Then he turned round to face Dr. Bremen, who had also risen.
This evening he had something new to tell him. He raised
himself on the tips of his toes and whispered directly into Dr.
Bremen's ear:

"I'm on the point of discovering this for certain: It's very likely that the sisters are keeping their husbands here in Berlin, but hidden away. Do you understand or not? They leave us asleep here, and they themselves go off to spend the night with their husbands. . . ."

By now it was late. The two lodgers parted and went cheerlessly to bed, but with the latent hope that possibly . . . even so . . . perhaps a mistake had been made. Both made an accounting of how extravagantly much the boardinghouse had cost them until now, and sooner or later both thought:

And the cost of living here . . . No small matter, the cost of living here! . . .

★ ☾ ★

DAVID BERGELSON *is one of the best prose stylists in Yiddish fiction. Born into a wealthy Chasidic family in the Ukraine in 1884, he received a traditional Jewish education and was fluent in Yiddish, Hebrew, and Russian by the time he was a teenager. He started writing in early youth in both Russian and Hebrew but soon settled on Yiddish, his mother tongue, the language he used for the rest of his writing career. I. L. Peretz encouraged his first work, and he published his first story, "Arum vokzal" [At the Depot], in Warsaw in 1909. Much of his best work, published before the Russian Revolution of 1917, dealt with the decay of the traditional Jewish shtetl and the plight of the wealthy Jewish bourgeoisie, who were fully at home neither in the traditional world of Orthodox Jewish observance nor in the Gentile world of czarist Russia. Bergelson, along with a dozen other writers and artists, was arrested during Stalin's anti-Jewish purges in 1948, and he was murdered, together with the cream of Soviet Yiddish literary talent, in August 1952.*

BRYNA'S MENDL

I. L. Peretz

Translated by Goldie Morgentaler

ryna's Mendl—there were no family names in those days—was a "tent dweller," as it was said of Jacob: he was a man who liked to devote his time to study. This meant that Mendl belonged to the spiritual elite of his town—more or less. He was not a great scholar, but he did recite psalms before praying, peruse the Eyn Yakov after praying, and in the evening read a chapter from the Mishnah. Quite often he brought home a guest, and every morning he put money into the charity box of Rabbi Meir the Miracle Worker. He was also called upon to read the portion from the prophet Jonah on Yom Kippur and to join the consortium of those who opened the Holy Ark. In addition, he was a man much preoccupied with doing good. When a preacher came to town, or someone had to collect alms for the poor so that they would have matzos, or firewood, or potatoes; when the Sabbath limits needed to be marked, or a monument erected over a tomb, or any such matter, then Bryna's Mendl would assume an air of expansive sagacity, take in hand his thick walking stick with the brass knob, and venture forth with the rabbi, or the inspector, or some other distinguished member of the community. He considered it a good deed to carry the collection box himself, even though the sexton walked just behind him.

During the winter he did not have a moment to himself. He recited psalms, prayed, read the Eyn Yakov, breakfasted, gave alms, attended the afternoon service, then the evening service, studied a chapter of the Mishnah, ate supper, recited the evening prayer, slept, awoke for the midnight service, and slept some more. There was never any time left to spare from his day. But to make up for this, during the summer he would have a long stretch of unscheduled time after the evening meal. This time too he spent in the study house, but then he would discuss worldly matters, the latest inventions, politics.

Bryna's Mendl was not clever. In *cheder* he had been called Stupid Mendl. When he got married, the general opinion softened and he became known as Foolish Mendl. It was only after he had stopped boarding at his father-in-law's and become master in his own house, when his wife, Bryna, had opened a grocery shop and was earning her weight in gold, that he was crowned with the title "Bryna's Mendl." And since Bryna's Mendl stood in no one's way, never said a mean word to anybody, and profited the study house and the community with his contributions, no one recalled what once had been, and no one laughed aloud when he punctuated every fifth word with, "I'm no fool now, am I? Don't you agree that I am clever?"

"It is true that I'm no fool," Reb Mendl once said. "Nevertheless, I don't understand how they can produce such thin, hollow strands of straw to fill the straw mattresses. I purposely pulled out about forty straws, one after the other. All are hollow as whistles. I wanted to ask my Bryna, but she had already left for the shop."

Before anybody had time to laugh, he answered his own question. "The peasants probably import the straw from England." Bryna's Mendl had heard a lot about England. He thought the world of that country—and then some.

This occurred after the battle of Sevastopol. The entire study house was abuzz with news of the latest English military strategies. The stories were circulated by war veterans who had witnessed the marvels with their own eyes.

Truly, there had been wonders, recounted a prominent member of the study house. For instance, a cannon. What, my friends, is the use of a cannon? A cannon fires a cannonball. So what? First, you have to convince the enemy to stand in the line of fire. Since the enemy is by no means a fool, he won't be talked into any such thing. Sometimes he even resorts to tricks. He stands, you shoot, and he sneaks away. Matters had so degenerated on the battlefield, you would have thought that the end of the world was at hand. But those clever bastards, the English, had heard the story of the plague of frogs in Egypt, so they too looked for something that multiplies. They invented an enormous cannon that fired not cannonballs, but entire cannons. And each of these cannons, when it fell, crashed into the ground, exploded, and disgorged ten new cannons, and those cannons fired the cannonballs. Well, try to hide from that! Now you can appreciate what kind of slaughter this caused. You think it was magic? Heaven forbid! It worked by means of a simple lever.

If someone asked why, after the war, the Russian Empire did not reproduce just such cannons, the answer was that immediately after the end of hostilities all the kingdoms had come together to make a pact among themselves, each one swearing, on oath, that in order not to destroy the world, they would never fire on anyone again, not with sheets of boiling millet and not with such cannons.

From that time on, Bryna's Mendl thought the world of England and then some. Whenever he saw something that his mind could not comprehend, then it was clear that the thing must come from England. That watches originated in England—about that there could be no doubt. But the first lever must also have been made by an English smith. Bryna's Mendl spoke with great enthusiasm about England, her wise men, and her blacksmiths. "They must all have great minds over there!"

Bryna's Mendl would have liked to live in England, but he wanted to die—after 120 years—in the land of Israel. First, for reasons of faith. Second, it was simply his nature to enjoy a peaceful existence, and whenever he recalled that at the time of the Resurrection the dead were required to roll underground until they reached the holy land, he lost his appetite for three days. But since he nevertheless continued eating despite his loss of appetite, he suffered from stomachache for six days after that. So he was overjoyed to learn from a reliable source that the land of Israel was even farther than England. Good, he thought. And from that time on, he seriously began making plans for a trip to Israel, because the way to the holy land must lead through England.

He would long since have sold the grocery store with all the household effects and set out on the road, if not for Bryna.

Bryna was very devoted to her Mendl. She wished nothing better for herself than to be his footstool in Paradise. She pampered him and stuffed him with food. She worked like a donkey to support him, to shoe and clothe him and their five children—three girls and two boys. The greatest pleasure she took in this world was to look out from the shop and see her Mendl pass by carrying the charity box in his left hand and holding the walking stick with the brass knob in his right. For a pittance she sold her seat in the women's gallery, because the window there looked out on the synagogue. She then paid an extravagant sum for a seat near the study house window, so that she could see how Mendl was called up to read the Torah and how sweetly he pronounced the blessing. Her heart melted when Mendl prompted the cantor to announce that "for the sake of the woman Bryna, daughter of the honorable . . . ," he pledged a contribution of eighteen times eighteen.

She was never happier than on Sabbaths and holidays, when she accompanied him to the synagogue to pray. When they parted in front of the two staircases, she would remain standing on the bottom step of the women's staircase and look back to see how her Mendl walked up the men's stairs. After the service she waited for him in the entranceway to the synagogue, and when she saw him and heard him call out, "Good *Shabbes*," she would blush, as if she were a bride who had just emerged from under the wedding canopy. Nevertheless, she was aware that Mendl was not clever in the foolish ways of the world, that his intelligence was limited to the domain of the printed word. He was brilliant in the study house, but otherwise, in more mundane matters—not quite. That was her province.

"No, Mendl, my dear," she objected placidly, "we can't just get up and leave. We can't just sell off all our merchandise. Maybe later, when the children are all married and the sons-in-law have boarded with us, and we have lived to see at least one grandchild born and maybe even a great-grandchild—then, you see, I wouldn't mind. Then we could transfer the business to the children."

Mendl knew that Bryna was an absolute wizard when it came to worldly affairs, so he waited, because after Jerusalem and England, Bryna was the closest thing to his heart.

Not all of his children had yet been married off, however, when he came home one day very downhearted. "You see, Bryna," he said, "I have received a summons to the heavenly court." He showed her a gray hair in his beard.

Bryna consoled him. "Don't talk nonsense, Mendl. You are not knowledgeable in these matters. My father, may he rest in peace, went gray at the age of fifty. And, may you live a long life—"

"May we both live long lives," Mendl corrected her.

"May we both live long lives—my father lived for another thirty years."

"But our generation is weaker. We don't have the strength of our forefathers," Mendl said, lowering his eyes.

Bryna talked him out of his distress and began to pamper him even more. From the butcher she bought an additional half pound of meat for supper.

"Eh, Bryntcha," said the butcher. "You must be having the in-laws over for dinner. May it bring you good luck."

"No," Bryna answered. "It's just that our generation is so weak." And at mealtimes, she always added to Mendl's plate another piece of this and another bite of that. "Eat this. This is a delight," she would say. And as she looked at Mendl, she prayed, "May he eat in good health. People today are not what they used to be."

She claimed that, having washed her hands at a neighbor's, she had eaten a roll at the shop. Once she said that a relative had cooked a new type of potato soup and brought her a few spoonfuls to taste. Another time, she maintained that she had eaten at a cir-cumcision, although she could not remember the name of the child's mother. In any case, she was not hungry at mealtimes and only pleaded: "Eat, Mendl, eat. Why do you compare yourself to me? Studying Torah takes strength."

"You mean it gives strength, Bryna."

"Let it be 'gives strength.' Or, as it is written in Chapters of the Fathers, 'Im ein torah, ein kemach'—'If you study Torah, you must eat.'"

Mendl smiled at this new mistake. Bryna had reversed the order of the Hebrew saying.

"As for me," continued Bryna, "what do I do? Either I sit around all day with nothing to do, or I warm myself at the firepot. If a customer comes in, I measure out a quart of beans, or cereal, or flour. If no one comes, then I don't. That's why I don't need to eat so much."

Mendl believed in the roll, in the potato soup, in the circumcision, even though he had just recited the prayer of supplication and should have known that no circumcision had taken place. Perhaps he really did need to eat more. It was no small matter to read two portions from the Psalms, a chapter of the Mishnah, and a few pages of the Eyn Yakov and, on top of it all, to recite the daily prayers, carry the charity box, and drag along his walking stick.

He was very pleased that his virtuous Bryna led such a quiet life, sitting idly next to the firepot, her hands folded, awaiting a customer. If a customer appeared, then he appeared, and if not, not. That was as it should be. Let her, at least, not work as hard as he did. Let her, at least, rest her bones. So Mendl stuffed himself with even more food, that he might have the strength to prolong his days and live to see England and then die in Jerusalem.

Apart from the pleasure he took in Bryna, Mendl also rejoiced in his children. His eldest son had been married to a girl from another town. The son was now boarding at his father-in-law's. God be praised, ever since his wedding he had not written a single letter home. This was a sign that all was well, that he was in good health. Whoever arrived from the town where his son lived brought regards.

Next in line was Mendl's second son, a *cheder* boy, who would soon also be of marriageable age. Bryna hired tutors, paid their fees, made sure that the boy studied on the level of his peers. For his part, Mendl tested him on his lesson every Sabbath. But he hated doing this before the meal. After dinner was better, more comfortable. Which was also the reason why Mendl always dozed off during the recitation and did not awaken again until he heard the tutor toast, *"L'chayim."* Then he pinched his son's cheek, and that was that.

In addition, Mendl had three daughters, young children who still played at marbles, fine girls all. Respectful children. Quiet children. Always clean and washed, a pleasure to look at. He did not actually notice when they were washed or combed or when Bryna patched or mended their clothes. He could hardly comprehend how they came to be so clever and well-bred.

These really are my children, he thought with pride. They take after me. He thanked and praised the Holy Name that Bryna led such a peaceful life, not like other mothers whose children drove them crazy. And the children were so obedient! For instance, if he asked for a glass of water. Bryna had a habit of repeating everything he said, so no sooner had she repeated, "Bring your father a glass of water," than a child would run and bring it. It was a pleasure to have such children. When he walked into the house, Bryna had only to say, "Your father is home," and the house fell silent.

Praised be God, a match was proposed for the second son, and an excellent match it was, too. Bryna thought they should go and view the bride. She told Mendl that she wanted to make the trip during the Christian holidays. But when Mendl found out that the road to his future in-laws did not pass through England, he decided to relinquish the honor of the voyage to his wife. Let her have the pleasure of the journey. Why not? All in all, she made only four trips a year and those were to buy merchandise. From these trips she returned tired and worn out from running around, appraising, and bargaining. At least once let her take pleasure in her travels, and let the world see what a wonderful wife he had. He himself would reserve his appearance for the engagement ceremony, perhaps even for the wedding itself. It was Bryna who had gone alone to interview the prospective bride of the eldest son, and the result proved that she was fortunate in such matters. As for him, he would in any case be doing his share of traveling. . . .

A few more years passed. When God bestows blessings, He does so with a free hand. He even bestows peace of mind. The second son also married, and married well, and now he too was boarding with his in-laws. Mendl, however, knew very little of the what and the how. It had all floated past him like a dream. The wedding did not even cause him to miss a single day's recitation of the Psalms. He suffered no headaches, except on the morning after the big night, when he did not get enough sleep.

And Mendl rejoiced. It only remained for the three girls to be married off—Bryna managed these things quickly—and then, finished! They would transfer the business to the children, rent a wagon wide enough to lie down in, bed it down with English straw, and off they would go! In truth, Mendl felt that somehow his legs were no longer what they used to be, and recently he had begun to have trouble breathing. But Bryna would not let him despair. She consoled him and doted on him even more. She assured him that he would live to realize all his dreams.

One day, as he was sitting over the Eyn Yakov in the study house, Mendl heard a scream. It sounded like his daughter, but that could not be. What business would his daughter have in the courtyard of the study house? And a girl of marriageable age did not cry. Someone was running up the stairs shouting, "Father! Father!" Surely that was her voice. But after all, it was not possible.

He wanted to consider the matter and took out a pinch of snuff. But even before he could insert the snuff into his nostrils, his daughter stood before him, pulling at his lapels. "Help, Father! Mother has collapsed."

And before Mendl could fully grasp what she was saying and run home, Bryna was dead.

In the space of one day, Mendl's hair did indeed turn gray. Now he really did have trouble breathing, and his feet were truly swollen. It had never occurred to him that Bryna would not outlive him. Not with such a husband, such children, such comfort.

Bryna, who had attracted no notice in life, was barely visible on her deathbed. She was so thin!

✴ ☾ ✴

ISAAC LEYBUSH PERETZ *is heralded as one of the most significant figures of modern Jewish culture. Born in 1852 in Zamosc, a
small city in Poland, he was well schooled in Jewish ideology as well
as secular/Christian literature. Peretz began his literary career writing
Hebrew poetry in the 1870s and practiced law until a false accusation
ended his career. His new job was as an official in charge of the
Jewish cemeteries in Warsaw; while not as lucrative, the position gave
him more time to dedicate to his writing and his socialist activities. A
great proponent of Yiddish as a national language of the Jewish people,
he received vast acclaim as a Yiddish writer. When he died in 1915,
one hundred thousand people followed his coffin to the cemetery.*

BUBBE HENYA

Dvora Baron

Translated by Naomi Seidman with Chana Kronfeld

Swaddled in a gray shawl, a wig perched on her head and a walking stick in her hand, that was how she used to go down to the gulch every morning. She would make her way with small, quiet steps. Whenever she passed anyone, she would take the time to greet them with a smile, to brighten their day.

"Good morning to you and to all good people everywhere!"

If she encountered a band of schoolboys, she always stopped to pass out filberts to some, almonds to others:

"Eat, children, so you'll have strength to study the holy Torah."

If she saw someone who was in pain, she would stroke them with her sad, moist eyes:

"I have just the herb for you, it will cure what ails you, make the pain disappear."

She had a voice, Bubbe Henya, a soft voice that always rang with sympathy.

The women of the gulch would greet her with beaming faces:

269

"I have a whole pot of leftover cream soup, Bubbe. I tucked it away for your poor folk."

"I saved up three bagels for you. Open your apron, Bubbe, dear."

Bubbe Henya would nod: "For that mitzvah, you won't end up depending on the kindness of strangers."

And with short, sprightly steps she would continue on her way.

They would follow her down the street with long, reverent gazes:

"They say that she takes from her own pocket even more than she collects from others."

"But where does she get it? What does she survive on?"

The neighbor women explain:

Night after night, when the last fire in the gulch houses has been extinguished and the lamp blown out, she wakes up, opens her little book of psalms, and starts praising the Creator, may His name be a blessing. Next to the table she has a sack of feathers, and she takes a fistful and plucks the down from the quill, and takes another fistful and plucks some more. From the money she earns from this, she takes what she needs for herself, and she takes a share to distribute in the poorhouse, and she also puts a little aside toward the redemption of her soul.

For a long while, the gulch folk would whisper and shake their heads:

"What a woman."

And much later in the night, when a mute darkness surrounded the gulch houses, quick, sure footsteps would break the silence of the town. Those were Bubbe Henya's steps. Her wig disheveled, her shawl slipping down one shoulder, she would emerge from the poorhouse. Her thin hands would be clutching two small bodies close to her breast. Caressing them in the stillness, she would whisper a warm secret in each of their ears.

They were two little orphans, sick and abandoned after their mother had died. Bubbe Henya took them in, to recite psalms over their little heads in the night, to wash them with her tears in the daytime. After they had recuperated but their legs were still weak, she would carry them to school every morning, hugging them close to her breast, so they could learn God's Torah. In the evening she would bring them back home. Her feet sure, her legs quick, in those days she didn't yet need a cane.

And this, now, is what the gulch women say about Bubbe Henya's arrival in town:

It happened once on a quiet and peaceful summer evening. The day had been a hot one. Everyone was sitting on their front steps, half-naked, talking and chattering away. Suddenly a commotion was heard, and down the hill, with a huge clanging, rolled a large carriage, followed by a column of dust, and inside that column, it turned out, an old woman was walking.

"Is there anyplace around here where I can spend the night?"

An hour later, she could be seen walking around town, moving from house to house.

"Are you looking for something, *bubbe?*"

She shook her head happily.

"That's right, call me 'Bubbe.' That suits me just fine."

And her eyes slid over the children's pale faces and snatched glimpses of the corners of the dilapidated little houses around.

People stared after her, unsettled and suspicious.

Who was she? Where had she come from? Had anyone asked her to come here?

But by the next morning, even before the sun had appeared at the top of the hill, everybody knew that, on that very night, they had been brushed by a hand bearing blessings from afar.

Children who had been sick energetically ran around the street, their cheeks a healthy, rosy color, their eyes shining; on their thin wrists, now, were tied red threads as talismans. Frail old people discovered bottles of an elixir on their doorsteps, which they drank, and felt their youthful vigor restored. And in the poorhouse alley, there was a feast on every table, on each and every table.

Soon after that, the following story made the rounds in the shtetl:

Her name was Henya. She came from the big city. There she had been a real lady, played an important role in community affairs. But tragedy struck: On the very day her first child was born, her husband passed away. She bathed that boy in her tears, she wrapped him in her own hair, and she loved him enough for two. But once, when she was lying in bed with the child, taking too much pleasure in him, a death sentence descended upon her from the heavens. And her husband arose from his grave, appeared before her, and pleaded:

"Wake up, rouse yourself from sleep, and take a look at what you're doing to our child: You're suffocating him with your own two hands. . . ." She heard every word he said, but somehow she couldn't move a muscle. And when she awoke the next morning and found, lying beside her, a bloody little corpse, she opened her prayer book, recited, "Blessed is the Righteous Judge," and then lifted her arms toward heaven and said:

"The Lord giveth and the Lord taketh away."

After the week of mourning, she disposed of her property, distributing it among the poor, took up a walking stick—and arrived here in our shtetl.

Others told it differently:

The truth is she came from a nearby shtetl. There she had a husband and seven sons—all of them renowned, all of them sitting day and night over the Talmud. And she herself—she took in laundry, shelled chickpeas, and supported her family. And late, late in the night, when she had finished her work, she—as worn out and exhausted as she was—she would steal into the women's gallery of the synagogue, rest her head against the lattice, and listen. Eight voices, eight melodious and clear voices, would flow together in one sad chant, filling the study hall with supernal light and floating up, up . . . At the eastern wall burned the lamp, illuminating the velvet curtain covering the Ark and the eight faces of her husband and children. She would take it all in and brim with pride and joy:

"Yes, that's my man . . . yes, these are my babies."

But the One above did not, as it were, care for these proud words, and a fire descended from heaven and engulfed the holy house while all eight souls were between its high walls. The next morning, the wife and mother picked their scorched bones from the ashes with her bare hands. And when she returned home from the graveyard, she looked at the house and it was empty. From the bookshelves, entire rows of holy books looked out at her in speechless shame, and in a corner, she saw eight pairs of desolate phylacteries in a neat pile—so she tore her clothes in mourning, took off her shoes, sat on the ground, and raised both hands to God:

"You are just and Your judgment is just."

Not a single tear did she shed, but her face became covered with deep wrinkles all over.

And when she arose from the seven days of mourning, she donated her house for Torah study and swore a solemn oath that she would devote her life to charity. Since then, there was no decree from God, blessed be He, so harsh that Bubbe Henya could not annul it with her tears. . . .

That same evening, the gulch folk added another prayer to their nighttime Shema:

"May it be God's will that the providence of this woman here shall never be removed from our midst."

Old people, on that same night, saw in their dreams:

Entire bands of angels, all of them pure, all of them radiant, spread their wings over the squat shacks of the gulch, floating above them and protecting them.

And in the gulch, the women told yet another story:

The shtetl had about a dozen or so orphan girls. Some of these girls' braids were already turning gray and they were starting to lose their teeth, others were getting wrinkled and withered, and every single one of them was gnawed by hunger and wretchedly poor. Bubbe Henya put together a few coins, one penny at a time, to sew them wedding dresses, she looked high and low for nice boys for them to marry, and then married them off one by one. It so happened that the last of these orphan girls had moved to a village and the wedding was held there, so Henya was gone from the gulch for two days. But before the first day had passed, awful news rattled every heart.

A mother of six small children was having terrible labor pains, the midwife wasn't holding out much hope, and where was Bubbe Henya now?

In the gulch, chaos reigned. Young wives carried boiling water from the bathhouse, filling basins, old women wrung their hands and argued with God, blessed be He . . . relatives banged their heads against the wall, wailing loudly. In the synagogue, ten old men gathered to rend the heavens with their psalms.

Toward evening, the laboring woman recited her deathbed confession and took leave of her children. That was when the people of the gulch declared with one voice:

"We've got to bring Bubbe Henya back."

With quiet steps, with small steps, she came back to town. Deep sorrow shrouded her wan face. Her good, moist eyes looked off, over there, toward the graveyard. And that, in fact, was where she headed.

As they saw her coming back down the hill, with a confident step, her face shining with joy, people's hearts beat happily and they breathed ever so easily, ever so calmly:

"When Bubbe Henya puts her mind to something, it gets done."

When the gulch folk gathered on the eighth day for the circumcision, the baby's mother served the guests herself. . . . That Bubbe Henya was destined to live out her full allotment of seventy years was clear as day to them all. But she was torn from this world in the sixty-fifth year of her life, and this, now, is how it happened:

One fine summer day, a black cloud loomed over the gulch folk: their rabbi had laid himself down with no warning, become paralyzed, and lost the power of speech, and the doctor from up the hill had given up hope for his recovery.

The whole community, shaken to the core, gathered in the synagogue. A fast day was decreed, psalms were recited, loud sobs rose from the women's section, even the little children prayed their hearts out—but to no avail; in the midst of it all, the rabbi's wife stormed into the synagogue. Her face was as white as a sheet, she was screaming to high heavens:

"Friends, we are losing the crown of our shtetl. He already sees the grim old man wrapped in black before his very eyes."

When the crowd turned toward the door, they found their way blocked by a gaunt body:

"Where are you going?"

It was Bubbe Henya.

Her two radiant eyes—two seas of compassion—looked first at one of them, then at another:

"Friends, seventy are the years of a person's life. I am sixty-five—the rest I give to our rabbi—let anyone whose heart is so moved give a share, too. . . ."

And two days later, Bubbe Henya was going from house to house, saying:

"I'm donating a Torah scroll to the old synagogue—come celebrate with me."

By now she was walking with two canes.

And when the sun set and evening came, tens of thousands of little flames flickered in the air. It was the gulch folk, lighting the way for Bubbe Henya's canopy with candles and torches, lanterns and lamps. Klezmer musicians with long trumpets led the way for her, women adorned in satin and silk and the elderly rabbi surrounded by dignified old men walked behind her, and Bubbe Henya floated along under the wedding canopy with her Torah, the holy scroll pressed to her heart, two glistening tears in her eyes.

And when they placed the Torah scroll beside its sisters and closed the Holy Ark and covered it with its velvet curtain, Bubbe Henya jumped up to the pulpit, flung aside her two canes, and stretched her arms heavenward.

Suddenly she stood tall, her face became youthful, and her eyes—two black suns.

"Ay, ay, Father in heaven . . . Ay, ay, Master of the Universe! . . ."

With quick and sure steps she circled the pulpit, walked out of the synagogue, and turned toward the poorhouse:

"Ay, ay, Father in heaven . . . Ay, ay, Master of the Universe! . . ."

And now, hands linked together and a great circle formed, a beautiful circle, the klezmorim blew their trumpets, old folk snapped their fingers, women clapped their hands, and they surged and streamed closer and closer to the poorhouse. Ten thousand flames flickered in the still air. Far away, in the distant east, a pale morning star stared with amazement at the gulch.

The next night, the gulch folk made their way home from the graveyard, their faces white as shrouds. Every once in a while a sigh would escape one of them, quiver for a moment, and then fade away. A great darkness reigned, and each of them walked down that mountain alone, groping for solid ground beneath their feet. . . .

From the mountain glowed the enormous church, threatening them all with its uncanny pallor. Down in the gulch, the dogs howled.

✳ ☽ ✳

DVORA BARON *was born in a small town in Lithuania in 1887.*
Her father was a rabbi, and unlike most of his contemporaries, not only was he interested in educating his daughter in typical women's subjects, but he allowed her to attend the classes he taught the boys of the town (she sat behind a partition in the synagogue). She arrived on the literary scene in 1902, writing mostly in Hebrew—an instant marvel because she was female and was only fourteen years old, which was unheard of among Eastern European Hebrew writers at that time. She immigrated to Palestine in 1910. The first modern Hebrew woman writer, her stories focus on the shtetl and women's experiences in Jewish Eastern Europe. She died in 1956 in her apartment in Tel Aviv, having spent the previous thirty-three years as a shut-in and the last twenty years of her life completely bedridden. The stories reprinted in this collection are from her earlier Yiddish works.

BUBBE MALKE

Shira Gorshman

Translated by Jennifer Kronovet

Next to the old cemetery stood her tiny house with its short windows. All winter, the snow covered the roof down to those windows like a large wool hat over the eyes of a small child. During the summer, the earthen roof became overgrown with mint and chamomile. Tall flowers with white specks grew around the chimney from between the fallen leaves, forming a trim that decorated the smoke. Nasturtiums, with their red, velvety petals that Bubbe Malke was so fond of, tightened the narrow footpath that led to her little pine doorway.

The trees in the cemetery would reach the house and rustle green reminders in Bubbe's windows. These trees were useful to Bubbe. She gathered linden blossoms, which were good for warming up the bones, and picked mushrooms from under the aspens. She drilled small holes in the birches and attached clay jugs to catch the sap. The people of the town washed down the aftertaste of Sabbath meals with the birch brandy Malke made from this. Bubbe Malke often buried empty, uncorked bottles in the anthills. The clever ants would creep into the bottles like fools, and Bubbe Malke would pour whiskey over them. Old men and women with rheumatism used to praise this cure, saying, "If my bones are still creaking, thanks are due to Him first, but then to you. . . ." To which Bubbe Malke would tip back a small glass and respond modestly, "From Him or from me, from me or from the ants, as long as the bones are still creaking."

People in the town said that the old rabbi called on Malke and scolded her, saying, "You pick mushrooms from the cemetery and make scrub brushes with the straw you find out there. Shouldn't that be enough for you?! But you also plant carrots and beans between the graves—don't you have anything better to do? I've even heard that you brag that the carrots are so big they can't be pulled up, and that every bean pod is stuffed with beans like a woman's tongue with words."

From then on only wild leeks grew between the graves. Yet, Bubbe Malke maintained, her leek tzimmes tasted as if it were made with honey. Who needs carrots?

She always came—through winter snow, through autumn leaves—when a woman was giving birth, and each town urged her to move there.

"A person alone, long nights, it's sad. . . ."

Bubbe would answer, "First of all, in all my life I've never considered myself unhappy. Secondly, my craft needs a calm spirit. I can't count the number of times I felt as if I were the one giving birth. But I've barely cut the umbilical cord and already I've forgotten it all."

Once, at a lavish bris, Bubbe Malke drank cherry brandy from a teacup and ate an entire platter of chopped liver from rim to rim. As she was edging a deep glass bowl of gingerroots toward her, she noticed how Mendl, the servant, was looking at her in an oddly severe manner. Accidentally, she knocked over the bowl, and while shuffling to scrape up the ginger, she yelled, "Don't look at me like that. I've more than earned this food. The child, heaven help us, was breeched!"

And so a life stretched forward with childbirths, brises, weddings, funerals. . . .

Bubbe Malke—airing out her possessions—used to inspect her one woven shroud and then stow it away again at the very bottom of the trunk, thinking cheerlessly: This is no bridal veil, it can wait a bit. Her life was filled with reminders of the far past, with hopes of "in two years" and "in five years." Then, in an instant, everything became razed and emptied. . . .

The whole town is already vacant, and she has been forgotten. At night she sits by her small, curtained windows, running her finger over the crooked rows in a yellowed log book, remembering: "Abram, Rose, and their children: Hershel, Fyvish, Dina, Frieda, Joshua, Hannah, and their Benny, Nichola, Saul, Menachem, and Jonah." She follows their names with her finger until she begins shaking and closes her eyes, unable to rise. . . . Circles turn around yellow flames in which babies are burning. Her small house is filled with the cries of children . . . and she sits throughout the night, clothed, opening her eyes sporadically to chase this horror away. . . . She remains like this for weeks, waiting for the Angel of Death. . . .

But one night she rose, put on her garnet coat with the burgundy velvet lapel, and, without extinguishing the fire, without closing the door, left her home. In one of the villages she bartered her coat for a sheep's skin and a loaf of bread. Her sunken and wrinkled face was exposed above the collar like a piece of yellow, dry hide, and her blue, fully faded eyes looked like two deeply set stones. Now no one would mistake her for anything other than a peasant who had spent her whole life working in the fields. In a second town, she removed her large amber beads from her neck and used them to pay rent: an old couple let her their anteroom where the pig lived. Each night the old man would put a wool sock on the pig's nose so its snorting would not hinder Bubbe Malke's sleep, but she hardly slept. At dawn she would collect nettles and other grasses for the pig. She told the landlady that she was a skillful healer, but the town already had its own. No one would come to the stranger. Yet it didn't occur to anyone that she was a Jew, and Bubbe Malke began to believe that her craft could be of no use to her.

One evening when she was chopping nettles for the pig, an old peasant woman rushed into the anteroom, yanked on Bubbe Malke's sleeve, and said, "Come quickly! Vlades's wife has been in labor for two days and is about to die."

The old woman led Bubbe Malke into a spacious house with clean floors. Plaster walls had not yet been built; coarse wooden beams, still greenish from the moss that had grown on them, marked where the rooms would be. On top of plentiful bedding, with an icon hanging above her head, lay the woman in labor; her legs were supine, and her abdomen eclipsed her face. Back and forth, from the mirror to the stove, the master of the house paced.

"Sir! Put up some water! Give me a drink and something to eat also!"

She gulped down the drink, quickly ate a couple of roasted eggs, then attached two hand towels to the headboard and, leaning over the woman in labor, said sternly, "Do you want to live? Then help yourself! I have seen more women in child-birth than you have hair on your head. So, make a move! Take the towels, tighter, pull them toward you with all your strength! . . . Even harder! Bend in your knees, my clever girl,

no one can exit from a shut door! . . . Again, dear, harder. . . .
Sir! A cup of tea—half honey, half water . . . quicker! Now,
drink. One sip! One swallow! Again the towels—pull them to
you! Help yourself! Harder!"

This was how Bubbe Malke commanded, until the woman
giving birth let out an unearthly roar. Then Bubbe Malke
rolled up her sleeves and called to the master, "Pour for me!"
Holding her cleansed hands in front of her, she ran back to the
bed. With a muffled voice, as if she were afraid of scaring
someone, she beckoned: "Come quicker, fool, there is no place
for you in there anyhow. . . ."

She spoke more and more softly while the woman in labor
roared louder and louder, until a quiet smacking sound was
heard and a soft, brand-new "Ooh-ah."

Vlades stood and looked at the blue-brown, openmouthed,
squirming soul that Bubbe Malke held in her left palm. With
her right hand, she poured the lukewarm water over the baby
and joked, "My goodness, you have a peasant, weighs twelve
pounds!" She swaddled the baby and addressed Vlades. "So,
give me something to eat."

Vlades brought out the home brew again and filled two
glasses.

"No, no more is necessary. Enough! I'm not a drunk! I just
needed a drop of courage before. You drink and give me something to eat."

Vlades brought out butter and honey and a round loaf of
wheat bread, and Bubbe Malke smeared slice after slice.

"Ay, Bobke, you've done a day's work. If we fed you up a
little bit, you could have babies yourself."

"You think your wife had this baby? I had it for her. And
now it's time to go to sleep, because you're beginning to say
foolish things. Go, lie down, and I'll sit by the mother."

Days went by, and Bubbe Malke soon realized that Vlades

was the German-appointed governor of the town. Soon the mother started walking again. The newborn turned from red to pink, and his wide, flat nose became narrow. Bubbe Malke cured the thrush that grew in the baby's mouth by regularly wrapping soft linen around her little finger, dipping it in salt water, and wiping his tongue and gums. Each day she ate from one dish with the governor and his wife and quickly scraped up the fat with a spoon. She filled out into her own body again.

When Vlades was not in the house, his wife, Marina, would open a green trunk and, while presenting silver utensils, linens, and other items, ask, "What do you think, dear, that this is a sin? If we did not take it, as you know, others would take it. Isn't that so?"

Bubbe Malke would shake her head silently.

Every night she had the same dream: She is bringing the child to be circumcised and the *mohel* has Vlades's face. He unwraps the swaddling clothes and throws them back to her— and from them scatter many, many bloody little arms and legs. She screams in her sleep, and the governor screams at her, "Go make a bed in the summer half of the house. You're not letting me sleep, Bobke, and I've got enough unpleasant things in my head already."

Bubbe Malke would go beyond the summer half, to where her eyes would lead her. Her feeling for Vlades, even from their first meeting, was not mere hatred. It was a feeling blended from disgust, hatred, and curiosity.

One afternoon a peasant woman came into the house and frantically announced, "Three miles from here partisans burned the command post with the Germans inside it."

Marina burrowed into the soft bedclothes and howled. Vlades came in from the street and screamed, "How many times have I said not to let anyone enter the house. Their eyes are practically popping out with envy! They can't wait to get after me. You think I'm the only one who stole anything, and they're such honest people? Get out of bed, you pig!" He lifted his fists as if to punch Marina.

"Vlades, I'm scared, I have no strength . . . burn everything, throw everything away, I don't need anything!" she sobbed.

"Throw everything away?! You stinking lump! You didn't carry this all in, you won't be the one to throw it all away."

And Bubbe Malke, rocking the cradle, thought: Dear God, he doesn't deserve to hear one sound from his baby.

Up until then the house had been completely stuffed with possessions—silver utensils, dozens of Dutch linens, unused copper pots turning green on the stove with their lids upside down. All of this was stowed away. They ate with wooden forks and spoons and slept on their own woven burlap. The pillows were among the only objects still being used, patiently holding their heads each night. The clock told hour after hour, the mirror now reflecting merely a corner of the stove and the four ropes holding the crib, instead of everything that Vlades had showed off.

In the mornings, when Vlades combed his hair, Bubbe Malke was always reminded of Tessa, her neighbor Isaac's little girl: she had stood with raised hands by the mirror, winding her braid around her head—there was a mirror just like this in Isaac's house. Everyone in the town said that someone would surely snap Tessa up—the way she held herself . . . and now she lay with her parents and so many others in a huge grave.

From the mirror, Vlades would look around with his flax forelock over his indifferent face. Unable to hold back, Bubbe Malke once blurted, "Vlades, cover the mirror, it is the type of glass that is sensitive to heat, and being in this house is like being in a bath. Take good care of the mirror, it is obviously yours now!"

Vlades, covering up the mirror, said to himself, "Yes, why should we draw more attention to ourselves? In a year, I'll build a new house with a high ceiling made to measure for the mirror."

Bubbe Malke, mashing a boiled potato for the chicken with the handle of a hatchet, murmured into the cast-iron pot, "You should not live to see your son grown. May he be your last child."

The hatred Bubbe Malke felt toward Vlades kept her from sleep. At night she peered out from behind the stove, and no matter how dark it was in the house, she saw his face and the teeth in his open, snoring mouth. At one point he was delayed several days in a neighboring town. If he had bothered to read her look on his return, he would have realized that she had been waiting for him in dread.

About Marina she had long since made up her mind: bland porridge without salt or pepper. But because she thought of Vlades in an entirely different manner, she began spending whole days planning how to send Marina away with the baby. To add to all of this, Marina went around sighing and moaning about something she was clearly concealing from Bubbe Malke. Bubbe Malke didn't ask any questions, but eventually Marina unburdened herself to Bubbe when Vlades was not in the house. "A week from Sunday," she said, "Germans will enter the town. Vlades says that he will invite them to our house and ordered me to make roasted geese with apples. I can cook geese with cabbage, but this is the first time I've heard of cooking them with apples . . . and you know him. Right? If he says something, it must be done."

"So, next Sunday, there is still time! And anyway, what does it matter to him how they're roasted, as long as they're roasted!" Bubbe Malke consoled Marina.

They whispered for hours until Marina burst into tears in

front of Vlades. "I want to go to my parents, dear Vlades, I miss them!"

Bubbe Malke cut in, "If you had common sense, you would say, 'Go, my wife, take this child and go!' Is it necessary that she pace the house? Your guests are German, don't forget, and Germans don't deny themselves anything. Refreshments are refreshments, roasted geese are, of course, delicious, and after several glasses of whiskey a young wife is not too bad, either! And while I'm speaking, I should say, Vlades . . . I think it is enough of my eating your bread. It is time to move on. Thirty miles from here I have relatives. When spring comes, I will help them manage the house."

"Have you suddenly taken it into your head that I am going to lay gunpowder under your ass? Can I say something? My wife can go! And you stay! She will return, you see," Vlades said, interrupting Bubbe Malke's speech.

In the morning, he himself drove Marina away. When he came back, he could not stop fussing and repeating, "The oven is whitewashed, the walls are thoroughly scraped, and the floors—we could eat porridge off of them."

Now alone with Vlades, Bubbe Malke became as restless and strained as she had been when she first arrived in the town. Then, the idea that the peasants and townspeople might realize she was a Jew had plagued her. She had slowly adjusted to this fear, but now she tensed up at every step, every squeak of the door, every move Vlades made—everything set her trembling. She did not for one moment let go of the strength and obstinacy that had served her all her life. She maintained an outward calm, but it was only outward calm: her old mind and her observant heart did not rest. Sometimes it seemed to her that it would have been simpler and better had she stayed in her village. There are only empty cradles there and the wind can rock them, she thought, watching how Vlades controlled the town.

After Marina went away with the baby, Vlades worked all the time. He was a wealthy miller's son, and it was not for nothing that the Germans had made him a governor. Vlades brought the Angel of Death to those who had sons, brothers, and fathers in the Red Army or the partisan forces. He shared with the Germans the belongings of those who were slaughtered, and he never knew the meaning of enough. Everything suited him: an iron pole unscrewed from a neighbor's house, fruit trees dug up with the roots from a stranger's orchard.

"He should be damned, no cradle should exist in his house. He should never hear the scream of a newborn again," Bubbe Malke whispered, and then cursed herself: "Senile, base creature! You live in Vlades's house and yet don't choke on your food!" She was bewildered and split in two. One Bubbe Malke wandered over ruins in her village, another never took her eyes off of Vlades. He plundered and helped to kill my people—his people should also be plundered and slaughtered, she thought at night, trembling, hearing voices say, "Save us!"

The awaited Sunday came. Bubbe Malke stuffed the geese with fat and grains of wheat. She put them in a scoured copper pan, topped them with herbs and onions, and stuck everything in the oven. When the geese were finished and she took them out, they were perfectly browned and smelled so wonderful that Vlades bolted the door. She taught him how to make a delicious liquor from the home brew: she laid dried cherries and plums in the samovar, poured in the home brew and a little bit of honey, and boiled it. Tasting the liquor, Vlades praised it forcefully, "At my house, they will swallow their tongues. Ah, Bobke, you have Lithuanian hands and a Lithuanian head on your shoulders!"

When Vlades went off to meet the guests, Bubbe Malke scrubbed and washed the house, put a cast-iron pot of lye on the stove to boil, and placed the roasted geese and the samovar on the table. Dinnertime came and it was unclear why Vlades had not returned with the guests. Alone all day, she had not eaten anything. For her, it had been a day to fast; the odors from the roasting food repulsed her. Eventually she climbed behind the stove and covered herself with a pelt. No cradle should stay near him, dear God, she thought, falling asleep. In her dream, people knocked on the door and cried, "Get up, we're saved, the Red Army is coming!" She stumbled out from her sleeping place and let Vlades in.

"What is with you, Bobke, I thought someone had killed you. I've been knocking and knocking, damn you. These three lovely geese are to be wasted! They came, they took who they wanted, and they didn't come to me!"

"Oh well, the geese won't get thrown out," Bubbe Malke consoled Vlades.

But Vlades did not hear what she said. He had already comforted himself. He sat at the table, sliced the geese, and toasted himself.

And she stood near the stove with her hands behind her apron.

"Bobke! You aren't pleasing me! Sit at the table!"

"No, roasted food is not for my teeth, I already ate potato kasha," she answered.

"Potato kasha!" Vlades repeated drunkenly. Bubbe Malke remained near the stove and watched as he drank glass after glass. Her eyes were half-shut but she could clearly see that it was the right time.

"Enough drinking!" she announced.

"I will drink as much as I want, old thorn! Watch your prodding words," he exclaimed, and made as if to come at her.

Bubbe Malke began to sense that her resolve could go up like smoke. You have trampled green shoots and blossoms and chopped down oak trees, and I should watch my sharp words? she thought without lifting her eyes from him. Seeing that he had cut off a drumstick and put it in his mouth, she grabbed the cast-iron pot with immense force, as if she were saving a woman in childbirth from the last, hardest pangs of labor, ran over, and poured the boiling liquid on him.

Heavy steam filled the house. She dragged a pelt from behind the oven, pulled it over her shoulders, and went outside. It seemed as if the street should have been full of people. She looked around in wonder: a star-filled night, a light chill. She put her hands in her sleeves, buttoned up, and thought: Thank the One whose Name cannot be uttered—that man will not look at any more cradles. She raised her eyes to the stars and asked, If possible, Father above, let me live, let me live a tiny bit more, no more than that. . . .

★ ☾ ★

SHIRA GORSHMAN *was born in 1906 in Krakes, Lithuania. She and her family fled to Odessa during World War I. Gorshman left her family before she was fourteen and had a daughter at sixteen. In 1924, Gorshman, active in the Zionist movement, moved to Palestine, where she worked on a left-wing commune and for the poet Hayyim Nahman Bialik. In the late 1920s, Gorshman moved to the Soviet Crimea to help build Jewish agricultural collectives. In Crimea, she met the painter Mendel Gorshman. They married and moved to Odessa and then to Moscow. Gorshman began writing stories in the 1930s; these stories were published in Russian, anti-Fascist newspapers and in anthologies. Her first book, 33 noveln [33 short stories], was not published until 1961. She went on to publish three additional books, the last in 1998. Gorshman died in Israel in 2001.*

Scenes on a Bare Canvas

Blume Lempel

Translated by Sheva Zucker

Over the sun-drenched streets of Tel Aviv, I followed the coffin that took Zosie, the girl from my hometown, to her eternal rest. Black crows in the background of my thoughts hovered noisily around the deceased, blocking the roads, the passersby, the black car that drove ahead, not letting me reach the paths and detours that had led Zosie to prostitution.

It was my first visit to Israel. I was getting ready to go to Eilat. I had already checked out of my room in Tel Aviv and packed my toothbrush in my valise, when the head of my hometown association called me and asked me to attend the funeral.

I had long ago learned to pass over the place where my cradle had stood and to find my beginnings in the stony strata of history: I searched for the living source beneath the time-covered sands of the Negev, setting sail through its gates and steering my ship on its destined course.

With make-believe frost I froze the window to the past. White trees and dead roses are always in bloom there, not as a memorial, but as a reminder that the layer of ice is thin, deceptive, an illusory film over the black abyss, where snakes and scorpions still feed on the remains of the unburied sacrificial victim.

Whenever I chance to meet a person who escaped from the abyss, I look at him with fear and expectation, lest I uncover something beyond my comprehension.

I sit in the car and watch the carriage carrying Zosie's martyred remains. I imagine the sounds of the letters *samech* and *zayin* dangerously sharpened in her Polish name. Zosie, Zoshke the bookkeeper's spoiled daughter, is racing around on her bicycle. Her windblown hair, blond like the furniture in her father's parlor. Zosie laughs, and the two rows of trees respond with a resounding "Yes!"

Many girls in our town spoke Polish. Zosie's Polish had deep roots, she had drunk it in with the milk of her Gentile nanny. In her Polish lay the stamp of her divided personality.

I turn the pages that are running through my mind. The black crows in the background recede. The road, open and free, leads back into our town. I follow the local princess over the shadowy corners of the earth. I follow her to the sea, to the blue shores of the Mediterranean, into which she had thrown herself. I do not see how she looks now. Nailed in her coffin, she is safe from human curiosity. She is no longer for sale, neither for bread nor out of despair. Against her will she came into this world, and against her will she is leaving it.

Three other people are sitting in the car with me. They, too, turn pages, readied with judgment. "She lived with an Arab, hung around on the streets." They recount facts that they had seen with their own eyes. I try to sense the unseen. I don't trust the eye, which relies on facts. Half-truths can mislead, turn the guilt away from the murderer, and cast it onto the victim. The corpse is silent, and the murderer—comfortable in his respectable status as citizen, father, and perhaps even grandfather—lightheartedly sips his beer, growing fatter day by day.

"Why didn't she adjust to the new way of life? Why didn't she become a productive individual like all the other new immigrants?"

I don't answer these questions. The truth, concealed beneath bloody bandages, keeps one from touching the painful wound. The surface also shows that fixed measurements do not fit all bodies. I think that no suicide is committed by accident. Every hour, every moment, the suicide holds the slaughtering knife to his throat. Zosie took her life in Felix's attic—her first spiritual suicide. The physical act came later, in degrees, step by step.

I wander about on the victim's strange paths. I know her murderer. For a piece of bread and ham, he gorged himself on her white, fully blossomed, sun-ripened young body. And perhaps she had even taken her life before this? Perhaps her life had come to its end on that wild autumn night when Felix came riding like a prince on a white horse? Under his arm he carried a loaf of bread, a peasant skirt, a vest, and a blouse. Zosie put on this clothing, kissed her mother's wet face, black as that autumn night. . . . She kissed the dog that lay at the door, who did not know that the house he was guarding was now a prison. She kissed her father's bullet-ridden body, which lay abandoned in the middle of the marketplace. She kissed the piano, the garden bordering the house. Everything, she gathered everything into herself, and hid it as ransom in the cellars of her being.

Behind Felix's stable, on the downhill path, was a quiet pond framed by laurel trees. Green slime covered the surface.

Beneath the tightly drawn film, fish spawned. On a sunny day Zosie could see the fish moving about. She could see the black rings on the green, mirrorlike surface. Through the narrow crevices of her hiding place in Felix's attic, the rings became the sole departure point for her hungry glance. She could look and think about the ring that she would create when she threw herself into the water. Buried deep in the hay, she had time to mourn her own death, to follow her own funeral.

Now, on the way to her funeral, I wanted to tell her that I was looking through her eyes, feeling with her sensibility. I try on situations in sweaty beds for size, with her fingers I caress bodies of purchased air. I do it in the spirit of the child whom I knew. I search for a hint of the present in the sunken world of the past. By that light, or rather, by its shadow, I want to touch upon the why. In my thoughts I descend into the abyss, covering the overgrown path to the past.

Long, long ago, when I used to bring my father's coffee to the butcher shop, I would stop in front of Zosie's beautiful garden on my way home. I would stand on tiptoe and, from over the fence, gaze in wonder at the golden lilies that grew around her house.

With great regret, I would think about that which could have been but never was. If my grandfather hadn't been so fanatically honest and had promised Zosie's father's parents the dowry they demanded, I would have been the bookkeeper's daughter, played the piano, and been preparing to go to Lemberg to study. But my grandfather did not want to, and perhaps could not, go against his deeply rooted ethical-religious spirit and make a promise that he knew he could not keep. The bookkeeper and my mother parted forever. He married the rich man's daughter, my mother—a butcher boy.

I would stand in front of the fence and fantasize about how it would have been if it had been, had been . . .

Now I am escorting the bookkeeper's daughter to her eternal rest. I, the tourist from Paris, remember how willingly I would have given up my worldly ambitions to study in Lemberg.

Through the little roof window of my Paris mansard, I would gaze at the four-cornered piece of sky that my destiny had allotted me and think of Zosie's luxuriant slumbering garden. I would curse the luck that had, on my way to Israel, left me stuck in Paris.

Zosie didn't want to, and didn't have to, go to Israel. For her the vine blossomed with all the magic hues of the preening peacock that inhabits the dreams of every young woman.

How could she have known that the very civilization whose fingers wrote the notes she charmed forth from the piano was, with those same fingers, drawing up the death sentence for her people? How could she have known that form and harmony were the seductive song of the Lorelei, the cannibal's facade behind which he sharpens his crooked teeth? Protected and sheltered, like the golden lily in her father's garden, Zosie did not see the cannibal's teeth. With the strength and right of every living being she shone toward the light of the sun. Endowed with all the attributes necessary to grow and thrive, Zosie was ripe for scattering her own seeds in God's ready earth.

The pages that I turn are unwritten. They go round and round like images in a broken mirror. I am thinking that the earth to which Zosie is now returning holds the bones of another harlot, the biblical harlot Tamar. Tamar sat at the fork in the road where the constellations part and conquered men with her seductive charm. I search for a spark of Tamar's passion in the image of Zosie lodged deeply in my memory. I look for the whore's lust in her dimples, in her pink, Polish-speaking lips that surely did not know what the word *whore* even meant. I look into her eyes, the reflection of her soul. Her character, not yet ripened, torn out by the root, is borne by the wind to the corners of the earth. I search for the continuation of generations of female modesty. I search for her father's clearly defined path, and another image rises up before me: her uncle Shloyme the Russian. I don't force the image; I let it grow to full size. I relive the fear that his death cast upon me, penetrating my dreams long after I had left my town. His imposing figure lifts itself out of the fog: gray eyes, black bushy eyebrows, shoulders broad, proud, and straight. It was from his mouth that I first heard the words *All is vanity*. When Shloyme the Russian spoke, every word was aflame, reflecting the sorrow and anger that had gradually consumed him. I imagined then that this was how Job must have looked sitting in the ashes. "What's the difference between man and beast," he would say, "when even the rabbi touches his wife on the tit?"

These words, said just like that, Saturday afternoon at our house caused a revolution in my thinking. I too began to ask questions that led me away from the beaten path. When Shloyme the Russian lay on his deathbed, he wanted only one thing: that God give him strength enough to get out of bed, set the house on fire, and, together with his possessions, burn on God's sacrificial altar of life. And this was what he actually did. People said that years before, he had been excommunicated for reading Spinoza and for walking beyond the limits allowed on the Sabbath.

Had Zosie also sought a path to God through alien gardens? Had the tragic worm that had eaten away at Shloyme the Russian also lodged itself in her soul and forced her to go, not on the main road, but off the beaten path, to the side? Forced her to walk beyond the limit, to excommunicate herself?

Shloyme the Russian had a legitimate complaint against his Maker. His wife, who was barren, was the first to turn away from God. She called upon all sorts of black powers, demons, and spirits, witches who fed her wild herbs and cheated her out of a fortune, promising that help would come to her if she followed all their instructions. So Shorke the Russian did as she was told. Around her neck she strung the claws of a crow, in her bosom she placed the hairs of a panther. Around midnight she would bathe in the milk of a pregnant cow, she outlined her navel with the blood of a bull. Her hair loose, her eyes painted with soot, her cheeks reddened by chicory paper— Shorke the Russian came to her husband to make her fertile.

It's quiet in the car. I look out at the winding streets of Jaffa. The sky is clear, blue as the blue of a prayer shawl, without a single cloud on which to anchor one's thoughts. The carriage carrying the corpse is in front of us. The parallels get longer and longer. Characters that on the surface bear no relationship to one another form connections like roots beneath the earth. Through secret underground channels they penetrate Zosie's personal frame. Out of the former child, they help me to construct—a woman.

I see the woman in Felix's attic. She too speaks to God. She begs him to take care of her mother, her little sister. She prays for so long that there remains nothing more for her to pray for. The city is destroyed. The past is destroyed. And maybe there was no past at all. The abyss into which she gazes has lost all distinguishing features. No trace of yesterday. No hint of tomorrow. The woods, in their innocence, blossom. The fish in the pond spawn. The cicadas call to one another. They seek one another out amid the long grass of the meadow. He and She meet. Zosie knows that she is pregnant. The cow in the stable is also pregnant. Both are silent. The cow chews her cud and ruminates. Zosie picks up a piece of straw and does the same. She thinks mostly about food. Not about the wild strawberries and cream that her mother used to serve her, but about bread and salt and perhaps also about a clove of garlic.

The hens in the yard peck at the seeds and go on with their quarrels. The hens in the yard don't know that man, out of his own self-interest, locked them up a ghetto and with cynical cold human calculation set up in a comfortable death camp for them. Whenever he gets the urge he'll grab the cleaver and chop off the head of a white hen as he whistles himself a tune. Zosie is not afraid of death. She, like the cicadas in the grass, accepts Felix's favors. She doesn't tell him she is pregnant.

Felix has a wife and children. He keeps Zosie hidden away in his mother's attic. He holds his mother responsible for Zosie's safety. Felix's mother knows that her son is not fooling around. She knows her son's passions. So she is anxious about the Jewess and doesn't let her come down from the attic. Hidden in the oats for the cow, she brings her food. Felix's mother is talkative. She loves to recount in as much detail as possible how the Nazis shot all the Jews to death, piled them together like fathoms of wood, poured kerosene on them, and set them on fire. Felix's mother does not hide her satisfaction. Although she hates the Germans, she enjoys their cruelty. "We should have gotten rid of them long ago," she says.

Zosie doesn't tell Felix what his mother said. She stopped expecting any indulgence a long time ago, both from God and from man. She lies in the attic listening to the front drawing nearer day by day. The stable vibrates from the heavy grenades that roll like spring thunder. Zosie doesn't wait for tomorrow. She also doesn't put much stock in today. Now that liberation is near, for some reason, she just wants to sleep. In her dreams she had a past. She has a father, a mother, a clearly defined path; a straight line between two mountains of snow. She is gliding on skates, diamonds gleam in the sun. Unable to bear her great happiness, she closes her eyes, but only for a moment—then loses her way in a fierce blizzard.

Zosie is sleeping. She wants to gorge herself on the dream. She wants to choke on the dream. Precisely now, when the liberator is knocking at the door, she cannot find the strength to get up and open it. So she lies there listening to the cells dividing in her bloodstream. She takes her pulse, her heartbeat. Deeper and deeper she descends into the black shafts of consciousness. Inch by inch, Zosie withdraws into herself. The footsteps of the liberator resound rhythmically on the road. She has no road. Her paths are overgrown with grass. She digs beneath the earth, under the weeds, touches the root with its suicidal poison—then she gets up. Climbs down from the attic. She stops at the cow. They look at each other for a long time, mutely and full of understanding.

Downhill, among freshly planted flower beds, Zosie walks slowly and deliberately. She goes over to the slimy green pond, closes her eyes, and throws herself in.

Zosie opened her eyes in the hospital. A congealed piece of blood quivered in a glass next to her bed. "Four months old," said the nurse. "Everything in you had to be removed. Everything in you was rotten."

Zosie smiles and says nothing. She doesn't ask, she doesn't want to know. And perhaps she is thinking of her aunt, Shorke the Barren? It really makes no difference to her. She lies in bed so long that she has to be taken out. She roams from camp to camp together with other wind-driven wanderers. But here, too, she is alone. Zosie tries to go with the current. But the torn branches, the leaves, and the stones that the current had carried off—blocked her path, placed their dead weight on her young shoulders, atrophied her will, separated her from the living course of history, drew her to the abyss, to the bottom.

Sometimes, when Felix would torment her, the tears

would come like a kindly rainfall. He was a rod of chastise-
ment, and she accepted his lashes for the sin of having let her
mother and sister go to their deaths alone. Each bite of bread
she ransomed through inflicting pain on herself and through
self-hate. This feeling of guilt also followed her to Israel.

In conflict with herself, in conflict with the reality to which
she couldn't adjust, Zosie looked for and found a meaning in
self-abasement; the deeper she sank into the swamp, the more
justified she felt in walking about on God's earth.

Zosie lay on the bottom, letting herself waste away. Like
the legendary Prometheus, she stood with her belly open,
exposed to the vultures of the world. And when the birds
found nothing more to peck at—she went off to the sea, just
as she had once gone to the pond, and threw herself in.

I am sitting alone in the car, wrapped in deadly silence. I,
too, am avoiding reality. From afar I see them covering the
grave. A Jew with a long beard and a broad hat recites a prayer.
I see that he's in a hurry. He'll soon repeat the prayer that he's
saying at another grave. I don't hear what he's saying. I listen
to the prayer that is trembling inside me. The prayer that can
never be repeated. It is a prayer without words, deeply interred
in the collective conscience of my people. The Jew with the
long beard is in a hurry. Somewhere another corpse waits for
him. The prayer that I'm saying has no end. It is seething and
fermenting like a chemical mixture on the eve of becoming. In
the mixture I seek the lost symbol. I must find it, cleanse it of
the filth, of the impurity of shame.

I know I shall return, perhaps tomorrow or maybe even in
a year. I will erect a tombstone out of the newly found symbol,
with no words at all, a bare stone. The passerby who stops will
have to construct her image himself from that which was not
said. He will stand before the stone like a master before his

bare canvas. Among all the possible pictures that will come to mind—he must also come to realize that Zosie is the crow that pecks at my conscience.

✡   ☾   ✡

BLUME LEMPEL *was born in Khorostkov, Galicia, in 1907. There she attended* cheder *and a Hebrew elementary school. In 1929 she moved to Paris, and in 1939 she settled in New York. She made her literary debut with a story in the Yiddish newspaper* Der tog *under the pseudonym Rochel Halperin and her work appeared in the most prestigious Yiddish newspapers and magazines, including* Morgn frayhayt, Di goldene keyt, Tsukunft, Zayn, *and* Kheshbn. *She published two collections of short stories,* A rege fun emes *[A Moment of Truth] and* Balade fun a cholem *[Ballad of a Dream]. Although she herself did not live through the Holocaust, she wrote often of those who did. Her stories are remarkable for their deep psychological probing, emotional intensity, and haunting imagery. She died in 1999.*

THE FOURTH MITZVAH

From "Tulye Shor Tells"

Kadya Molodowsky

Translated by Kathryn Hellerstein

A person would not be able to live in this world if not for the bit of goodness that he has seen with his own eyes—this is what Tulye Shor said to me. She was sitting on the steps of a large building, the way you sit on your own earthen stoop in Frampolye. She looked at the noisy street, at the automobiles, with such eyes—as if there were no automobiles, but only sheep walking back from the fields; sheep hurrying home, as a storm approaches. She was gray, and I was of the opinion that she was old. And I gave her a perhaps somewhat astonished look when she said to me, as if I were an old acquaintance of hers:

"Have a seat. What's the hurry?"

This was the first time in my life that a complete stranger had out of the blue started talking to me and then invited me to sit down.

So I sat down next to her.

"Where do you come from?" I asked her.

"I know, does it make a difference where one comes from? . . . From the world. From Frampolye. Fate decreed that I should see America, and it is identical, identical."

"Who did you come to here?"

"I came to join a son. So he took me off the ship, dressed me like an empress, and gave me a few dollars. 'I'll give you the same every week,' he said, and he gives."

The woman dressed like an empress sat on the steps in a red-and-white-checked cotton dress.

"You're looking at my dress? This is a comfortable dress. I like comfortable things. These shoes are comfortable, too."

I glanced at her shoes. Thick, black shoes.

"Ten dollars a week he gives me, my son, every Thursday. Thursday evening he comes, gives me the money, gives me a kiss, and goes away until the next Thursday. This is the way I live, with his money and with a kiss. If not for the goodness I've seen with my eyes, I wouldn't be able to live."

"He has children, your son?"

She made a motion with her head that meant neither yes nor no. It meant only one thing—that she didn't want to talk about it.

"And your husband?"

"My husband?" She pronounced the words with a hopeless indifference. "And how did I come here? Soon after the wedding, my husband left for America. Left, so I received letters from him for half a year, and after that, it was as if he'd drowned. I used to be unable to sleep for entire nights. I lay there, thinking, Where is he? Where on earth am I? What's one to do? Then my son was born . . . enough thinking."

She scraped both her hands over her gray hair.

"That's when I turned gray, not from now. At age twenty-four, the snow fell out of me . . . until I was helped. . . ."

"Helped?"

"Yes, back home in Frampolye there was a 'Little Tatar,' as they called him; a Jew, he had a small soap factory. Made soap. The entire shtetl bought from him, all the villages around. The Little Tatar became rich. A short man, always walking around in a green jacket, raking up money from the shtetl. Who ever thought about him? Not even once a year.

"Once I was lying there before dawn. My child was sleeping near me in the cradle. The sky had already begun to turn gray—when suddenly someone knocked at my window. The window faced the street. My heart knocked! Maybe my husband had suddenly remembered me. . . . Maybe he had sent a telegram. I looked at the window—lo! There stood the Little Tatar in his green jacket. I almost spat! What was he doing here? So he says to me, the Little Tatar:

"'Tulye, come over to my place later, I need to speak with you.' And he went away.

"I could not lie still anymore. I got up, cooked up some food for the child, straightened up the house, could hardly wait until the moment the sun came up, and I took off for the Little Tatar's. His factory stood in a narrow alley. I arrived, he was standing on the porch in his green jacket.

"'Good morning,' I said to him, and waited.

"'Good morning yourself,' he answered me, and put a question to me:

"'From what do you live, Tulye?'

"'What?' I answered him, and I shouted, 'What? Should I go tell a Little Tatar a story?'

"'A person has to live from something,' he said to me. 'You will collect money from the stores, and I will pay you by the week. . . .'

"And he handed me a list of his customers, the store-keepers. I earned so much from him that a wealthy house-holder in the city would have made a fine living from it. I sewed myself a dress and walked around every day, collecting the money. Like a grande dame, I walked about through the city, raised the child, my son, gave alms generously, and joined the association that provides dowries for poor brides. Collected coins for them. All the funds used to pass through my hands. I grew prosperous. But however many times I tried to learn from the Little Tatar why it had occurred to him to knock on my windowpane at dawn, so that I should become prosperous—I could not find this out from him. He had the habit of smoking a pipe, like a Gentile. He used to smoke the pipe and ask me again:

"'Things bad for you, working for me?'

"'God forbid, as good as in Paradise, but I want to know.'

"Nevertheless, one time I found out. The Little Tatar, Kabaner, they called him, fell ill. He had a wife somewhere in Galicia, but he lived with an elderly mother. Since he was sick, I went to him—to cook for him, to serve him something, to place a cloth on his head, what wouldn't I do for him? He was my savior. He lay in a fever and calculated the accounts for his soap factory. I asked him with a laugh:

"'Honorable Mr. Kabaner, what on earth possessed you that time, to come to my house before dawn and knock on the windowpane?'

"'You really want to know? Ha?'

"When a person lies in a fever, he keeps nothing hidden. When a person's head is burning, his tongue loosens.

"I changed the washcloth on his forehead.

"'Good,' he said. 'Good. . . .' And he told me this story:

"His mother had four little boys. He was the fourth. His three brothers all died before the age of thirteen. When he turned twelve, his mother almost went out of her mind with fear. Everyone was terrified that something would happen to him. And there was a Jewish shoemaker in their shtetl, a joker. So Kabaner's mother went to the shoemaker, ordered a pair of shoes for the child for Passover.

"'He should only wear them in good health,' she said.

"'Why not?' said the shoemaker.

"'He should only be healthy,' answered his mother.

"'Why not, who would prevent him?' said the shoemaker, the way a joker speaks.

"'He should only have long years.'

"'Why not?' said the joker. 'Is living long a trick? Absolutely not a trick. All you have to do is to drink a shot of schnapps every day and, every ten years, do a good deed without expecting thanks.' Thus pronounced the shoemaker and licked the cobbler's thread. 'There are no tricks in the world,' he said. 'Whoever wants to, can live a long life.'

"'Coming home, my mother implored me to do a good deed every ten years without expecting thanks. The fourth decade had ended, so I knocked on your windowpane. My eyes were opened,' the little Tarter concluded. 'No need to wear out my feet going to collect money from the stores. I'd rather pay you, Tulye.'

"When the Little Tatar got well, he asked me once:

"'Tulye, did I perhaps talk deliriously in my fever?'

"'No, didn't say a thing,' I told him.

"'Didn't tell you about a shoemaker?'

"'What shoemaker? . . . I don't know anything.'

"'I know, a person with a fever . . .' And he puffed on his pipe, greatly satisfied.

"But I had learned the story."

The woman suddenly rose to her feet.

"Today is Thursday. I've got to go. My son will come soon, Thursday."

It seemed a shame to me that the woman was leaving. I caught up to her and asked:

"And what were the three good deeds he'd already done, the Little Tatar?"

"What do I need with his good deeds, since I have my own? A person has enough to tell about oneself . . . and especially concerning Tulye Shor. Enough has been revealed about my life."

When Tulye Shor stood up, I saw that her red-and-white-checked dress was not exactly new. A small patch was sewn with delicate stitches between the pleats. She noticed that I was looking at her dress and said:

"You think that I don't have any dresses. I could be dressed up like an empress. But I like comfortable things."

✹ ☾ ✹

KADYA MOLODOWSKY, *born in 1894, was a major figure in the Yiddish literary scene both in Warsaw (from the 1920s through 1935) and in New York (where she lived from 1935 until her death in 1975). A teacher in the Yiddish schools in Warsaw as a young woman, she was best known for her children's poems. After she came to the United States, she wrote for the Yiddish press and founded and edited a literary journal,* Sviva, *which she published for three decades. In addition to six major books of poems, published between 1927 and 1965, as well as plays and essays, Molodowsky published two novels—*Fun lublin biz nyu-york: togbuch fun Rivke Zilberg *[From Lublin to New York: Diary of Rivke Zilberg] (1942) and* Baym toyer: roman fun dem lebn in yisroel *[At the Gate: a Novel of Life in Israel] (1967)—and a collection of short stories,* A shtub mit zibn fentster *[A House with Seven Windows] (1957), from which "The Fourth Mitzvah" is translated.*

THE DEATH OF MY AUNT

Blume Lempel

Translated by Ellen Cassedy

In the early hours after midnight, the telephone sounds entirely different. At any rate, so it seemed to me when the metallic jangle pounced like a thief, putting a swift end to my dreams and rousing me from bed. I ran down the long, dark corridor to the dining room and reached for the receiver.

"Yes?" I croaked.

At first I couldn't catch who was on the line. "Who did you say is speaking?" I asked again.

"The old age home on Howard Avenue," a voice answered.

I felt for a chair and sat down, because the spiders that nest in hidden places had come out into the open and with their thin, hairy little legs were tightening the loose strands of their webs. I clutched the receiver with both hands and waited.

"Are you all right, Mrs. Lempel?" His feigned politeness was enraging. I was tempted to ask whether he'd called at two o'clock in the morning just to find out how I was. But my throat closed up.

The voice on the other side of the night started up again. "I'm sorry to say we have some sad news for you. Your aunt— your aunt—Rochel Halperin is no longer among the living."

The flush that had broken out all over my body turned into a chill; then I was hot again. With the receiver still at my ear, I managed to open the window. A cold gust of wind swept over me. A car sped by; in the glow of the headlights I could see it was snowing. The grass around the house was already white.

"Mrs. Lempel?"

"Yes?"

"We'll be arranging for the funeral first thing in the morning. We'd like you to be here then."

I waited a moment. "When did it happen?"

"Saturday at five in the afternoon," he answered.

His cool demeanor made me want to scream, curse, scratch, and claw. Why, why had they waited until two o'clock in the morning before calling me? Why had they allowed her to die alone?

"Mrs. Lempel, I see that you're upset. I understand your situation, and I don't want to argue with you. But you must understand—"

I closed the window and tried to understand why he was calling on Sunday, when she'd suffered the first heart attack Thursday. From what he said, on Friday she'd improved a bit; then Saturday morning she'd had the second attack. She'd wrestled with the Angel of Death, held out till late afternoon. . . .

I couldn't listen anymore, so I hung up the phone and went back to bed.

My husband and children had slept through the whole thing. I didn't want to wake them now—what for?

So she'd waited for me, hoping I'd come to her. *Got mayner,* why hadn't they called? Why had they inflicted this torment on her—on me? Abruptly I sat up in bed. I wanted to call the home and scream: "Murderers! Robbers! For the cost of a lousy phone call you destroy the lifelong dream of a poor old woman?"

But instead of going to the telephone, I went to the window and parted the curtains. I looked out at the tree swaying in the wind. The snow had turned into a heavy rain, and I saw that the bare branches of my tree were filled with keening women wrapped in black shawls. They had settled on the bushes and on the barbed-wire fence, too, and in my aunt's voice they were speaking to me: "Remember, be sure to give me a decent burial the way I asked you to. . . . Do not disgrace my dead body. . . . No lipstick, no powder. . . . Examine my shroud, make sure it hasn't, God forbid, picked up any mites. . . . Do not forget the Willett Street rabbis. For the sake of charity, they should say kaddish and study Mishnah. Remember! Remember!"

"I remember," I answered into the pillow.

I pulled the covers over my head, but the wailing women in the March wind kept up their lament. They demanded that I read and understand the windblown pages of my aunt's life. Eyes shut, I gazed upon the narrow lane where my aunt was born and where she grew up in the home of her father the *melamed*. Here she was as a little girl, playing with the boys who studied at the *cheder* with her father. Here she was as a grown woman, sitting at the machine, sewing bridal garments for other women's weddings. She sewed and sewed, until white began to show in her jet-black braids. Then my aunt bowed to her father's wishes and married a widower with grown children. When her father the *melamed* died, her husband took over the *cheder*, and his children left for America. My aunt's mother moved away to live with her older daughter, my own mother. Just before the Second World War, my aunt and her husband arrived in New York.

Her husband didn't last long. The strange new country sapped his will to live. He fell ill and soon died. After his death, his children washed their hands of her. Alone in a strange world, without a relative or a protector, her old home in ruins, my aunt drifted from place to place, hungry, not knowing where to turn, until someone suggested she clean houses for a living.

To ward off the humiliations of the outside world, my aunt took refuge in the secret passages of her own being. There she found a strength that guided her, motivated her to go on with her life. With every punishment in this world of lies and false-hoods, she attained a higher moral standing in the World of Truth beyond the grave. She looked forward to the just and agreeable World to Come, knowing that there she would be rewarded. Every moment of every day, every day of the year, she prepared herself for the journey to the other world. Mondays and Thursdays, in accordance with the old custom, she fasted half the day.

When we arrived in America, we tracked down my aunt on Powell Street in Brownsville. She was living in a dark cubicle; the landlady kept the toilet locked. That very day, we moved my aunt to our house on Ocean Avenue. We gave her a room with a window overlooking Prospect Park. My aunt, who was barely sixty years old, was already well along on the road to the other world. She didn't interfere with the running of the household. She cooked for herself in her room, kept kosher, prayed in the morning and in the evening. Forever bent over her holy books, she rarely lifted her eyes to see what was happening here on God's earth.

As evening fell, when her room began to grow dark and the shadows pressed in from every corner, when she had finished eating, said her prayers, made up her bed, and placed a bowl of water on the night table for the next morning's ritual hand washing—then my aunt would emerge from her room to tell the children a story.

She'd recount the tale of the little old lady who had lots and lots of children—dark, charming little girls and boys—Yiddish-speaking, Torah-studying, God-fearing Jewish children.

Once, when the little old lady had to go into the forest to gather kindling, she warned the children to be good and say their prayers before bed, so that no evil would befall them.

The children did as they were told. They said their prayers and went to sleep.

Then a brown bear came running, not from the forest but from far away, from the great cities of the civilized world. And this bear gobbled up all the children. But it so happened that the youngest, the weakest and most delicate of them all, little Yisrolik, was spared.

Yisrolik was a stargazer. The distant stars called to him. He conducted nighttime vigils high up in the mountains or deep in the valleys. There he read the signs of the zodiac as they migrated across the heavens. When Yisrolik came home and saw the disaster that had occurred, he took up his spyglass and set off for the land of his ancestors.

On Friday nights, with the beginning of the Sabbath, my aunt came to life. A special spirit shone forth from her gray eyes and the wrinkles disappeared from her face. She bought meat from the Glatt kosher butcher. She stewed carrots and baked a sweet kugel. She took her best dress from the closet and laid it on the bed, next to the white silk kerchief with golden fringes that she wore to bless the candles.

My aunt had brought this kerchief with her from Poland. It was the only memento she had from her mother. My aunt had decided to wear this kerchief on her head when the time came to stand before the Lord of the Universe. She had also sewn for herself a shroud with long sleeves and a high, ruffled collar, as befitted a pious woman.

With every passing day, my aunt became more devout, more observant. She withdrew all the more from the material world.

"Why don't you go to the park once in a while?" I would sometimes ask. "Fill your lungs with a little fresh air, visit with the other women. . . ."

"I don't have time, my child," she'd say. "I still have so much to do . . . and for me the sun is already going down."

When our family expanded and the apartment on Ocean Avenue became too crowded, we decided to buy a house on Long Island. Unexpectedly, my aunt refused to come with us. She wasn't familiar with the neighborhood—maybe there wasn't a synagogue there. Now, in her old age, she wasn't about to live among Gentiles—not even Jewish Gentiles.

My aunt was seventy years old when she went into the old age home. All that she owned she turned over to them, and then she began to save again. Every penny I gave her she put away—for the rabbis, the scholars, after her death. She wouldn't allow herself to buy a piece of fruit or a dress. Everything went into the little purse that hung around her neck like an amulet.

My aunt had no children of her own. No matter how much I did for her, it always seemed that children of her own would have been better: a son would have said kaddish, a daughter would have donated to charity to save her soul from disgrace in the other world. The way things were, the entire burden fell on her shoulders.

Every Sunday, I visited my aunt in the old age home. She was busy there, perhaps reciting a psalm for a sick person or penning a letter for some poor woman who didn't know how to write. As time went by, I noticed that some odd remarks had begun to creep into her speech.

"You see that woman over there? She's our *shoychet's* youngest daughter—you must remember her from back home. There she was a big shot—here she's just a sad case, poor thing.

She's ashamed to look me in the eye. She wants to convince me she's from Warsaw—imagine! Well, if it makes her feel good . . ."

This wasn't the only such example. In fact, my aunt peopled the home with characters from the old country. The rope maker from the shtetl had turned up here as a *mashgiach*, overseeing the kitchen. The tenant farmer's son had become the house doctor. The cantor was the same one who used to lead the prayers in the big synagogue. I talked to the doctor about this phenomenon. He assured me that it was caused by hardening of the arteries. I had my own interpretation. My aunt was simply running away from the old age home, escaping back to the shtetl. She was going home, back to her youth, back to her roots. Step by step, as if descending a ladder, she was returning to her own beginnings, her own Genesis.

One Sunday evening, she called me by the name of her sister, my mother.

"Pesenyu," she said, "I have to tell you something, but remember, don't repeat a word to anyone." She moved her chair closer to mine. Her eyes sparkled, and her white hair peeked out from under her kerchief like the unruly curls of a young girl.

"Listen to this," she said. "Motele Shoyber has shown up again. I have no idea how he found out where I live. Please, Pesenyu, don't say a word in front of Papa."

She looked me in the eye, then smiled as if to someone behind me. I turned aside—I didn't want her to see that I knew she was rambling.

"He's walking back and forth in front of the window," she said, "just like in the good old days. I plead with him—'How can this be, Motele? You have a wife and children, what do you want with me?'

"'You're mine,' he answers. 'It was ordained in heaven.'

"Last night I had just finished saying the prayer for the close of the Sabbath. No light had yet been turned on. All of a sudden I hear someone rapping at the window—not banging, God forbid, but gently, pleadingly. I look out—it's Motl.

"'What are you doing here in all this rain?' I ask.

"'Open up, Rochele,' he begs me. He flashes a look with his Gypsy eyes. I go hot and cold. I'm scared to death—Papa could walk in at any moment. But Motl won't give up.

"'Rochele, darling, open the window, I'm dying for you!' His red-hot eyes burn holes in the windowpane. I cover my face. I don't want to look at him. I don't want to see the net he's spreading for me. I grab the holy book lying on the table. All the virtues of my mother and father come to my aid. And even though I don't turn around, I feel that he's still there—so sad, so forlorn."

My aunt cried, and I cried along with her.

She fantasized about Motele for the whole summer. By the beginning of autumn, she was slipping rapidly. Around Chanukah, she had become a little girl . . . running around barefoot, washing her mother's noodle board in the river . . . setting down the noodle board in the water and swimming away with the current.

Her mind didn't always wander. These excursions into the past took place mostly in the evening, when she would lay aside her prayer book and remain alone in her room with only the walls for company. She seldom complained about her fate. She even stopped envying the women who had children of their own.

"God works in mysterious ways," she would say. "Man with his limited wisdom cannot comprehend God's ways."

I lay in bed and thought about man's limited wisdom. The March wind had blustered away somewhere, taking with it the keening women who spoke to me in my aunt's voice. I also thought about the philosopher who once said that a little knowledge is a dangerous thing. Indeed, I knew a little. Lately, when she'd begun calling me Mama, I knew that her end was near. I'd even asked the secretary to call me promptly at the slightest change in her condition.

Well, they had let me know after it was too late, and now God's mysterious ways were enough to drive me crazy.

Again and again I imagined her despair. She'd been counting on my last visit. She'd had so much to say—so much she wanted to hear. I imagined how she'd wrestled with Death, mounted her brave resistance, waited and hoped that at any moment the door would open and I would arrive. Until five in the evening she held off the Angel of Death. When night fell, her thoughts naturally became muddled, her wits distracted. Then, only then, did she manage her escape—her triumph, as it were.

If only they had called me in time, I could have been standing at her deathbed, perhaps with the white wings of the angel Gabriel. I would have opened the gates of the Garden of Eden for her. With all due ceremony, I would have shown her to the seat she so richly deserved, where the patriarchs and the matriarchs and all righteous men and women sing the Song of Praise before the throne of God.

At daybreak I arose, ironed the garment she'd sewn for herself, wrapped it in tissue paper, and set off for the funeral. In the lobby, the women fell upon me: "How can anyone have such a heart of stone? Her wailing could have moved a rock—yet you didn't find it necessary to respond. They said in the office that they'd called you—the poor woman was waiting for you until the moment her soul departed."

I followed a man who led me down to the basement to iden-tify my aunt's body. She was lying in an open coffin, wrapped in cheap linen basted together with big stitches.

Frozen with fear, I stood and looked at her. I had to do it—I had to—the idea took hold of me with iron claws. I looked at my escort. "Get out!" I said in a voice that allowed no opposition. He stared at me, surprised, but said not a word.

When he had gone, I unwrapped the shroud with the ruffled collar and the frills around the sleeves. I pulled it over her thin frame, all the way from her feet to her blue lips. I covered her head with the special burial cap, and over the cap I put on her mother's white silk kerchief edged with the golden fringe. I pulled the kerchief down over her closed eyes. Only her long, pointy nose poked out at me.

Bracing myself against fear, against death, against my own feelings, I touched my lips to the silk kerchief, and it seemed to me that with this gesture I freed the imprisoned soul, which then rose, fluttering softly, and wafted away to the exalted place for which it was destined, leaving behind the body as a gift for Mother Earth.

✦ ☾ ✦

BLUME LEMPEL *was born in Khorostkov, Galicia, in 1907. There she attended* cheder *and a Hebrew elementary school. From 1929 to 1939, she lived in Paris, and in 1939 she settled in New York. She made her literary debut with a story in the Yiddish newspaper* Der tog *under the pseudonym Rochel Halperin, and her work appeared in the most prestigious Yiddish newspapers and magazines, including* Morgn frayhayt, Di goldene keyt, Tsukunft, Zayn, *and* Kheshbn. *She has published two collections of short stories,* A rege fun emes *[A Moment of Truth] and* Balade fun a cholem *[Ballad of a Dream]. Although she herself did not live through the Holocaust, she wrote often of those who did. Her stories are remarkable for their deep psychological probing, emotional intensity, and haunting imagery. She died in 1999.*

Glossary

bal-darshn—a Jewish preacher or orator.

bris—ritual circumcision on the eighth day of a male infant's life.

bubbe—grandmother.

Chasidic—pertains to members of Chasidism, a movement begun by mystics, that stresses joy, faith, and ecstatic prayer.

chazzen—cantor.

cheder—a Jewish elementary school.

cholent—a stew of beans and meat, traditionally eaten for lunch on Shabbes.

dreidel—a four-sided top with a Hebrew letter on each side that is played with on Chanukah.

Elul—an autumn month on the Jewish calendar during which the High Holy Days take place.

Eyn Yakov—a book of Talmudic morality tales.

Gehenna—a place where the wicked are tormented after death.

Gemora—part of the Talmud, a book of discussions on the Mishnah.

Glatt kosher—held to the strictest level of *kashres*.

Got mayner—exclamation; literally "my God."

gymnazium—a European secondary school that prepares students for the university.

havdalah—prayer that marks the end of *Shabbes*.

High Holidays—Rosh Hashanah and Yom Kippur.

Hoshanah Rabbah—the last day of Succos.

kaddish—the mourner's prayer; recited for eleven months after the loss of a close relative.

kapote—traditional black caftan.

kasha—porridge made from buckwheat groats.

kashres—being kosher.

kedushah—literally "holiness"; prayer said to praise God.

kiddush—a ceremonial blessing pronounced over wine.

Kiddush Hashem—sanctification of God's Name.

klezmer—traditional Eastern European music played by klezmorim.

kugel—a pudding.

L'chayim—traditional toast; literally "to life."

mashgiach—person who watches over the preparation of food to ensure its *kashres*.

matzo—unleavened bread eaten on Passover.

mazel tov—congratulations; literally "good luck."

melamed—a teacher of Jewish children.

menorah—candelabra.

mezuzah—a scroll affixed to doorposts of Jewish homes.

midrash—a body of rabbinic commentary that is of an anecdotal or allegorical nature.

Mishnah—Judaism's Oral Law, legal commentary on the Torah (Written Law).

Misnagdim—opponents of the Chasidim known for their skepticism; singular is Misnagid.

mitzvahs—good deeds.

mohel—person who performs the bris.

Pesach—Passover.

pletzl—Polish onion cookie.

rebbe—rabbi.

rebbitsin—the rabbi's wife.

Sefer Torah—Torah scroll.

Shabbes—the Jewish Sabbath, which begins at sundown on Friday evening and ends after sundown on Saturday evening.

shatnez—the mixing of linen and wool in one garment, which is forbidden by Jewish law.

Shema—traditional prayer; "Hear O Israel, the Lord is God, the Lord is One."

shikse—a non-Jewish woman.

shlemiel—someone who is clumsy and always unlucky.

shlimazl—an unlucky person.

shnorrer—one who habitually takes advantage of the generosity of others.

shofar—ram's horn; blown during the High Holidays.

shoychet—ritual slaughterer.

shtetl—a little European town, often predominantly Jewish. Plural, *shtetlech*.

shtreyml—fur hat worn by Chasidim.

shul—synagogue.

Shulchan Aruch—a book of Jewish law.

Simchas Torah—holiday celebrating the Torah; celebrated after Succos.

sliches—penitential prayers recited during the High Holidays.

succah—booth built for the festival of Succos; the family eats their meals in the succah during the holiday.

Succos—Festival of the Tabernacles; a Jewish harvest festival.

tallis—ritual prayer shawl.

Talmud—discussions and commentaries on the Mishnah.

Targum—Aramaic translations of the Torah.

Tishe Bov—a fast day during the summer and the saddest day on the Jewish calendar; marks the destruction of the Temple.

tzimmes—stew usually made from carrots, raisins, and honey.

yeshiva—Jewish school for religious instruction.

zeyde—grandfather.

Selected Source Notes

"Spring"
The Yiddish text of this story, under the title "Shvester" [Sisters], was first published in the collection of David Bergelson's stories entitled *Velt-oys velt-ayn* [A World Goes, a World Comes], volume 6 of *Geklibene verk fun Dovid Bergelson* [Selected works of Dovid Bergelson] (Vilna: Boris Kletskin, 1930), pp. 77–97. An ideologically revised version of the same story, under the new title "Friling" [Spring], was subsequently published in a post-Stalin volume of Yiddish writing assembled by Izrail Aizikovich Serebrianyi and edited by T. Gen, entitled *Dertseylungen fun yidishe sovietishe shrayber* [Stories by Yiddish Soviet Writers] (Moscow: Sovietski pisatel, 1969), pp. 91–107. The present translation has been made from the original text (1930).

"In the Boardinghouse"
The Yiddish text of this story, under the title "In pansyon fun di dray shvester" [In the Pension of the Three Sisters], was first published in the collection of David Bergelson's stories entitled *Velt-oys velt-ayn* [A

323

World Goes, a World Comes], volume 6 of *Geklibene verk fun Dovid Bergelson* [Selected works of Dovid Bergelson] (Vilna: Boris Kletskin, 1930), pp. 99–111. The present translation has been made from this text.

"At the Rich Relatives" and "Bella Fell in Love"
Dropkin, Celia, *In heysn vint* [In the Hot Wind] (New York: John J. Dropkin, 1959).

"My First Readers"
Rochel Faygenberg's story was published in Yiddish in the journal *Di goldene keyt,* vol. 37 (Tel Aviv, 1960).

"Bubbe Malke"
Gorshman, Shira, *Dertseylungen fun yidishe sovetishe shrayber* [Stories by yiddish soviet writers], assembled by Izrail Aizikovich Serebrianyi and edited by T. Gen (Moscow: Sovietski pisatel, 1969).

"The Sack with Pink Stripes"
Rachel H. Korn wrote "Dos roz-geshtrayfte zekele" near the end of her life. It is one of two completed chapters of a proposed autobiographical memoir titled *Mayn heym un ich* [My Home and I] (1969). It has not been published before in Yiddish or in translation.

"A Satin Coat"
Kreitman, Esther Singer, from *Ichus: Short Stories* [Yikhes (Pedigree)] (London: Narod Press, 1950).

"Scenes on a Bare Canvas" and "The Death of My Aunt"
Lempel, Blume, *A rege fun emes* [A Moment of Truth] (Tel Aviv: I. L. Peretz Publishing House, 1981).

"The Four-Ruble War"
Excerpt from Helen Londynski, *In shpigl fun nekhtn* [In the Mirror of Yesterday] (New York: Knight Printing Corporation, with support from the Helen Londynski Book Committee, 1972), pp. 11–21, 25–29.

"The Fourth Mitzvah"
Molodowsky, Kadya, in *A shtub mit zibn fenster* [A House with Seven Windows] (New York: Farlog Matones, 1957), pp. 70–73.

"Winter Berries" and "At the Mill"
Schtok, Fradel, *Dertseylungen* (New York: 1919).

"Rosh Hashanah" and "Two Heads"
Serdatzky, Yente, *Geklibene shriftn* [Selected works] (New York: Hebrew Publishing Company, 1913).

"Androgynous"
Singer, Isaac Bashevis, "Andruginus," in *Der shpigl un andere derstey-lungen*, with introduction and notes by Khone Shmeruk (Jerusalem: Magnes Press, 1975; repr. 1979), pp. 180–193.

Selected Bibliography

Aleichem, Sholom. *Tevye's Daughters*. New York: Sholom Aleichem Family Publications, 1999.

Baron, Dvora. *The First Day and Other Stories*. Berkeley: University of California Press, 2001.

Baskin, Judith R. *Women of the Word: Jewish Women and Jewish Writing*. Detroit: Wayne State University Press, 1994.

Chametzky, Jules et al. *Jewish American Literature*. New York: Norton, 2001.

Forman, Frieda et al. *Found Treasures: Stories by Yiddish Women Writers*. Toronto: Second Story Press, 1994.

Howe, Irving and Eliezer Greenberg, ed. *A Treasury of Yiddish Poetry*. Holt, Rinehart and Winston, 1969.

Howe, Irving et al. *The Penguin Book of Modern Yiddish Verse*. New York: Viking Press, 1987.

Miron, Dan. *A Traveler Disguised: The Rise of Modern Yiddish Fiction in the Nineteenth Century*. Syracuse: Syracuse University Press, 1996.

Neugroschel, Joachim. *No Star Too Beautiful: An Anthology of Yiddish*

Stories, 1382 to the Present. New York: Norton, 2002.

Peretz, I. L. *The I. L. Peretz Reader*. New Haven: Yale University Press, 2002.

Seidman, Naomi. *A Marriage Made in Heaven: The Sexual Politics of Hebrew and Yiddish*. Berkeley: University of California Press, 1997.

Singer, Isaac Bashevis. *The Collected Stories*. New York: Farrar, Straus and Giroux, 1982.

Weinstein, Miriam. *Yiddish: A Nation of Words*. South Royalton, VT: Steerforth Press, 2002.

Copyrights and Permissions

About the Translators

ELLEN CASSEDY began studying Yiddish in 1989 as a memorial to her mother. The late Max Rosenfeld, a translator, was a beloved teacher. Her account of her daughter's Yiddish-flavored bat mitzvah appeared in *Bridges* and *Utne Reader*. A founder of 9 to 5, the national organization for working women, she is the author of two books for women workers, a former columnist for the *Philadelphia Daily News*, and winner of national awards for fiction and drama. She lives near Washington, D.C.

KATHRYN HELLERSTEIN is the Ruth Meltzer Senior Lecturer in Yiddish and Jewish Studies in the Department of Germanic Languages and Literatures at the University of Pennsylvania. Her books include her translation and study of Moyshe-Leyb Halpern's poems, *In New York: A Selection* (Philadelphia: Jewish Publication Society, 1982), *Paper Bridges: Selected Poems of Kadya Molodowsky* (Detroit: Wayne State University Press, 1999), and *Jewish American Literature: A Norton Anthology* (New York: W. W.

Norton, 2000), of which she is coeditor. Her current projects include *Anthology of Women Yiddish Poets* and a critical book, *A Question of Tradition: Women Poets in Yiddish*, supported in 1999–2000 by a fellowship from the Guggenheim Foundation.

FAITH JONES is a short-story writer and translator and a researcher of book and library history. Her work has been published in anthologies and in scholarly and literary journals such as *Canadian Jewish Studies, Lyric, Bridges, Fiddlehead,* and *Geist.* She is a librarian in the Dorot Jewish Division of the New York Public Library and is active in Yiddish, feminist, and peace organizations.

IRENA KLEPFISZ is a writer, scholar, translator, and activist. She is the author of *A Few Words in the Mother Tongue* (poetry) (Portland: Eighth Mountain Press, 1990) and *Dreams of an Insomniac* (essays) (Portland: Eighth Mountain Press, 1990), coeditor of *The Tribe of Dina: A Jewish Women's Anthology* (Boston: Beacon Press, 1989), and has written extensively on Yiddish women writers and Eastern European Jewish women activists. Her essay "Queens of Contradiction" serves as the introduction to *Found Treasures: Stories by Yiddish Women Writers* (Toronto: Second Story Press, 1994). She teaches courses on Jewish women at Barnard College and on Yiddish women writers and Yiddish translation at YIVO Institute for Jewish Research. For the past three decades, she has been an activist for gay and lesbian rights and for peace and reconciliation between Israelis and Palestinians.

JENNIFER KRONOVET was born and raised in New York City. She holds an MFA in creative writing from Washington University in St. Louis. Her poems have appeared in *Meridian, Ploughshares, Poetry Northwest, Post Road,* and other literary journals. She is the coeditor of *Circumference,* a journal of poetry in translation. Currently, she works at the Poetry Society of America.

SEYMOUR LEVITAN's translations of Yiddish poems and stories are
included in numerous anthologies, among them *The Penguin
Book of Yiddish Verse* (New York: Viking Penguin, 1987), *A Trea-
sury of Yiddish Stories* (New York: Viking Penguin, 1989), *The
I. L. Peretz Reader* (New York: Schocken, 1990), and *The Second
First Art* (Editions d'Autrui, 1996). His translation of Rachel
Korn's memoir *The New House* appeared in *Pakntreger* (winter
2001). *Paper Roses,* his selection and translation of Rachel H.
Korn's poetry, was the 1988 winner of the Robert Payne Award
of the Translation Center at Columbia University. *I Want to Fall
Like This,* his selection and translation of Ruchl Fishman's
poems, was published by Wayne State University Press in 1994.
He lives in Vancouver, British Columbia.

JOSEPH SHERMAN is currently Corob Fellow in Yiddish Studies,
Oxford Centre for Hebrew and Jewish Studies, University of
Oxford. The author of over forty academic articles and the editor
of nine books, he has lectured widely in the United States, the
United Kingdom, and South Africa. His major field of research is
Yiddish literature, on which he has published widely in interna-
tional journals, including *Prooftexts, Judaism, Studies in American
Jewish Literature, The Journal of Narrative Technique,* and, in South
Africa, *English Studies in Africa, Journal of Semitics, Acta Academica.*
He is a specialist in the work of the 1978 Nobel laureate Isaac
Bashevis Singer, whom he interviewed in Miami Beach in 1983
and on whose work he wrote his doctorate. He translated into
English the most recent of Singer's hitherto untranslated novels,
Shadows on the Hudson (New York: Farrar, Straus & Giroux, 1987),
for which he was awarded the Modern Language Association of
America's first Yakov and Fenia Leviant Prize for Yiddish Translation at the end of 2002. His other field of specialization is the work
of the great Yiddish prose writer David Bergelson (1884–1952), and
he has recently published a new English translation, together with

a newly redacted Yiddish text, of Bergelson's masterly 1913 novella *Opgang* [Descent]. His current projects include translating two major South African novels from Yiddish into English and making new translations of work by Sholem Asch and Isaac Bashevis Singer.

SAMUEL SOLOMON studies comparative literature, writing, semiotics, and literary translation at Brown University. He is currently co-translating the complete poems of Celia Dropkin into English.

SARAH SILBERSTEIN SWARTZ was born in Berlin, Germany, the daughter of Yiddish-speaking Polish Holocaust survivors. She has studied Yiddish at Columbia University and the University of Toronto. A book editor and writer by profession, she has helped produce numerous prize-winning volumes on Yiddish, Jewish, and Jewish women's topics in Canada and the United States. She is coeditor of *Found Treasures: Stories by Yiddish Women Writers* (Toronto: Second Story Press, 1994), in which she translated the autobiographical writings of Malka Lee; coeditor and contributor to *From Memory to Transformation: Jewish Women's Voices* (Toronto: Second Story Press, 1998); and author of *Bar Mitzvah* (New York: Doubleday, 1985). She also served as editor in chief of *Jewish Women in America: An Historical Encyclopedia* (New York: Routledge, 1997), in which her articles on Yiddish poets Malka Lee and Anna Margolin are included.

SHEVA ZUCKER is the author of the textbooks *Yiddish: An Introduction to the Language, Literature & Culture, Vols. I and II*. She teaches Yiddish and Jewish literature at Duke University in Durham, North Carolina, and in the Uriel Weinreich Summer Program in New York City. She has taught and lectured on Yiddish language, literature, and culture on five continents and at major universities, including Columbia, Bar-Ilan, and Russian

State Humanities University. She was, for several years, the translation editor of *Pakn Treger*, the magazine of the national Yiddish Book Center. She writes and translates mostly on topics related to women in Yiddish literature.

About the Editor

SANDRA BARK is a writer and editor who lives in Brooklyn, New York. She grew up in an active Jewish community, attending yeshiva day schools and trying to understand what her grandparents were saying about her in Yiddish. Her first year of college was spent at Bar-Ilan University in Ramat Gan, Israel, where she furthered her studies in Jewish culture and history. With a strong interest in Jewish literature, she began researching Yiddish women writers when she realized how little of their work was available for English-speaking readers.

THALIA THEATRE.

טהאליא טהעאטער, 48-46 בּאָוורי.

עקסטרא!

צום ערשטען מאהל ביים יודישען
טהעאטער עקזיסטירט

עקסטרא!

צום ערשטען מאהל ביים יודישען
טהעאטער עקזיסטירט

מאדאם
בּערטהא קאליש
אלס האמלעט

מאדאם
בּערטהא קאליש
אלס האמלעט

עהרען בּענעפֿים פֿאָרשטעללונג
פֿיר

עהרען בּענעפֿים פֿאָרשטעללונג
פֿיר

מאדאם בּערטהא קאליש

מיטוואָך אבֿענדס 30 יאנואר

צור אויפֿפֿיהרונג קומט
שעקספּיערס בּעריהמטע דראמא

האמלעט

מאדאם בּערטהא קאליש אלס האמלעט

איין גוואַלדיגע און פֿערזאממעלהויב־זאַלע וועלכע איז ביז יעדע בלויז פֿון סענירן גענעראלע געווארען, שפּיעלט צום ערשטען מאהל מאר. קאליש
מיט דער מיטווירקונג דער גאַנצע טהאַליא טהעאטער טרופּ קאמפּאַני.

וועראטהעם פּובּליקום: —האמלעט איז ביז יעצם געשפּיעלם געווארען פֿאַן די נרעסטע קינסטלער דער וועלם און סענירט. די איינציגע פֿרויע
וועלכע האם זיך אונטערגעשטאנדען צו שפּיעלען די ראַלע פֿאַן האמלעט וואר נור סאראה בּערנהארד. מאדאם קאליש וועלכע האם אוממער
גענאַמהן איהר בּעסטעם אין איהרער וועלכע ראַלע דורכצוטהרען מיט גרויסער פּאַריכמזניקיים, נעטם אויף זיך יעצט די נרעסטע אויפֿנאָבּע צור
די ראַלע ערהן בּענעפֿים און שפּיעלען די שפּיעלען די ראַלע פֿאַן האמלעט.
ביים 6 מאנאטען וואס האט זא שטאריטא די נעשיכטע זא שטאריטא איהר ראַלע וועלכע פֿאַן זיא נרעסטע
נרעסטע פֿראַפֿעסאָרען אין דעמען פֿאַך אונטער דעם נאמען ל. מ. נאַללאָטן שמאַם, דער זעלבּער פֿראַפֿעסאָר האם אונטערערווינטען די גרעסטע
קינסטלער, ווא: שַאַנדערין, מאוד אדאמס, עני רעסעל אונד נאַך אנדערע, אונד זיא פֿערשפּרעכם אַללע אנצוואונדרען דאַס דער אבּענד פֿאַן
30סטן יאַנואר וועל מערובּליבּען פֿיר איין אַנגענעהמער פֿר אַ טהעאטער קאמפּאַני זאַן אונזער ליעבּע צושוער.
ווערדען צור עהרן אונזער קאלענע קינסטלערין וועלכע האַם פֿערשאַפֿם עהרע אונד כבֿוד מים מיר ערטהיילען מים אונד צוזאַמ מען
אויף איין ביהנע וועלכע די נאַטור זעלבּסם האם איהר נעשענקען מים די דראַמע זא אויך אין אַפֿעראַ. פֿיר וועלכע די נרעסטע
קריטיקער אונד בּראַפֿעסאָל אונד אונערע האַבּען איהר נעקרוינט מים דעם כאַמיאַן קינסטלערין, ווערדען מיר האַנ מענליבּעם אום מעמאוהל־
זאַן איהר איהרע שוינע ראַלע דורכצוטהרען מים פֿראכט אונד נלאַנץ. קלָאַין זוּ יאַסענטיל אונד זעהרע טהאליע אונד זעהרע דער וערהד עבֿורתם.
אבּמונדסנאַלל.

די מאהליא טהעאטער קאמפּאַני.

ביים אויפֿמערקזאם אויף דעם דעל וועלכע האמלעם האם מים לעארטום.

קינדער אונטער 5 יאהר ווערדען נים אריינגעלאַזען.

טיקעטס זינד שוין צו בּעקומען אין באָקס אפֿים פֿון טהאליא טהעאטער.

ז. ליעבּשם. יונאָן סטים פּרינטערי, 1801 נרעדע סטריט, ניו יאָרק.